E.B.E.

Extra Biological Entity

Michael Christopher
Carter

Golden Hill

CONTENTS

E.B.E.

Extra Biological Entity

The second installment of The HUM series

PRAISE FOR THE HUM...

"Enjoyed it from beginning to end. I can't wait for the sequel!!"

"Well written, creepy, tense, fantastic book..."

"Captivating, page turning fun..."

"One of those books I had to force myself to put down to get anything else done!"

"Like an intense high-impact movie, but different to your usual sci-fi..."

"The more I read the better it got. The surprise ending was terricfic!"

"It takes a really interesting book to hold my attention and I read this in one day!"

"This book leaves you feeling like you can

actually hear the hum..."

ONE

The phone call

Royston, a small town in England 1993

Brenda planned to ignore the phone. Saturday calls were usually double glazing, or wall coating, or fitted kitchen, sales calls, and she couldn't be doing with any of those. Magazine paused between table and inches from her face, where she was admiring a feature on who was sexier: Brad Pitt, or George Clooney, she was struggling to tune out the persistent ringing. "All right, all right!" she slammed the article down, rocking a cold cup of coffee which, if it spilled, would ignite a fire the salesperson on the other end of the line would live to regret. "Hello," she answered; not the forceful, suffer-no-fools tone she promised herself, but a mild polite Britishness she shrugged and allowed.

"Hello, is it possible to speak to Stephen, please?"

"Hold on. I'll see if he's in. Who's speaking?"

"Carys Ellis."

Brenda dropped the phone. It was that girl! What should she do? Her boy had been missing for days and had scarcely settled home and everyone said *she* did something to him.

"Who is it, Mum?"

Brenda flapped. "Oh, it's no-one. Just one of those sales calls, you know."

"I don't believe you. You look terrible. Who is it? What's happened?"

Shoulders slumped. She couldn't lie. Not after the barrage of accusations thrown at her boy as she and his dad tried to find out what had transpired and where he'd disappeared to for days. "It's that girl."

Stephen frowned and lifted his palms up to question. Sniffing the air, he glared. How did she expect him to know what she was going on about? He wasn't psychic. "What girl?" It was no exaggeration that saying there was a girl on the phone narrowed it down to the entire female population of the town; under a certain age, of course. He should have known. He should have understood exactly which girl was '*That girl*'.

"Carys Ellis."

Blood drained from his face and he leant on the telephone table for support. After making such a fuss, he couldn't decline the call now. Not without facing some difficult questions later. "I'll take it, Mum. But, do you mind? I'd like a bit of privacy, please." He held the handset to his shoulder, shielding the mouthpiece with the fabric of his shirt. Waiting until his mum disappeared back into the kitchen, and delaying further for her to close the door, he eventually spoke. "Hello?"

"Stephen, this is Carys Ellis." There was a breathy pause before she dropped her bomb. "I won't bother with 'How are you?' because I don't care. The reason I'm phoning is merely out of common courtesy to inform you that you are going to be a father. I am six weeks pregnant."

Stephen gulped. What should he say? What *could* he say? Leaning on the telephone table wasn't enough now. He had to sit.

"Did you hear me?"

Of course, he heard her. The words would echo around his head forever, but there was one thing he was sure of, and he had to tell her. "I can't be. Nothing happened. Don't you remember?" Stephen waited for the silence to answer the question. "Look, I am truly sorry for my behaviour. I thought you liked me. Every other girl does. I was frustrated. I assumed you were…" he toyed with countering with something more biting but chose, "Playing hard to get."

Her breath told him she was listening. "You don't remember, do you? It's taken a while for things to come back to me, and I can't recall everything. But some parts are crystal clear. Believe me. Like I've said," he persisted, "I deeply apologise for how I behaved, but nothing happened that could cause you to be pregnant. I promise. Nothing."

Re-living that night flooded him with a nausea he was struggling to control. "You must remember the bright light? And those... Those things?" Retching faltering his voice, he closed his eyes for calm. "I couldn't have done anything with you then, even if you'd begged." No reply came from Carys, but the line went dead and Stephen didn't blame her. Because if he wasn't the father of her baby, they both knew who was.

OCTOBER 2019

PEMBROKESHIRE

"Happy now?"

Ebe hid his face as he reached for his seatbelt. Unable to speak, he recognised Marco wasn't really interested. Not in how he was at any rate; only whether he was ready for their mission. And there had never been any question of that. He'd been born ready.

"Well, let's go. The sooner we get packed, the sooner we can leave."

Ebe gulped. He hated packing. Mum had always

done that for him, and the fact she wasn't rasped in his throat.

"What's the matter? Want your mummy?" Marco scoffed, regretting it immediately. If Ebe chickened out, especially if they blamed him, well, it didn't bear thinking about.

He hid his smile as his protégé batted tears from his face and announced in steely determination, "I'm fine," and stared out of the windshield.

He'd made him cross, but it wouldn't last. And Marco knew the surest way to snap him out of his mood. "McDonalds?" Hands rubbing on his thighs, sadness evaporated as his thoughts travelled to his last meal. He'd miss the convenience of fast food in Alaska. Not for him, the love of 'getting away from it all', although he did enjoy occasional camping trips. The excitement of their mission outweighed the inconvenience. And it wasn't forever.

Marco could be annoying. And why hadn't he shown his mum his true self sooner? He recalled the terror in her eyes and understood, but it made him sad to consider the shock she must have gone through. "When did you tell Mum about, you know, your other identity?"

Marco blew through his lips. How should he play it? "Only recently, son." A glance showed Ebe hadn't reacted to the endearment. He never had and never would, but Marco was proud. Associating with this boy who would change the world was a desirable stance.

Expecting more, the golden arches tore Ebe's attention and if he made a mental note to mention it again later, it didn't show in his face. "What are you going to have, Ebe?" Marco took a hand from the wheel and pinched the bridge of his nose, anticipating the protracted deliberations that would follow.

Ebe shuffled to get closer to the menu. "What's new?" he craned his neck and jiggled in his seat, which creaked sending shudders through the chassis.

"Calm down, Ebe, you can read. Look for yourself." The harsh tone did nothing to speed Ebe's decision-making skills. Sweat beaded on his high hairline and his chewed-to-the-quick fingernails found their way to his mouth to be gnawed.

Marco sighed. "Sorry, Ebe. I know you find this hard and it is meant to be a treat." The calming effect of the apology was immediate but not enough. "Wait a minute and I'll pull into a bay and we'll read it properly. Where's your phone?"

"Out of battery."

How someone so into technology let their phone die as often as Ebe did was something Marco would never understand. Especially as he relied upon the information provided by the world-wide-web to make most of his decisions. It was the reason he was so angsty now, wasn't it? The phone app had the menu easily accessible and anything now promoted in vibrant OLED colour. “Look, there’s this... New Spicy Chicken...”

“Ooh!” Ebe bobbed in excitement, then stopped. “But I don’t know if I want to risk it. My tummy and flying tomorrow.”

Tomorrow? where did he get these ideas? “Don’t worry, Ebe. The flight isn’t that soon. We’ve got a couple of weeks.” Distress showed in his pulled features and Marco wished Carys could be here to calm him. Sometimes there seemed no right words. “But at least you can have the spicy wings.”

It had been a struggle limiting Ebe’s luggage to legally permitted weights and types. Some things he wanted to bring made no sense. Some ‘raspberry pie’ computers he’d been programming were deemed essential, and he had almost come to tears when Marco persuaded him they weren’t a good idea.

But now they were at London Heathrow Airport in hot anticipation of a thirty-six-hour journey to Alaska including two stops, one overnight in Seattle. It had taken effort to persuade Ebe staying in a hotel would be okay. More so than setting up an entirely new life away from everything he’d grown to love in Cambridge. “It’s like Wales,” he had encouraged. A bit. But more remote; a lot more remote. He would point out the mountains looking similar to North Wales and Snowdonia where they'd holidayed during his childhood. Ebe had shown enthusiasm for the industrial scars on the landscape, and thrilled at visiting remains of slate mines and copper mines, comfortable and enthralled in the miles of subterranean passages. Auspicious, Marco had thought, the relocation to Alaska a plan even then.

Duty-free tech took Ebe's eye and Marco was happy to indulge him. His prize. His ticket to a future not promised (or in his mind, even likely) for most. It had been a while since Marco had flown, but he liked to choose Cardiff, Bristol, or even Birmingham, or Manchester, airports over anywhere in London. And Europe's busiest airport was plagued by delays. With more passengers and flights than anywhere else on the continent, there was always some technical fault or other to delay the whole take-off and landing schedule. But today, a little after a fast food lunch, they were called to board exactly on time.

The tunnel joining the plane felt like leaving the galaxy. And from what they would experience when they arrived, it might as well be.

The seats were big and comfortable. Marco had insisted on window seating and made sure his protégé was closest to the action. As the huge aeroplane taxied to the runway, Ebe never took his stare from the little oval pane as the terminal building shrank to a speck in the distance and they accelerated to over one-hundred-and sixty miles-per-hour and left the tarmac, the British Isles, and everything he'd ever known behind.

After an hour, Ebe tapped Marco's arm. "There's Wales down there."

Marco leaned over and smiled. The snow-capped peaks of the Cambrian Mountains reached out waving hands and bid them farewell. Marco shook his head; grateful Carys wasn't there to lead the other passengers in a rousing *'We'll Keep a Welcome In The Valley'.* The part of him that still pretended to be Marco wished she was. But that fragment would become a distant memory soon. There was no role for the son of a preacher man where they were going.

Fourteen hours in Seattle left some time to explore the city. They had thousands of miles to go, but the fact they were two stops from their destination made Ebe feel civilization was closer than it was.

Despite Marco's attempts to venture into somewhere upmarket, Ebe craved the comforts of home, so they sought the golden arches again. It quickly became clear Ebe had found his new home from home. Huge portions of the familiar taste filled even his greedy stomach, and overlooked by the famous space needle, it seemed a very fitting last meal before their adventure began.

A different city in a different time zone, eight

hours behind, made anything but a couple of grasped hours of sleep impossible. When it was time to catch the flight for the next leg of their journey, they were both exhausted.

Four hours on the plane, then another five on a stopover in Anchorage, where it would be dark when they landed. With only two hours of daylight available, unless there was a big delay, those wouldn't coincide with their brief stay. Sleep came before then and they were woken to instructions to refasten their seatbelts, even though they'd fallen unconscious before taking them off.

"Come on, you two sleepyheads!" a flight attendant said at close range. "We'll be landing in Anchorage in five minutes."

Ebe shuffled in his seat and looked out of the window at darkness stretching forever. Distant lights for the runway were visible, but the night skyline was not exactly what he expected from the remote capital of this U.S. state and he felt even more in touch with civilisation. As they flew lower in preparation for landing, bright illuminations and tall buildings of a bustling city filled the view and Ebe gazed in awe.

Behind the city, huge mountains, taller than their flight, wowed him more. Alaska was going to be much easier to cope with than he'd feared. "There has to be McDonald's there, Marco, doesn't there?"

"I bet," Marco agreed, stretching his legs,

readying to walk when they touched down.

"Why did you worry me? This is better than Cambridge. I'm going to love it here."

Had he forgotten, Marco wondered. He didn't have the energy for a discussion with Ebe if he had. He'd remember soon enough. "Do you want to get a burger now? Are you hungry?"

Ebe's lips pressed together and his eyebrows rose and dropped a couple of times. "I'm always hungry, Marco. You know that."

"You're always starving, Ebe."

Sampling McDonald's in the third city in twenty-four hours didn't dampen Ebe's enthusiasm. Despite larger portions, he ordered an extra burger to eat on the way back to the airport. "It'll be nice to see the sights in daylight, Marco. It's cold at night."

Marco shook his head. For a genius, he could be dumb. And it wasn't even cold. No colder than winter in the UK, anyway. "Come on, we have to get the next flight in an hour."

Ebe's bottom lip trembled. "Another flight? But I like it here."

"Well, we can visit again."

His face brightened, and then his eyes narrowed. "When? Soon?"

Marco's head wobbled from side to side. "I suppose it will depend upon how quickly you can help with what needs to be done, Ebe."

Filled with confidence in his own ability to do whatever it was with ease, Ebe grinned. "Book us in for tomorrow night then, Marco!" his eyebrows danced above his sparking eyes set in his bulbous face, and he laughed.

The five hours dragged. McDonald's had taken the time expected for somewhere purporting to be fast food, so that left, after walking there and back, three and a half hours to hang around the airport. Marco noted with dismay that several restaurants in the concourse described themselves as some of the best food in the city. And they'd had burgers again. Well, anything to keep Ebe happy, he supposed.

It was still dark when they were called to their flight. In the light from the city and the airport, the snow on the vast mountains glistened eerily. The crashing waves of the sparkling sea gave a surreal soundtrack beneath the sound of jet engines warming up for take-off.

"I thought it would be a little Cessna, or a helicopter, or something," Ebe halted in front of the large aircraft. "How far is it?"

"Another three or four hours."

"What!? You said it was an island off Alaska."

"It is. Over a thousand miles off Alaska. What were you expecting, Caldey Island?"

"Well, no. But maybe more like Anglesey."

"You expected a bridge?" Marco was never sure if Ebe was deliberately playing the fool to make conversation; something he'd never quite mastered the purpose of, or if he genuinely had ignorant expectations of where they were headed. He'd soon be swept up in the gravity of the task to be bothered for long.

TWO

A dream come true

1993

Marco looked at the photograph. She was beautiful. His eyes flitted from her pretty symmetrical facial features to her full breasts, and then back up to her dark blonde hair. He only tore his gaze from the picture because it seemed unbefitting for a Christian son of a minister to stare for longer. And because he'd seen her before...

For weeks he had woken in a cold sweat. A smiling face from across the room. A girl on a train; in a bar; reaching for the same thing in a supermarket and sharing a smile. The attraction had been instant, and why wouldn't it. He had constructed his ideal woman in his mind as a fantasy upon which his strict Christian parents couldn't proffer opinions.

She was perfect: thick dark blonde hair framing the prettiest face atop an athletic, but full-figured frame. On the mornings after dreams of her, he'd been quite pleased with himself. There was no question back then that she was real; one of the mousy girls who swooned at him when he played his guitar before Sunday worship would end up becoming his wife. It's what kept his carnal desires at bay.

But recently, he'd woken in cringing discomfort in full fantasy coitus and incriminating sheet stains. He had even started wearing underpants in bed to hide his embarrassment. It was all perfectly normal, of course, but denying those types of feelings was much easier than the excruciating exploratory conversations his mum and dad thought were oh-so-subtle at mealtimes. 'Any girls taken your fancy in the congregation, son?' they'd ask. 'Your mother and I were already married when we were your age, you know. And I hope you remember our religion forbids anything of the sort of thing you may be thinking about until after you're wedded. I'm not saying you would, but it would be an affront to God. You remember that, right?' And he would have to swear again that he hadn't been improper with anyone; including himself, because that was a sin, too.

So, seeing a photo of the girl who had prompted equal joy and distress was, to say the least, a shock.

"Who is this?" he forced a smile.

"That's our daughter, Carys. She'll be moving down here to Wales once she's finished her A-levels. It would be nice if you showed her around."

Marco's smile dropped, but he pried it back on his face. It was literally a dream come true; and his worst nightmare. How could he resist such temptation? 'The Lord tempts us to test us,' he thought.

Looking at the middle-aged woman in front of him, he marvelled how he hadn't noticed before and felt a twinge in his loins at recognising some of his dream girl's features on her mother. Aware acutely of eyes boring into him, he stuttered his answer. "I'd be delighted. And don't worry. I won't let anything happen to her." And he wouldn't. His upbringing had made performing that task an impossibility. Every erection enveloped in guilt; they didn't tend to last.

Ensconced behind his guitar on stage, his sweaty fingers fluffed most of the chords and he paused to tune it, shaking his head, passing blame to his faulty instrument and not his lack of skill. Grimacing and frowning as though he didn't understand what was happening, he allowed the rest of the band to cover for him and played a semi-rhythmic muted pattern over the bass and drums and vocals.

Feet tapping and head nodding, he tried desperately to appear as though he was getting into it. A compulsion to bolt from the stage was anchored, ironically, in his sudden inability to move without humiliating himself and causing extreme discomfort to his nether regions. Certain his guitar covered his embarrassment, he was grateful for that at least. But if the protrusion remained, what could he do? His only wish was that guilt did its thing and relieved him of it soon.

With a jerk, he gasped, as the reason he wore pants in bed unleashed its sticky fury. It was a relief and a torment. When the music stopped, he'd have to rush to the toilet and trust nobody would see his shame.

Strumming the flat strings through another hymn, his face burned. Singing about Jesus, with the Devil's juices cooling in his boxers, encasing his mercifully shrivelling self in a snail-slime cocoon, he felt sick. Fingers tugging at his collar, he couldn't faint. He just couldn't. If he fell from his stool and dropped his guitar, he was sure it would cascade out of him like a thick waterfall and God would come down and smite him right there. 'I'm sorry, God. I'm sorry, Jesus. I'm so sorry,' he repeated over and over in his mind whilst the words branded on his soul after repletion and rehearsal flowed effortlessly from his lips:

"There will come a day
When a trial comes our way
What am I going to do right now
I'm at a loss and I don't know how

I need some help in this situation
Please deliver me from this tribulation
Oh Lord, I'm crying out to you
I haven't got a clue, I don't know what to do,"

And they'd never felt truer. 'What do you want me to do, Lord? I'll do anything. Please forgive me.

Someone watching, not God, something else, did have a plan for Marco. And had for some time. He would be in no doubt the path his higher power was leading him. And he would certainly have no choice.

2019

It was strange, daylight developing as they flew. But as they travelled south and west, the sunshine was bright. Below them, endless ocean glistened until, after nearly four hours, a small island rose into view.

Dotted with identical houses, it didn't seem real; more like a model village where the modeller had bought a job lot of unimaginative buildings.

"It probably won't interest you, Ebe, but there are a lot of relics from the cold war down there."

"The cold war? Was that in Alaska?"

Marco couldn't bother himself to answer. If Ebe really didn't know, it was too much to explain in the short time before they landed. And there were far more important things to be thinking about. Ebe didn't push him further, and he was grateful.

"Ladies and gentlemen. Thank you for flying Alaska Airways flight 162 to Adak. We will be landing in approximately eight minutes, so please return to your seats and fasten your seatbelts as we prepare to descend. The weather on the ground is bright and sunny and seventy-one degrees, or twenty-two Celsius, for our European passengers today. The time when we land will be 1.15pm local time.

The lower they got, the worse it looked. None of the bright lights of Seattle or Anchorage, and none of the charm of the Outer Hebrides they had holidayed once. Ebe didn't know why Marco hadn't appreciated his cold war joke. He understood as much as anyone, and more than most. And he realised perfectly where they were heading. It was just a part of him needed to deny it. And that part was about to be more horrified by their bleak reality than his protestations had readied it for. He gulped. He had to hope it was worth it.

Ebe expected to be met by military personnel, but he and Marco were left to exit the airport on their own. Standing outside in daylight for the first time, the bleakness of it all hit Ebe hard. "I don't like it, Marco."

Marco clenched his fists. You're not here to like it, you little twerp. You are here to do the most important thing you've ever done. And all thanks to me. Your brain is big, but you would have wasted it if it wasn't for me, he didn't say. "It's not unlike Wales, really, is it?" he pushed the idea. "Mountains, sea, even the weather feels similar. Not bad at all."

Ebe gasped for breath. "It's nothing like it. It looks like Colditz or somewhere."

"What do you know about that?" Marco fought the urge to morph into his stronger, forceful form. Then he spotted something that would make all the difference. "Look, Ebe... McDonalds."

It worked. Momentarily, Ebe was distracted enough to release his attachment to the familiar back home and embrace the familiar six thousand miles away from it. Cajoling his bulk into an unpleasant jog, Ebe rushed towards the recognisable looking building. It didn't appear open. Usually, his nose would twitch at the delicious aromas of griddled beef and French Fries and fried onions. And it wasn't only his favourite eatery that disappointed; nowhere was trading, and the number of tourists on the flight would be expecting to eat, so that didn't make sense. But as he neared, closed was the least of his worries.

Shutters at broken windows, the golden arches faded by years of arctic sun hung forlornly from their sign. Grabbing hold of the handles, Ebe shook the doors, determined they should open and grant him access to the comfort food he loved.

"It's been abandoned for a while, Ebe, by the looks of it," Marco said calmly, inside the furnace of fury grew hotter. "Come on. Nice try, but we have to go."

"But I don't like it here, Marco. I want to go home."

"Well, you're not going home. *This* is your home! Now, next week, forever for all I know. Move your fat arse before I kick it all the way there." He remembered to smile and pass it off as a joke. Ebe was a big strong lad, easily overpowered by his true self, but now, in front of naïve tourists, was not the time. "Okay, Ebe. You're right. It's nothing like Wales, but when we get where we're going, you'll say it's the best place you've ever been." It seemed a much better idea than saying, 'The beings you'd disappoint if you got back on the plane to Wales are not the sort of people you want to fuck about with. The 'finding out' would be brisk and lethal. Much better to lie and say how great it was. "Come on,

Ebe. You're gonna love it."

THREE

Mothers know best

1993

Marco gripped the sheets. Despite protection, there was still seepage. He closed his eyes and a tear squeezed down his cheek. "What can I do? How should I serve you?" he asked in the direction of his ceiling. In answer, his mind recalled his dream. A baby. And her. Was she going to be his and they would make a life together? He shook his head. Wishful thinking. Was it his conscience desperately trying to demonstrate the consequences his lustful desires could create? Well, it hadn't worked. He desired her more than ever.

He'd asked God how he should minister; what

he required of him, and still he had dreamt constantly of the girl he now knew to be Carys Ellis. He had to consider, as unrealistically optimistic as it seemed, that being with her in some way was indeed what he was being called to do. "Please, God, give me a sign."

It was a few more weeks before the object of Marco's affection appeared in the flesh, and when she did, it was hard to keep his cool. He had to trust that if Jesus wanted them to be together, it would happen in spite of his insecurities. But it had become more than a desire to please his lord and saviour. It was burgeoning on obsession and Marco understood that might be a test itself. If it turned out he'd been kidding himself all along, which the nagging voice in his head assured him was the case, he wasn't sure how he would cope.

But then, one Sunday morning, after Geraint and Diane had been absent for a few weeks, and as he was tuning his guitar behind the scenes on the stage where he and some others would perform songs of worship before the service, he glimpsed her.

Neither the photo, nor his fertile imagination, did her justice, but at the same time the picture of her was oddly flattering; her beauty undeniable, and far greater than could be conveyed on celluloid, her expression was that of defeat. His insecurities may well be exactly what she needed to bring her out of herself. It was all falling into place.

Resting his guitar on its stand, he hopped off the stage. As he approached, he was grateful he seemed to have already caught her attention. "You're Diane and Geraint's daughter," he said with a wink. "I recognise you from your photos. Even more beautiful in real life." She blushed suitably. "Marco," he introduced himself, then in the spirit of not wanting to appear overly keen, and to cover the fact that he had not thought beyond his opening gambit, he turned to speak with somebody involved with the sound system.

A confident grin set on his lips, he faced Carys again. "We'll have to grab a coffee later?" he said with a nod. His question carefully crafted. Despite his lack of opportunity to woo the opposite sex under the scrutiny of his parents, he had taken note that appearing too eager was never recommended.

Her coy smile gratified him, and he sauntered away with a contented, casual, well-rehearsed stride. Springing back onto the stage, he plucked his guitar from the stand and hoped she noticed.

As the other musicians joined him, he forced his gaze around the full room. Determined not to look at her, he would bide his time. They were songs of praise, but pointedly glancing at his intended every point love occurred in the lyrics, he was hopeful would be as seductive as it sounded.

After service coffee was customary, and he took his opportunity to sit with Carys. It was easy to continue his show of charm and sophistication as cakes and drinks were prolifically proffered by enthusiastic members of the congregation. Leaving her nursing a plateful of snacks, Marco made his excuses of needing to help pack away.

Acutely aware of every glance she shot his way, Marco controlled his breathing. 'Thank you, Lord,' he thought. 'This actually seems to be working.

Further meetings were equally inhibited by other people; at weekly sermons, and at bible study groups. They shared smiles and the occasional superficial comment, which Marco tried to keep complimentary but never needy.

And then she'd stopped coming. Weeks had passed, and he hadn't seen nor heard from her. The ache in his chest seemed ridiculous, considering how little he knew about her. And then there were the dreams. Night after night, he'd wake from disturbed sleep where it appeared the only solution to his torment was to be with her.

So, it was with delight and relief he received the invitation from Diane after church to call at their house.

A very pleasant dwelling, Marco forced his eyes to enjoy the scenery rather than flit to every window, wondering which one housed the beautiful girl. If she was watching his approach, better to look cool and non-plussed than like a nervous psychopath. And anyway, the panorama calmed him. Views across the valley to the distant Preseli Hills, ten miles north, gave the sensation of being on the edge of greatness. He drank it in because he expected that when he saw Carys, she'd be all he could stare at.

"Come in," Geraint Ellis: *Sergeant* Geraint Ellis, invited as he opened the door. Diane bustled from a doorway beyond and took his hands in hers.

"Thanks for coming, Marco. Sit down, please."

Marco took a seat at the kitchen table; a little disappointed Carys wasn't around. He'd assumed seeing her was the reason for the invitation.

"Carys isn't well," Geraint said.

Marco pressed his lips together to mask his distress.

"She's found out something rather delicate. I'm sure you heard what happened to her in England?"

"Diane! I don't think Carys would want her private business discussed."

Diane glared. "It's not fair on Marco to hide things... She's pregnant!" she blurted before Geraint might succeed in silencing her. "And she's not been well."

"Morning sickness," Geraint simplified.

"It's more than that. I'm sure. She's heading to a deep depression. You see..." Diane wrestled with her loyalties. “She was raped.” Her hands covered her mouth and she wished she could push the words back in. But there was a satisfaction in her honesty. She was sure that saying was the right thing, only it did feel disloyal. It excused her daughter’s behaviour, and so gave her a better chance with Marco. That was reason enough, she decided. “We can’t get her out of her room,” she felt comfortable apprising. “Sorry to ask, but she likes you, and I… *We*… wondered…”

Marco couldn’t hide the reddening in his cheeks.

“If you manage to persuade her out, you’ll be helping her more than you can know.”

Marco gulped. Who better to reassure a delicate damsel than a virgin minister’s son? With a nod, he realised he was performing the will of the almighty and took his mantle with pride and determination. “I’ll see what I can do. I’ve grown extremely fond of your daughter in the past few weeks and I don’t like the idea of her suffering.” He smiled and pushed up from his chair.

Geraint glared after Marco as he heeded Diane’s directions to their daughter’s bedroom, but he hoped too that it would work. “Do you think a boy arriving unannounced is the best thing? After what happened.”

“Believe me, it’s the only thing.”

It felt wrong, but he had to trust God’s will, didn’t he? And if, by some personal bias, he’d misread what that was, he had to trust her own mother. Treading carefully, reluctant not to stomp and sound like a raid, but not wanting to creep up on her either. With a quick count of the doors, he was sure he'd reached the right one, so he gently knocked.

Silence. Knocking again, a sound of Carys rushing reached his ears, but still the door remained shut. He wouldn't go downstairs yet. If she was so miserable she refused to be seen, then interceding was the right thing to do. It made a good excuse for selfishly doing the wrong thing, anyway. Handle turned, Marco pushed the door open a crack and peered. Staring back at him was Carys's beautiful eye pressed against the door.

What would she do? Would she be angry and scream at him to go? He was relieved when, instead of anger or indifference, she laughed. He laughed too, and they laughed together. Mothers know best, don't they. And then when she accepted his invitation to leave the house and go for a drink, he was doubly sure.

FOUR

Marco's calling

The bar was busy and Marco felt proud to be out with the most beautiful girl there. "What will you have?"

Carys reddened. "Just a lemonade, thanks."

Not unexpected, it did make him pause still. Should he let on he'd been told she was pregnant? Better to be honest and defend it; and it wasn't his secret to keep, anyway. "You've not been feeling too great, your Mam told me. Morning sickness, right?" She seemed relieved, and then they talked about everything but her time before and babies, and they laughed some more.

At home, in bed, for the first time in a long time, Marco felt satisfied with himself. Guilt assuaged, he was sure he was on the correct path. As a result of his intervention, she'd promised to come back to church. Admittedly, not just for the usual reasons, but specifically to watch him play his guitar. His heart raced. It was a date.

Another fitful night had him waking in a pool of sweat. An ache in his side like his ribs levered apart made him touch it and wince, but it wasn't a real pain; not a physical pain. It was an ache. Heartache? His mind lurched, and he knew what he had to do.

Dan Paulo peered at his only son over his half-moon reading spectacles. "I am quite busy. There's all this to get through before bible study on Thursday." He wafted his arm over papers on his desk.

"I just want your advice, Dad. Man to man."

Dan's eyes squeezed to slits and he sniffed. He'd avoided a 'birds and bees' talk in favour of a celibate stone talk instead. Not that they'd actually spoken of the matter over announcing how certain things had to wait until marriage. Not that sex itself was a sin, but the sort of sex one indulged in with people you didn't love led to enough heartache. They wanted to spare their son that; and anyone he showed an interest in. But now this Ellis girl had moved from England to join their conversation, he had half-expected a foray into a insinuation of bending the rules. But they were not his rules. They weren't rules at all. Just ways of behaving that pleased God. And he believed his son wanted that.

"The thing is, Dad. I've grown fond of Carys

Ellis, as I'm sure you've noticed." He thumbed his pocket and dipped his stare to the ground. "You are probably aware she was raped?" he said, looking up.

Dan continued nodding.

"Well, she told me today she's pregnant." Marco left a long pause, but his dad said nothing. "How will she cope?"

"What are you suggesting? You're asking me something. What is it?"

"I haven't told you, Dad, but before I met her; before I ever saw even a photo or heard her name, I knew her. God showed me in a dream. I didn't understand at first, but the dreams kept coming, night after night."

"What did you dream?" Dan had overheard his wife's dismay at their son's sheets a while ago, and now underpants were washed with a frown and a held nose. What version of the truth was his son about to spin him?

"In lots of the dreams, we're together." Marco's face burned, and he hoped his meaning wasn't too obvious. "Then God showed me a baby. I thought it was a warning not to succumb to temptation – and I never would, of course. But now it's evident! I'm being called to care for Carys and her baby."

Dan gasped. His knee-jerk reaction was 'No'. An unmarried mother was not who he saw his son ending up with. But there were extenuating circumstances. Marco might so easily be tempted to the pathway of sin, himself. If by 'care for' he meant 'marry' then it might be the making of him. Joined in God's sacred eyes and not succumbing to temptation. And he must mean marriage, because if he merely planned to be a good friend and provide practical help, it hardly seemed the topic of a 'man to man' chat. "You may be right; if you think God is leading you that way. What does your mother say?"

Marco frowned and rubbed the corner of the desk with the fat of his thumb. Looking away, he brought his eyes back, not quite meeting his father's. "I haven't told her. I came to you first." They both knew the answer. Justification might need to be broached, but in no time, she'd be beside herself with joy. A wedding was a blessing.

FIVE

A new world… And a proposal

2019

Marco appeared to Ebe to know where he was going, and it didn't make sense. Meandering through abandoned buildings gave him an odd, lifeless sensation. He hoped his step-father was right.

Row upon row of tin houses. Despite jolly red and blue roofs that were also interesting in their design; gables and valleys breaking up the monotony, it still looked as bleak and unwelcoming as a POW camp. Beside a deep blue ocean, backed by dramatic mountain scenery. What was it that filled him with dread?

Ebe stared, trying to work it out. In another setting, the same elements might be the primary features of a gushing brochure. The description could be applied to Wales or Scotland and coastal

England and Ireland, too; all places they had visited and raved about the beauty. All places that attracted tourists in their millions every year. What was different?

Ebe imagined the same place bustling with people. He struggled with crowds when they wanted something from him, but blending into the background in a city was easy. Eyeing round he decided that was it. The lack of human life.

It seemed somehow fake, like a set of a movie, or documentaries he'd seen of countries governed by military dictators showing a false window to the world of all their lovely houses. Staged and wrong. That's how it felt.

As they rounded a corner into another deserted street the same as the rest, Marco quickened his pace. "Just along here," he pointed. They stopped outside a building that looked even more decrepit than the others they had passed. Through broken glass, Marco reached inside and turned a handle to open the door. "Come on. It's down here."

Ebe obeyed. What was down the dark corridor? Not the place he would love, then, what?

A heavy steel door barricaded further progress. Marco stepped back, adjusting his feet particularly. Briefly, he morphed into the figure Ebe had grown accustomed to but still feared. From behind the steel, a buzz echoed, and the door swung open. Once they moved over the threshold, it swung back again and buzzed shut.

In total darkness, they waited, Ebe fighting the urge to cry out. This was the plan. It had to be safe.

Brightness flashed on, lighting a long corridor. "This way," Marco jerked his head. There was no alternative route, but Ebe didn't have the energy to point it out. Arcing to the left, the tunnel seemed never ending. After five minutes of walking, they reached another fortified entrance. Marco remained in his human guise and they stood and waited. Just as Ebe was growing impatient, that door clicked too, but this time it opened towards them and two armed military personnel stepped out.

"Arms against the wall. Spread your legs."

As one frisked them, the other pointed an automatic rifle at close range. Ebe was sure they wouldn't want to hurt him, but just knowing there was armour piercing steel ready to unleash into his back at a thousand rounds per minute at the squeeze of a trigger finger made him want to run. There was a time when that's exactly what he would do. His mum and Marco had grabbed him by the hood as he darted into traffic, or headed perilously near a cliff edge. But he'd learned, over painstaking years, to control those human emotions. Fear was rarely an ally. Noticing the sensation and detecting its source was the only benefit. And so logic had quashed terror in Ebe, allowing him to perform even better under terrifying circumstances. Now the most dangerous times were when the threat seemed menial; too small to trigger the overpowering logic, and too big to ignore. A simple worry about if they would run out of whatever speciality burger was flavour of the month was more of a risk than this situation. Acknowledging his shortcomings and unusual strengths, Ebe smiled and laughed under his breath.

"What's so fucking funny there, sport?" the man holding the gun sneered.

"He doesn't mean it. He's autistic."

The man rolled his eyes. "He'll be in good company here then. What are your names?"

"Marco Paulo, and Ebe Ellis."

1995

He knew she was coming. She had promised. But tuning his guitar, he felt sick. He hadn't told anyone, but from the buzz in the room, he could tell that everybody knew. And if he was about to receive a rejection, it would be a day no-one would ever forget.

And then she walked in. They'd only been alone a handful of times. There had been no intimacy; not even a kiss. And now he was about to ask her to commit her life, and the life of her unborn child, to his care. It was ridiculous. He couldn't go through with it. The expectant faces and winks told him he had no choice. It would be agonising whatever happened. And whilst her uncertainty would be understandable, he felt totally sure, himself. Uncertainty would be an affront to God. Or, worse, an admission he'd deluded himself for weeks.

Deeper and deeper breaths inhaled, he shook his head to rid the giddiness wobbling him. His guitar on his knee surprised him. He didn't remember picking it up. And now everyone was singing and playing around him, so he jigged along, opening and closing his mouth until recognition of the song sparked and he was able to join in.

There she was, smiling up at him as he strummed and fluffed his way through the set. He'd be forgiven. There was only one person there who didn't realise his nerves were shredded this morning.

When he had taken Geraint aside and asked for his daughter's hand, he could tell the gesture had secured him in the affections of his hopefully future father-in-law. A tearful handshake, and a jokey, 'I hope you know what you're letting yourself in for', had been the only response. And he must have told Diane, because she sat next to Carys and grinned in a way only the expected marriage proposal could explain. It was almost as though they'd be keen to be shot of her.

The set finished and the strain of expectation fell to his shoulders. She was beautiful, there was no denying. But he worried he might have been too hasty. People took years to decide on such matters. Was it all lust? Had he persuaded himself it was God's will to hasten the wedding night?

It was likely, apart from the dreams. They'd happened before he even laid eyes on her. And who cared if it wasn't love? It would be one day. She fitted in with the church – his life. His parents approved; her parents approved. What could go wrong?

As the silence threatened to envelop him, he made his announcement. "Carys, will you join me on the stage, please?" If she expected a duet, his bad playing might have put her off. But as she stood before him, and he dropped to one knee; in amongst the *oohs* and *ahs* of the gathered congregation, Carys appeared surprised. Her answer was lost in the noise, but from her smile and moist eyes he was sure it was a yes. So, he asked her to repeat it into the microphone. Confirmed, the crowd cheered and Marco grinned. This was what it was to have the Lord on your side.

SIX

On the same page

"Don't worry, my dear. Leave it all to me."

Marco kissed his mother on the forehead. "Thank you. But make sure you include Carys and Diane in the arrangements. We don't want to offend them, do we?"

It was a little late for that. Geraint's offer to pay for whatever Carys wanted was pushed aside by the sheer convenience of Pastor Dan Paulo being able to perform the necessary. And so soon. By the time Carys's favourite day—Christmas Day—was offered as the most suitable, and that it wouldn't cost anything at all because the church always provided a Christmas dinner for everybody anyway, it seemed churlish to argue. But that didn't mean they weren't seething in silence.

With a whistle, Marco walked to the buildings

behind the church. "Need a hand?" he called, as the finishing touches were being applied to the parish's carnival float.

"Typical, Marco. You've left it too late."

Marco grinned. "Really? What a shame."

The sonographer looked out from her darkened room at the ladies waiting for her services. There was a strange buzz in the air; some wanted to be told the sex of their little one, others were awaiting reassurance that there were no terrible conditions rearing their ugly heads to the echo-sound monitor.

Typically, they were not alone, and that was the case today. One girl was with an older doppelganger, obviously her mother. Another was with a doting husband, and yet another had brought the whole family. But the pretty blonde girl in the corner sat on her own. Her only company was the ferocious frown that ravaged her otherwise flawless features. What was her story? An unsupported single mum? A history of Downs in the family? She'd seen the look before. It was the expression of someone not able to take much-needed meds for the health of the foetus.

There was no mention of mental illness on any of the notes she had to hand. When she found out who this girl was, she'd try to tip off the midwives and the health visitor that she was a ripe one for post-natal depression.

After performing a number of scans, she'd

forgotten about the forlorn figure until last on her notes, she called her in. “Carys Ellis?” the furtive girl scurried past her and waited to be invited to sit.

“Nobody with you?” she inquired as she applied freezing gel to her fingers and slathered it over the girl’s bulbous belly. Moving the paddle around, it didn’t take long to locate the pulse, and she liked to reassure. A miracle; a little life created from one miniscule moment and now well on its way to being a living breathing human the same as them. In ten years, it had never stopped being miraculous.

“A good strong heartbeat. That’s what we like. Hopefully, baby will turn and give us a nice photograph. They cost three pounds if you’d care to keep it.”

Barely perceiving a nod, she carried on examining the cavern in front of her. Face turned away, hiding a frown, she pulled at her collar. ‘Have you seen the obstetrician?’ she had on her lips to say, but she didn’t want to worry her. Not yet.

The image spun round and round but there was no denying, this baby’s head was alarmingly large. There had to be a bad swelling. And if it was as enormous as it seemed, the brain remaining intact and unharmed would be unlikely.

They trained her not to jump to conclusions. Measure twice, write down once. So, she measured twice, and then thrice more, to be sure.

"Everything okay?"

The girl had picked up on her obvious tension. She couldn't say yes, and she didn't have enough data to say no, so she said nothing. Just kept clicking away. If there was good news, she'd find it now.

"Is something wrong?" the girl asked again.

It was time to pass the buck. If there was terrible news, she wasn't about to ruin her day imparting it. That was what consultants got paid to do. "I'm sure everything's fine..." she began, "But I will just go and get a colleague. Okay?"

Hurrying from the room, she struggled to contain her relief as she bolted for the sanctuary of a senior colleague's opinion. Shared, this particular problem could be more than halved. It may perhaps be removed from her responsibility altogether.

A gentle knock received no answer, but she was in. When the door opened and a mum-to-be ushered out with cheery farewell, the large nursing sister glared at her. "Maureen, can I help you?"

"Er, hi, Sheila. I'd like a second opinion, please."

The glare turned to glee. There were few things more gratifying than the recognition of others of one's pre-eminence. "Of course. What seems to be the trouble?"

Maureen sighed and resisted chewing a fingernail as her hand made its way automatically to her mouth. Lowering it, she smiled. "Baby's head is awfully large."

"Well, advise Mr Overton of a C-Section then, surely?"

"Well, yes. I'd already decided that. It's just, well, it's *really* big. Odd, in fact."

"Cephalitis."

"Of course, but I'm worried it's so severe the baby won't escape severe brain damage.

"And you want me to break it to your patient?"

"Oh, no. I don't think either of us should do that... We wouldn't want to deny dear Mr Overton of that pleasure."

Sheila nodded. "So, you want me to back you up? Confirm that you haven't got in a muddle with your measurements?"

"Something like that."

Sheila consulted her pocket watch. There were no more appointments today, so it was just for show. "Very well. Lead on."

Maureen felt a sudden panic that she'd left the odd girl on her own for a while and was keen to get back to the room. She pushed open the door a little too enthusiastically and saw the girl gasp. Before she had a chance to apologise, Sheila barged in and past her and took her place at the ultrasound machine.

Remembering her manners, she turned abruptly to Carys and greeted, "Okay, dear?" but her manners didn't extend to waiting for a response. And Maureen was right. This foetus displayed a lot of problems.

Measurements corroborated. She glanced at Maureen and gave a confirmatory nod before wiping the sticky gel from their patient and helping her sit round. "You aren't here with anybody, are you, dear?"

The girl didn't speak but shook her head.

"I don't want to worry you," she persisted, "But I'm going to refer you to the consultant obstetrician, Mr Overton. He's ever so nice."

"Wha... what's wrong?" the girl rasped

Sheila did her best to dress up a bad situation. It was easier than she thought. She was good at this. Perhaps she'd missed a vocation in politics. She told the truth. At least a palatable version of it. "None of the anomalies we look for were detected... but we are a little concerned with the size of your baby's head. It is unusually large. It may be that it will even out later on in the gestation,"

I don't see that happening, Maureen hid the thought behind a cough as her senior continued.

"...But you might have to bring your due date forward, and you might need to have a Caesarean section. Like I say, the consultant will tell you all about it." She patted her arm and squinted her eyes as she smiled. Careful, Sheila. Too much sympathy and she'll detect disaster.

"Is there any reason to think that Mr Ov..."

Sheila frowned. Here we go. The name never came, so she completed it for her, "Overton."

Nodding, the girl asked her question "...Will recommend termination?"

He may very well. It would depend on how optimistic he was about possible brain damage, but Sheila kept it politically non-committal. "I can't predict what Mr Overton will say, but I very much doubt *that* will be his recommendation," she regretted adding. Now if he did terminate this pregnancy, she might personally be held up as – she could barely bring herself to consider it – *fallible*. "It's probably nothing to worry about," she concluded and bit her lip as she put herself in the potential firing line again.

Maureen, as keen as Sheila to change the subject, thrust the little photograph at Carys. "You wanted to keep this, didn't you?" she received a glare from Sheila as a quick glance showed a foetal photo like neither had ever seen before. They only hoped the oddness didn't strike their inexperienced patient in the same way. And that she didn't show it to anybody.

Affronted that she hadn't made her plans clear, Marco conceded that she didn't have to tell him everywhere she went. And it was unlikely she was doing anything he wouldn't approve of. Jealousy was natural, he knew. And unattractive.

He was just musing the possibilities of her whereabouts when he spotted her leaving the bus from Haverfordwest. What was there? The hospital, of course. Why wouldn't she include him? Conscious he wasn't the father, but he was as good as, wasn't he?

Diane, of course. That was fair enough. But why catch the bus then? And wait, no, her mum wasn't with her. Staring, half-expecting to see her leave with another boy, his head slumped. "You're being an idiot," he slapped his cheek. Window winding down, he called out, "Hello, beautiful! Need a ride?"

Head shaking as she seemed to struggle to recognise him, she finally moved. "Can we go somewhere? For a coffee or something? I really want to talk to you."

A worried frown creased his forehead, "Er... okay. Everything all right?"

She refused to answer, but as he guided her into a small coffee shop near the bus stop, she warmed to his hand on her back. Once hot-chocolates arrived and they looked at one another over the steam escaping from beneath a cloud of whipped cream and marsh-mallow, she spoke. "I hope you meant what you said the other day?"

"What I said?" It took a while to realise it was the proposal. "Asking you to marry me? What do you think? Of course, I meant it!"

She reached her hands around the mugs and touched the ends of his fingers with hers. "You see, I don't want to wait. If I am going to be a good Christian wife, I can't exactly give birth before I'm married."

Calmed that their bulldozer plans fitted in with hers, he declared, "Christmas day soon enough?"

Gasping, her relief thrilled him. But then the first cloud of doubt circled in his head. It seemed plausible, but why was she so keen? And after a trip to the hospital, too. Had they told her something off-putting about the baby? Was he going to be a dad to some hideously deformed child? He reined his unkindness. If that was why God had called him to this role, then sobeit. Then he smiled. Maybe the baby wasn't going to make it. She might have lost it already. Didn't it take a while for the bump to diminish fully? So, if she thought the only reason he wanted to marry her was to be a helpful Samaritan, she might worry he wouldn't want her if she wasn't pregnant. The callousness returned. He couldn't help pondering how a childless Carys might be even more appealing.

SEVEN

The beginning of the end

It seemed like a bit of an anti-climax. Instead of being their special day, it had been Christmas morning like every other; except that in place of wearing what he wanted to church and playing in the band, he wore a suit and everyone seemed stressed.

It wasn't even just their day. The wedding was to be tagged on at the end of the usual service. They hadn't discussed guests, or table plans, or any of the expected arrangements, and Marco had been grateful. But now a creeping dread caked each step. With a jolting shake of his head, he brought himself back to his senses. It was God's will, remember?

The weeks since Carys begged him over coffee to make their marriage happen as soon as possible had been difficult. She had been distant, and every inquiry into why had met with nonchalant shrugs or irritation.

Convinced she'd been to the hospital without telling anyone, he just couldn't persuade her to comment and he'd become more swayed to the idea she had lost the baby. He hadn't asked directly. It was hard to voice without risking showing his true feelings. And he wasn't even certain what those feelings were. It was just her caginess putting worries in his head. But he trusted God. If it ended being a challenge, then it was because he needed it.

Doubts were appeased when he saw her. Committing to someone so alluring couldn't be that risky, could it? And the smiles and good wishes of his church family would get him through anything. Whatever happened, Marco was convinced it would be fine. And then there was the honeymoon. His loins twitched at the thought.

His dad's Christmas day service dragged more than normal. He wasn't even separated from his bride-to-be, and so the customary wait at the altar, turning to see her, wouldn't happen. He hoped it didn't matter.

"Thank you all for coming this morning. You won't regret it. Apart from my scintillating Christmas message, you have the wedding of my one-and-only son—you may have wondered why he was missing from the band today."

Marco wondered too. It was the only concession to the special day.

"—to the beautiful and lovely Carys Ellis." The congregation cheered and whooped and added some 'Praise the Lord' and 'Thank you, Jesus' to the congratulations.

"You're all invited, and afterwards there will be the usual Christmas dinner with a bit of a wedding twist. And as well as figgy pudding and mince pies, everyone will leave with some lovely cake that Natalia has baked and decorated." Gestures to the kitchen alluded to the said cake being hidden within, and the crowd *ooohed*.

"For now, if you could make your way to the back of the hall so we can set things up at the front. After the ceremony and dinner - 'Wedding Breakfast' we're calling it, the band– minus Marco, will play and we can all let our hair down and have a boogie." His wide eyes skimmed around the group, spreading his glee. Marco hoped Carys was feeling better about it all than he was.

Thankfully, he was excused from helping shift the chairs to form an aisle, and spared coffee duties too. Anxious glances around the room didn't help him spot Carys. With a gulp, he hoped she hadn't changed her mind. After a tense few minutes of nudges and surprising crude remarks about wedding night expectations, someone ushered Marco to the front of the hall. Behind him, the wedding march echoed, strummed on a guitar.

A few bars into it, Marco gulped as Carys walked

in. She'd got changed into a wonderful wedding gown, and walked perched on the arm of Geraint, smart in his full police uniform. There was no regret in the lump in his throat.

As she wafted down the aisle, he squinted at her bump, or lack of. She'd undoubtedly chosen a dress to hide her pregnancy, but he was suspicious it was doing such a good job. Her expression was numb. Not the glowing bride he'd hoped. If she had lost her baby, that would explain it. It was too late for doubts as she came to a halt in front of him.

As always, Dan didn't waste an opportunity to let everyone hear his voice, and it took forever to get to the part where they said 'I do.'

And when it arrived, it went off without issue. Carys spoke first and expressed some lovely vows she had written. Impressed, Marco embellished his dad's words on the spot with heartfelt but contrite messages of loving her for better and for worse.

Something in her eyes at the promise made him wince and convinced him that worse was beyond doubt where they were heading.

The dancing was okay, but most people there were much older than the two of them and overly keen to let their hair down. And the band seemed only to know a handful of songs that weren't praise, and one of those was The Birdie Song. Watching staid and reserved Christians flapping their elbows to the ridiculous record made Marco long for it to be over.

And then it was, but for a final announcement. Called onto the stage together, Marco held Carys's hand and they gazed at one another as Dan spoke into the microphone. "I'm sure our blushing bride and groom might be wondering where their presents are, but they can wonder no more, because here it is. A little something from us and your parents, Carys." He handed them an envelope for them both to open. Marco let his new wife do the honours.

Carys's slender fingers cut through the envelope flap and she pulled a card out.

"What does it say, dear?" Dan prompted with a grin, pushing the microphone towards her.

"A honeymoon. Two weeks in Mauritius. Oh, thank you, that's amazing!"

"Wow, yes, Dad. That is incredible. Thank you, and thank you, too, Geraint and Diane."

His new in-laws beamed up at him as his dad tapped him on the shoulder. "There's a car outside with suitcases packed. Your passports and tickets are in a bag on the front seat and it's ready to take you to the airport. Off you go. Enjoy!" He pulled Marco and Carys in to him for a hug and smiled as they eschewed through the parting crowd.

Confetti flew, good cheers shouted, and soon the new bride and her groom were alone in the back of the car. It was the first time they'd been alone all day. It was the first time they'd been alone ever…

EIGHT

A difficult start

Marco smiled as his bride squeezed his hand. He wanted her. They were married, and he wanted her right now. But they'd have to wait. He'd waited twenty-one years. Another few hours wouldn't matter, he supposed.

Their alone time didn't extend to even a kiss before they were interrupted by their driver, someone familiar from the church who tended to help a lot with the cooking, but Marco didn't know his name. "Hello, you two. Congratulations. But if you could leave that sort of thing until you're at your destination, I would appreciate it. Some things are best to be private."

Marco replaced Carys's hand to her lap and sat on his own. No, another few hours wouldn't matter.

The car pulled into Cardiff International Airport and their driver, whose name they still hadn't learned, and after the poor welcome were quite pleased about it, stopped at a drop-off-only bay. "Bags are in the boot. Here are your passports and tickets. Have a lovely time, and, don't do anything I wouldn't do," he laughed at his own joke, and when Marco and Carys failed to join in, he wobbled his head and threw open his door. Without words, he yanked the boot lid and slung the cases to one side. Bending so he could be seen through the rear windscreen, he shouted, "You two coming, or what?"

They edged to their respective doors and out of the car. As they reached their driver and their bags, Marco checked the documents were as handy as he'd been told. "Thanks for the lift. See you in a couple of weeks."

The man scoffed. "Not likely! You get back on a Saturday. Your dad's picking you up, I think. You'll have to check with him. Right, got everything?" he waited for the briefest of nods, then clapped his hands together and sniffed. "That's me off then. Bye bye."

They watched as he drove in the wrong direction as dictated by the airports one-way system, and then observed as he negotiated a roundabout and drove towards them. As he approached, his window wound down and he called out, "Get yourselves inside. You don't want to miss your flight."

Marco smiled and defiantly took his wife's hand. "Come on, Mrs Paulo."

"I'm still Ellis. Check the register. I didn't take your last name."

"Wha... What? Why?"

Carys shrugged. "We didn't talk about it. You could have taken my lovely Welsh name. I mean, we live in Wales, not Italy, don't we."

It can't be too late to persuade her, Marco thought. But did he want to? Alone at last; insomuch as no-one who knew them was anywhere near, Marco felt a cringing doubt. This was a bit much. He shouldn't have assumed, but why had she married him if she didn't want to?

"The main thing is, this little one won't be born out of wedlock," she said, cradling her bump.

"Mmm hmm," Marco mumbled. "Come on. Let's check in."

The concourse was crowded, and finding the British Airways desk wasn't immediately apparent. Screens flashing above them at every conceivable location had one word prominently displayed: Delayed.

They didn't know which was their flight, but Mauritius seemed likely to be the MRU shown midway on all the boards. As they spotted the Union Jack of the British Airways livery and approached the check in desk, the weary face of the uniformed attendant confirmed the annoyance.

"Sorry, your flight's been delayed. It should board soon, but they need to perform some last-minute checks after some issues landing."

Marco gulped. Waiting seemed the best option, definitely. Checked in with nowhere to go, he hardly felt like eating anything after the large Christmas wedding fayre they'd feasted on, but what else was there to do? And for how long?

His new wife agreed to a diet cola and an unimaginative jacket potato, which she picked at as they stared at the screen for updates.

Marco took a deep breath. Before the doubts about the baby, and doubts Carys wanted to marry him at all, there'd been the weeks and months of dreams and desire. He needed to remember that and rekindle a romance. Reaching across the table, he squeezed her hand and smiled. "What do we look like in our wedding clothes? You'd have thought we might get some special treatment, but no-one seems to have even noticed!"

"Yeah, I know," Carys grinned. "I can't wait to get bargains at duty-free. Maybe people will want to wish us well with extra discounts!"

The ice was broken. Carys might have been relieved Marco wasn't making a big deal about the name thing, and she let herself laugh. At last, Marco was enjoying her company, and looking across his glass, he couldn't wait to get her into their wedding night bed.

A few shopping bags dotted around them, already unconvinced at the supposed tax-free bargains they'd allowed to tempt them while they waited, Carys pushed away the diet coke she'd been nursing for the past two-and-a-half hours.

"Another?" Marco asked, and she shook her head. "Hungry?" He wasn't even peckish, himself. Bored? Definitely. "I'll go and ask again."

For the sixth time, Marco shuffled up to the check in desk, and for the sixth time, shuffled back shaking his head. Adding a shrug for good measure, he reported. "They're not sure, but it probably won't be too much longer."

Another four hours, and having succumbed to the free food vouchers offered due to missing the in-flight meal, they bit into dry burgers and sipped at unwanted drinks.

Despite a lack of hunger and thirst, they still found it incredibly annoying that before they even finished their 'meal' their flight was called.

With a furtive tapping, Marco began to stand. "Come on. This is us!" Briskly hurrying down the concourse, he aimed to side-step the conveyer. "We'll be faster if we run." He jerked back as his new wife halted like a stubborn mule.

"In case you'd forgotten, I'm pregnant." Marco sighed and turned towards the moving pavement. They wouldn't leave without them now. There was really no need to rush. Their hands rested on the shifting handrail, which as usual travelled faster than the walkway, tilting them both forwards.

The wrestle to find it amusing, or act disgruntled that her new husband had decided on a strenuous walk to the plane without even consulting her, showed in Carys's eyes. The occasion, and the excitement of finally boarding, seemingly won through and she laughed too. And where she'd flinched from his touch when he had first tried to hold her hand, she now allowed a squeeze.

They, along with a couple of hundred others, shuffled down the tunnel to inside the plane. The struggle to fasten seatbelts around a suit and a wedding dress reminded them how no-one had commented on why. Nobody uttered, 'Congratulations', or, 'Well done'. With so many marriages ending in divorce, Marco hoped it wasn't an omen.

It was dark, and they were tired. There were various options for movies and entertainment at their seats, but instead of enjoying any of that, they were woken by the duty-free trolley rattling down the aisle.

Eyes opening, the break of dawn lit under the slits of the window blinds and. They were due to arrive at what at home would have been 10.00am and lunchtime in Mauritius, but thanks to the delay, they were arriving in the evening, and so close to the equator, it was about to get suddenly dark.

Views of the beautiful islands from the aeroplane bubbled excitement in Marco as he leaned over Carys. “What do you think?”

“Breath taking.”

By the time luggage was retrieved and a taxi procured to take them on to their hotel, darkness had woven completely around them. It was a shame they hadn’t been able to view more on their first day, but they were here safe and sound, and although not technically their wedding night, it was night time, and there were certain matters which needed attending.

Shown to their room by a smiling tanned man, he offered them their first congratulations since they’d left Wales, and bid them a wonderful stay.

Champagne and a bowl of delicious fruit and snacks rested with a beautiful bouquet on the dressing table.

‘Mr and Mrs Paulo’

It read. Carys placed the card down and tapped it. “That’s not my name.”

Marco sighed. “They weren’t to know, were they. Our parents booked it. They must have assumed you’d follow tradition and take your husband’s.” Like I did, Marco thought, but instead of bothering saying again, he raised placatory palms and said, “Look, I can cross it out, if you want.”

Carys stared at it for a moment before

wordlessly turning it over. "I'm going to get washed and changed. I'm exhausted."

Part of Marco expected his new bride to put the finishing touches to a beauty routine before returning to woo him beneath the sheets. But he wasn't surprised when she came out wearing what appeared to be a t-shirt.

"Oh," he said. "I thought someone might have known to pack something a little more appropriate for the occasion. I suppose that's what you get, having a minister for a dad!"

Carys sighed. "There were some… other things. But I'm absolutely shattered."

"But it's our wedding night!"

"Technically, it's not, is it. Our wedding night was spent thirty thousand feet above the Indian Ocean."

Marco chewed his lip. Why hadn't he pushed to persuade her to join the 'Mile High' club? "If our marriage is unconsummated, it's not really a marriage."

Carys glared. "If that's the only reason you married me, perhaps we shouldn't be."

Pulling back the covers, she climbed into bed and hauled them over her head.

Marco sighed. The champagne and the fruit looked surprised they remained untouched. The romantic evening and passionate night promised by the spectacular location didn't look possible. Marco wasn't even sure if he was welcome in the bed. There was nowhere else to sleep though. All the other furniture in the beach-shack room was designed strictly for sitting. When the first snores echoed, Marco risked climbing quietly beside her.

Sorrow for himself eased when he thought more. This wasn't a normal wedding night. His beautiful bride was carrying the child of the boy who raped her. He'd never experienced intimacy, and her only experience was against her will. Of course, she wasn't going to wear sexy underwear and seduce him. He had been an idiot. Tomorrow, he would be the non-threatening, lovely guy, who God placed in front of Carys in the first place.

There was much to enjoy apart from carnal flesh. And, put at ease in this romantic setting, it was likely to lead to what he desired. But she was right. If that was all he wanted, he shouldn't have married her. And despite some doubts, he knew he can't really have gone to all this trouble just to fulfil his lustful desires. "Start again, Marco," he said under his breath. "She deserves to be wooed."

NINE

Closeness at last

Breakfast in bed, whilst brought to their room by hotel staff, would still be pampering if he made sure he jumped up and got it for her. Tray in hand, he closed the door swinging his hip, and sashayed over. "Good morning, wonderful wife." Was that a bit much considering she would know he was disappointed about last night's non-existent nuptial celebration? He retained his grin, and lay the tray on folded down sheets. "This looks amazing, doesn't it."

There could be no denying it, but Carys looked less than impressed. "Can't we eat it outside in the sunshine?"

Careful to keep the smile in place, it was a mission now. Don't take offence. This is a test from God. "Lovely idea, my love." Jumping up, he skipped to the window and pulled back the curtain, and they both gasped.

More like a film set than reality, the turquoise ocean lapped right up to their room. There was even a slide straight into the crystal waters. “We could swim before food, couldn’t we? Work up an appetite. We won’t want to ‘wait twenty minutes after eating’, will we!”

Carys grinned. Nobody could maintain melancholy in these surroundings. “Last one in the water is a rotten egg,” she screamed, sounding like an Enid Blighton novel as she scurried to the slide. Marco ran too and jumped straight from the veranda and they hit the water together.

“A draw, I think,” he laughed.

Carys’s bright eyes flashed. “Okay, a lap around our hut. First back on the deck is the winner.”

Choosing the direction by swimming first, she had an unfair advantage as the slide cut off some of the circuit. Despite a slender build, she wasn’t a fast swimmer. Her overly large breasts made her too buoyant, and she struggled to keep her face in the water.

Marco finished at the steps several seconds before her, but instead of rushing up for the win, he waited. As she reached him, she smiled. “You could have won easily.”

“I’ve already won. I’ve married you.”

Carys swam up and put her arms around him. Ruffling his hair, she pulled him close and kissed him on the lips.

Water beaded around the curve of her breasts and as she pressed against him, his genitals thrust from stasis, desperate to get in on the action, but Carys pressed her hand on his chest and pushed him away. "Sorry. Not yet." She kissed him again and dived into the water. Splashing salty spray, she squealed. Come on, let's race again."

Marco grinned. This was torture. Paralysed by his swollen shorts, he laughed. "In a minute. I just need to catch my breath."

Intimate encounters were left alone for the first week of the honeymoon. Marco endured, frustrated, but proud. He'd waited long enough, gaining the trust of his beautiful bride was worth waiting a while longer.

They had relaxed, and cuddled, and kissed. And they'd swum and eaten and travelled to tourist recommended hot spots of the incredible island.

Discovering the mountainous interior of Black River Gorges National Park together brought them closer, then on a sunset cruise Carys was so cuddly Marco thought that would be the night. She slept in his arms and that had been enough.

It transpired the vital ingredient that had been missing was alcohol. Alcohol and dancing in beach club bars they'd missed entirely on their first week, having been booked into an expensive and exclusive couples' retreat. From their sunset boat, they'd spotted vibrant nightlife and sought it out the next day. Company and music, closeness, and vibrancy: all the ingredients for a great New Year's Eve.

As 1993 blurred into 1994, the significance washed over them like the Mauritian sea cleansing the perfect white sand. "This is paradise," Carys whispered into Marco's ear as he leaned in over the loud music. Hands above her head, beer bottle in hand, Carys moved like a natural, and despite the opulence of beach-body-ready girls, her curves garnered the most attention.

They danced until they were the only ones left. Ushered away with fond farewells, Carys grabbed Marco's hand and skipped away, giggling to the shore.

Behind some rocks, far from the bar, she pulled him onto the sand and kissed him passionately, and this time when he responded, she thrust her hand down his shorts. "Thank you for being patient."

Marco smiled and kissed her hard as he wriggled free from his restraints. On top of their clothes, the sea lapped their feet as, naked, Marco climbed atop her and looked deep into her eyes. 'I love you' poised on his lips, but he stopped himself saying. First of all, he wasn't sure he did, and even less convinced she loved him too. And it might create awkwardness.

Noticing him pause, Carys stalled too. Pulling back, she said, "Are you worried about hurting the baby?"

He hadn't been, but saying so cooled his ardour rapidly, and combined with the cool lapping water, his robust libido softened. His flagging was short lived when she whispered in sultry tones, "Don't worry, it's fine." His apparent display of caring turned her on, and she grabbed him passionately.

Barely able to appreciate the moment, as soon as he caressed the moist welcoming warmth between her legs, everything took on a surrealism. Ecstasy reached almost at once, Marco collapsed beside his new bride with a groan in a fit of paralysis.

His senses returned to the sound of her laughing. "Well, that's what I get for making you wait, I suppose!" Taking him in her hand, and mouth, he was soon ready again. Sliding her legs around him, she straddled him and reached to put him back inside her.

In total connection, they writhed back and forth and Marco was relieved that just before he reached the point of bliss again, he saw the same look in her and they achieved the closeness they had both craved but been denied their whole lives. This was worth the wait. This was special. Marco held her and stroked her hair, closer to her than anyone else in his life, and he liked it.

TEN

The honeymoon is over

The Welsh weather, a metaphor. A new year, and a return from paradise to mundanity. Moving into the marital home wasn't much of a chore. Marcus had mortgaged a townhouse in the centre of Narberth a couple of years ago and had given notice to the occupants who rented it from him that he would need it. It seemed harsh over Christmas, but as is often the way with God's plans, it coincided with their own requirements to return to family in the Midlands.

The furniture was his – it had been included in the purchase when he bought it. The corner terraced house had been the show home, as it was the first one anyone coming into the close would see. Not his taste, perhaps, but stylish none-the-less, and now at least there was the nursery to consider. A chance to put their stamp on the place.

Carys had not been as enthused as he expected, and opted for a neutral colour scheme. It was a good idea. They didn't know what she was having and they might have more children of their own soon.

They'd made love only once since they returned. A christening of their new bed, but Carys complained it was getting a bit uncomfortable now. Marco presumed that would be it for a while. She would only get bigger and more painful, and then how long did you have to wait afterwards? Mauritius had been wonderful, eventually, but the honeymoon was physically and metaphorically over.

Back to work had filled him with dread, but being away from home gave him something to concentrate on where he didn't have to second guess every choice he made and didn't have to please his wife. Leaning backward in his chair in County Hall, he filed another claim for housing benefit and notified another department of a recently deceased tenant and broke for lunch. With such excitement, no wonder he'd become so enamoured with getting married. Anything for some satisfaction.

When he pulled into the close and parked outside their home, the lack of life within was a shock. He didn't know what he expected; not Carys running out to greet him, throwing her arms around him, but it would have been nice.

Presumably she was still at college if she wasn't home. With a frown he commented how late it was, but he wasn't really accustomed with her routine. With a sigh, he tried not to think about how he wasn't really familiar with her at all.

The gate unbolted with a creak and he opened the door into the kitchen, grunting in disappointment that no cooking smells greeted him and he was even more sure she wasn't home. A scowl grew on his face and he assumed the loud blaring of a television was coming from one of the nearby neighbours.

Pulling his phone from his pocket, his thumb scrolled to 'Carys Mobile' and pressed send. Voicemail began its message, and he ended the call. Out of battery, he supposed.

Apprehension mounted as he walked from the kitchen into the hallway to the toilet. Drying his hands, he shook his head and squinted. The loud television was upstairs. How was that possible? Two at a time he bounded up, then flung the door open.

Carys barely glanced in his direction before staring back at the screen. A moustached man commented on the Pyramids' connection to ancient aliens.

Marco glared at the TV and back at his wife. "What on earth are you doing?" It was as though he'd said nothing. "I thought dinner would be started. How long have you been home from college, anyway?" Struck by a notion, he raised his voice. "Why are you watching television in the bedroom and not in the lounge? Have you even been to class today?"

Carys still didn't look up or speak.

"You haven't, have you? Have you been in bed gawking at this... this... crap all day?"

The scowl Carys gave him in reply made him hanker for silence again. "Leave me alone," she growled with quiet rancour.

"*I'll* make dinner then, shall I?" he hissed, half-placatory, half-antagonistically.

"Do what you fucking want," she spat, her face glowing with hateful rage.

Marco retreated like a wounded puppy, went back downstairs, and looked around the kitchen for inspiration. They'd only shopped for basics but there was enough to make a decent Bolognese, and that was something he took an Italian's pride in. As well as the benefits of occupying his thoughts, he was sure the delicious smell would tempt her.

As it was quick to prepare, it didn't give long for Carys to calm down; and he didn't want to risk more abuse by calling up that dinner was ready. He shouldn't eat without telling her, so he allowed it simmer. "Let the flavour develop," he said out loud to himself.

He nearly died of shock when Carys put a conciliatory hand on his shoulder while he stirred the sauce. He hadn't noticed her coming downstairs.

"Sorry," she said.

The aroma of fresh cooking had worked its magic. He fought the urge to press her on why she'd spent the day in bed. The return to normality must have hit her harder than him. And college was arguably less important. They didn't pay her for a start. "Dinner's ready." He smiled.

Spooning the long pasta expertly onto two plates and ladling on the juicy red sauce, he carried them to the kitchen table and placed them with silver service precision.

Winding the steaming pasta around his fork, he was several mouthfuls in, when, mid-slurp, he noticed she wasn't eating.

Dinner pushed about the plate, she caught his eye, "Sorry," she whispered. "I'm not feeling very well today."

Marco sat up. He'd been quick to temper and hadn't even thought she might be unwell. Why had he been so quick to assume she was being lazy? He pushed back his chair and wrapped his arms round her shoulders. "No, I'm sorry. I was horrible to you, and you're not well."

Carys squeezed him back. "Come on, let's snuggle up and watch a film."

He'd dodged a bullet. This was harder than he thought. But an only child embarking on their first and only relationship might be forgiven inconsiderateness. It was a learning curve. The Lord wouldn't give him more than he could handle.

As he sat with Carys leaning against him, he twirled her long hair around his fingers. Suddenly, she pulled away. What had he done now?

"What do you think about UFO's?" she blurted.

Not a lot, was his immediate thought, but he was already learning. Discounting a topic which she was clearly interested in without consideration would not win him any favour. And fortunately, the prospect had been discussed at a recent Bible group. "The church doesn't deny the possibility that other life may exist on one or more of the infinite number of stars and planets out there," he explained. "I'm not sure how I feel about it, but it's nice to think that God and the concept of life on other planets aren't mutually exclusive."

It seemed like he'd got the answer right as Carys slid back down the couch and rested her head once again on his shoulder and purred at his stroking of her hair. Marco smiled to himself. A little consideration. That's all it would take.

ELEVEN

Carys cracks

It had been the weirdest dream. He blamed Carys. The stupid documentaries about aliens had obviously seeped into his subconscious. And now, in the bright of dawn, he didn't remember much.

Big heads, skinny bodies, huge eyes; peering down at him; examining him. He shuddered. They talked to him and he understood what they were saying. He remembered that, but not a thing that was said.

His gaze fell to his wife. She really was beautiful. Should he wake her and find out if she was any better? If she wasn't, resting would be best. He decided to bring her a cup of tea. If that woke her, then she wouldn't mind.

With a yawn, he staggered downstairs to the kitchen and returned with tea for both of them. Leaving his to cool while he quickly showered,

Carys still hadn't stirred when he dried off, dressed, and glugged down his own cup. "Bye, lovely," he whispered hoarsely and gently closed the door.

Sat behind his steering wheel, he knew something was wrong. A sense of dread crept from his stomach, whirling around his body from his chest and down his arms. He tensed to free himself from the feeling but it remained.

He turned the key and started the engine. Work, he hoped, would be the distraction he needed.

Chat at the photocopier was easy going and helpful. Mandy, an older colleague, reassured how normal their relationship sounded; how disruptive pregnancy hormones can be. Collin, another colleague confirmed his wife had lost interest in the bedroom when she fell pregnant. Both agreed everything would be okay, and he felt better.

When he pulled up, he knew what to expect. If she was home and in bed, it was because she wasn't well and he would make sure to treat her as a doting husband should.

Hand paused on the handle as he took a breath, he pushed open the door. Silence greeted the same as yesterday. He sprang up the stairs but paused outside the bedroom before going in. Propped up on pillows, Carys snored loudly above the noise of the television which again showed a program about extra-terrestrials.

Deliberately ignoring it, hoping it didn't plague his dreams tonight, Marco leant over and swept hair from her face before planting a gentle kiss on her forehead. "Is there anything you'd like for dinner, sweetheart?"

She smiled up at him. He was getting good at this. Mandy and Collin were right. Everything would be okay. Returning her smile, he went back downstairs, had a look around for dinner ideas while the kettle boiled, and returned with a cup of tea for her.

As the door swung back on his hinges, his grin crinkled in the tense atmosphere. He placed the cup of tea next to her and scanned her face to work out what was wrong. "How are you feeling? Anything interesting on the telly today? Don't let your tea go cold." She said nothing. Marco backed away with the promise of dinner. As he retreated downstairs, his heart dropped with every step.

As he reached the bottom, a crash halted his heart. Hurrying back up again, he recognised the sound of breaking crockery but couldn't work out how it had happened. Had she fallen reaching for it?

She sat on the bed. Something in her calmness unnerved him. His eyes followed where she stared. A large stain on the wall above the smashed cup on the floor raised his eyebrows. Why had she done that? Hormones. Mandy and Collin's warnings echoed in his mind. There was no point asking why she'd done it, was there. It wasn't rational so he shouldn't expect a rational explanation. The Lord won't give you more than you can handle, he reminded himself again.

He backed away and padded, defeated, downstairs to make their meal. His appetite had left him, but he had to try to be normal. Like fighting evil with love, he would fight his wife's hormonal abnormal behaviour with the most normal behaviour he could muster.

Marco found inspiration hard to come by in the edgy environment. After a brief look through kitchen supplies, he decided on sausage and mash. Not a favourite, but it was something.

Cooking, like going into the office, was becoming a mindless comfort. With scissors he snipped the little piece of skin in-between each link. Three each seemed greedy, perhaps he should put a couple back in the fridge for a sandwich to take to work.

Potato peeling was therapeutic too, and when he'd boiled them and grated butter and cheese into them and pounded them to death with the masher, a lot of his tension released. But now it was ready, he would have to call his wife, and he wasn't sure he wanted to.

It wasn't worth risking antagonising her, he decided. He popped his head around the kitchen door and called, "Carys!" He waited, not expecting a reply, and none was forthcoming. "Carys!!" He called a little louder. "Dinner is on the table." Injecting a sense of considerate firmness, like he was determined not to take any nonsense. Still no answer. What was he supposed to do?

Sat staring at his plate, after all that work, he didn't want it now. He pushed his towards hers and sighed. He'd have to go and check on her, wouldn't he. It all was getting a bit ridiculous.

With another huge sigh, he slumped up the stairs without bothering to disguise the sound of his footsteps, nor his displeasure. Pausing half way, the silence disconcerted him. What was she doing up there? Sleeping? He hoped so. Maybe she'd wake in a better mood.

Hesitating outside, the bedroom door was now closed when it had been ajar. Peeved that he should be unwelcome in his own room, he raised a reluctant hand to knock. There was no response to his gentle rapping. Twisting the handle, he pushed it open.

Carys sat in the middle of the bed rocking forwards and backwards. Blood on her wrists clotted and was starting to scab. Wounds, raw and painful. There was a scarlet stain on the bedsheet; thankfully not enough for Marco to worry she was in danger, but he couldn't contain his distress at what he saw and let out a wail of anguish. "What have you done you silly, silly girl? How is that going to help, hey?" How could he accept his beautiful wife of only a few weeks was in such a state? Why disfigure herself like this? "God made those wrists you're abusing!"

Carys flung what was left of the cup, missing him by inches. Either her aim wasn't brilliant, or she hadn't meant to hit him. "Hey! There's no need for that."

Carys screamed. A primordial, hair-raising scream that shook the ceiling and hurt his ears. "You don't understand!" she yelled. "You don't care about me!"

Marco gasped. "Of course, I care!"

She leaped up, and in one bound made it round the bed to him where she unleashed her clenched fists on his broad chest. He wasn't hurt, but he was angry. This was a step too far. "Behave yourself. You're acting like a spoiled little brat."

"Huh! Like you care? You haven't even asked what's wrong!"

She had a point, but he was loath to give her any leeway after her appalling behaviour. Looking again at her blooded wrists, he accepted this wasn't a rational human being he was dealing with. He tried to keep calm. "I'm sorry," he forced through gritted teeth. "You're right. I haven't." her shoulders dropped in response to his mollifying tone. "What's wrong, my darling?" he finally asked.

"I can't tell you," she said shyly. "You wouldn't believe me."

Marco squeezed his eyes shut. For heaven's sake, there was no winning. With a fake smile he opened them again. "Try me."

Fiddling with the duvet, damp and stained with

her blood, she mumbled, "I have an alien baby growing inside me, and I don't know if I can cope." As soon as the words left her lips, her hand shot to her mouth to silence them.

Well, he had asked. What could he say? Noticing Carys twitching her hands from the corner of his eye. A sharp piece of the broken cup was gripped in her right hand, she didn't seem aware of it as she fidgeted with her nightie. He knew silence wasn't an option. "Why do you think that, my love?"

"I don't think it. I *know* it!"

Marco slowly released his breath. "How?" was all he thought to ask.

Carys glared at him, as though she didn't grasp how he could be so thick. "Because I only had one encounter before you. I don't remember it because that's what they do. They wipe your memory. At first, I thought this boy, Stephen Holmes was the father, but after I asked him, I'm sure he's not. He sounded adamant and really believable that nothing had happened between us. He told me about the figures walking towards the car."

"I know who Stephen Holmes is," Marco said. "Your mum and dad were frantic about him raping you. Why would you believe him? He abused you and got you pregnant. Of course he's going to deny it!" he noticed his tone getting loud and took another calming breath. "I can't understand, for a second, why you'd buy anything he says." Despite his best intentions he was shouting now. "And what have you come up with to excuse his lies? An alien pregnancy!"

His speech hoarse, he couldn't stop, "I know you have hormones raging through your body, and since meeting me the idea of that scum touching you probably makes your skin crawl even more, but come on. Get real!" He tried to cough away the frog in his throat. "He raped you. He's covering for himself by taking advantage of your fragile state. That's all. That's all it is." Too late, he added, "But I'm here now, and everything's going to be okay."

He caught a glimpse of how he may have got things catastrophically wrong in Carys's catatonic stare. "Let us pray," he suggested in desperation. "In the name of Jesus," he began, and then he mumbled something that basically amounted to helping her see sense, but calling God onside.

Words dried up, and he gulped. It hadn't gone well. Logic was what she needed, but she looked ready to refuse it forever. But what else might he have said? 'Oooh, an alien. That's interesting. What shall we call him, Jar Jar Binks? Meesa no think so.' Remembering dinner was still untouched downstairs he muttered, "Dinner's ready," and slumped from the room.

His appetite hadn't returned, but he forced the sausages and mashed potato down with dogged determination. She wouldn't make him abnormal as well.

After the first mouthful, the taste awoke a hunger in him and, for a moment, he debated eating hers. He didn't. If she did come down, finding he'd eaten her dinner may well set her off again. There were the sausages in the fridge, though.

Pushing back his chair, he stood with the refrigerator door open, the light illuminating as he poured brown sauce along the length of the sausage and wolfed it in two bites. There seemed little point saving the last one, so he ate that as well.

A glance toward their room fed him no new information, and he allowed furtive hope she was asleep to push him into the lounge and flick through the TV channels. Mindless action seemed most likely to take his attention, and he chanced upon something with Sylvester Stallone and thought that will do.

A crash from upstairs made him sigh and squint at the ceiling. What now? As he peeped from the lounge, Carys was hurrying down. Dinner had worked its magic again. He should right a recipe book – *'How to Calm The Mentally Ill With Food'* – he thought as he scurried to the kitchen. Deftly removing her saved plate from the fridge, Marco was blocked from getting to the microwave to reheat it by Carys as she pushed past him to the cereal cupboard. Oh well. If she didn't fancy sausages, at least it would be something.

Standing with the plate in his hand, his gazed followed Carys as she slid her finger under the cardboard flap on the box and peeled open the plastic bag. But she didn't continue to prepare a bowl of cornflakes as he expected. Instead, she poured the entire contents of the box onto the kitchen floor.

In disbelief, Marco felt paralysed and also curious. Why was she doing this? Without a word or even a look his way, she crunched over the floor and opened the fridge to take out the large six-pint bottle from the door.

Surely not, Marco widened his eyes. Yes, she was. Determined not to react; attention must be what she wants, he thought. Sucking in his cheeks, he watched as she poured the milk to meet the cornflakes. Her next move was swift and took him by surprise, but as soon as she'd swiped the plate of food from his hands onto the floor, he knew he should have expected it. And what happened next.

Carys was already out of the kitchen and heading for the front door. "Where are you going?" Her rapid pace jolted him to action. As he witnessed the door close with Carys the other side, he rushed after her and grabbed the handle, desperately aware of the final turn of the key in the lock.

Through the kitchen to the back door, he skidded on the milk and cornflakes, just making it across the room without falling. The door fumbled open, he burst into the garden. The temperamental gate catch conspired to hinder him, but he wobbled it free, then erupted, breathlessly, onto the street.

Of course, she wasn't there, and he had no idea which direction she'd gone. Eyes squinting, he glared at each corner desperate for clues, but nothing struck him.

Come on, think! Where is she likely to have headed? The Drang—Pembrokeshire slang for alleyway—was to the left, down which dark tunnel the town centre sat in a neat circle around them. The other way led to the communal garden of a warden-controlled complex for elderly residents. Straight ahead was clearly in view and he was confident he'd have spotted her. The gates to the residents' flats creaking was usually a source of irritation. Marco was sure he hadn't heard it. That left the Drang, apart from a gap through the fence to the fire station, but at five months pregnant, that was unlikely.

Hurtling down covered alley and into the main street, he could see a long way up and down the road. She wasn't there so he raced back up and past the old peoples' complex onto the street the other side of the town.

Out of breath, he shook his head. She was large and pregnant; how had she outmanoeuvred him? A sniff of the air sucked cold reality into his lungs. He couldn't just leave her out here. It was bitter. Her wellbeing, and the health of the baby, were not all he had to consider. Teeth pulled at his lips until it hurt. He had to admit she was a danger, to herself, her baby, and to the public. He had no choice: he needed help.

Reaching the front door, he remembered it was locked. He saw with relief, Carys had left the key protruding from the barrel. Inside, he yanked the phone from its cradle on the hallway table and dialled 999.

"Emergency services. Which service do you require?"

"Er," he needed the police, he knew that, but requiring an ambulance wasn't inconceivable. His head quivered in confusion, and he blurted, "Police, please." The line was quiet for a brief but tense minute and then the police answered.

When he replaced the handset, he couldn't even remember what he'd said. Had he mentioned cornflakes? He wasn't sure. They were coming, and that was all that mattered. Restless, what more could he do? Geraint, his police sergeant father-in-law. Of course. Phoning required him to paw through the telephone book they kept by the phone. It rang with no answer. Marco sighed. It was late. He was probably asleep, or working a night shift. He might even attend. That would be weird.

He couldn't rest. From memory, he phoned his parent's number but there was no answer there either. Hopes to mobilise a posse of Fellowship members to search for her faded. Embarrassing her was the last thing he wanted to do, but he had to try everything to help her and their baby.

Still wondering what more he could be doing; who else he should call, a squad car with flashing lights appeared at the front of the house and he answered the door before it was knocked. Two officers, a sturdy male and efficient female waited to be invited inside and Marco showed them into the lounge.

"Has your wife been diagnosed with any mental health conditions?"

Marco shrugged. "I don't think so. It might be hormones because she's pregnant."

The police woman gave him a watery smile, and a lump rose in his throat. It had been testing. The honeymoon hadn't been perfect, and setting up their marital home had been far removed from the bliss everyone seeing them may expect. He smiled back and fought the stinging in his eyes.

"Do you think she could be a danger to herself or others?"

He'd already said on the phone, but he confirmed, "I really do, yes. Definitely to herself and her baby. And I don't know how she'd react if a stranger tried to get near her. She was aggressive enough towards me. I'll show you the kitchen in a minute."

Wedding and honeymoon photos were the

most recent. Armed with those, they began their search. As they left with those and instructions for Marco to wait at home in case she returned, he leaned against the door and sighed. God won't give me more than I can handle, he confirmed to himself yet again. But it felt like it at the moment. How sure was he that helping a rape victim overcome her abuse and settle into a normal family life was his calling? He suspected more and more that he may have been the victim of his suffocated libido. If he'd been allowed girlfriends; or rather, to be intimate, sexually with girls before now, would he have been so ready to commit himself to Carys?

Perhaps that was the point. It made him perfect for the role. He sighed again. But doing God's work would bring him joy, even if it was anything but at the moment.

He felt trapped. Being responsible for Carys was not what he wanted. Eyes turned to heaven, accompanied by more sighing as his tears stung anew. His own mental health was in danger at this rate. If he could be assured it was God's will, that would give him the strength to persevere. If it was a desperate foray to get laid, then this was his punishment for giving into such base instincts. Yes, that's exactly what it feels like. I've been a fool, haven't I?

Before his question received any discerned reply from the realms of greatness, the door knocked. What if it was her? Or, what if someone had found her in the worst possible way? For a fleeting moment that would haunt him, he wished they had. That an officer on the doorstep would say, 'I'm sorry to have to tell you this, but I'm afraid we've identified your wife, and it's not good news.'

No, that would be terrible. It was an errant, demonic thought. But if he was doing God's will, no demon would dare come near him. Was this the sign he'd asked for? Having such an evil image, even just for a second, and even if he didn't mean it—and of course he didn't—that must be a sign: a bad omen? The door opened to a uniformed man and Marco swallowed. What had he done? What had he wished for? "Yes?" He squeaked. "Any news?"

In a gruff tone, the officer answered. "No sign of her. That's why they called me out." Marco stared for a while before noticing the 'Dog Unit' badge on the man's jacket. "Could you bring something of your wife's for Rufus to smell while I get him ready?"

The choice was obvious. There were no recent clothes. The tracksuit-like pyjamas she'd been wearing for days, she was still wearing. That left the pillows. Upstairs, he grabbed her used case and discarded the pillow inner onto the bed.

"Go on Rufus. Get that scent in your nostrils."

Rufus, an enormous German Shepherd Dog, looked clearly excited to do his job. Amber eyes, bright as neon as his nose twitched at the smell, and he strained at the lead. Marco wished he enjoyed his office so much.

Given the go-ahead and the command to 'Go find,' Rufus raced off with his handler past the old peoples complex and up to the main road.

If Marco had known that was the way she'd headed, he could have caught her easily, but it had seemed the least likely. How had she made it through the gate without him hearing? It would have been while he was crunching over milk and cornflakes and wrestling the back gate catch. She probably thought he had heard; possibly waited for him to come and make amends. He'd got it wrong again. That didn't sound like the will of God. To keep making errors of judgement struck far more akin to instruction from a different source altogether. Marco shuddered and re-closed the door.

They'd find her soon. There was no way she was outrunning Rufus. He should try to sleep while he had the chance. He didn't know how he would cope when she returned. If this wasn't his calling after all, perhaps he wouldn't have to.

TWELVE

You must do as we say

The bedroom uninviting, and he didn't want to be too far into unconsciousness when she came back. A rest on the sofa would be better. Eyes screwed closed, despite the darkness and the quiet, sleep proved elusive.

The same monologue played round his head: He'd made a mistake. He couldn't care for Carys. Things were due to grow graver when the baby arrived. That was the real reason she needed him: she didn't want her baby born out of wedlock. It was against his teachings to divorce, but given the exceptional circumstances, surely God would understand.

Now they were married, it wouldn't be born a bastard as Carys was so keen to avoid. That didn't mean they had to stay together, did it? Couldn't they live 'estranged'?

Sighing was so deep his lungs threatened to

explode on his out breath. Could he defend leaving her? Abandoning his wife was a terrible idea. The evil thought clearly coming from demons and not his Lord and saviour was contention raging in his head again. But even if his actions pursuing and marrying Carys Ellis had not been the result of divine guidance, that didn't mean deliberately doing wrong now was justified. He had made his bed, and he'd have to lie in it.

But not now. Now, he would lie on the sofa.

Lights off, the only illumination came from the satellite box, whose faint light grew more irritating as Marco's eyes became accustomed. Pillows propped, he flattened them, pummelling harder with his fists as frustration at his situation and the cushion's refusal to conform to a comfy shape irritated him. He sat bolt upright and leaned hard against the back of the couch. Feet planted firmly, he released his breath and began a prayer, the gist of which was to provide him with strength to do the right thing, and again asked for a sign.

Being careful what one wishes for was a phrase Marco would soon bring to mind.

The darkness—which had become a blinking blue haze Marco scarcely believed emanated from the tiny display of the receiver box beneath the television screen, and which made him appreciate how much energy might be consumed worldwide if millions of these little lights lit up homes twenty-four hours a day—suddenly changed.

From nowhere, dazzling luminosity flooded every corner of the room. His first thought was a helicopter searchlight, but their lounge seemed an odd place for that. Then he wondered if floodlights from the Fire Station might be polluting the night sky from a training exercise, but then he realised whilst it was next door, the houses opposite would block, or at least, diffuse their floodlights.

Whatever generated this glare was much closer. With a frown, he tried to distinguish an odd noise; a humming from outside. It's direction indiscernible, it came from everywhere. Pulling back the curtains and peering out seemed the natural thing to do, but instinct clutched him. It must be the tension of his wife's behaviour because he couldn't understand why he felt so scared.

Hands gripped the arms of the sofa and the cushion beside him, fingernails digging into his palms until pain brought his awareness rushing, returning to the room. Feet firmly on the floor lacked the power to push him to stand.

Paralysed, the humming noise got louder and the searing light shone so fiercely he couldn't see: like looking directly at the sun. Gasping for breath, he knew it must be the sign he asked for. An angel would appear and tell him the child in Carys's womb was special. And like Joseph, he would be asked to care for a child of God.

But it wasn't an angel who emerged from the light. Not like any angel Marco had ever imagined. The creature in the doorway, grey, and naked, and angry, and as far removed from Marco's accepted view of angels as it was possible for him to conceive.

Welded to the sofa, the wetness he sat in didn't even register in his head. He had to get away, but paralysis fused him to his seat.

The creature shifted towards him. Breath caught in his throat and he wriggled his quivering backside as far as the cushion allowed. It shouted at him in a voice like the death squeals of a large tortured animal – an elephant fighting its last fight while poachers held it down to cut its tusks from its face. Marco's mind cramped as he realised he understood. In his brain, words flowed as easily as hearing plain English: "Listen. You must do as I say. I will not harm you if you do as I say."

Marco opened his mouth but his lips wouldn't wrap around shaping words, so he bobbed his head. He would do whatever this thing asked him to. He knew he didn't have a choice.

"The child is coming. You must protect it and teach it."

'Teach it what?' he desperately needed to ask, but even the thought was hard to coax. With a gulp, he awaited instruction.

"There is vital work he will be of great help

with. No harm must come to him. That means no harm must come to his mother. Do you understand? You must not cause harm, or take any action you consider might cause harm, to the mother. We are always watching, and we cannot allow you to fail in this endeavour."

The bright light left, and Marco stared into the darkness as if he had just woken. With a sigh, he sucked rapid breaths and calmed his racing heart. "A nightmare, that's all," he spoke in a loud voice, challenging the room to show him he was wrong; defying the whatever-it-was to contradict him. His heart sprinting once again, he wished he hadn't been so bold. As the room lingered in silent dimness, his anxiety subsided.

"A dream, that was all. A bright light. An unearthly being. Orders to care for an important child. It all sounds like a visit from one of God's angels. I must have turned it into an alien because of all those documentaries Carys insists on watching."

Marco knew he'd had his sign. The nightmare was real, but he duped himself to trust its divinity. If he told anyone, he knew he would convince them, too, that an angelic visitation was exactly what it was.

And the result was the same either way: He wasn't about to leave Carys. Despite the appeal of being away from the difficulties, he was glad to accept his fate. At least he could continue his notion that pursuing her had been deific will, and not merely human lust. As the light of dawn broke through a gap in the curtains, he lay back on the couch and closed his eyes.

THIRTEEN

Unwelcome appearance

The knocking woke him and he jumped up ready to fight or flee aliens. Echoing in the hallway, he recognised it as the knocking and felt foolish. Arms numb, he struggled to push himself to his feet and stagger to the door. With sensation not fully returned, he fumbled it open. Only when he saw the uniforms did he consider that exercising more caution might have been sensible. But he didn't really think he was in danger from his wife, did he?

"Mr Paulo. May we come in?"

With a gulp, he stood aside. What were they about to tell him? Eyes squeezed almost closed, readying him to hide away from guilt if his dark prayers had been answered to be rid of his destructive spouse.

As the officers stepped inside, Marco saw two tall, blonde men in suits standing across the street. They watched as the police came inside. "Are they with you?"

With a glance over her shoulder, one of the police turned, then quickly back again with a frown and a shake of her head. "Are who with us, sir?"

"The two men over the road."

Without looking again, she reassured, "We are not with anyone else. People often stare when they see us. It goes with the territory... Nosey buggers!"

Inside now, they both smiled sympathetically. "As I say, we've found your wife."

"Is she okay?"

"Physically, she seems fine. Although, she has sustained some minor injuries... Self-inflicted injuries."

Marco sighed.

"She is currently on the maternity ward in Withybush. As a result of her self-harm there has been some bleeding. You might want to visit, or call the hospital to check on your baby."

It's not mine, Marco thought, and then with a shudder remembered last night's nightmare (he would insist on calling it that for his own sanity). The creature of his dream made it clear the child coming to harm would be bad news for him. Paling, he leaned against the wall. "Okay. I'll have a shower and go."

"Best check visiting times. You don't want a wasted trip. We recommended she see someone who can help her. You know, somebody specialised. Hopefully she'll be a bit calmer."

It was the first glimmer of hope he'd had to grasp for a while. "Thank you," he blew through round lips. "Is there anything else?"

The officers shared a glance. "No, I don't think so. Just, when your wife does come home, don't hesitate to call us if you're worried again, okay? You did the right thing."

"Thanks." Marco opened the door. The men across the road still stood watching. Why so interested? They didn't look like passers-by. As the police denied a connection, might they be from a secret agency?

Satisfied briefly with his explanation, he stalled in his thoughts. What agency? With last night's visions swirling in his head, Men in Black soon joined the cocktail. Holding their gaze, he waved the police farewell, and only broke eye-contact when the door closed. Weird. One eye shut, the other pressed against the spy-hole, he saw them. And they were staring right at him.

He jerked his eye away and leaned breathlessly against the wall. With a gulp, he scurried upstairs for a shower, whistling, convincing himself all was normal. All was perfectly normal.

After showering and dressing, he toasted some bread and forced it down, spread with jam and butter. The sweet carbs would give him a boost, if not sustain him, to leave the house and visit his wife. A glance at his watch showed he was due at work, so he paused on his way out to make the call to excuse himself. No need for a cover story. His voice, from stress and so little sleep, sounded awful.

'Get back in when you can,' they implored. In the background, he detected offers to cook him dinner if he needed. They were a good bunch after all, but he had no need of their culinary sympathy. Only he cooked since getting married.

The maternity ward advised no specific visiting hours for spouses, and so he had no excuse but to leave right away. Last night's vision played in his head and he whispered a prayer the baby was unharmed. The source of his change of heart wasn't what he recognised as divine, but at least he was free from his own disgusting notion that losing them might be the best thing; even though it had been by force.

Spy-hole uncovered, he peered through again, relieved to see no-one in view. Keys jangling as he spun the keyring around his finger, he halted as the rainwater drain caught his eye and he played through a disaster where he dropped them through the grating and couldn't go to the hospital and *they* would know and do goodness-knows-what about it. As they came to rest after their final spin, Marco gripped them tight in his palm.

Thrusting the key into the ignition, the car started first time, which was never guaranteed on these cold January mornings. Perhaps God was smiling upon him again - a thought he desperately wanted to cling to.

The early hour didn't afford the ample parking opportunities he had expected as he'd driven beside the mountains to the hospital. What was everybody doing?

He circled around the first car park, and then the *'Staff Only'* bays, receiving a glare from a nurse on the zebra-crossing. 'Sorry,' he mouthed, hoping she'd believe he hadn't been about to steal an NHS worker's space and delay them from providing vital patient care.

Around the back of the hospital, between grey buildings, pipes, Portakabins, and chimneys, spaces dotted sporadically but all seemed full. Close to doors were unoccupied 'Disabled' bays, but he dreaded the looks he might garner by using those. And why was he in such a hurry, anyway? He had come, as required. There was no precise time he needed to get there.

Guilt eased only briefly as, turning right around the building and returning to the start of the car park, he recognised his in-law's car in a prime location. If he'd been as early and conscientious as they had, he would be parked too. Finger pressed firmly into the bridge of his nose, he caught the smell of strawberries. Jam. He sniffed his fingers. Where was it? Hands turning different ways showed no sign of stickiness and so detective work led him eventually to his sleeve where sweet buttery residue smeared all the way to his elbow.

Leaning on the worktop rather than crunching over the cornflakes to use the table had been lazy. The milk had already soured, but he hadn't cleaned it. He planned to do it later. But what if Carys came home right now? Seeing it might set her back off on a mental breakdown instantly. For the countless time, he wished something distressing for Carys to convenience himself and he felt disgusted. "Be honest, you coward. If she's coming now, tell her you rushed here and haven't cleaned up yet. She may even apologise. After all, it was her mess."

A middle-aged man sneered at him, and as he walked past he shook his head. He flushed red, but sometimes speaking his thoughts out loud helped to make them real. And if God was listening, he'd have the chance to influence him: to show him a sign.

Eyes down, he walked through a hedgeway bisected by the tarmac path that led to a crossing and onto the main reception. A large signpost below directions for 'Accident and Emergency' and stating the main entrance in the opposite direction said, *'Have you paid and displayed?'* "You have to be joking!" Marco spoke to himself again. Returning to his car, he rummaged for change for the ticket machine. "In a hospital car park? This is appalling; an effrontery." An old fifty-pence piece reluctantly relinquished its hiding place between the footplate and the seat, but was it enough?

A squint at the sign near the tariff showed he'd get twenty-minutes for his paltry sum. It was barely worth getting out of the car. But he was here. Perhaps he could borrow some change from his in-laws.

After the walk to the machine with his coin, and then walking back to stick it inside the windscreen, as he flicked the little paper strip to separate it from the adhesive coating below, he gritted his teeth. Neck rolling to calm him, he saw the car next to him displayed a dozen or more stuck on rectangles left from previous days' parking.

Picturing an elderly man, perhaps visiting his wife at death's door, being forced to fuss around with the unethical ticket system, or face hefty fines, he shook his head. Some people; faceless associates behind desks in the very building he worked in, were responsible for this. With a sharp nod, he thought he could find out who, and persuade them to change it. The inconvenience now had a holy air and placed Marco in God's good books again. Good, that was, until he got closer to the entrance. There, outside, as conspicuous as clowns, were the two tall blonde, suited men.

Eyes bulging, Marco's legs buckled and he leant against the wall for support. If he wondered if he was imagining their interest, they didn't help and put him at ease. Both stared at him.

The doors into the hospital the reception area slid open and closed again behind them, but nobody else took their attention. Options whirled around his head. He already admitted to himself that he wasn't expected at any particular time. That meant he didn't have to go past these odd men, did he? He made a show of patting down his pockets and shaking his head. Now he could return to his car and get whatever he was pretending he'd forgotten.

Why was he afraid? He had nothing to hide; he had done nothing wrong. It was just that stupid dream putting him on edge. Perched up in his seat, the doors weren't visible from the car; the hedge blocked his view. Finger poised, he considered listening to the radio. Unable to resist, he pushed the on switch bringing a news program blaring into life. He would give it until the end of the bulletin before venturing out again.

"And here's the weather report for your area..."

The news update had ended far too quickly and Marco developed a rapid interest in the forecast, smiling along to predictions of fine weather. Then a song came on he liked, then one he didn't. Should he wait for the ad break to end to see what they'd play next? Blonde, suited men loomed in his mind. Who were they? The stern instruction of his nightmare struck starkly. *'You must not let any harm come to the mother or her child...'* and he couldn't help connecting their appearance. They were checking up on him. And he had hidden in the car. It didn't give evidence he was taking the best care, did it.

The door creaked open, his leaden feet swung round onto the tarmac, and Marco hauled himself out. Wallet clutched in hand propelled the pretence he'd forgotten it. So what if the radio distracted him? Edging beyond the hedge, his heart skipped. They weren't there.

Rapid steps over the crossing brought him to the doors which swished open to sanctuary inside. But what would stop the men from lurking there? Flinching at the possibility, his breath calmed when furtive glances to each available corner didn't expose them. His hoot of relief came out awkwardly loud and attracted irritated frowns.

He might have been a bit overdramatic, he smiled to himself. Of course they were staring. They were most likely police and he had acted very suspiciously. Law Enforcement waiting outside a hospital suddenly seemed like the most normal thing in the world. They might be reporting on a drunk driver, or, given their lack of uniform, a more serious crime. What was unfeasibly abnormal was that they were checking on him under instruction from an alien force that resided exclusively within his subconscious.

Fairly skipping up the stairs, he saw signs

directing him to the maternity ward and hurried along the corridor, keen not to test his new theory, yet, conversely enthusiastic to show the powers-that-be he had arrived to care for Carys.

Introducing himself as Mr Paulo, the receptionist buzzed him through security doors and directed him to the third door on the left. "She's in a side room, what with... Everything."

What with her behaving like a complete madwoman, he supposed she meant. He gave a smile and a nod and slowed his pace. Beyond the door, his mother-in-law and his wife were in full discussion about the pros and cons of various psychiatric medications. He shuffled away for a moment, not wanting to interrupt.

In the corridor, his thoughts wandered. Safe in the knowledge he was doing as he had been ordered, the strange men took on another role in his mind. Angels! He was meant to wait outside so Carys and Diane could have their important chat. They were there to stop him, and when he obeyed their desire, they left because there was no need for them anymore.

His smile and nod grew into an uneasy rhythm, leaving him unconvinced he was capable of a sensible thought. Never mind his wife's struggle with mental health, he feared he might be completely cracking up himself.

Somehow, despite his clandestine retreat, Diane spotted him and rose from the bed. Reaching the door, she offered a hazy sneer and ushered him.

"I bet you'll want to see your wife, young man."

With a resigned swallow, Marco said, "Of course, yes." As soon as he stepped in, Diane made her excuses.

"I'll leave you two to it. I bet you have a lot to catch up on."

Marco smiled his thanks, but being alone with Carys had rarely been the coveted experience he had presumed it would since seeing her photograph months ago. And now he felt uneasy. What could he say? He opted for nothing. Hurrying to her side, he leaned in and hugged her instead.

FOURTEEN

Angelic visitation

"So, when's she coming home?"

"Later, I think, Dad." The expression in his father's eyes was disappointment. It wasn't fair. He was doing a good and brave thing. He understood, of course, why his father might have concerns he'd made a rash choice marrying Carys, and for all the wrong reasons. That was why he shared the weirdness of last night and today. "I know that look, Dad. And trust me, I've had my doubts too. But when you're doing God's will..." his mouth dried; still unconvinced, he fervently hoped his father saw the truth, "... Trust is so important."

"If you're trying to do His will. It can be so easy to convince ourselves that what we want is what He wants. It's the way of temptation. You must know that, son."

"Of course, but doubts are natural, aren't they?

I'm completely sure now though, because I was visited by angels."

Dan nearly spat out his morning coffee. "What do you mean? What did they say?"

"They said I had to look after Carys and that her baby was special."

"Be careful, son." Dan glowered. "What you're saying could be seen as blasphemous."

"How?"

"How?! You're comparing yourselves to the story of our Lord and saviour, Jesus Christ."

"Jesus isn't the only child of significance in the Bible."

Dan's face reddened, and he looked ready to strike the heathen words from his son.

"This morning, the angels were outside the house, and then I saw them again beside the hospital. I think they were making sure I was caring for Carys as I'd been asked."

Dan widened, then at once squinted his eyes. "What did these angels look like?"

Marco gulped. "What do angels look like? There was no burning bush, if that's what you mean. I suppose, perfect human males. Tall, blonde."

"That's racist. What's so perfect about tall and blonde? What about short and dark? Are you suggesting God made some people less perfect, because we're *all* sinners? You're sounding like a Nazi, do you know that? We're all imperfect compared to Jesus, aren't we?"

"Of course. But I could tell they weren't normal

humans. That's all I'm saying." He was desperate now for his dad to say, 'That sounds just like an angelic intervention if ever I heard one', but he didn't. He stared. Marco's mouth dried and he became acutely aware of the cutting tang of dark roasted coffee and he felt sick.

They had to be angels. Anything else was unthinkable. But he had thought it. He'd thought it at the time and he thought it now. And he was pretty sure his dad thought so too. Why had he said they weren't human? He'd been convinced they were special agents this morning. Now, what was he suggesting?

The arms of the chair caught him as he swooned. His father moved over to him and put his hand on his head. "Let us pray," he instructed. Marco was too faint to hear what he said, but grateful. If not angels; and therefore not God asking him to stay with Carys and look after her baby, why would he? Love? Had he fallen for her completely as he'd expected after his dreams and seeing the photo? Perhaps. But Marco felt sure the reason was the exact opposite: fear. He was terrified that his dream and the strange tall men were exactly as they appeared to be if Carys's claims were true.

Unknown in-laws who are truly out of this world. What hell had he plunged himself into? Tears wet his cheek and he craned his neck to hear the comforting, holy words of his father as he wrought the wrath of God upon the demons troubling him.

Prayer usually helped. His choice was not what he'd pretended. Not do God's will and look after Carys and her baby, or selfishly return to bachelorhood at the first hurdle. The will of his Lord Almighty had nothing to do with it. It was something else: Stay with Carys and make sure no harm came to her or the baby, or face unthinkable consequences. Or, perhaps, accept he was even more insane than his clinically diagnosed wife.

Right now, he wasn't sure which was worse. Far from acting with God's assent, his *approval,* he was sure the creature in his dream and the odd men were the farthest from that.

And that's why he felt sick. But he couldn't let his dad see that. He'd know exactly why he was shying away from his holy presence. There was only one explanation.

The crinkled smile he forced onto his lips quivered under his father's intense glare, and he looked away.

"What's wrong? You seem very troubled. As you should." What did he mean? Marco's mouth dried, and he coughed. "Your lustful weakness has attracted the worst sort of entity into your life. Do you suppose you'd look and feel like this if they had been angels you had seen?"

"I'm rough because I've had a really worrying night with Carys in hospital." The stern look wouldn't waver. "If you think marrying Carys was such a bad idea, why didn't you say something sooner? You seemed right behind it. You conducted the ceremony!"

"I was behind it. It doesn't mean I didn't have doubts. But I thought if my son was going to succumb to those desires, at least he should do it in wedlock!" He slammed his palm on the table. "She's not the type of girl to wait, is she? How far along is she with the child that isn't yours?"

Marco almost swore. "She was raped, Dad! I'm doing a good thing, supporting her. I thought you'd be proud."

Dan Paulo sighed. "I would be. But these demons coming into your life show me a different story." His tone mellowed and he smiled. "But we've prayed now. They may not trouble you again. If they do, you must inform me. There are other, more stringent measures we can take."

Marco closed his eyes. He had seen exorcisms before and they scared him. Why would he suffer such an attack alone? All he could do now was pray that he was going mad and that his dad's prayer had helped.

FIFTEEN

E.B.E.

1994

For months it seemed it had. He thought he glimpsed them a couple of times, in the supermarket, and on the street, but when he turned, he was sure he must have been mistaken.

Today, that changed.

He'd had the call. Carys's waters had broken when she was out shopping and he had to hurry to the hospital to see the birth of his baby—so the frantic midwife had told him. They'd discussed countless times with numerous nurses and healthcare professionals that he wasn't the father. In fact, it had annoyed him.

A father was exactly what he had planned to be from the moment he accepted the role. A role he'd re-convinced himself had divine purpose since Carys returned from hospital and benefitted from medication. So, he was chuffed whoever he spoke to insisted, biological or not, he was to be a dad.

As instructed, he rushed and was happily surprised when parking proved easier than he'd anticipated. He strode to the ticket machine, not even begrudging the fee. His smile grew, imagining the fun he would have. There were the sleepless nights, of course. He wasn't sure how prepared he was for those. No-one was, yet people managed, and he would manage, too.

First words; 'Daddy'. First steps. Baby bottles. Packing enough to mobilise an army every time they went out in the car. It sounded a nightmare, but it made Marco feel important. Grown up. He would never put their kids under the Same scrutiny he had suffered.

And that was the thing; it would not stop here with this one child that wasn't technically his. This was just the first. How many would they have? Four? Five? His cousin had seven. Seven little lives to mould. Seven little humans to love.

Making the babies would be fun, too. Intimacy with Carys, had been non-existent since their honeymoon. First, she was mental. And then she was too huge. Not that he didn't fancy her. She became more beautiful the more she budded. There was the miracle of existence growing within. And there were her huge breasts. Large before, they'd grown to humongous proportions now they were fit to burst with life-affirming nutrients for their little one. It was just, knowing how uneasy she was around intimacy, and indeed how physically uncomfortable she would find it, he hadn't pressed her.

All this joy wrapped around him fell apart when the men loomed outside the entrance where he'd seen them before. Again, they stared right at him. He had done nothing suspicious this time, unless smiling was an intergalactic no-no.

Determined to walk closer to see what they would do; to learn if they even were watching him, or if he was paranoid, he took a route straight at them.

Their gaze never left him, and as he grew closer, the one nearest stepped towards him. With no introduction, he leered, "Remember, you must make sure nothing happens to the baby."

Fighting the faintness with rugged breaths, Marco clenched his fists. If they needed him, they needed him unharmed. "What about Carys? I was told no harm must come to her. Does she not matter anymore?"

The man's expression remained unchanged. "You must make sure no harm comes to the child. When you see him, he may seem strange, but you need to make him welcome and care for him. You must do as we say."

Marco trembled, praying insanity was the answer, his gaze flitted to passers-by and he let out a nervous chuckle. One man passed, and as ancient cigarette odour assaulted Marco's nose from a raggedy cardigan, evidently worn for the purpose of countless fag breaks in-between washes (if it had ever actually seen detergent in its life), sucked his teeth and scowled.

"Excuse me," Marco couldn't fight the compulsion to ask this complete stranger. "Do you know these men? Have you seen them here before?"

The man jumped back and hit a karate pose. He must have been seventy. "Keep away from me, nutter. Talking to yourself. Crazy man."

With a sigh, Marco shuffled inside and was assailed by fresh stenches; a mixture of disinfectant and uncontrolled bowels. It seemed his prayer had been answered. Diagnosing himself with insanity, the diagnosis didn't stop him worrying what the baby would look like. And picturing everything from E.T. to Yoda as he forced his heavy legs to climb the stairs, didn't prepare him for what he witnessed.

That he hadn't been whisked away by special forces and a war of the worlds declared was a mystery. A bulbous balloon head with oversized dark almond shaped eyes swayed atop a scrawny neck which joined an equally skinny body. If he could stand, he'd make an excellent extra for a science fiction film.

Cheeks pinching, saliva trickling into his mouth, Marco peered through the tinted Perspex of the incubator.

"His head will need supporting for a while," a nurse pointed out the obvious.

Marco's own head moved slowly up and down.

"It is rather large," she added. "I'm sure he'll grow into it. We had one yesterday covered in hair and looked exactly like a monkey!"

Her attempts to comfort were tactless and would have missed the mark if he had been the baby's father. As it was, he doubted anyone would even know the target they were aiming for. A target to dispel his fears that the weird men and his frightening dream had been just that – his imagination. "Where's my wife?"

The nurse creased her neck giving her double-chin some wobbling friends. "Haven't you seen her yet?" It seemed a pointless question but Marco wasn't about to turn on a friendly face to boost his esteem and sufficed with a quick headshake. "You best follow me, then, young man."

Down the corridor and into a side room, Carys, as she had been last time he visited her in hospital, was with her mum. And again, he felt intrusive. Beckoned in, his mind whirred as he worried what to say. Admit she was right, and that he believed her alien baby story now he'd seen him? That seemed foolish. She might have forgotten about it and be really offended. But, if she was doing her thing of waiting for him to guess what she was thinking or risk her wrath, he should say.

Her irritability only really showed when she was unwell, though. Medication had done a great job battling the hormones and there was no reason to suppose they weren't, still. And once said, things couldn't be un-said. He'd stay quiet and gauge her feelings before broaching his own.

"Hello," he scurried over and enveloped her in a big hug. It meant he didn't have to look at her face, or rather, allow her to see into his and read his every thought. Pressing her into him, he was aiming for loving husband whilst he waited for Diane to say something that might give a clue to what they'd been talking about prior to his arrival. "Have you seen..." he nearly said 'Our son', but didn't know if that was allowed. And saying 'Carys's son,' would sound like he didn't want him; which, of course, he didn't. He was just terrified he had no choice. "The baby?" he responded neutrally.

"He's lovely, isn't he. Carys was a funny looking baby, too!" she chuckled. "Big head, sticky-out ears and the darkest eyes I'd ever seen."

Marco's legs buckled; something that was happening a lot. Was it a reaction to all the weirdness or did he have an iron deficiency or something? Hearing his mother-in-law's description, he had the fleeting fear his own wife was some type of hybrid too. Diane had suffered from a variety of mental health problems, herself, and she was terrified of the idea of extra-terrestrials. He blew through his lips. It was crazy. There was no way that odd little new-born in the incubator would grow into the beauty his mother was. Marco thought he'd be relieved if he achieved a normal life at all.

It would be a test, but he'd known people with severely deformed and disabled children. It seemed to make them even closer. Tears welling to lubricate the lump in his throat made him smile. He was going to be a great dad to that little boy, whatever his needs and whatever his purpose. And not just because he'd been forced.

SIXTEEN

Don't go changing...

He stared into the mirror. What had he seen?

He'd had optimistic expectations, being alone for a few days while Carys stayed at the hospital to feed the incubated baby, who now had a name: Ebe. Apparently, it was Dutch, but why a name from The Netherlands was significant, Marco didn't know. He hadn't been consulted.

His attempts to feel like the baby's father were struggling, and voicing his disquiet fell on the deaf ears of his new bride. "I thought we could name him together," he'd said and she'd shrugged. He wasn't the father. He had no rights, but he wasn't enjoying being taken for granted. Respectability, security, and a father to her unfortunately conceived child was what he offered when he asked her to marry him. Why had she consented if that wasn't what she'd wanted?

So being away from her, on his own, with whatever he chose on TV, anything he wished for dinner, and without it being thrown on the floor, had been something to look forward to. Guilt at feeling that way, aside—with the reason being the baby wasn't well enough to bring home—he was now surprised to crave Carys's company.

And the reason for that was what was making him sweat and cling onto the sink in the downstairs toilet.

It couldn't be, he knew that really, it was outlandish; but for a second; perhaps not even that long; for a *fraction* of a second the face reflecting back at him was not his own. For a fraction of a second the face reflected wasn't human.

Chest squeezing, reluctance to stare and confirm what he thought he'd glimpsed was being rewarded by having not seen it again. And he stared for over five minutes.

Why crave Carys? Because she would understand. Probably. Given all the things she'd told him it seemed likely she would believe him. That didn't mean she'd welcome it. And what was it anyway? Unearthly overlords scrutinising him? Why? Carys would be terrified they were coming for Ebe as she rambled weeks ago.

And the alternative: that her new supportive husband was as crazy as she was wouldn't go down well either.

Throughout his life his parents had been his best friends, and the ones to call on in times of trouble. But this type of trouble had a name in Narberth Christian Fellowship. And that name was possession.

His dad had already had his suspicions.

He couldn't stay here. Not after what he saw. Not with mirrors and reflective windows everywhere he turned. If he witnessed it again, what would he do? He wasn't going to wait to find out. Grabbing his coat, he opened the door, stepped out, and slammed it behind him in one fluid motion. He didn't know where he was going, but for now, away from the house was enough.

When troubled, his instincts would take his footsteps to church, or his parents, and usually both simultaneously. Now, he joined the ranks of the average married man and found himself outside the Dragon Public House.

The stench of old pints soaking into beer mats and the regulars propping up the bar repelled him at first, then beckoned him like a warm hug. 'Come on, leave your troubles outside,' it said.

Not against drinking alcohol, he had a dim view of those who used it as a crutch, always careful to dress it up as compassionate sympathy. He thought he understood. Anxiety created his hallucinations; or the hallucinations were triggering the anxiety. Either way, a drink to blur the edges might help.

Unusually for or a young man, there were few drinks in his repertoire. He wasn't fond of beer and wanted something faster working, anyway. Looks of disdain floated across the bar as he ordered spirit with a soft lemonade mixer. Rum first, then bourbon, and then vodka. Feeling nothing from the first shot, he slugged down two more before realising he had metabolised none of them and they suddenly all hit at once.

"What do you see when you look at me?" he slurred to the patient barmaid. She'd heard it all before so was relieved at his next question. "You see a plain old human, right? There's nothing... *not*human about me, is there?"

Reluctant to commit, suspecting some 'out of this world' chat up line to follow, accustomed to that from countless other patrons; many her own age, and plenty of what her dad would call 'dirty old men'. She was safe and not too busy so she bit. "You look perfectly human to me. The only thing odd about you is the weird questions."

Marco laughed. "Thank you. Thank you... Wos your name?"

It was on her badge, so answering, whilst unnecessary, seemed innocuous enough. "Cally," she answered.

"Call-y," Marco sounded out. "C-a-ll-y," he laughed. "That's a funny name."

"Is it?" she grimaced. What a strange conversation. Maybe he was an alien if he'd never met anyone who shared her name before. “And what’s your name?” Annoyed now, she had to see what he was on about.

“Marco. Marco Paulo.”

She was relieved she hadn’t taken a sip of the cola she’d been nursing her entire shift since someone offered to ‘Put one behind the bar for yourself’ hours ago. “That’s a really odd name.”

Marco scowled. “It’s Italian.”

“It sounds like you’re saying Marco Polo with a funny accent. Wait, *are* you saying Paulo, or Polo?”

“Marco Polo, *was* an Italian. But my name is Paulo. Not Polo.”

“I reckon you might not be human after all. If you’ll excuse me, I need to serve other customers.”

“Is he bothering you, Cally?”

Cally looked at the large man offering help. If she accepted, she’d be indebted. “I think I’m all right for now,” she glared at Marco. “Right?”

If he was forced to leave, there were plenty of pubs and bars within sight, but why bother. Swill enough to make sleep inevitable and stagger home. “Of course. I’m sorry, I meant no offence. Let me buy you and your friend a drink.”

The large man awaited Cally’s response, but then gladly accepted when she looked at him and said, “The usual?”

Place secured for the evening, Marco handed his money over with a smile. When he got another vodka, he hopped from the barstool, staggered forward and shuffled to a corner table.

Inebriation already making him sleepy, he rested his face on his hands. When his chin fell off and he caught himself awake, he considered pulling up a cushion and sleeping there. God glaring down at him made him jolt up straight. Then with anger in his voice he mumbled, "If you don't want me to behave like this, help me! Keep those whatever-they-ares away from me." And then he realised how foolish he had been seeking solace in the pub and not the church.

He flinched from the memory of his dad's sneering disappointment and felt trapped again. His eyes creaked open and a new clarity fought its way to his mind. Of course, Narberth Christian Fellowship wasn't the only church. Far from it. He could pick one of the others and speak to the pastor, reverend, or priest and make them swear discretion before he said anything.

Picturing himself in a confessional box, the thought was comforting. He knew little about Catholicism, but he wanted more than prescribed 'Hail Mary's' and 'Our Fathers'. He didn't know yet, but he was sure one of them would offer a more open-minded access to his lord.

A plan formed, he pushed himself up from the seat, the door in sight helped him aim, but didn't allow for the tabletop full of drinks in front of him. As his knee collided with the leg, and expensive liquor slopped everywhere, his apologies were lost in confusion as his feet left the floor. "Sorry, I didn't mean to. I've just had a lot on my mind and a lot to drink. I'll buy more, don't worry."

His offer was declined as he landed with a thud on the pavement. The door slammed behind him. Memory of where he was seemed frustratingly elusive and he squinted at the streetlights as landmarks flicked recognition in his head: Rebecca's cell; the war memorial, the entrance to The Drang. He lived up there, didn't he.

Reptile scales on a face not his own stared back from the mirror in his memory. He turned just in time to prevent the contents of his stomach exploding down his front and watched in fascination instead as lumpy liquid trickled on the slabs, down the hill in revolting rivulets, to the drain.

He couldn't go home. Not to risk witnessing what he'd seen again. But what was safer about being out here? He was just as vulnerable anywhere. There was nowhere they wouldn't find him. If they were real. They weren't real, were they? His head throbbed and he could only stomach one eye open at a time. Tears streaked his cheeks. He didn't know. Certainty he was imagining it, and conversely, that they were unquestionably about to thrust him into a spaceship full of unimaginable terrors, swung in a pendulum of discomfort that propelled him slowly homeward.

Prayers whispered under his breath, he opened the door. Drunkenness gave him the perfect excuse not to stumble upstairs and crash on the couch instead. He knew really, he wanted to be close to an escape route. The memory of Carys's pretty face made him smile. It was a comfort, and that was good. But at the same time, her return would mean the introduction of Ebe into their lives. And if he was who she said he was; who his own visions told him he was? Well, that was no comfort at all.

SEVENTEEN

Running away

"I should be bringing him home soon," Carys looked pleased and exhausted. Hearing spoken what he'd spent the night fearing gave him the same wrestle inside. It was nice to need her. He was stuck with her, all things considered, and so a growing fondness would help.

The determination to be a wonderful dad no matter what, swelled within him. Alone with Carys, and away from the house and his silly thoughts, it all seemed so positive. She caught him sighing and gave him a quizzical look. Should he tell her what was troubling him? Would she feel supported in a struggle only the two of them knew? Or would she be terrified and not return? A third notion; that she would suspect him of taking the piss was the one that finally quashed the desire to speak out.

When she asked, “Is everything okay?” he answered with a brisk nod and a hasty smile. “I have a list of things I need before I can bring Ebe home.” Her face fell, and she glowered. “Are you going to get a pen and paper?”

A sigh for another reason dropped heavily from his chest. What sort of life had he foisted upon himself with his hasty proposal? His apathy may have been from circumstance. Or from a premonition of a future no-one would believe.

Orders clutched in a sweaty fist, he kissed Carys’s cheeks and left the ward. Smiles from other new mums were warmer than from his own wife. He sighed again,
stuffing the list into his pocket, he had to get away.

The call of Cally and her soothing tincture made him shake his head. It was barely lunchtime. Reaching the car in a daze, he sat behind the wheel and clutched the key in the ignition. It surprised him to remember his thoughts from last night about seeking other religious input, but that seemed like running away. And what would his dad say if he found out? It was almost as bad as what he was afraid of. No, he could avoid them no longer. With a decisive turn of the key, the engine grumbled into life. He hoped his parents would provide the comfort he craved.

As the door opened, Dan Paulo regarded his son. He was already scouring for clues to unholiness.

"Come in, Marco. What are you waiting for?"

"You. You're looking at me peculiarly." Let's have it, then. The brave thought surprised Marco. Pride in his assertiveness wavered at recognition it wasn't like him. Not to his father, at any rate.

Throughout his childhood, and now early adulthood, challenging thoughts were discouraged in favour of obedience to the Lord, and by proxy – as His representative through the church – himself.

"That's because the last time you we were here we prayed together for a very specific reason and I am trying to ascertain our success."

"I'm fine, Dad. Honestly." And now he was lying. "Mum!" He had never been more pleased to see her. "How are you?" he rushed over and planted a kiss on each cheek and hugged her to him.

She squeezed him, but then pushed him away a little. "It's only been two days, Marco. Are you sure you're all right?"

Marco stretched his eyes open to allay tears threatening to expose him. "It is an emotional time. I guess I'm worried if I'll make a good father."

"You *guess*? What, are you American?"

His assertiveness withered, and the apology rose to his lips without consideration. "Sorry, I'm worried I might not be good enough."

"Everyone feels like that." Implying: you're not special. "You just get on with it and you get good at it. You took on this role, and you said it was ordained from on high. Do you not trust our Lord?"

"Oh, of course. Perhaps I don't trust myself to follow his instructions."

"I understand. His is an impossible standard. But He never gives us more than we can handle. If it's hard, you should be flattered. He knows you are strong enough."

Well, he expected to be extremely 'flattered' if any of what he'd witnessed was true.

"I'm just finishing some ravioli. Then it will only take a few minutes to cook. I was going to put some by for lunch tomorrow—your father likes them cold—so there'll be plenty for you to stay for dinner."

"That sounds fabulous, Mum. I'll freshen up." As he walked upstairs to the bathroom, the phrase stuck in his mind. 'Freshen up'? He'd never said it before. Reprimanding for 'Going for a slash/whizz/piss' was the usual. Why was he behaving like an awkward guest? As he unzipped and aimed, he smiled. Nothing unusual. The strangeness perfectly normal for a son moved out of the family home. Especially as things weren't exactly marital bliss.

With a shake, he realised the seat was wet with droplets that he needed to wipe and he grew red at not having lifted it. He let the water run hot before soaping his hands. He wasn't even looking in the mirror. All his attention focussed on being clean and presentable for dinner.

Satisfied at last, he turned off the tap and reached for the fluffy hand towel. A sniff of his fingers convinced him they were clean, and the scent of his childhood soap brought a comforting confidence. A quick glance at his reflection to check all was well and,

It wasn't him.

A split second, but longer than last time, reptilian scales covered a face that was not his own.

Marco stumbled, jerking his gaze backward, as though someone standing behind him in a horror mask would provide the solution. Collapsed on the floor, he hauled himself up using the ceramic toilet bowl.

Don't look again, he failed to fight the compulsion. His own face shone back at him and he grasped a tentative relief.

It came again.

"Who are you? What do you want?"

It vanished once more leaving his boyishly handsome features reflected again.

Just like normal.

But things were far from normal.

Was he insane? Or would others see the change, as well? Would Dan and Natalia?

Picturing his mother dropping the entire pot of tomato ravioli in a spectacular mess; his dad commanding him from the house with a crucifix in hand, he knew he couldn't risk being seen like this. He had to get away.

Two at a time, he sprang down the stairs and flew to the front door. “Sorry, Mum, sorry, Dad. I’ve got to go.” He had no idea what excuse to use, but he’d be away before they asked and with time to think, he hoped to come up with something convincing.

Car keys thrust into the lock, the front door opened and his dad ran down the drive. Had he seen?

With a gushing smile, Marco started the engine and thrust the car into gear. Spinning shingle into the air, he flinched knowing he’d be in trouble for that if nothing else, he waved and spun onto the road. “I had this overwhelming sense Carys needed me,” he rehearsed lying. It sounded ridiculous, perhaps he’d come up with something better. He suspected he wouldn’t need to. His mum and dad dealt with things they didn’t like by pretending they hadn’t happened. It was part of their ‘give all your troubles to Jesus’ philosophy.

Where should he go. The only place no-one would see him was home. And he had Carys’s list to work through: some shopping, and plenty of cleaning. That would occupy him. He’d have to brave the shops at some point. But for now, he wouldn’t worry about that. Not having Ebe’s essentials was the least of his concerns right now. And what he was bothered with he had no idea what to do about. No idea at all

EIGHTEEN

Ahead of the game

He started in the bedroom, considering Carys was most likely to want to crash into bed after an exhausting week at the hospital. First, he changed the bedding so that any crumbs and loose cotton would be vacuumed afterwards. Furniture polish sprayed and wiped from the bedside tables as a finishing touch, the aroma of 'fresh linen and lavender' wafted and he was proud of himself.

The duvet fought him for its cover. Did the stripes of quilting run vertically or horizontally? Did it matter? He discovered it did matter, and after three attempts finally wrestled it into the corners by turning it inside out and safety-pinning them and removing them once the other corners were firmly in place.

He wiped sweat from his hairline and proceeded to wrestle the fitted sheet onto all four corners at once. Gratitude at the pillows and their ease of operation almost persuaded him into bed to hug them, especially when smoothing the duvet always seemed to crease the side he wasn't on and knock a pillow over. He hadn't realised making a bed was such an artform.

A glance back at the wonky creased bed satisfied him even less than he feared. He closed the door.

The stair carpet looked a lot better, and the lounge was ready for guests once he'd picked up three or four pairs of shoes; three, or four, because only three were complete. One boot languished without its partner, its location in another room struck Marco as improbable. He had got drunk and must have stumbled around with one boot. For now, at least it was clear and smelled of polish.

Slumped on an armchair, he tried to decide what to do next. Carys wasn't coming home today, so he didn't have to complete the list. He hadn't eaten, having missed out on delicious home-cooked ravioli.

Takeaway, or eating out? People seeing his reptile demon face was a risk. Incredulity flooded his thought in an effort to restore sanity. It couldn't be real. A crazy hallucination was all it was. As convincing as he believed he'd been, he opted for a bowl of cereal, then fell asleep on the sofa watching telly. At least the bed would stay tidy.

Mid-week parking wasn't too difficult at Withybush General Hospital and Marco was soon striding towards the entrance; no tall, blonde, weirdos; and his reflection walking towards him was entirely human, if not a little less dashing than he was used to. That's what nights without sleep did for you.

With a whistle he weaved through the corridors and up the stairs to maternity. Buzzed in quickly; he'd become quite the fixture over the last few weeks, he smiled and greeted midwives as he made his way to Carys's room.

He arrived mid-conversation with an official looking, bespectacled woman who paused mid-sentence to look at him. Turning back to Carys, she received a nod to continue and smiled to include him in the conversation. "As I was saying, we can't recommend Ebe leaving our care for at least another two weeks."

Marco gasped. The jelly of emotion swirling around was hard to pinpoint. More excruciating time alone, although at least it was time he wasn't responsible for Ebe. But the longer it went on, the more it pointed to the child being severely disabled. He raised his chin to the heavens and offered a silent prayer, 'Your Will be done, oh Lord'. Turning his smile to the room, there was nothing to say, but 'Oh dear', and, 'What a shame', sprayed easily from his mouth.

"Whatever is best," Carys said to the doctor and her husband. Marco took it that she was as keen as he was to put off their fate. "We've waited nearly nine months. A couple more weeks won't make a difference in the long run."

Affection missing from their goodbyes as usual, he hoped work might be the distraction he needed. If his peculiar affliction struck there and everyone saw, his life would be over. Or he'd be forced to get help. The distant strings of sensibility pulled but he wasn't ready to accept assistance just yet. Fear of what professionals may find, or might not find kept him from that endeavour.

He set off the short distance to County Hall. He couldn't promise effective work, but he could promise long hours—if nothing weird happened again.

"Marco! Feeling better?" the same sentiment repeated by each colleague in turn. With smiles and reassurances, he set about opening emails he'd missed. After reading three without actioning anything, he decided on a walk to get coffee.

The day passed in a haze of occasional banter, a bit of photocopying, and one of the three emails receiving his warranted attention.

"We're all heading for an after-work drink. Fancy joining us?"

He could exchange the pretence of overtime where he might deal with another email for company, albeit not the most scintillating? Despite logistical complications regarding getting home without driving drunk, Marco couldn't resist the pull of the pub. "That sounds great."

Five Pembrokeshire County Council civil servants walked over the bridge to the nearest public house, named, *The Bristol Trader*. Without much persuasion from Marco, they ordered food as well as drinks. His night was sorted. Just another thirteen to go. At least.

The pie he had opted for soaked up some of the whisky, and at some point, he'd been persuaded onto beer. Given his unfamiliarity with alcohol, his capacity was small. Although he felt perfectly fine, he was pretty sure driving would be a bad idea. He didn't feel dangerous, but if he had it in his system and got stopped by the police, losing his licence would be a terrible embarrassment, and a massive inconvenience. That left sleeping in his car, or back in the office.

There were things to catch up on, and whilst he couldn't get answers he needed from other departments, he could still organise things so that tomorrow he'd get more work done. And he was closer to Carys.

As his monitor went dark loading, he caught his reflection. It wasn't a reptilian face that grabbed his attention this time, but his own contented smile. Being useful felt good.

By morning, he was ahead of tasks and he was hungry again. And he smelled. Showers were located somewhere in the building. He didn't understand why, because staying after hours and sleeping in the office was unlikely to be encouraged no matter how much work he finished.

Consulting a map of the building, he found the showers on the top floor and made his way there. No towels. How long would it take to drip dry sufficiently to put his clothes back on?

He pushed the bin in front of the door and opted instead for sploshing soapy water from the sink under his arms and nether regions, and drying himself under the hand dryer. With clean water he washed his face and soaked his hair. Hand soap as shampoo was better than nothing and the blower was a useful hairdryer.

Smelling clean in body brought to his attention the offensive odour of his clothes, but there was not much he could do about them. Laundry was too much to ask of the facilities he had at his disposal, but perhaps a walk in the fresh air for food would be sufficient for now.

On the window sill he noticed a can of Airwick room deodoriser and decided to freshen his clothes with that. Still coughing halfway down the corridor, he was relieved to reach the front door.

Handle gripped, a sudden fear of what he'd seen

and somehow been free of in this complicated building made him reluctant to open the door. Is this how agoraphobia started? There was no point in hiding. He would have to take his fate no matter what. But bravado was easier as the memories faded.

Stomach full of a Subway roll and a large maximum caffeinated cola, Marco felt more himself than he had in ages. Arriving at the office along with everyone else, the surprised faces told him he succeeded in not looking like he'd spent the night there. "I'll head out at lunchtime and visit my wife, if that's okay."

"Fine, I'll cover. Make sure you're up to date with correspondence first, though, please."

Marco grinned. 'All done', he thought; "I will," he assured and spent the morning giving more attention to issues than he was usually able. This may well be a long-term solution. What a way to escape the rigours of a demanding baby and wife than to serve the community.

Carys's blank expression didn't faze him, and by the time he was ready to leave, wouldn't you know it but he'd made her smile.

"You've really cheered me up today, Marco. It will be all right when we come home, won't it?"

It hadn't occurred to him she might be worried if he would still be willing to accept the odd lifeform she'd brought into the world. Her gratitude pleased him. Things were coming together after all.

The visions? Stress. It was obvious. With the love of his good woman, perhaps it wouldn't be so bad. And whilst it was early days to call it love, as his eyes drank in her curvaceous beauty, he had to concede there were perks while they waited for that to develop.

Reluctant to spoil the mood and be presumptuous asking when normal marital liaisons could resume; it couldn't be too long. Even after a c-section—maybe even sooner because of it, he didn't know but the point excited him. "Of course, it will, my lovely. We'll be a proper family." She beamed back and Marco left her happy for once.

At the end of the working day, he felt confident enough to go home. As if to prove his hypothesis that stress had been the cause of his troubles, his mirrors didn't betray him. He even slept in bed.

NINETEEN

Bringing Ebe home

He'd spent the morning cleaning up again. Willingness to return to the house had caused its problems in two weeks of man-on-his-own housework schedule, but now Carys and Ebe were coming home at last and he had taken the morning off work to get it back to standard.

The duvet was just as perplexing as the time before and he hoped he wouldn't have to change it soon. A final glance around made him smile. They were coming home, and after weeks of dread, he had to admit, he was pleased.

When he arrived at the ward, Carys was sitting on the bed fully dressed and busily shoving things into a carrier bag. "Oh, good, Marco. Did you bring me a nice holdall to put all this in?"

Her face as he had to report that he hadn't

remembered to bring anything worried him it might not be as ideal as he'd built in his mind. Overacting his apologies, determined not let anxiety do what it had before, he made sure he was convincing.

"Oh, leave the poor boy alone," a hand stroked his back and Diane stepped into the room. "He's done a great job keeping the house spick and span."

Carys smiled. "Sorry, Marco. I didn't want to stress you out. I've just been struggling to cram everything into this." She held up the ward-supplied green bag. Marco grabbed it and disappeared to return with another. "Oh, that'll work, thank you."

It would have been nice to come home with his wife and baby alone under normal circumstances, but he had to concede these were not, and so Diane's presence was a godsend. Responsibility for working the car seat was something he was happy to pass on to his experienced mother-in-law.

"Where is he then?" It was an obvious question. Why wasn't their young charge in the room with them? He hoped there wouldn't be another delay.

"You just missed him," Carys smiled. "I've been practising feeding him all week but the doctor just wants to check a couple of things to be sure he can come home today."

"Really? I thought it was definite." Marco sighed. Ready to wait a long time, he was surprised when a midwife backed into the room holding something.

"Doctor wants him to wear this until he can check him next week." In her hands was a tiny surgical collar. "We're still concerned for his neck. He's been lying down, so far. If he can start to support his own head, then Doctor will look at removing the collar."

Marco frowned. "Won't it push progress back? I mean it's a heavy thing to have to lift as well as his head."

"It is a factor, but it offers such support. Right now, his head is just too much weight for his neck. If it's something you are worried about, we can consider him staying in a bit longer."

Marco looked frantically at Carys, "No, I'm sure you know what's best. We'll get by at home, won't we?"

Carys nodded too, "We'll manage."

The car seat they'd bought didn't work. With measurements allowing for his head, he and Carys walked to Halfords and after much deliberation, selected one that would suffice.

With Ebe strapped safely into place, and passing the midwives safety inspection, they sat in the car park in nervous anticipation.

For ease of access, Ebe was in the front seat. The airbag had been decommissioned and his new seat fitted perfectly. In the rear-view mirror, Marco watched Carys eagerly scrutinising her new baby as she waited for the car to start.

He couldn't stop himself looking. It's what any father would do, but for Marco it was for some peculiar reasons. All babies looked like Winston Churchill as far as he was concerned, but for Ebe, that would have been an improvement.

Staring at him, he sighed. It was a wonder they were allowed to take him; that he wasn't in a huge tent with people is hazmat suits prodding him and keeping them outside for their safety. Or, that men in dark suits weren't pointing flashy pens at them and sending them on their way.

He had a face that required explanation. Hopefully everyone would be too polite to inquire what was wrong. Ebe regarded him with unseeing eyes as dark as the deepest ocean and Marco looked away.

In the mirror, he worried Carys might catch his looks of dismay so he plastered on a big grin. "Right, we'll get you two home, then."

It felt special. Surreal. To be driving with the new and odd life. He allowed beautiful Carys to fill his view and squeezed his lips together as he thought how her beauty would be his strength in his struggle to make this work.

He pulled up carefully, grateful the space nearest the house was clear to fend off questions from doting neighbours as well as for convenience with carrying things inside. Unplugging the seat from the car, Marco plucked the whole thing up and whisked him the few steps inside the house.

Diane arrived just after. Should he wait and hand Ebe to her, or let her help her daughter inside. The question answered itself when Diane smiled and made her way to the back to steady Carys.

Marco held onto him, reluctant to place him on the floor and not sure where else was safe. The other two stepped into the hallway.

"Marco! I thought you said you'd cleaned."

At first, he assumed she was joking. She bent her fragile frame to the floor and wiped the baseboard with her finger. "This is filthy! I wouldn't have brought a baby into this, if I'd known."

"But I spent ages cleaning. I didn't think to do the skirting board, sorry."

"I'm going to have to do it, aren't I. And then I'll feed Ebe. I'll make you a four-course meal as well, shall I?"

"I'll do it." Marco marched to the kitchen and began filling a bowl with soapy water. By the time he returned, Diane and Carys were gone. For a moment, he wondered if they really had returned to hospital, but then he heard cooing upstairs as Ebe was shown his bedroom. No more banshee screams, Evidently, he'd done enough cleaning upstairs.

Angry and unappreciated, as the water in the bowl grew greyer and filthier, he realised that perhaps his unreasonable wife had a point. It was early days, but one day Ebe would be the crawling around those germs. Even now, he was the one closest to them. Satisfied at their cleanliness at last, he loaded a tray with tea and biscuits and made his way to find them.

They were in the bedroom, Ebe laying on the bed between Mum and Gran.

"Ah, Marco," Diane cooed. Carys has something she wants to say, don't you, love."

"Sorry." She said with the look of a child being forced.

"It's okay. You were right. I didn't realise I should wash them. I've done it now, and they were very dirty. You were perfectly fair to be disappointed."

Diane copped the next dirty glare, and she shared an eye-roll and smile with her son-in-law. 'Hormones,' she mouthed. 'Just hormones.'

Diane made sure they were getting on before she left, but as soon as the door closed and the echo of her cooed goodbyes died down, the tension grew fast.

"Well, what do you reckon? Pleased to have us home?" Carys asked, laying staring at the ceiling.

Marco rolled towards her. "Yes, of course. I missed you so much I've barely been here. I just couldn't stand it without you." He felt her stiffen and wondered what he'd done wrong now.

"So, where have you been sleeping," she asked

after a while.

So that was it. She was jealous. Flattered, he did his best to reassure her, “Believe it or not, I’ve been staying at work; showering there and everything. I got loads done, I’m really pleased. The idea hung to share the reasons he’d missed her, but he quickly dismissed it. Now was not the time.

“What do you think of Ebe, then?”

It was a tough question. She’d see through platitudes, and they weren’t appropriate for a surrogate father who was expected to love him and treat him as his own. Pondering, he said, “Worried, I suppose. They didn’t sound very reassuring. And that neck-brace can’t be comfortable.”

Carys smiled and rubbed his arm affectionately. “We’ll manage. I hope he grows into that head!”

Marco gasped. “Yes, but I bet he’s pretty smart if his brain is as big as it looks.” That was something to anticipate. He was never going to be a looker, but they both knew, even if they didn’t share it with one-another that there were big plans for their little liability.

TWENTY

Difficult baby

It was all new to both of them. Seeing the huge cranium dwarfing Carys's ample bosom, Marco marvelled at how much he guzzled. Swapping sides, Carys shook her head. "He's hungry. I'll be glad when he can eat food."

"When's that?"

"Oh, ages yet, unfortunately." When at last he unlatched, Carys held him over her shoulder to burp him and conceded the neck brace seemed vital. Hopefully not for long if he kept eating as well as he was. He'd be growing big and strong in no time.

"How do we put him to bed?"

"In the hospital the nurses took him after feeding and put him back in the incubator. The last few nights he's been in a crib beside me. That's why I asked you to buy one. You did get one, didn't you? Only, I can't see it."

"It's in the nursery. Mum got it." Why did he say that? He'd been involved in choosing too, but now his volatile wife was twitching again. "I'll fetch it."

By the time he returned, she seemed normal and was bouncing Ebe in the window - showing him his real dad, probably, Marco considered wryly. His head was nearly as big as Carys's. His blank little face peered unseeingly over her shoulder in Marco's general direction. "Here," he said and braced for the criticism of how he'd got it wrong again, but she surprised him.

"Oh, that's lovely, Marco. Very retro. Shall we try to settle him?"

Visions of a sleeping infant as he lay with his beautiful bride aroused him and he squirmed in embarrassed twitches. Jiggling him, Carys laid him as she'd been shown in hospital, making sure his head had extra support. As soon as her hands left his side, he screamed. "The midwives said to ignore his cries."

"Yeah, I'm confident he'll settle soon."

Carys twirled her wedding ring around her finger as the screams grew louder. With a frown, she said, "Well, he can't be hungry. And he burped. Can you check his nappy?"

Would that mean picking him up. Marco would prefer professional supervision before tackling that. Instead, reaching inside the crib, he sniffed close to his bum. "Smells fine."

"You'll have to check to see if he's sore with wee,

then."

Marco winced at feelings of ineptitude, sweating at figuring out the baby-grow, and how to get it past his neck-brace obstruction, then sticking the nappy together correctly so it contained what it was supposed to without leaks. As his hands hovered over his stepson, he became aware of Carys moving behind him.

"Oh, for goodness' sake, give him here." Grabbing him deftly and swinging him onto the bed, Carys manipulated the baby-grow from him and peeled back the nappy. "It seems fine but I'll change him anyway, whilst I'm here. You'll have to learn how to do this too, you know."

"Of course, Marco soothed. "I plan to."

Fed, burped, nappy changed, the crying continued. "What shall we do? Should I call the hospital and tell them he's unwell. They were happy for him to stay on the ward a bit longer, weren't they?"

While they deliberated, Ebe snuffled his way around until his huge head rested on Carys's chest whilst his little face pressed firmly into hers. It was the only position that brought peace. Any attempts at removing him, even onto the bed, met with vicious screams.

Pictures of them being lovingly intimate faded as Marco imagined a different outcome. And in this one, his needs didn't get a look in as Ebe took every ounce of Carys's attention. It was probably normal and he was undoubtedly being unreasonable. Resolved to his disappointment, he sighed. "That's done the trick," he forced a smile.

"You look tired!"

Everyone at work knew about the new baby. Or, rather, they all knew a baby had been born and had just come home. They didn't know he looked like ET's little brother or that he only ever slept if his face was pressed onto his wife's.

The subject of post-birth intimacy was a difficult one to broach. His friends were too young and he couldn't ask his parents. They'd just tell him he was being vulgar and that reproductive sex was the only kind to pursue. Not that they'd even call it sex. It was a wonder he had been born.

Across the desk he smiled at his colleague, Julie. As she grinned back, her lips parting caused a stirring inside that unnerved him. She was forty, at least, and he'd never noticed her before. Noticed that, to a certain way of thinking, and to someone much older than him, she was devastatingly attractive.

He shouldn't ask her for advice now, should he. But talking about sex, even innocently, felt so compelling he couldn't help it. The desire grew inside him, and within his trousers and he couldn't reason. A tear welled in his eye. This wasn't right. This wasn't how he was brought up.

The need to flee to the bathroom was hindered

by the protrusion hidden under his desk and he had no choice but to stay where he was, but he couldn't speak. Through his thick throat, he garbled, "The baby." Julie smiled and looked back down at her computer screen. Marco cursed the missed opportunity and fought to re-kindle it.

After a round of throat clearing, he coughed one more time and smiled. "Julie, you've got children, haven't you?"

Julie beamed, swivelled her chair away from her desk and slid over to him. "Yes, two. Questions?"

He wanted to ask how long it was before she had sex with her husband afterwards; desperately. Instead, he inquired after baby bedtime tips.

"A lavender bath helped a lot with my eldest boy, Brandon, who was a nightmare to get down. But then Lauren slept like a dream from day one. My sister's boy, Zach, never slept at all. Unless she was rocking his crib, he'd be screaming. Marco's heart sank. He knew Ebe was going to be one of those. "Your boy not sleeping? What's his name again?"

"It's Ebe. And he only sleeps pressed into my wife's face."

"Well, it's early days. Try the lavender." Her legs tensed ready to propel her back to her desk, but Marco's desperate eyes made her pause. "Was there something else, Marco?"

His cheeks burned, "This is embarrassing."

"Never mind. I'm a woman of the world. I'm

sure you won't shock me."

Marco sighed. "The thing is, I was just wondering... How long after having a baby did you... You know... When did you... Have a proper marriage again?"

Julie laughed and stared right at him as if that was exactly the question she'd expected. "I think they say leave it a month or so. We couldn't wait that long, and there were no complications. It's not recommended to rush things, though."

"Your husband's very lucky."

"Someone should have told him that. He left me for a younger model, I'm afraid. Such a cliché."

"Oh, that's terrible. I'm so sorry." As she cooed her replies, Marco had already lost his ardour and was thankful. His frustration quelled knowing that with it having only been three weeks since Ebe was born, expectation would be reckless, let alone unreasonable. "Thanks, Julie," he inadvertently cut her off mid-sentence and she slid off behind her desk with a frown.

"No problem."

At last able to leave and go to the bathroom, Marco excused himself. Splashing water over his face, he stared at his reflection. That didn't look like a twenty-something success story. His finger brushed his hairline. Was it receding? Surely not. Brushing it off his face he scrutinised his image and judged his hair was a few millimetres higher than it had been.

He flapped it back and forth trying to recall

what he'd looked like before and then, on the down sweep of hair, he saw it. Quicker than ever it was gone, but there was no mistaking it.

Marco stumbled away from the mirror, crashing into the next person. "Sorry," he stuttered.

"Are you all right? You look terrible."

He wasn't all right, but he didn't want to be excused to go home. He'd felt safer here. Safe enough to sleep for nights, but all that had changed in that fraction of a second.

Julie, miffed, barely looked up as he came back in, and he was grateful. Hiding behind his desk, he opened up his to do list and picked the first task. He'd do them all. Keeping busy was his only hope.

TWENTY-ONE

A desire for normality

Julie had ignored him for the rest of the day and five o'clock was fast approaching. His throat constricted and chest tightened as he tried to figure out why she was so peeved. Squinting and peering up, he tried to remember the last words of conversation as when he interrupted, but recalling something he hadn't listened to in the first place was impossible.

He noticed her move from the corner of his eye. "Are you off, then, Julie?" she didn't reply. "I want to say sorry for earlier."

She paused. "Go on."

Marco smiled. "I asked your advice and in the middle of you giving it, I cut you off. It was just that what you said made so much sense it got me thinking and I stopped listening. It's a man thing."

"You got that dammed right." Marco flinched at

the profanity. "I was telling you how my husband had left me for a younger model and you went blank. You obviously believe he had a point."

"No, not at all. I was thinking how attractive you are."

Julie smiled. "Oh, Marco, really? Well, maybe if you buy me a drink on the way home from work, I'll forgive you."

He didn't want to. Getting back to Carys now his expectations had been managed was what he wanted, but now he felt obligated. And she'd supported him eating in the Bristol Trader to keep him company when he needed it. It was the least he could do. "Okay. One will be fine." He already felt bad that he was trying to restrict her. "Or maybe two," he grinned. As she turned to put on her coat, his face dropped, but he quickly regained a joyful demeanour when she turned back again. "Ready?"

Perhaps it was the lighting, or merely that he was a normal red-blooded male, but as Julie leaned in towards him and laughed at his crappy jokes, golden curls twisting between her fingers as she ran the tip on the other hand around the rim of her glass, feelings began to stir. Why couldn't Carys be more like this?

She had only ever shown him reluctant affection and he strongly suspected he'd been accepted as a best of a bad job; that no-one else would have wanted her when she was pregnant, and a secure home for Ebe was the most important thing to her. Meal ticket, that was the term, wasn't it? He'd known, of course, but it made resisting the charm of a beautiful woman harder.

Unused to drinking, and choosing beer for reasons that escaped him now, he found his need for the toilet annoyingly persistent. No matter. Julie's ardour didn't seem like a brief absence would dampen it. "So, sorry, Julie, but nature calls."

"Ooh, need a hand?"

Marco stopped cold. What was happening to him? Weeks ago, he was a righteous virgin. Since succumbing to the desires of the flesh, even under God's blessing of marriage, he'd changed. He drank alcohol when he never used to, and he was seriously considering taking this woman by the hand and having sex in the pub toilet.

He couldn't. Debauchery and adultery in one brief temptation. He'd never even noticed Julie's charms until today, he wouldn't argue they were irresistible. But the pounding in his pants was draining his resolve. He had to be strong now or it would be too late.

Damn himself to hell, he couldn't resist. Leaning forward, he allowed his lips to brush Julie's face below her ear and he whispered, "That sounds like a great idea. Come on."

He felt her bite his lip. She pulled away and began to whisper, "Are you sure," when instead she screamed and dropped her full glass, smashing on the floor. "How are you doing that? Oh, my god, that's disgusting, stop it."

"Doing what?" it wasn't his voice.

Julie fell back off the barstool. "Stop it! Oh, my god, please, no!"

His hands flew to his cheeks. Scales, smooth and warm is what he expected, but instead he was sure it was the regular stubbled chin he always had. Why was she being like this then?

A noise came from the back of the bar. "Everything okay?" the barman said in a loud strong tone.

Marco stood up and saw his face in the mirrors behind the optics. Perfectly normal.

The barman asked again, "Everything all right in here? Madam?" Julie couldn't speak, struggling to get back to her feet. "Aren't you going to help the lady up?"

Marco offered his hand to Julie.

"Get away from me!" she squealed.

"I think you'd better leave, pal, don't you?"

Marco put up his hands. "Fine. I'll leave. I believe the lady has had a bit too much to drink, that's all."

"Just leave now or I'll call the police."

Marco reached the door and glanced back. He'd had a lucky escape. He'd escaped becoming someone he loathed, and now he got to go back to his stunning wife, guiltlessly.

She was foolish to believe she didn't have

options. He'd never seen anyone more beautiful, and that's why he acted. It was like he struck at the perfect time to take advantage of her at her neediest. And that didn't sound very Christian. No wonder she didn't yet love him. He'd do better. If he treated her the way he knew he should, closeness was an inevitability, surely. And why would he want it any other way?

On the journey home, he looked into a garage forecourt selling flowers. The steering wheel twitched as he considered purchasing, then twitched the other way when he decided it was a sign of a guilty conscience. "Treat her well and buy flowers for a different reason," he said to himself, and he had to get home to relieve himself. As he looked in the mirror to catch his eye and aid making his statement real, he added, "Lord, please help me be the best husband and father I can be."

Traffic lights changed to amber and despite a brush of the accelerator, he didn't make it through before they turned red and he braked a little too hard. Panting at his foolishness, he glanced in the mirror again to see if anyone had witnessed his roguish driving. There, immediately behind him in a black saloon car were the two tall blonde men.

His fingers drummed the wheel desperately. Home, anywhere away from them, he had to go. Car in gear and foot on the clutch, he revved and as soon as the lights changed, he floored the accelerator and drove as fast as he could.

The black sedan kept up effortlessly. Every bend he flew around convinced he'd lost them, their lights flashed in his mirror again.

There was no reason to lose them. The first time he'd seen them they were outside his house. They knew where he lived.

He slowed the car. Whoever they were, he couldn't escape them and behaving suspiciously only gave them more reason to trail him.

Once, he'd suggested to himself that they were angels. What if they were a response to his prayer to be a better husband? Angels showing up to escort him home and encourage him to do the right thing? He feared he knew what they were, but his mind grasped onto anything as the perfect solution. He'd be the perfect husband. It's what everybody wanted.

Marco liked a lie-in on a Saturday, but with Ebe around that wasn't likely to happen. So, when the inevitable sniffling of his hunting baby gums sought Carys's sore nipples, he leapt up to make tea and breakfast.

Returning with a laden tray, Carys smiled pleasantly. "That's a nice thing to do, Marco, thank you."

"It's the least I can do. You've gone through such a lot and I've been wrapped up in my own problems the last few weeks. I'm sorry." He balanced the cup and the croissants on the duvet. Ebe clung on and he realised actually eating would still be a problem. If Carys was unable to enjoy hers, starting his own was awkward too. "I'll take Ebe, if you like?"

Carys glared, "Your breasts are full of milk now, are they?" As his face dropped, she moderated her tone. "Sorry. It was a stupid thing to say though. When he's finished feeding, you can burp him whilst I eat, if you like."

"I meant when he'd finished. Yes, of course." He pushed his food around awhile, unsure if beginning was rude.

"Start yours," Carys ordered.

Permission granted, he felt an emasculated fool, but tucked in anyway, and his eating seemed to correspond to Ebe finishing too. Arms stretched toward them, he plucked him up, careful of his head despite the neck brace. "If he keeps drinking at this rate, he might not need this for much longer." Already, his body had caught up a little with his giant head. Marco gazed down at him, forcing himself to hide his disgust. "There you go, Ebe, there's a good boy," he jiggled and cooed, tapping his back to release a violent burp. And then the tears and screams of anguish that for nearly a minute he hadn't been pressed into Carys's face.

She sighed a deep breath. "I guess I won't be having breakfast in bed, then."

Marco stood, "No, don't worry. I'll distract him."

He strode to the window, "Look, Ebe, what's that?" his finger pointed indiscriminately, ready to hone in on anything Ebe showed interest. The screams grew louder and as he turned to see if Carys was able to enjoy even a mouthful, he saw milk spurting through her nightdress onto the plate. "Oh, just give him here, Marco!" Snatching him away, she smiled a cardboard smile and plopped her nipple back in his mouth. After a brief glug, he was settled again. A warble began in his chest and Carys pressed him into her, willing him to sleep.

"I've had an idea. How about coming to church with me tomorrow? See people again. What do you think?"

Without looking up she sneered, "Don't be ridiculous. How am I going to bring Ebe? He'll either be stuck on my tits, or pressed into my face. I won't see or hear anything and I'll be really embarrassed."

"There are plenty of people to pass Ebe around to. You'll get a bit of an uplifting break."

"Pass him around? We'd need to vet everyone to make sure they'd cope with him. He's not built the same as other babies. No-one will be experienced, will they."

"I suppose not. It was just a thought."

"But you go. Have a lovely time leaving me here with this," she gripped his baby-grow tight and breathed hard. The tension made him cry and Marco feared for her sanity; and Ebe's safety. If something happened to him, that would be sad, of course, but more pressing were the strangers' threats. "I am in the band, but I guess I could stay." hearing the words fall unsupportively from his lips, he caught himself. This wasn't being the best husband. "No, I'll stay home, of course I will. My duty is to you." He regretted the word as soon as he said it. With relief, either she hadn't heard, or chose not to bite. Whatever reason, 'Duty,' was not mentioned again.

"Is it okay if I practise for a bit?"

"What, just in case Ebe has miraculously learned not to be such a pain in the arse overnight."

"I need to practise. We will go back one day. No rush, of course, but I can't be forgetting how to play! I could have a strum of a few songs in here, if you like. Ebe might find it soothing."

"He might," Carys whispered, "But let's not let the first time you try be when I've finally fucking got him to sleep!"

He didn't pick up her vulgarity.

"Where are you planning to play? Because if you wake him, I'll..." she didn't finish but didn't need to.

"I'll go to Mum and Dad's if you want to be left in peace."

"Peace? Yes. Left? no."

Marco smiled. "I'll be really quiet."

Strumming away at his guitar and singing

songs to Jesus under his breath didn't bring the usual uplifting to his spirits, and he knew the reason: guilt. The things he saw, and things it had tempted him to do didn't fit in with the kind Christian son-of-a-minister he had always been.

Prayers suffered unanswered. He wanted to believe he was being tested, as all men were. Without temptation, righteousness can have no value. And he'd come through lacking having sinned. Not properly, anyway. But he knew he would have; and at the first enticement.

Julie could have made him an adulterer with little effort and the only thing that stopped her was the sudden revulsion she showed. And that was what really troubled him. No-one had witnessed what he had before. He couldn't be sure that's what it was now; he hadn't seen it himself and the barman certainly hadn't either.

The fact that was the conclusion he had immediately jumped to was reason enough to be afraid. There was no good explanation for the hallucinations. The most hopeful was that he was crazy. That he'd succumbed to the pressures of becoming a new dad to a baby he had no rights over and who appeared was likely to experience problems. That was the best case, and he didn't like it.

Of the other two reasons, which was more unpalatable was hard to decide, but he plumped for demonic possession. How it even happened in the loving bosom of Christian fellowship was a mystery. Maybe not. He had just sinned, and that was how you invited demons into your life.

As awful as that scenario would be, he knew the help to deal with it was on hand. He'd be loath to ask, and beyond embarrassed he had succumbed to such evil as soon as he ventured into the adult world. And he wasn't ready to give in yet. He needed to be a good husband, but he needed to go to church too. To bask in the holy words of his father and feel his spirit lift as they sang exalted praise to their Lord. That would sort him out.

So that left the third and worst of the three afflictions. And, right now it was the one he trusted the most. Carys really had been impregnated by beings not of this world, and he was charged, on pain of death, to care for the hybrid child. Every time he showed sign of being dissatisfied with his lot, he hallucinated a hideous alien reptile and met up with odd looking men; either aliens living among us, or agents making sure he didn't break some secret intergalactic treaty to care for extra-terrestrial offspring.

It was terrifying, but so ridiculous that whenever he outlined the problem in his mind, cynicism pushed aside the terror. It can't be true, can it? Absolutely preposterous. That led back to the preferable option two. Good. He knew what to do about that

TWENTY-TWO

Trickery and solace

Saturday was no relaxing day. Ebe was so demanding that a walk to the local Chinese takeaway was a relief. It was difficult to enjoy Saturday evening television with Ebe needing constant attention, but it was what he signed up for. Knowing he wouldn't be going to church tomorrow gave him a tenseness he wasn't used to, but he was up for the challenge.

Another night next to the most beautiful girl, unable to touch her, and the probability of that happening again seemingly ever-distant. On Sunday morning he persisted with the good husband routine and brushed off the terse remarks, forgiving them in the name of hormones, but it wasn't fun. Being a perfect partner would be a lot easier if he were able to enjoy at least some of the perks that go with the job: companionship, support, a clean house, food, closeness; all of which he provided, and some of which were unwelcome. He was no sexist, his independent and ferocious mother had taught him well in that department, but receiving no help was hard to take. But he couldn't blame her. If Ebe moved an inch away from his mummy, he screamed like he'd been run over. He was shocked to realise he was actually eager to get back to work.

Monday, and his enthusiasm was soon unrewarded. On top of the mundanity and frustration of attempting to provide solutions to the undeserving, and find no resolutions forthcoming for those in desperate need, was Julie's refusal to even look his way.

It made things easier. Temptation had disappeared. But a growing curiosity of exactly what had upset her was inescapable. What had she seen in his face? "Julie," he grinned from his workstation to hers. "Julie, can I have a word?"

She ignored him, and on his next attempt to speak, got up and fiddled with the photocopier. Was it avoidance, or the opportunity to talk away from the others' desks? Marco pushed his own chair back and, trying not to appear too obvious, stood up, stretched, and walked over to join her.

She watched him the entire time, and as he drew closer; close enough where he'd look suspicious if he didn't print something, she jerked away and strode from the room.

But Marco didn't care about looking shady. Quickly, he stormed after her and dashed down the corridor. At the double doors which led outside, he grabbed her arm. "Julie, wait!"

"Get off me. I'll scream the bloody place down."

Marco let go. "I'm not trying to pursue anything improper. I just want to know what I did wrong?"

The door wouldn't open and Julie was cornered. "Listen, you freak. I don't know who, or what, you are, but you keep away from me, you understand me?" She shoved the doors one last time, realising she would have to return to her desk. "Keep away!"

"Did you see a lizard?"

The question shocked her. Eyes moist, she gave short little nods. "What *was* that?"

Marco said, "I don't know. I thought I was hallucinating, but if you saw it too… What can it mean?"

"You're possessed. You're a monster, that's what it means."

And despite the dread, Marco was relieved. 'Possessed' not 'Alien'. And he knew what to do about that.

For the rest of the day, it was difficult to concentrate with Julie pointedly refusing to ever look in his direction. Every time he sniffed or coughed, she visibly jumped, and when he walked past to get to the photocopier for genuine reasons, she let out a whimper.

It was no surprise when the next day she'd called in sick. He felt guilty, of course, but he had no control over what was happening to him, and who may or may not witness it.

Carys hadn't seemed to mind, but now he was here, he was worried. "Marco! Good to see you!" several of the congregation clapped him on the arm. "Dan and Natalia never mentioned you were coming."

Marco had avoided them for two weeks. "No? funny." The heaviness of their scrutiny hit him already. "It's my wife, Carys. She's struggling with her self-esteem, you know? Says she needs to lose the baby weight. I don't get what she means. She looks fantastic to me."

"She is a splendid looking girl, I must admit," one of the older members leaned into the conversation.

Marco grinned but wondered if it wasn't more of a dig than a compliment; like they could see all his doubts around his virtues. "Well, I best let the band know I'm here. We'll have to grab a coffee afterwards," he said, with no intention of seeking their company again.

As he walked away, he was sure he caught the word 'Odd' and was equally sure it was directed at him.

Odd? They didn't know the half of it. Enthusiasm continued from everybody who saw him, but each time he left, he burned, believing they were saying things behind his back. Even the rest of the band looked as though they wished he hadn't bothered, though their words said otherwise.

"Who's going to tell Jake he's not playing guitar today?" one of them joked.

Replaced already. "I don't want to step on anybody's toes. Why don't we have two guitars this week?"

"We could. But we've been working on some new arrangements."

Marco smiled and raised his palms. "Fair enough. I had been practising, too, but I don't want to spoil things."

"Oh, are you sure? Thanks for being so understanding."

There was no coming back from that. "I'll try to give you all a bit more notice next time."

"Yeah, exactly. Then we can all jam together, like usual."

He'd yearned for this, but he had no choice. It wasn't too much of them to expect to perform how they had rehearsed when it mattered; in front of an audience. Smile creased onto his face, Marco made his way to the back of the hall.

Skilfully avoiding his parents, in the middle of his dad's sermon, he ducked, avoiding eye-contact as he worked the crowd with this week's message of forgiveness. He hoped he was ready to practise what he preached. Not that he'd done anything to be forgiven for. Not yet.

When the band was invited on stage to close the morning, Marco took his leave and ventured to the toilets. Not to get out of clearing the space for coffee time, although that would be reason enough, he struggled to watch the musicians without feeling jealous. And he couldn't afford another sin on his record this week.

Shuffling from the back of the crowd, no-one seemed to notice his exit. Head down, as he pushed open the door, he was surprised when someone else was coming out. "Oh, sorry," he said, and lifted his head to acknowledge who he'd addressed.

The man said nothing, but his very presence rendered Marco speechless. With a gasp, he collapsed against the wall and watched as the tall, blonde gentleman weaved through the mass and left the church from the back door.

Stuck to the wall, Marco made the mistake of looking across to the bank of mirrors. There he saw his face was not his. The entire image didn't fit. The being reflected back at him seemed much larger. How was this happening?

Footsteps. He couldn't let anyone see him like this. Forcing himself free from his paralysis, Marco bolted for the cubicles and slammed it shut, sliding the feeble bolt across, designed to allow access to children, or the infirm.

Etiquette decreed that one-another's presence was not acknowledged.

Marco waited in excruciating silence for the

other occupant to finish and noted with dismay not hearing the soap dispenser, tap, or dryer operate before the door swung open and re-closed.

Gasping hard, he listened to his breaths. Did they sound normal? Would somebody be able to tell all was not well? He couldn't risk finding out. He would stay in here until everybody left, and if someone came in, he would hold his breath.

Coffee cups clanked, and the smell of baking and fresh brews reached the toilet block to fight with the smells of stale piss and urinal cakes. The battle was valiant, and neither side won, leaving a combined effluvium which was worse than the original stench, tricking his mind that he was expected to eat what he smelled.

He felt normal. Dare he open the cubicle to glance in the mirror? Marco creaked it ajar and listened. The clatter of crockery and hubbub of chatting filled the air. He had enough time.

Two steps and he almost reached the mirrors, but just then the door opened before he checked.

"Ah, you are here!" Dan's booming voice echoed around the hard surfaces.

Marco's mind whirled. He must be seeing him as normal, but how soon before there came a glimpse of the demon within?

"Everyone said they'd seen you, and someone was sure they'd spotted you heading in here over an hour ago. Whatever are you doing in here?"

"I just wasn't myself." It felt good to be almost

truthful.

"What's got into you, son? Three weeks you've missed. Don't you love Jesus anymore? And how does it make me look if my own offspring can't even be bothered? Hey?"

"Sorry. It's Carys. I wanted her to come too, but she's been acting strangely."

"When has she not? You want to hear what I think? That girl needs some spiritual intervention. Obviously got the devil on her shoulder."

"What should I do?"

"You need to bring her in. Let her remember the power of the Lord."

"She says she can't come because of Ebe. He really would scream the place down if she didn't give him one-hundred percent of her attention."

"He's another one who needs to come, if ever there was."

"Come on, let's not discuss this any more in here. Grab a coffee and a slice of cake before it's devoured."

Marco took a deep breath and prayed the darker side of him kept under wraps in front of everyone.

Natalia and her cronies came up with a solution. "If Carys can't come because of Ebe, perhaps we could offer to babysit."

"Oh, that's very kind. We could do with some alone time."

"And then, when she comes to drop Ebe

off, we'll perform an intervention and exorcise whatever dark entity is troubling her."

Marco feared Carys wouldn't be up for that. The secrecy was obviously dishonest, but necessary. A demonic entity would explain her crazy mood swings. Although his mother-in-law had said it was her hormones, he had another reason to be enthusiastic: he might get rid of his own scaly demon without having to admit its existence! "That's a brilliant idea. I'll try to persuade her. When?"

"No time like the present. How about tonight?"

Marco gulped, but yes. Why not?

Despite his trepidation, and how unwelcome he felt in his own church, and how close a call he'd had with his demon being spotted, Marco acknowledged a bubbling of, if not excitement, perhaps something positive. Relief? That his episode of whatever he was experiencing was about to be over?

Walking with a rapid pace, he soon reached The Drang and scurried up; away from the parishioners and on to the challenge ahead.

He arrived at the back door, and with a deep breath, pushed it open. Silence. This had happened before. "Carys?" He called up the stairs. A rudimentary plan in mind to deceive her and ambush her into a ceremony that he hoped would relieve them both of the darkness plaguing their lives.

"Carys?" he called again, halfway up the stairs.

It was still quite early for a Sunday. She was probably asleep. "Carys," he said as he reached the top, "How does getting out for a nice meal sound? My mum and dad have offered to babysit!" He stopped mid-sentence when he saw what had been going on in his absence.

The look of rancour on Carys's face was replaced with one of fear and regret as she sat on the bed, blood seeping from her arms where she'd cut them. Marco glanced around for what weapon she'd used this time, and spotted the broken photo frame which had held a picture of the two of them on their wedding day. Shards of glass scattered haphazardly whilst she used one of them to carve gruesome wounds into both her arms.

Tonight's plan was happening just in time, he thought and said, "It's okay. I'm here now," he soothed, rushing to cuddle her. "Everything will be okay." Where was Ebe? Why couldn't he hear him crying?

"It's okay," Carys whispered, sensing the stiffness in his embrace. "He actually settled to sleep."

Marco checked she was telling the truth and had done nothing regrettable. For the first time since he'd brought them home, Ebe was sleeping peacefully, chest rising easily up and down.

"I don't feel like going out for a meal, but I would like to get out of the house," suggested Carys in response to the invitation Marco had assumed went unheard.

"That's fine, babe," Marco said. "We'll drop our little man off with Mum and Dad, and we can decide from there." Marco was pleased with how it had gone. The meal was only the bait to initiate his plan. "Why don't you get in the bath and have a soak. I'll jiggle him if he wakes up... It won't be good enough, I'm sure, but I'll try everything to let you get some peace."

"I'll settle for a hot shower. I don't think I'd relax knowing I might have to hop out of the tub any minute. A shower will be just fine." As she reached the landing, she turned, "Thank you." Stepping into the bathroom, she turned again, "And I'm sorry."

Marco's smile diluted. What should he say? It's okay you've defaced your beautiful arm? It wasn't his arm, and it wasn't her rational self doing it. Before he came up with a sensible answer, she'd disappeared into the splattering sounds of the steamy shower.

When she returned, in what seemed like far too little time, she looked more relaxed than he'd seen her in months. He enjoyed watching her pick out clothes and applying a little make-up. Almost moved to say, 'You don't need that,' warning bells sounded, and he realised it might be taken as criticism that she usually wears too much, rather than the compliment to her fine features that needed no adornment to outshine anyone he'd ever met. He fidgeted, remembering how close he came to being seduced by Julie. The supposed demon had done him a favour by showing his face. Encouraging him to be a faithful and better husband didn't sound very monstruous.

"You look fantastic, my angel," he beamed, and she grinned back. "We can get going as soon as you like."

"I'm enjoying the peace, but we'll go once Ebe wakes for a feed."

This was easier than he had expected. Ebe remained peaceful after his milk and even allowed Marco to buckle him into his car seat without objection. It was only a quick drive to Dan and Natalia Paulo's.

An aspect of his plan that he hadn't considered threatened its ease of execution as they pulled into the driveway.

"Are you sure your mum and dad are happy to babysit?"

Marco frowned. "Of course, why?"

"Well, they've obviously got company. Oh, I don't want to get on the wrong side of your mother if she's not wanting to. You go in and make sure it's all right."

"I'm sure it's fine. Totally."

"Well, I'm not going to wrestle the car seat back out if it turns out you've got it all wrong. Go and ask!"

Marco sighed. "Don't give it away," he said under his breath as he walked from the car to the front door. "Not now!"

Natalia quickly answered. "What's going on, Marco?"

"She saw all the cars."

"Come on, I'll get her out. She needs to understand this dispossession is exactly the right thing for her."

"She knows nothing about that. She just thinks you've got company and that you hadn't agreed to babysit Ebe after all. Smile and wave, beckon her in and I'm hoping I can still persuade her inside."

"You really should be firmer, Marco. Don't be such a pushover."

"Gently, gently, catch a monkey," he said and didn't know why.

When it was clear Carys had seen his mother's attempts at a warm welcome, he bounded over to the car to help her out. "I hadn't got it wrong at all. The guests are just leaving."

"Should we come back?"

"No! Mum's really excited to have Ebe."

Carys smiled doubtfully.

The door had closed again and Marco scowled. Where had his mother gone? He supposed watching as they collected all the things Ebe needed for an evening wasn't fun, and she wouldn't want to let the heat out, but still...

"Are you sure your mum and dad are expecting to babysit?"

"Yeah. We're a bit early, I suppose. Mum said the

cars will be gone soon, and not to worry about it. Using his foot to push the door, he was irritated it was locked. He gripped his hoard harder in his fists as Carys leaned over him and rang the bell.

"Hello," Natalia beckoned them in. Seeing the bustling of people beyond, Marco realised they were trying to hide, and that was why the door had been closed as they hoped for a few more minutes to prepare. "Come here, little man," she said, but instead of unstrapping him and cuddling him, she passed him to a church elder.

Carys paused. "Where's your dad? We should thank him."

Marco flushed red. This was it. "Er, just in his study, I think. Hold on and I'll come with you." They strode down the hallway, sensing Carys's reluctance with everyone acting so suspiciously. Why couldn't they have been more subtle? When she paused, he offered a hand of encouragement and pushed her over the threshold. "G… Go on in."

Carys was in the study. In the centre of the room, his dad paced, crucifix in hand, pastors' robes flowing with every step.

More churchgoers bustled through and guided Carys to a chair in front of him. Would she go along with it? She could easily shove past and run away, but that would mean leaving Ebe and, whilst he was sure she trusted they wouldn't hurt him, he hoped her reluctance to leave him would be enough.

She sat.

"In the name of Jesus Christ, Our Lord, I command you to leave Carys's body and leave this house!" Dan thrust the crucifix further into her face and she jerked from his reach. "In the name of Jesus, we command you to leave the body of Carys Ellis in peace, now!" Over and over, "May the name of Jesus compel you!"

Marco should have known what to expect, but specifying Carys wouldn't serve his own plight. Under his breath he added, 'And Marco, or and me,' wondering if the third-person directive was more powerful than asking for deliverance himself. His dad splashed holy water and Marco made sure he received a good dash as the orders to leave Carys and him in peace in Jesus's name flowed over him.

The screaming made them all jump. Leaning forwards in the chair, Cary contorted grotesquely, and she shrieked incoherently. It was a clear sign to Marco she was troubled by more than mental illness. He latched onto the purging affirmations as his wife wailed and squealed.

Laughter was next. Manic, sickening mirth at first, but then the conviviality gave Dan the cue to stop. What now?

Dan blessed her, commanding the demons never to return, and Marco repeated everything he said, inserting his own name. Please, God, let it have been enough. "We'll have to get you baptised, and soon. This wouldn't have happened if you'd been baptised," Dan admonished. "We'll get little Ebe dedicated as well."

"Thank you, thank you," Carys cried, eyes flitting around the crowd, and then to Marco, "Thank you for what you organised here. I wouldn't have come if I'd known, but I feel so much better."

Marco smiled. No-one comprehended his selfish reasons. It had gone well even though it skirted disaster that could have pushed his fragile wife too far.

"Does this mean you aren't going to babysit?"

Dan glanced at his Natalia, who smiled her superior smile. "We're happy to look after him. You two go and enjoy yourselves. You deserve it," she said and bustled them out before Carys could voice any subsequent objections to the deception used to garner her cooperation

TWENTY-THREE

Disappointment

"That went well," the older man jiggling Ebe's car seat/rocker said, successfully forestalling cries.

"Well done keeping the little one quiet. "I think if she'd heard him cry, it would have been the clincher in her throwing a fit and leaving. Consider poor Marco, then!" Natalia huffed.

"He has been very odd lately, hasn't he," another churchgoer commented.

"It's no wonder, is it? Not with all the trouble Carys causes. Did you see her arms?" she said with a shake of her head. The others were unwilling to comment on her complicated mental health, and Natalia sensed she was losing her audience. "Let's hope tonight has done the trick."

Before anyone agreed, horrific screams filled the room from Ebe's tiny mouth.

"Oh, my gosh, he's got some lungs, hasn't he!"

"It's not human," the man rocking him scowled into the seat. "Sounds like an animal."

Face puce, bald head throbbing with purple veins, the squeals of despair were like nothing any of them had ever heard before.

"Who's the father, a gorilla?"

Laughter rippled through some of the more acerbic members of the congregation. "He hasn't got a hair on him. What's not hairy and sounds like that?" silence spread and no-one answered, just stared as Natalia tried to hug him as his back arched away from her. "Get me his bottle from that bag, someone, please!" she pulled her own head back as little arms flailed.

Grandmaternal instinct was tested to its full extent as Ebe's fist reached her eye as he knocked his bottle to the floor.

"Maybe, he isn't hungry?"

"Well, he isn't tired, he's only just woken up." Natalia was desperate to pass him on. Everyone mumbled how she was doing such a good job and he'd settle for his grandma soon. It was a fair point. She was the closest one to him. She was where the buck stopped.

Moving over to the window, he showed no interest in looking outside; and wasn't distracted by his Nonna's keys, or ornaments, or toys from his bag. "He's far too young for any of this," she snorted.

"Is he too cold... Or, hot?" they put Cardigans on

and off to no avail. "You've smelt his nappy, have you?"

Natalia didn't shout, but of course she had. It was the first thing she'd thought of and it was dry. But it was worth checking again, she grudgingly conceded.

Ebe lay kicking and shrieking on the cold change mat. "Help me hold him," Natalia begged. Every limb held down, Natalia struggled his baby-grow off and saw the nappy was a bit wet. It shouldn't cause the distress it seemed to be, but she might as well change it now she'd started.

When he was finally in a clean towelling baby-grow and cardigan, the adults involved in changing him sat back breathless and sweating. Still, Ebe screamed.

"Marco said he only settled with his mum. He wasn't joking."

"We have to get him dedicated as soon as we can."

"We should all pray now," Dan's deep voice carried over anguished Ebe's screams. The congregation encircled him and followed the lead of their pastor in prayer.

As the squeals grew ferociously louder, they took little persuasion to believe the freakish looking baby in front of them was deeply troubled and possessed by a spirit of unpleasant origin. "We can't wait for Carys and Marco. We have to do a casting out ceremony now, Dan ordered.

He began in a similar procedure to that he performed a couple of hours before with his daughter-in-law. Ebe writhed and kicked and screamed and cried, snot and tears flooding from him in sticky streams.

"Stop. He'll ruin his clothes again and you weren't the one who had to change him," Natalia reproved.

"We can't stop now. Finishing is vital," Dan thrust his crucifix at Ebe and incited obedience in the name of his Lord Jesus Christ.

"Well, you've been doing it for a while and it hasn't done anything. What if he isn't possessed. Perhaps he's just fed up and missing his mum." Natalia scooped him back up again and whisked him away from the crowd to their bedroom.

"Thank you for your help today. I'm sure it will have worked," Dan gestured everyone to leave. "The crowds might be a bit much for him. It has been tense, I suppose."

One by one the exorcists disappeared and manoeuvred their cars from the drive. As the last engine putted up the road, the Paulo residence was returned to silence.

But for the animal screeches of their grandson.

Arm in arm, Marco and Carys strolled back to the car after the most romantic and relaxing evening they had ever spent together. "Thank you," she cooed into his ear as they neared where they'd parked. "That was lovely."

A stroll on the sand followed by a relaxed meal in a hotel bar overlooking another stretch of sand on Tenby's South Beach had been the reward for seeking the spiritual guidance of Narberth Christian Fellowship.

"We'll have to do this more often," Marco encouraged, receiving a squeeze of his arm as confirmation Carys favoured the idea.

Their peace lasted for nearly five minutes as the drive back to Dan and Natalia's was four minutes and it took them the other minute to reach the front door. In fact, four minutes and forty seconds was all it truly lasted, because Ebe's screams were heard before they'd closed the car.

"Is that Ebe crying?" Carys gasped. Marco's first thought was that it was an odd question, but so unhuman did he sound, if the situation were not known, one might have several guesses to what could be making the noise, and human baby may not feature in the top three.

Before they pondered further, the door flew open. Dan stood on the doorstep, a lopsided smile quivered below eyes bulging with doggedness. "You're back. Did you have a nice time? Come in, come in," he beckoned.

Carys hurried past. In the lounge, Natalia was trying to hold him to her and he was writhing and kicking away.

"Carys, dear. I've tried everything; feeding, changing, playing, ignoring, he hasn't stopped from the minute you left." It was regrettable. For a moment, she wished she could take it back when she saw the panic set in Carys's face and realised all the enjoyment she may have felt on an evening out with her son was now replaced by guilt. But it didn't do to hide from the truth. She needed her to understand that caring for Ebe wasn't something she would offer to do again for the foreseeable future. If anything had happened to him, administering care would have been impossible. And her nerves were shredded. Despite her objections during the prolonged dispossession, she wasn't at all convinced there wasn't something seriously spiritually wrong with her grandson.

Face clouded by a brewing storm, Carys grabbed him from Natalia, "There, there, Ebe, Mummy's here." Sitting on the couch, she unstrapped her bosom and offered a nipple to his mouth. Proximity of his mother's smell made his little lips hunt and he latched on. He couldn't scream and suckle at the same time, and so, for the first time in hours, peace returned to the lounge. "Didn't you think to contact us?"

"We had no idea where you'd be."

Guilt washed over Carys, then anger as the thought she should be able to leave her son with his grandparents once in a while without it turning into this. She didn't answer. Neither did she ask if they'd be able to repeat it. The answer was obvious, and she couldn't subject Ebe to this distress, anyway, so that was that.

TWENTY-FOUR

It's not me, it's you

Returning to work on Monday morning after a night of no sleep as Carys had riled at the deception of the day before after it turned out the way it did, Marco was ready to make amends with Julie and assure her that what had troubled him had been 'dealt with.'

"Good weekend?" a familiar face smiled up at him as he entered the room, but not Julie's.

"Okay. Had a lovely romantic night out with my wife, but our baby terrorised my mum and dad, so it looks like a repeat is off the cards. Shame."

"Shame," the colleague repeated. "And before you ask, Julie isn't here."

Why would I ask, Marco wondered? Apart from the mild flirting last week, they'd never been close. Not that other people would have noticed, he wouldn't have thought. "Why, where is she?" he took the bait.

"Gone."

"Gone? What do you mean, gone?"

"Quit. Couldn't stand to be around you, apparently. What happened between you two, anyway? You kept that quiet! If I'd known she was up for extra-maritals, I'd have thrown my hat in," the man chortled, failing to acknowledge Marco's superior youth and good looks over his middle-aged balding paunchy dad-bod.

Marco smiled. So, she'd told everyone. That's how they knew. Good job he hadn't done anything that relied on her discretion.

"Are you going to tell me? As if I didn't know! What's she like? Cracking tits, I'll give her that, even if her face is a bit, you know..."

Marco didn't know. It was nicer than his, that was for sure. "Nothing happened."

"Oh, come on!"

"I'm telling you. We went for a drink because I had questions about bringing up a new baby. She got a bit flirty and I guess I must have offended her because she stormed off and hasn't spoken to me since. Now, I don't suppose she ever will," Marco shrugged.

"So you didn't... You know?"

"No!" The man lost interest and bumbled off, shuffling papers and mumbling excuses. If Julie had seen what he had seen, he understood her fear. But how could she have seen it? His reflection had appeared lizard-like, and he'd entertained theories it was alien overlords making sure he was frightened enough to stay with Carys. He had assumed a mind-altering frequency or something, not that he had actually turned into a lizard. And then he realised he had answered his own question. People close might hear it, if that hypothesis was correct to him and they would see whatever the aliens, or demons—as he'd since decided they were, wanted them to.

Julie seeing it too didn't make it any more real. A shared hallucination; one that after Sunday's ritual wouldn't be bothering him again. With that thought, he found peace and got on with his work.

TWENTY-FIVE

A clutched straw

Angela pulled up outside her patient's house and took a few deep breaths. Carys Ellis was a difficult patient. Full of smiles, she brought her bag from the boot and struggled to the front door. She heard the bell ring and footsteps.

It was difficult to maintain her smiling seeing the blank, dark mood radiating from her patient. But she did her best. It was her job. "Hello, Carys, dear. Had you remembered I was coming?"

Carys didn't answer but pulled the door open more and made space for her to squeeze past. "Lounge or kitchen?" she asked, visits had been split between them. There came no answer so she decided for them. "Lounge would be best today, I think. I've got to weigh baby Ebe and he'll prefer to do that on the carpet, I expect."

Carys followed her in and sat beside Ebe in his

rocker.

"In his rocker again. Doesn't he like to play under the baby-gym? He'll never learn to roll over and crawl if he's always in this, will he?" Angela chuckled in her attempt to not sound critical. "Pop his clothes off and we'll give him a little weigh. Where's his red book?"

"He never stops screaming unless I am breast-feeding him, or I've just breast fed him and he's in that bloody car seat. I have to rock him in it if he wakes up."

"Mmm hmm," Angela noted without looking up. "But maybe if he could entertain himself, he'd be more contented. Give it a try, eh?"

Carys said nothing.

Ten pounds, eleven ounces. That puts him at around the thirtieth percentile. Be good to get that up a bit. Especially as a lot of that weight's going to be his large head, isn't it."

Carys stared blackly.

"If you're struggling with anything, Carys, you let me know, won't you?" As she finished the sentence, she saw the red raw gashes on her arm. "How did you do those?" she asked with a smile.

Carys shrugged.

"It might be a good idea to stop breast-feeding him, my lovely."

"But that's the only thing that settles him."

"The only thing right now with him strapped to a rocker all day. How about if he's playing and getting properly hungry, you can put some extra calories into a bottle. It won't be long and he'll be able to hold the bottle himself. You'll feel obsolete then," she grinned.

"The thing is, you'll be able to take some better medication. It must rub off on baby if mum's not happy, eh?" She crammed things into her bag. "Well, you think about what I've said. Call me if you need any help. I'll show myself out, don't worry. Bye bye, Ebe, Aunty Angela will see you again soon."

She turned to Carys. "You'll get a letter. I see in your notes the Community Psychiatric Nurse is visiting you as well. Tell her what I've said about stopping breast-feeding and show her your arm. She might be able to speed things up with the psychiatrist. We'll want to make sure you're okay and that Ebe grows into that big brain of his, or he may need some help."

Bag lugged behind her she reached the hallway and called out again, "By, Carys, bye, Ebe." Pulling the door closed she was pleased to get back to the car. The next mum and baby were the cutest, and they always gave her a nice slice of cake and a pot of tea.

Marco was dreading coming home. Work was weird with everyone sniggering behind fingers over what they imagined happened between him and Julie, and at home, his wife hadn't been as enthusiastic about his clever exorcism.

As he opened the front door, it did not surprise

him no cooking smells greeted him. He found Carys staring at an early evening TV quiz show. "Hi, babe. How's things?"

"I haven't cooked, or cleaned, or even showered. I can't. I can't do anything but hug Ebe and let him suck my nipples until they bleed. How was your day?"

It was a sarcastic question, and Marco couldn't answer it, anyway. He could hardly describe how a woman he almost absconded into the toilets with for an improper liaison had left her job because she saw lizard-demon features morph onto his face, could he. "You poor girl," he said. He was getting good at this husband thing. "What do you fancy. I'll cook, and then try to get Ebe to settle while you have a shower."

"He won't relax, Marco. Nothing interests him apart from me. He's obsessed. I'm not even sure if I love him, he's suffocating me so much." Her hand flew to her mouth, "No, no, no, of course I love him, I didn't mean that."

"What did the health visitor say?"

"Blamed me for Ebe not settling. Said I need to stop breast-feeding so I can get onto better meds. I'm wondering if I need to after yesterday."

"You think it helped, then?"

"At the time, I suppose. I've been fed up today, but I haven't, you know, *done* anything."

"It's up to you, babe. Maybe you should go on tranquilisers and still breast-feed. That might give us some peace!" he laughed, and fortunately,

Carys did too.

"What was it they used to give babies, Laudanum?"

"Something like that. Tempting." Marco smiled. "I'll get dinner on and you relax, even if I have to take him for a stroll in his ever-loved rocker. He can upset the neighbours instead of you." Seeing the gratitude pool in her big eyes made it all worth it. One day, if Ebe settled for five-minutes off Carys's chest, they could try to make some more babies. Normal babies. That would be nice.

Chicken in herby tomato sauce with pasta, Marco rustled up in half-an-hour. He enjoyed it. Resentment that he'd had to do it didn't even occur to him. He'd been out at work all day, but he'd do ten days rather than have the odd little baby welded to him for just one.

Now, the food had been eaten and the dishes left to soak, Carys was showering and Marco had whisked the noisy baby away before she heard him. Down the Drang tunnel and out through an alleyway at the end that led to fields.

He expected it would be peaceful; that he could scream without disturbing anyone, but as he looked down the valley, he knew the sound was permeating every home. "Sorry," he spoke over Ebe's cries. "Will you ever shut up, little man? What's wrong? Missing your real daddy? He closed down his train of thought. The middle of a field in the dark was not the place to invoke that sort of attention.

He jiggled, and sang, and bounced but Ebe didn't stop crying for a moment. "What on earth is wrong with you, Ebe? Eh? Are you going to cry your entire life?" Marco pictured a grown man with a big head wailing everywhere. "You'll end up in the nuthouse with your mother." And then I'll be blamed and goodness knows what would happen, Marco sighed.

Wheeling Ebe back, he pushed open the door and hoped Carys had enjoyed her break. Ebe cried in the hallway while Marco popped his face in the lounge and then the kitchen before heading upstairs where he found her bent over the bed tucking in a sheet wearing nothing but a towel.

"Oh, my goodness, you look stunning."

"It's nice to be clean. Shut the door."

Marco's eyebrows shot up. "Really, but Ebe?"

"What? He's fucking crying? He's always crying. I want to be close to my husband for half-an-hour. He can cry without my attention until then. He'll be perfectly safe strapped into his seat. What's going to happen?"

Marco didn't need telling twice. The door being closed dampened the worst of the noise, and by the time they were rocking in closeness they ignored him easily.

Laying back as satisfied as either of them had felt in months, Carys laughed. "The health visitor tried to persuade me that if I left him, he'd shut up eventually. Well, that didn't work."

"No, but at least we got to be a proper married

couple. I was giving up hope we ever would again." It surprised him Carys even wanted to. Maybe yesterday had freed her of those demons. And with a bone thrown his way, Marco felt for the first time that marrying Carys Ellis might not have been the biggest mistake.

"I suppose we best get him." Carys sighed and rolled onto Marco's chest, stroking slender fingers on his skin.

"I'd blocked him out until you said."

"Me too. It won't be forever, will it? He won't cry like this forever."

Marco smiled. "I don't think it's possible, to be honest. His vocal cords will give up one day."

"Can it be today? He's driving me insane."

Marco laughed. "What I wouldn't give, but I think today might be too optimistic." Her sanity was a difficult subject to broach, but ignoring her comment which could be a cry for help, would be foolish. "How are you? Mentally, I mean." He flinched in anticipation.

The chest patting paused. "Okay, considering. Remember, I said the midwife called today and suggested my mood was the reason Ebe is so distressed. She said I should stop breast-feeding and increase my medication."

"Don't you want to?"

"It's earlier than I planned, but he makes me really sore. Him suckling me is the only time he's quiet at all. If we don't have that to fall back on, what if he never shuts up? He already struggles to take my milk from a bottle. He likes the comfort of skin to skin, I suppose."

Marco reached his hand up and took hers. "For now, we have no choice. Do you believe you are affecting him negatively? I mean, if that were true, why is it you're the only one he likes?"

"I know. It's nice to believe there might be something we can do."

TWENTY-SIX

Wires

The plunge taken, Carys was on increased doses of medications and it was a decision that quickly became apparent was the right one.

Her mood was even-tempered and Marco appreciated his loving, caring wife. Enjoyment slightly marred by Ebe still only ever settling to sleep pressed to her face, at least there were times for closeness whilst he was occupied and lulled into unconsciousness by Marco's continued routine of taking him for a walk after work, even if their sporadic infrequency was less than satisfactory.

Where sleeping was an issue, walking was not. Marco went to work one morning with Ebe as a strong crawler, and on his return, he was walking around like he'd been doing it for years.

Neck muscles had grown to support his huge

head to the point where it noticed far less. Observers might be more inclined to comment on his weight-lifter's neck than his head.

Tufts of hair had begun to curl around his ears and onto his forehead and the nape of his neck, softening the starkness. He wasn't about to win any bonnie baby contests or win an advertising contract, but he was less likely to make people who saw him scream.

Carys greeted him grinning like he'd not seen before. Pride was an attractive emotion. And she had a lot to be proud about. She was coping with a troublesome child whilst managing her own mental health issues. She had built a home of Marco's investment into bricks and mortar and that was reason enough.

When Ebe toddled around the room, Marco welled up to see the joy in his wife's face. "Let the health visitor tell me he's backwards now! He can't talk yet, but how many nine-month-old babies can walk?"

Marco had no idea, but was willing to assume it was an impressive feat if it kept Carys happy. "What's he doing?"

"Following wires. He's fascinated with them. And when he reaches the end, whatever appliance he sees holds his attention for ages."

The oddness of his interest struck them both, but they resided in the warmth that at last he was doing something good; better than expected. It was a glimmer of hope that didn't need to be extinguished by either of them venturing into the world of wonder where they worried it might be because he was being prepared for some otherworldly potential.

TWENTY-SEVEN

Multi-species meet

2019

It was strange mingling with beings from different planets and dimensions. Gradually, it became natural; more ordinary perhaps than the time they'd gone to a comic convention in Cardiff and seen so many creatures from so many stories convincingly portrayed. Ebe understood the beings in front of him; their motivations and desires, more than he had on that day.

The feeling of belonging was enhanced further when he was taken to a large room filled with young people about his own age. After the tall reptilian roared his explanation Marco translated. "These are the other EBEs. They have skills introduced to the most promising of them and invited to join the research."

"Why are they here before me?"

"This project has been underway for a long time. It hasn't always been about you, Ebe. But when I reported your extra-special genius, excitement has grown."

Ebe's eyebrows were dancing as he squinted and opened his eyes wide in half-second cycles. He had seen someone do it once and liked it. Marcus recognised the oddity as Ebe's attempts at displaying incredulity. Why did they need him? What problem was so big that all these clever boys and girls hadn't come up with an answer? Finally, he grinned. Whatever it was, he was sure he'd be able to crack it like he solved every other conundrum set by professors of arguably the finest mathematics institution in the history of the world. He just had a knack of seeing the problem, usually so obvious he struggled to comprehend how it could be missed.

It had led to people saying to him on occasion, 'Why are you explaining that? Do you think I'm stupid?' The truthful answer was yes. He was so used to everyone not knowing things that were second nature to him, how was he supposed to know when he'd reached the level of their understanding. He never challenged them, though. Everything he understood was from his own research. He had long given up believing someone might have something to teach him beyond what he already comprehended.

Normally the thought of mixing with new

people would make him anxious, but after the strangeness of the past week, he welcomed the camaraderie of like-minded individuals.

As he let his gaze take in individuals in the room, he considered how odd they looked. Some were short little humans with no traits of mixed species biology whilst others made it hard to believe they had any human in them at all.

Different heights, pigments, and hair colour abounded. They all shared one thing: unattractively large heads. It would be the first time in his life he would feel accepted.

TWENTY-EIGHT

Molly

All the large almond eyes turned to him as he walked in.

"Make yourself at home, son," Marco ruffled his hair. He hated it, but he was determined to show, or remind, everyone watching that the genius they were about to encounter was partly down to him. "I'll collect you when it's time to eat again." Ebe pondered, rocking from one foot to the other, the pressure from all the attention burning in his cheeks and neck. "Go on, you'll be fine." Jerking his head, Marco and the other reptilian, and the big-headed grey alien, hurried from the room. The door closed and bolted behind them and an armed human guard took his post, cleverly concealed for Ebe's arrival so as not to put him off before he even got there.

"He'll be fine. Once he gets his brain into the

problem, he'll be happy, right in his element."

"Well, done, Marco. You have done well."

"Thank you, sir."

Ebe stood, arms flapping at his side. He was moments away from smacking his head with flat palms. A girl approached him, nervous at first, but then with a smile displaying all her teeth and most of her gums. "Hello," she greeted, offering her limp hand. Ebe glared at her and flapped harder. One leg cocked like a peeing hound, he balanced awkwardly and hopped, hands fluttering at his side like little wings.

The girl seemed not to notice. "I'm Molly," she said. "You're Ebe."

Her knowing his name befuddled him enough for him to stop. "Yes," he accused. "How do you know?"

Molly giggled. "Ah, that's for me to know," she teased. Ebe jumped on one foot again before Molly enlightened him. "They told us you were coming before you got here. Some of us don't react well to strangers, especially if they're unannounced."

"What did they say about me?" Ebe was ready to vehemently defend his privacy if he thought they knew too much.

"They said you were another genius who would probably help us find the answer to our problem." Ebe smiled. Yes, he doubtless would. Molly held out her hand. As Ebe's fingers slipped into her palm, she gripped hard. It felt awkward and blissful at once. "Come on," she said, "I'll introduce you to David."

"Who's David?" There had to be a hundred people in the big room. Why was David so special? Ebe scowled and pulled his hand away, but Molly gripped hard. "He's another friend. I think he'll like you. He's good at explaining stuff, so he's probably the best person to talk to."

Ebe squeezed Molly's hand, and she squeezed back, so Ebe pressed again, a little harder, and she gripped back a little harder. Ebe crushed her hand, eyebrows dancing over his flashing amber eyes. "Ebe! You're hurting me!" He dropped her hand.

"Sorry. I'm so sorry. I didn't mean to hurt you. I really like you, Molly. Are you okay? I'm sorry... Really sorry..."

Molly shook her hand and put it under her armpit before taking it out and shaking it again. "That's okay. You didn't mean it."

A tall boy approached, similar to Ebe in appearance; large head, odd stooping posture that fell lower with each awkward step. "Everything all right, Molly?" he folded his arms in a show of strength he'd seen on TV, but on him looked like a petulant toddler.

"Yes, thank you, David. This is Ebe."

"Greetings." David held up a flat palm like a mimic of Star Trek, or a native American.

"I told him you're good at explaining stuff."

"So they tell me," David's arms still crossed, his

twinkling smile showed he was no threat. "What do you want to know?"

Ebe thought, tapping his chin. "I don't know, because I don't know what I don't know."

"That is a confusing sentence, young man," David replied, even though they seemed the same age. "But I appreciate what you mean. Perhaps I should start at the beginning."

Ebe winced and let out short sighs. The beginning? That was an awful long time ago, and the origins were not undisputed. And if he meant species origin, rather than theories pertaining to the creation of the known universe, then which species was he referring?

David carried on, oblivious to Ebe's conundrum. "You and I, and many more, like us, have been created, *cross-bred*, if you like, in the hope we would combine the problem-solving abilities of one ancient species, with the adventurous, truth- seeking, capacity to love, from another, in order to find a solution to a problem.

Ebe itched to say, 'I know all that,' but he stood still, eyes boring into David's in a manner most unlike his typical flitting stare. Soon there would present an obstacle that had confounded this boy, and Ebe was determined to pounce on the answer. There was no escape, Ebe would be victorious and save the day, he had no doubt.

"The complication being, how to re-introduce the supreme beings, the creators, who have evolved to new levels of enlightened since previous visits thousands of years ago, without killing the humans and other species who currently inhabit Earth? Why return at all, people may ask? Well, they always promised they would. In the age of Aquarius, they planned to come again: right any wrongs and give benefit from what they had learned on their interdimensional travels.

"The planet is suffering some serious mismanagement issues, I'm sure you'll agree, Ebe?" Ebe just stared, expectant for his moment. "But they cannot risk destroying their creation - the human race - by arriving too hastily. David rested, problem posed. Smiling at Ebe, he seemed to be awaiting a response.

"Why? "Ebe questioned after a wait.

"They are vibrating at a super-high frequency now. They are not even sure what that equates to here on Earth's resonant 8hz. But if their arrival increases the planet's vibrational frequency too much, it could affect all matter on the planet."

"Affect? How?"

"Like a million, trillion solar flares all at one time."

"So, like a mega, mega atomic explosion."

"Mega, MEGA atomic explosion."

Ebe tapped his chin again. "What data do you have?"

David's cheeks turned bright pink. "Not very much. Just the basics. Earth vibrates, on average, at 8hz. Humans between 3 - 17hz on average. That's about it."

"Average? Mean? Mode? Median? What affects vibration? Who vibrates at the lower end of the spectrum, and who vibrates at the higher end? What are their characteristics? If the Aryans arrival increases the frequency, are those vibrating below Earth's modal 8hz at less risk?

David coughed. "I can see why you're the man for the job, Ebe. With insufficient data we haven't got very far. We kind of hit a wall."

Ebe grinned. He remembered what that was like. Medial tasks could be brought to a standstill by something as innocuous as pondering how a drawer separator might be useful for organising his socks. He would then need to calculate how many socks he owned, the approximate size, and if a particular folding method could maximise available space. Then of course, the size of the drawer in questions would need to be determined, and he didn't often know where to find a tape measure. The purchasing of a simple drawer divider could be a time-eating minefield. Any of the crucial information missing could bring Ebe to a complete standstill. And it certainly wasn't worth picking up any more socks from the pile of washing until answers had been established. He didn't have time to organise them twice.

But this wasn't menial. This was the most important period in his home planet's history.

1995

His first birthday was at their home. Both sets of grandparents attended and no-one else. There were no toddler friends to invite. And no grown-up friends they wanted to persuade. Carys's absence from the church made her unpopular, and Marco knew a day centred around Ebe wouldn't be the way to build bridges.

A knock at the door meant his in-laws had arrived. His own parents tended to treat the place like a home from home and let themselves in with a 'Cooee!' Marco and Carys weren't sure which they disliked more: the awkward guests, or the overfamiliar. "Diane, Geraint, come on in."

The pair stepped inside and waited in the square hallway until Marco thought to offer to take their coats and show them their seats like a Maître d'. "Thank you, Marco," they said.

Sat squashed at the kitchen table, Geraint shuffled on the bench and coughed. "Carys and Ebe joining us?"

It was an odd question, but given their understanding of their daughter's mental health challenges, perhaps not so peculiar. Carys had told him how many social engagements had been called off, or her mother's absence excused. The sudden need to hide away in their 'nest' never could be underestimated. "Yes. You're a teeny bit early, that's all."

The couple sat bolt upright and looked like they were making to leave. "Oh, so sorry. I thought we might be able to lend a hand, but if we're in the way..."

"No, not at all. You are so welcome." Marco didn't fully understand their uneasiness around him. He'd wondered if they felt bad bringing them together when things had been difficult. He speculated, too, if him being the goody-goody son of the church leader, now witnessing phenomena he was ill-equipped to cope with, was a factor. But most of all he fretted they'd seen something in him that scared them. The same something that caused his colleague to quit her job. "Tea, coffee?"

"Only if you're making one," Diane apologised.

Marco turned and filled the kettle. As soon as the click and fizz announced it was working, he excused himself on the pretext of helping Carys.

"When are you coming down? Your mum and dad are keen to see you and Ebe."

"You can entertain them for a bit, can't you. I need to get an outfit on Ebe and I'm struggling to fit them over his head. I think he's grown."

Just what he didn't need, Marco sighed. "I can, of course, but I could help you get Ebe ready and then we all go downstairs together."

Using his fingers to stretch the neck of a jumper, once Carys guided his unfeasible skull through the hole, the rest of it looked oversized like a woolly dress. "You can't even see his trousers. I don't know why I bother!"

"Your parents appreciate what Ebe's like." Her face flashed anger. "I think he looks cute, anyway," Marco soothed. "Ready?"

"Not quite. Take Ebe. I just want to finish my makeup."

"Are you sure? You don't need any, you look lovely."

"Well, I want to feel lovely, if that's okay. Give me ten minutes, please!"

"Okay," Marco breathed as he hoisted Ebe up to carry him down the stairs. Deliberately, he fussed over Ebe as he went back to the kitchen. "Here he is, the birthday boy. One-year old, can you believe it!" Without waiting for arms to raise in request of a cuddle, Marco leaned into Diane and began the handover. She could hardly refuse and it bothered him that it seemed that she might. Ebe was not the difficult child he had been even three months ago.

"Hello, Ebe," Diane said, but with none of the grandmotherly love Marco would have imagined. With even family's treatment of him being so distant, Marco felt proudly protective. He bit his lip for now. He didn't want a row before Carys had even made it down the stairs. "Was it tea or coffee? Milk and sugar?" He asked.

Spoon jingling away gaily broke the silence, and he hoped his wife would make it down before he was forced to chat.

Carefully placing the mugs beyond Ebe's reach out of adult instinct rather than caution needed; he showed zero interest in anything people did, only his own fascination with technology.

"Thank you," Geraint answered for them both.

Marco pulled out a chair opposite and braced for small talk. "Criminals keeping you busy, Geraint?"

The sergeant raised his eyebrows. "You'd be surprised. I moved here after the stress of Cambridge got too much, but there are some horrible things that happen here as well. I hadn't allowed for the four million tourists who come every year for a start. There was a stabbing at one of the caravan parks the other week."

Marco gasped appropriately.

"Easy case though. Loads of witnesses, but still. Very unpleasant. Not many burglaries, but drugs? There's a lot of drugs; cannabis, ecstasy, you name it."

"Well, I hope you're clearing up the streets then."

"I've come up with a few ideas which have been received very favourably, shall we say."

Marco was relived he didn't get the chance to regale him with details before Carys trouped in, breathless and beautiful. "You're not boring Marco with your operation whateverit's called, are you?"

Geraint tapped his nose. "You know I can't divulge the details; even to family."

"There's a shame," Carys laughed, and Geraint didn't seem to get the gibe.

"When are we giving Ebe his presents?" Diane asked.

Was she keen to spoil him or was she just looking for an excuse to take him off her lap? "My mum and dad need to be here first. They're late as per usual." Marco smiled.

"Do you think Ebe might like a play on the floor?" Diane smiled up at him. There was his answer.

"He's good at walking. Put him down if you've had enough of a cuddle."

"Oh, it's not that... maybe for now," she said, lowering him. Ebe stood exactly where he was placed, like a doll. "You run off and play then, there's a good boy," she said, reddening as it didn't happen.

Marco glanced at the clock. When would they arrive?" More refreshment was the only thing he could think to bridge the awkwardness. Fortunately, Carys seemed oblivious. She was used to them.

"He walks better than any baby I know," she smiled.

"Do you know some, then?" Diane tilted her head at the news.

"I see them around. At the surgery and things."

"He doesn't really look at people, does he. Not in the eyes. Have they said why that might be?"

Who are *they*? Carys wondered. "The health

visitor says everyone develops at their own pace. Ebe is interested in technology. He is really dexterous for his age."

"Well, that's good. He doesn't say anything yet, though?" She made the statement a question.

"It's early for him to talk, Mum."

"Oh, of course. But does he make sounds? Apart from screaming? Perhaps he's deaf? I mean, assuming you talk to him – I was always chattering away to you."

I bet you were, you nutty old bag, Marco thought through his forced smile.

"We chat to him all the time, Mum. He's not deaf. He loves music.

"Just a thought," she said.

The bang as the front door swung open and Natalia and Dan's Italian accents filled the hallway was a welcome diversion for everyone. "Hello, hello. The party can begin now!" Natalia bustled into the kitchen carrying a shiny bag. "Hello, Ebe, My darling. Look what Nonna's got for you!"

Ebe didn't notice. He was staring at the cable that ran around the room nailed to the skirting board for the tumble-dryer in the corner where there was no socket.

"And here's NonnoDan with more."

"I've left it outside. It's too big to bring inside and keep secret."

Diane sighed and shot a glance to Geraint and tried to include Carys too, but she didn't seem to share her dismay at the over exuberance for a simple one-year birthday. "You'll spoil him. Then we'll have to put up with a brat."

"Aw, don't be like that, Diane. It's his first birthday; our first grandchild, o' course-a we gonna spoil him!"

"I agree, Diane," Dan smiled, "But once she got me in Toys R Us, I couldn't resist. I think I've bought things I'd like to play with myself, actually!" he guffawed at his own joke and Ebe didn't look.

Carys hoisted him up and turned his reluctant face towards his family as his eyes shone with enthusiasm. But it wasn't for them. As soon as Carys freed his chin, his gaze shot back to the wire and his eyes blazed.

"Shall we sing?" Carys suggested.

The traditional '*Happy Birthday*' song was sung first in English, then '*Penblywth Happus*' in Welsh, and finally Marco, Dan, and Natalia gave a rendition of '*Buon Compleanno*'. If Ebe had understood any of it, he would have been bored and frustrated wanting his presents. As it was, the joyful verse did seem to get his attention. His eyes burned even if his delight was yet to display on his lips.

"Who's going first with presents?" Dan grinned, neck stretched like a child's hand in a classroom.

"Well, I think me and Carys should, then Geraint and Diane. They were here before you."

"Of course they were. We're always late," Dan

laughed again. "Saving the best until last, eh?"

"Probably." Geraint sat back, arms folded.

Fun learning toys: large shape wooden puzzles, and a wobbly doll that jingled when pushed, were greeted with little understanding and even less enthralment from Ebe. Geraint and Diane passed over a modest bag which Carys unwrapped for him. "Oh, what's this, Ebe?" As she pushed the buttons on a little plastic telephone and sounds blared and lights flashed, Ebe reached up to take it. With tears in her eyes, Carys croaked, "He loves it! Oh, thanks Mum and Dad. It's perfect."

"Sometimes small presents can be a lot of fun, can't they?" Natalia smiled and leaned forward. "Now see what Nonna and Nonno have got you."

Unfeasibly large soft toys would have made a lot of babies cry, but Ebe stared at the giant bear, challengingly.

"What did you have to leave outside?" Geraint felt confident to ask now that their phone had been so much better received than the giant plushies.

"Wait and see. You won't believe it!" Dan disappeared, and when he returned, his prediction proved correct.

"I don't believe it," Carys said. "It's very generous, but what did you think he would do with a car?"

"It's just one pedal, and he's got good strong legs from all that walking. It's electric. We know how he loves electric," Natalia shrugged, sad their generous gift wasn't getting more enthusiastic reception.

"I bet he'll love it," Marco defended. "Where do you think he'll use it? There's nowhere round here."

"He can keep it at ours, if you like. But I thought he could ride it around the house. It's quite a run from the kitchen to the lounge."

Marco blew through his lips. "If you say so, Dad. I reckon he'll crash into the door frames, if he's able to work it at all."

"Let's see, shall we." Dan stood and plucked Ebe from the floor. Sliding his sturdy legs into the seat, his feet didn't reach the pedals. His hand, however, did reach the horn button which played several different melodies in rotation. He did like that. "Until he grows a bit, he can have fun pushing that, look."

"What are you going to get him for Christmas," Geraint scoffed, "Drums?"

"I think it's great, Dad. Better to have something cool he can grow into than something he'll have grown out of in months."

"Like a baby-phone," Natalia sneered.

"I didn't mean that. The phone's great. But the car's great too. Seriously, thank you. All of you."

"Yes, thank you," Carys joined in. "Now who wants cake?"

TWENTY-NINE

Bunch of bitches

1996

For months, the mood in the house had been good. Medication had worked on Carys, and Ebe being forced to eat rather than simply drink milk had kept him more content. Walking and discovering new technology around every corner delighted him. They'd given up on the baby-gate that he had succeeded to open no matter how complicated a device they went for. He mastered the stairs with ease, ambling up with the support of his arms, and climbing back down like a ladder.

In many ways he was advanced. But apart from his peculiar looks, there was still one aspect of his development which, since his second birthday was approaching, had become a family worry. And upon Marco's return from work today, it reared its head when he found Carys sitting in the darkened lounge. "What's happened? Is everything okay?"

She was easy to distract from her introspection as he turned the light on. She looked surprised to see him. "Is that the time, goodness? I'm fine. Kind of. The Health Visitor came today." Carys sighed. "She was really impressed at first. He built things with blocks that she was stunned by, but then she upset me a bit."

"What did she say?"

"That Ebe should be speaking by now. Or at least *trying* to. *Mum, Dad,* basic language, minimum. She mentioned all sorts of diseases and syndromes because of his large head. There's no doubting his intelligence, so why doesn't he ever say anything?"

"My mum..."

"We both know what your mum thinks; that I'm a terrible mother who never speaks to him and that's why he's not learned any words. Yes, thank you for reminding me."

"I was going to say she thinks he might be autistic."

"Well, there will be all sorts of tests, so I suppose we'll know soon, won't we?" Marco leaned on the doorframe unsure what to say. "She said I should take him to mother-and-baby groups to socialise him."

Marco winced, and Carys's response was no surprise.

"I'm not going so people can laugh at me. This is such a small town. Everyone knows about my mental health issues, and when they see Ebe..."

"I'll take him, if you like."

Carys's mouth opened and closed a few times before she answered, "So you think it's my fault too, do you? I talk to him all the time, you know."

"I didn't mean it like that. I know you do. But if it will get my mum, and the midwife off your back, why not? I'll break the ice with the mums and fend off any awkward questions, and you can go another time if you feel like it."

"But your work..."

"I'm due a few days off. I'll lose them if I don't take them. Anyway, I could take a sickie if necessary. I want to make you feel better. It's important."

A reluctant smile grew on Cary's lips. "Well, there's one tomorrow in the community centre, apparently. If you want to take him, it's at eleven."

"Perfect. I'll go into work, feign illness mid-morning, and get home in plenty of time to take Ebe to the baby group."

"Won't you feel odd with all the mums?"

"I'll be fine. Don't worry."

A few bulging eyed sighs whilst rubbing his stomach had colleagues suggesting he go home. "You don't look right, Marco," they said. He even protested a few times before allowing them to persuade him to leave. At half-past ten he arrived home to Ebe gulping down baby-rice pudding from a plastic spoon Carys held. Dressed and clean, it was clear Carys was enthusiastic about the plan.

"Why don't you come too? We could go together."

The laden spoon paused between jar and Ebe's hunting lips, Carys sighed. "I'm tempted, but if someone laughs at me or Ebe, I might not react well."

Memories of smashed plates and the broken gate after one of her episodes flashed in Marco's mind and he didn't coax her further. "Okay, I'll check it out first; see if they're nice."

"… Or a bunch of bitches."

It didn't take long to establish Carys's predictions were accurate. Marco entered the community centre to raised eyebrows and a halt in conversation. "Is this the parent and baby group?" he corrected the sexist assumption on the posters.

No-one replied, but the proliferation of babies and mummies answered itself. "Hi, I'm Marco, and this is Ebe." As he unstrapped Ebe from his seat, breathy murmurs growled through the hall as they all whispered dismay at his appearance. Bunch of bitches, Marco agreed.

Affronted for himself, and for Ebe, and Carys, Marco decided to push it; make them cringe if needs be. How could they be so unsupportive?

With Ebe on his knee, he sat down amongst them. "Hi," he re-introduced. "This is Ebe. You probably didn't hear me from the door."

"Hello," the head mum said and turned away at once to begin a conversation without him.

"Is that what passes for hospitality here? Hello, and then ignoring me?"

The head mum paused her exchange. "I'm sorry, but we've known one another for weeks. There are things to sort out, to arrange. I'm sure you understand."

"I realise. But that is rude, don't you think? You could have introduced yourselves. And a smile probably wouldn't have caused any permanent damage. If I'm going to be coming here regularly, then it might be nice to include me in some of those plans, too."

"Coming regularly?" another mum gasped.

"The poster says it's a weekly meet, why not? Am I not welcome because I'm a dad, not a mum?"

"I'd rather you than your crazy wife," a voice from the background pushed through.

"You're familiar with my family, then? Perhaps you'll understand how valuable your support might be in that case."

"Aren't there like, therapy groups she can go to? Group counselling or something?"

"It really sounds like you're saying we're not welcome. Is that right?"

"Well, we are rather full. We have arranged events for our closed numbers for a while. Taking in more can be a nightmare."

"Perhaps you better take your posters down, then. Anyone could turn up and cause you untold headaches. I'm here now though, and I'd like to learn the sort of things we get up to, in case space opens up in the future." Marco was so angry, but he'd been brought up well and he was determined to remain calm and polite, even if he wished swearing was something that suited him. Carys would have knocked them all clean out by now.

His hanging around wasn't to see if it would benefit her. It was abundantly clear it wouldn't. And they looked the type to press charges for assault. While he was here, he wanted to at least try to show them how horrible they were being. "So, what are we doing?"

"It varies," chief mum suggested vaguely.

"Well, what are we doing, *tonight?*"

"Nothing. Just having a chat. Letting the babies socialise."

He didn't bother pointing out how that proved he had interrupted nothing and that they were just being rude. And instead, clapped his hands and said, "That sounds just what we need, hey, Ebe?"

To the sound of his clap, several of the babies finally reacted to the tension and bawled.

Chief mum sighed. "This is exactly the sort of

thing we try to avoid."

Marco plonked Ebe in the middle of the bevvy of babies. The cries turned to screams as he stood over them, and each child used whatever method their level of development allowed to escape Ebe's presence as though he'd just dumped a rattlesnake on the floor.

"What is wrong with him?" an unkind hiss reached Marco's ears.

Marco beamed. "We're not sure. The midwife said socialising might help. He tends to be a little distant."

"I wish he was distant. A long distance away from me and my kids," a large woman with pink and orange hair leaned threateningly forward. Odd this aggressive creature had been accepted into the fold of stuck-up mums when the polite preacher's son was ostracised. And all because Carys had mental health issues and Ebe looked unusual.

"You should all feel ashamed. Yes, Ebe is different, but we're all god's children."

"Oh, here we go. Get lost, god-boy. Take your little freak and leave. We come here for some peace and a gossip, not to listen to your sermons."

Head mum smiled as Marco picked Ebe up and returned him to his stroller. "Now do you see why we need time to integrate mums and babies? This morning's ruined because of you."

"If today has been spoilt, it's because of your

rudeness. But I can't see that socialising with you can possibly be a good influence, so I'll go." As he reached the door, he said, "I'll pray for you."

"Oh, fuck off," pink/orange woman sneered.

Wheeling back the way he'd come, he reached the car and strapped Ebe safely inside. "Well, that went well," he said, closing the door with a clunk that could have been a slam.

"You're back early. No good?"

Marco had considered his answer all the way home and decided, against his upbringing and religion, to tell a white lie; that is a lie that didn't benefit him, but did benefit his wife. Making her worry how Ebe would fit into school, and society generally was not something that would help her. And she would worry.

"It's no longer running. Some problem with the room being too cold and not having found alternatives yet. I bet you're right though. They would have been cliquey as anything anyway."

"Bunch of bitches, is what I said."

"Yes, that. You're probably correct. And I'm positive you talk to Ebe enough. I'll make sure I do my bit, too and before you know it," he was about to say, 'He'll be off to play school,' when alarm bells rang and he was reminded of being told how tough his mum had found it when she had let him go to nursery having had him with her twenty-four hours a day until then. "Before you know it, he'll be talking so much we'll wish

he'd shut up!"
Carys grinned. "You're right."

THIRTY

Disaster

Marco never told Carys what happened in the mothers-and-toddlers meet. They'd both spoken avidly to him, naming every item they picked up in front of him, despite him showing no interest in whatever it might be.

He seemed more content with the world. He still slept on Carys's face, and was yet to utter a word, or even an attempt at one, but he seemed... Happy? He never smiled, so that might have been a stretch. Perhaps, content. And it was such an improvement it was enough for now.

Tests booked by the health visitor were stressing Carys, but Marco had learned to live with the strange baby and his odd behaviour. He didn't see that adding a diagnosis was a bad thing. They might even get some help. "Shall I walk him like usual, or would you rather I stay home?" he asked when she seemed particularly stressed one evening.

"Walk him? He's not a dog!"

"You know what I mean. Shall I take him out in his stroller?"

"Why would you change the routine now? It's been working for months."

"I just thought you might need comforting, for heaven's sake."

Carys looked thoughtful. "Yes, sorry. Take Ebe. How about picking up some Chinese whilst you're out. I haven't prepared anything."

Sorry was a new word to Carys's vocabulary and Marco accepted it with a grin. "The usual?" he asked, as he strapped Ebe in his chair. "See you in a bit."

The strolls into town were a pleasant habit. Especially compared to when he'd be heard long before he was seen. There was a downside though. Where people avoided a screaming monster, a contented child attracted looks from those who adore babies and toddlers and fending off their questions after displaying ill-disguised looks of repulsion were unpleasant.

He'd taken to walking beyond the town and into the castle ruins. The grounds were unkempt and visitors discouraged, so it was always peaceful and offered wonderful views from its lofty perch. Tonight, with the promise of a Chinese takeaway, he was forced to walk into the centre of the charmingly small market town.

Past the war memorial and Rebecca's Cell with its sign depicting a rough-looking man in a dress and bonnet wielding an axe. Past boutique shops that attracted tourists by their tens of thousands this time of year but which were thankfully closed for the night, Marco realised he hadn't thought to ask if they needed anything else.

"Well, Ebe, we always need milk. I've never known anyone drink more of the stuff than your mother." Ebe did not react to his stepfather's voice, or to the coos of 'Aw, look at him sitting peacefully,' from the shopkeeper as he pulled the buggy in behind him. Conversations about what might be wrong with his antisocial, unfortunate-looking baby had already been had on earlier excursions, so Marco was happy to let it go with a smile.

Other essentials; bread, toilet rolls, cheese and jam struck him as likely requirements so he reached the till with quite a horde balanced on the hood of Ebe's pushchair. A lady in front turned to admire baby Ebe, and focussed on the queue again quickly.

Shoving things in her bag as soon as they were scanned, she looked at Marco before leaving the shop, "Sorry, I'm in a rush." He'd never seen her before. Her need to excuse herself didn't surprise him, though. A smile absolved any guilt and she bustled on her way muttering to herself, probably along the lines of 'What was wrong with that child?'

A carrier bag hooked to one handle of the stroller gave it an uneven wander that Marco had to correct constantly to prevent the wheels falling into the gutter. His concentration meant he reached the door of the Chinese takeaway before he noticed it wasn't open. Of course. They were always closed on Tuesdays. "How about fish and chips, Ebe?"

Back past all the shops he'd already seen, Marco was dismayed a queue had formed since their walk down the hill. "If I'd remembered the Tuesday opening times, we could have been home by now." To underline his blunder, spots of rain splashed on his head and on Ebe's chair lid. Was it worth queuing and getting Ebe soaked? He might get a chill or something.

Dinner abandoned, Marco rushed Ebe up the slope and sheltered from the downpour in the Drang. The smell as dry tarmac became wet filled the air with a comforting aroma. As soon as it began, it was over and Marco peeped his head from the alleyway to be sure. Black clouds loomed so Marco decided to take Ebe home and see if there wasn't something he could rustle up from the kitchen. He could always wrap up and come back out in the rain to get food if Carys insisted.

It didn't take long to ascertain the disappointment on Carys's face, and as the main reason he'd agreed to takeaway food was to cheer her up, he didn't hesitate when she proposed he drive the eight miles to Tenby where they favoured a Monday closure and so would be open tonight. And, of course, he offered to take Ebe.

Together, Ebe sitting up in the back looking out of the window thanks to the extra height his booster seat gave him, they set off to the pretty coastal town – The Jewel in Pembrokeshire's Crown, as brochures conveyed. Carys was enjoying a relaxing soak when they left and so, despite hunger, he opted for the scenic route whilst it was still light enough to enjoy it.

Through the sought-after village of St Florence where his parents had considered living before Dan took up his place with the church; on through Manorbier with its castle on the beach, and along the coast road through Goreston where a creepy looking Mediaeval church was just visible through the trees and a holy well promised vigorous health to all who drank its waters.

Over the brow of the hill, just offshore, Caldey island was just visible as the sun fizzed into the Irish Sea. Marco smiled at the stunning view and pointed it out to Ebe. A double-take showed Ebe's gaze was taken by something other than the setting sun… Something to the left of the island, and when Marco saw it, he wondered if the other cars slowing were looking at it or the sunset.

Fingers pointing out of windows seemed to

agree with Ebe that far more interesting than the sun setting, which happened every day, was the peculiar vision rising from the ocean.

Marco scoffed. It was just one of those weird optical illusions. He noticed how Caldey Island, a mile offshore, often looked much further away, and at other times, as though you could swim across without straining.

So, it wasn't that difficult to picture the bright lights rising from the deep for what they were. Across the bay in Llanelli, the Scarlet's Rugby Football Stadium nestled in the valley behind all the shops and houses. He'd never noticed it before, but that's the thing with strange phenomenon: they were unusual by definition.

Stolen glances weren't enough to confirm, and any other explanation why a stadium sized oval of searing lights might look as close as the community of Cistercian monks who lived on the island, was terrifying. But Marco was reluctant to stop and survey the view. And so were the other drivers. Despite lay-bys and view-points opening up along the route, nobody stopped.

Perhaps they were all compelled to collect Chinese takeaways for hungry spouses, or some other urgent duties, or perchance they were compelled to look away and go about their business by another force—An unseen force which dwelling upon only caused more cloudy confusion, until years later one might be struck with a sudden clarity; 'What did I see all those years ago?' But by then, no-one would listen or care. The world will have moved on. Your life will have moved on and you may never think about it ever again. And that would be the best you could hope for.

For now, it was Parc y Scarlet's Stadium thirty miles across the water in Llanelli. Such a dull thing to report, it wouldn't be worth troubling others with mentioning. Certainly not Carys. He knew already what ridiculous notions she'd come up with to explain it, and they could both do without the stress of that.

By the time he walked out of 'China Town' half-an-hour later, bag of hot food clutched in one hand, Ebe's stiff little fingers in the other, he'd forgotten all about it. He wouldn't for long...

Ten miles west along the coast at the entrance to the Milford Haven waterway, (in Welsh, Aberdaugleddau –Aber -meaning estuary, Dau -meaning two, and gleddau -meaning swords, and referring to the eastern and western Cleddau rivers which met to form the second deepest harbour in the world) the strange lights were about to play their part in Pembrokeshire history.

Pilot James Pearce had boarded the super tanker from Suez and introduced himself to the Russian captain to guide the huge ship into Milford Haven Port.

Sunlight had dipped two hours ago so James was mainly using the well-lit buoys to avoid a rocky outcrop in the middle of the haven. He wasn't the most experienced of the pilots employed by Milford Haven Port Authority, but it was still a manoeuvre he had performed countless times, and with some ships even larger than the 900 feet long Sea Empress.

It was with immense confidence he steered the bow away from the lights he could clearly see from the bridge.

The easy smile dropped from his face as the lights guiding him bubbled from beneath the water. A huge area he estimated to be the size of a football stadium disappeared beneath the hull, his eyes glued to the peculiar display as his mind raced for explanations. Underwater work on the harbour that he'd missed the briefing about; another tanker sunk and submerged beneath the waves?

By the time he'd run out of explanations, whatever it was had vanished into the deep waterway and its disappearance left pilot, James Pearce, confused.

Too late he realised the actual lights of the buoys, vital to his safe manoeuvre, were the wrong side of the vessel.

Screaming at the captain to help, he wheeled the ship around as the crunch of metal splitting on rock was felt by all on board. As the huge ship listed, James and the ship's crew fought to right it as it rocked to one side and the stench of crude oil filled the enclosed space.

Ashen, James radioed for tugs to rush to right them. If they could set the boat straight, perhaps they could contain the spillage before it damaged the delicate waterway, an international site of special scientific interest.

What was it he'd seen? What was it that had appeared and disappeared beneath the surface to confuse him? He couldn't identify it. Back at the port control, he would check with the radar team to find out what it was. If this disaster grew to the scale it could if the oil wasn't mopped up soon, he needed someone to pass the blame onto. He couldn't have the marine animals, and the entire tourist industry the people of Pembrokeshire relied upon as their main income, on his conscience.

The cost to lives and livelihood racking up in his mind. The oil industry and the tourist industry were unfortunate bedfellows. If this 'act of war' from one was met with forceful enough opposition from the other, it was likely they wouldn't both survive. He couldn't have that on his shoulders, he just couldn't.

The tug operation was equally awful. Perhaps they too were confused by the light anomaly, or more likely, whatever he'd seen disappearing beneath the waves had caused a wake to the surface which sucked them in. James had no choice but to watch in anguish as the enormous ship under his control leaned one way, then shot back the other as the little tugboats fought with not enough power to correct it.

The stench grew. Where it had seemed an easy to contain minor spillage, rocking the vessel had succeeded in splitting further along the hull wall and freeing more of their deadly cargo into the marine sanctuary of Milford Haven.

Pilot Pearce gulped down the foul taste as, from the bridge, he could now see the ever-growing slick reach from one side of the estuary to the other and wonder in horror how far it would travel on the tide, and how many creatures would die. What was that thing that came from nowhere and disappeared just as fast? Whoever and whatever it was, I had the blame for this disaster. Not him. There was nothing he could have done.

He had that to cling onto. The truth was uncertain, but his version of it could be the only thing to save his reputation, his career, and his livelihood. Unfortunately for Pilot James Pearce, his version would not be allowed to see the light of day.

THIRTY-ONE

The cover up

A room he didn't even know existed in the Milford Haven Port Authority headquarters had been his home for nearly twelve hours now. No communication with the outside world, he had been assured the authorities had told his wife and family how he was helping them with their inquiries and that he was safe. James didn't have too much faith in their last statement. He certainly didn't feel protected.

The tone of questioning had been anything but friendly: "What did you see? Tell us exactly what you saw. And, what do you think it was?" He had answered truthfully; that as far as he was concerned, he had no idea what it was which made it 'unidentified'. An unidentified submerged object.

USO his interrogators referred to it as. Having

a name alerted him to it being less uncommon than he might otherwise had thought. But alerting his suspicions didn't seem to be that much of a concern to whichever authority he was bound to now.

He'd already signed an official secrets document forbidding him to discuss the submersed vessel with anyone. A version where his supposed lack of experience and subsequent incompetence had led to him misreading the buoys' lights.

The tugs were not sucked into the wake of the non-existent submerged craft because how could they be? It didn't exist. They were simply underpowered to deal with the vastness of The Sea Empress.

A similar incident had occurred only three years before off the coast of Scotland so it was time to call for more government investment to ensure it didn't happen a third time. And revise single-hulled super tankers so that a simple grounding on rocks would only cause minor spillage and could be contained by the ship's crew easily.

Like The Titanic demonstrated the need for sufficient life boats, The Sea Empress would show the necessity for re-investment and redesign for oil containment safety. What it definitely wouldn't expose was that there might be more beneath the surface of Pembrokeshire's, and indeed British and international, waters than the civilian public were permitted to know.

He signed all that gladly, albeit with a clenched fist, and despite what he feared would happen to his career. Early objections had been met with thinly veiled threats and now he was just pleased to be going home instead of being listed as a heroic casualty of the disaster, giving his life, as all good captains did, and going down with his ship. And he'd never mention to anyone, not even his wife; *especially* not his lovely wife, what really happened on the fifteenth of February nineteen-ninety-six.

In the Paulo-Ellis household, the news breaking at nine o'clock, just as they sat down after clearing the Chinese takeaway remnants and washing up, filled them with sorrow.

"Our lovely beaches! Will they be okay, Marco?" Carys asked her husband, but he had no answers beyond what the news broadcaster was telling the world. Five-thousand tonnes of spilled crude oil had grown to ten thousand already and there was no hope of moving the huge craft.

Explanations for blame were sketchy. Freak weather conditions causing unusual currents the only explanation so far. If the lights anomaly had been mentioned, Marco may have worked out the cause, but it would just have been another secret to keep. For now, along with the rest of Wales and beyond, he was consumed enough with worry for the marine life and the tourist trade. So many people relied on the spring and summer business to survive after the bleak winter.

And, perhaps a little selfishly, although it was easy in his position to dress it up as an afront to God Almighty, he was concerned for the impact it would have on the stunning views.

One of life in Pembrokeshire's greatest treasures was being able to remove yourself from the stresses of life standing at the shoreline, aware the Pembrokeshire coast alone stretched one-hundred-and-eighty-six miles around you from Amroth in the south, to Poppit Sands on the Ceredigion border in the north.

It was a figure etched onto every frequenter of Pembrokeshire. As the only coastal national park in Britain, they promoted the famous unbroken coast path on leaflets and posters in so many shop windows. If you walked the entire length, you would scale and descend so many cliffs it would exceed the height of Mount Everest. Picturing that all coated in slimy oil; dead birds and dolphins washing up daily to the oil-stained beaches brought a tear to his eye. When the clean-up started, he'd make sure Narberth Christian Fellowship played their part.

For whatever reason, the containment operation was a disaster. The story was the tugs had proved underpowered, but James Pearce was suspicious. He'd been a pilot at the port authority for years. It was perfectly placed to serve the oil industry with tugboats designed for the very job of guiding the very tankers that came to the harbour. They would be useless otherwise. Now tugs from around the British Isles had been called in to help, was he to believe they were all incapable of the job?

Whatever the reason, a week had passed and the *Sea Empress* was still stricken on the rocks and haemorrhaging crude oil at a catastrophic rate. News reports were full of images of marine life and sea birds coated in the stuff. Thousands of animals had died and the ecology of Pembrokeshire's seas was feared never to recover.

The locals appeared in huge numbers on beaches, wiping sea gulls and mopping oil off rocks. It seemed a never-ending, pointless task, but you had to start somewhere, he supposed. And they'd have to do it without him; if someone recognised him—a reporter, perhaps, he couldn't guarantee he'd be able to keep his mouth shut about who was really to blame if hundreds of angry residents accosted him. He should stay away and protect him and his wife safe from the crowds, and the 'authorities' who had questioned him. If he kept his head down, he might find he could even save his career as well.

Marco wasn't the only church member to want to help, so Sunday's worship was curtailed in favour of a beach clean. Groups from the congregation made their way to Amroth and

Saundersfoot and Tenby as their most local beaches, and when they saw the damage to God's beautiful creation, they wept.

The journalists did not pick the reports of strange submerged lights around Caldey island up camped out in the area. The news was full with the single story. No-one linked what people were seeing with what happened on the haven. Not even those who witnessed it.

The worldwide web had a page dedicated to the sightings, and local 'nuts' uploaded fuzzy pictures that even amongst the scant followers of the blog garnered little enthusiasm. It was too hard to tell what they were, and the photos took so long to load onto the site, most gave up before they'd seen anything. The smokescreen, as one faithful commentator wrote under his own photo, was working. What the unidentified presences were doing off the coast of Pembrokeshire, they could only imagine. But none of them considered it might be because of an odd little boy born nearly two years ago.

THIRTY-TWO

Improbable achievement

Ebe's second birthday was a sombre affair. The guest list was identical to the previous year, and with another year passed, the lack of change—of progress, was underlined uncomfortably. Diane sensed the tension and was careful not to mention it, so Geraint had been briefed the same.

Dan, however, was always ready to judge, and combined with Natalia's tactlessness, the atmosphere had taken quite a nasty turn. "Still not talking, then?" she asked unnecessarily whilst posting cake between heavily rouged lips.

"Mum, you know he isn't. Why ask?"

"You're right. What I mean to say is, what are you doing about it? It's not normal. You had a huge vocabulary when you were two. Well, by eighteen months; fifteen, probably." She reached for another slice. "I did used to talk to you all the time in English and Italian. Do you speak any Italian to Ebe?"

"I must confess, no. Because he has yet to utter a word, I figured sticking with English would be best. Keep it simple."

"Why are you doing this, Natalia? Don't you think we're worried? Don't you think we realise it's not normal?" Carys scowled, knife in hand, jam from the madeira cake lining the blade in an ominous imitation of blood. "And, of course we talk to him. We aren't just doing it when you're here to witness it."

"Don't shoot the messenger. You know I'm right. We'll be celebrating his third, and fourth birthdays without a word at this rate."

"And what if we are? Ebe is just Ebe. He'll develop when he's ready. He's a genius at other things. The health visitor was stunned at the towers he constructed with blocks."

"Einstein didn't speak until he was four, apparently," Geraint defended his grandson.

"Well, let's hope that's why then. I hope his genius is the reason he hasn't spoken. But it is unusual. Peculiar, even."

"Rest assured we are as keen as anyone for Ebe to be as 'normal' as possible," Marco said.

"Well, that might be a bit difficult," Dan said with a nudge towards Diane and Carys.

Diane sat up straight. "Are you saying we're not normal? Are you saying that because we have suffered with our mental health, we're not *normal*?"

"I've made my views perfectly clear on a number of occasions, Diane, you know that. I think there's a strong correlation between your church attendance and what you describe as mental health issues."

"That's a terrible thing to say, Dad!"

Dan held up his hands. "It's not my intention to cause offence. I want to help. But first, I needed to get your attention."

"You think if I came to church, Ebe would be talking?" Carys lay the knife next to the cake and stepped back, as though recognising a danger. Dan pressed on.

"I'm not saying that... But it wouldn't hurt, would it?"

"It might. I get sick of the looks when I take him out. And I'd be subjected to more opinions about what a terrible mother I must be."

"You're not a terrible mother!" Diane squealed. "Ebe adores you. Anyone can see that."

"No-one's saying you're a bad mum, Carys, dear," Natalia stroked her arm, her hand left in mid-air as Carys flinched from her touch. "But if we can see where you might improve things, we have to say, don't we? For Ebe's sake, and yours."

"But you have said nothing. Nothing different anyway."

"Well, think about coming back to church, Carys. You felt better after we helped you before, didn't you?"

"When Marco lied, and you all ambushed me to do an exorcism because that's how little you understand complex mental health issues?"

She couldn't answer further because it had helped. Was she being foolish for allowing herself to be put off going and not grasping the opportunity? They might all think she's a bad mum, and that Ebe is weird, but they have a Christian obligation to at least disguise it. It might help take some of the responsibility off her. "Okay," she agreed with slumped shoulders. "I'll come back to church. Don't blame me if Ebe screams the place down."

Natalia smiled a smug smile and bit into her third slice of cake.

Geraint tried to coax his eyebrows down his forehead and resist from saying out loud, 'How on earth did that work?' Instead, he changed the subject completely. "How have the church been getting on with the clear up? Any news on what happened?"

Marco flinched. He feared his mum and dad might tell his father-in-law everything he now knew without him concluding the same thing: that the lights the Port Authority Pilot had tried to avoid, and which had caused him to move the ship the wrong side of the central sand bank, were from an unidentified submerged object. The same as he'd seen near Caldey Island the same night.

It had taken a while to piece it together, but

it made a lot more sense than someone trained to a position of expert in his field, making such an error as passing the buoy the wrong side. And what took him weeks to suss out, he feared Dianne and Carys would recognise immediately. Their paranoia was honed far more than his.

Nervous glances revealed no recognition as his dad regaled the details only those close to the action might have gleaned. The official version would gloss over who could have been to blame, quickly. Not a difficult task when the media was flooded with distressing pictures of oil-coated marine wildlife at every opportunity.

Marco joined them in their game with stories of birds he had cleaned to divert the focus. He hoped he'd been in time to stop the cogs of Carys's troubled mind from crunching to a halt on the disturbing truth. "They reckon the tourists will be back on the main beaches in the summer," he diverted again. A discussion about the merits of tourism and whether the council were glossing over the real issue to make money followed. Marco sat back and smiled at his probable success.

THIRTY-THREE

A chilly reception

"Come on, it'll be fine," Marco grinned at his angry-looking wife as she forced the clips of Ebe's stroller closed around his ever-growing body.

"It won't be fine, will it? They'll look, make snide remarks about how I am a terrible mum who never talks to her baby, probably because I'm some sort of nutcase. Then they'll snigger, saying he looks funny. Remind me, why am I doing this again?"

"Because going to church is good for you."

"Because I'm not mentally unwell, but I have demons inside me?"

"Whatever causes you to become ill is improved by being in His presence."

She didn't argue further because she'd already decided to go, and was worried she might talk herself out of it if she let the rage at feeling so misunderstood run unchecked. "Well, what are we waiting for? We're both ready."

Marco kept his smile in place as it nearly slipped and pulled open the door with a flourish. "After you. I'll lock up."

Marco tried to warm the way with a big grin and plenty of toothy 'Hellos' and, 'How are yous'. But whatever he achieved was immediately cooled by Carys's icy stare and the responding weak smiles.

Exactly as she had feared, there was muttering and whispering, quite unbecoming from a congregation who prided themselves on their Christian values.

"You bring it on yourself," Marco winced at his tactless retort to his wife expressing her displeasure. "They were all friendly when I smiled at them."

Instead of flouncing off, throwing the occasional chair to be found later cutting into her arms with whatever she had absconded with, she said, "I suppose I could try to make the effort... For Ebe."

Making a point of smiling graciously to anyone who caught her eye won some of them over. At least it gave them permission to flex their holier-than-thou muscles, dressed up as motherly advice.

Carys impressed herself with her strength. Not just to stay where she was, but in her restraint to not lash out at every eyebrow that raised from a glance at the occupant of her lap. Yes, he was odd-looking, but at least he wasn't screaming. Keeping him pressed close to her protected him from both the desire to scream and the unhelpful looks. Ebe wasn't going anywhere, and Carys knew at that moment they were in this together. If the world didn't like Ebe, the world could suffer because she loved him. He'd have a lot to give one day, she was sure.

If only she knew what, perhaps she would have shared the disdain.

The post-sermon coffee gave everyone the opportunity to speak to Carys. An opportunity the congregation seemed reluctant to take. As Carys sat awaiting her husband's imminent return with her coffee and cake, she allowed her gaze to flit around those nearest her and, every time, their eyes darted away.

The last occasion many of them would have seen her, she was screaming her head off and then laughing hysterically in Pastor Dan's study while they chanted Christian mumbo-jumbo at her. Why the fuck didn't they want to at least ask how she was? Fists clenching, she struggled to control a glowing temper burning in her storm-kettle resolve.

Marco returned and read her at once. Turning to one of the congregation, he changed his mind, choosing someone more reliably compliant,

"Ann, have you met my son, Ebe?"

Ann turned slowly and Carys fumed at her reluctance. When their eyes met, Ann dropped her stare to Ebe and her cheeks burned. "He's a bonny boy, isn't he."

Carys stared. If you don't want to be here making small talk, why don't you fuck off? You're not fooling anybody. Despite staying silent, she conveyed the message clearly through a stare that left no doubt.

"Uh, er, how're you getting on with him? Is he sleeping through the night?"

Carys continued her hateful stare, and Ann struggled to speak. "Er, um, well, I best leave you to it... Let some other people come and have a look." She took a step, then bravely turned back to say, "Aw, bless him," before scurrying away.

"Anyone else?" Carys inquired. Shock on Marco's face and the undeniable rudeness made her scream. "Anyone else want to come over and pretend to be fucking interested in my baby? Anyone!" she stood abruptly. "Come on. I know what you're all thinking!"

Words stalled on lips that really should have been a comfort. From nowhere, Carys felt arms around her shoulders and soon her face was hidden in the broad chest of the Pastor and her father-in-law, Dan Paulo. "Now, now, Carys, don't worry." Her face still pressed into him, he addressed the crowd. "My lovely daughter-in-law has been away from our little church for a few months. Do you know why? Do you know why?!" he shouted. Steps from side to side accompanied mumbled 'I don't knows' and incoherent apologies. "She thought after her cleansing, and the trouble she's had bringing up my grandson, who has some difficulties, she might attract the kind of attention that would make her feel worse."

"Well, let me tell you, I'm ashamed. Myself and Natalia persuaded her she was mistaken and that she would be welcomed with open arms and warm smiles. What are you all afraid of? Yes, Ebe looks a little unusual and you might not know what to say, but the Lord would, so you should call upon his grace. Come and meet my grandson, or feel the wrath of shame of Our Lord!"

"I don't want them to."

"They must, Carys."

"They don't deserve it!" she pulled herself away and screamed at the group. Her angst set Ebe off crying despite her proximity, and she hugged him closer.

Waving her arm, fending off the first well-wisher, as more and more came over and apologised, they wore her down and she broke in grateful sobs.

Hugs abounded and when she'd cried, the pit of her inners aching silently, she wiped away tears with a tissue that appeared before her, held in a liver-spotted hand. "Better?" a lovely old face peered at her, framed by a blue-rinsed perm.

Carys snivelled and nodded.

Another voice; a young voice, spoke softly. “It must be hard. I can tell how much Ebe loves and needs you. I bet you fear him going off to nursery. And I don’t mean just for his sake. I remember when Jake, that’s my three-year-old, went. I thought I’d be grateful for the peace, but I spent most of it crying and then staring at my kitchen clock. I’m not making it sound very appealing, am I!” the lady leaned over and patted Carys’s thigh. “The thing is, I learned to busy myself. And now he’s heading to school in a couple of months. I really am looking forward to getting more done. I’m going back to work.

Carys had been in denial about fears for herself if Ebe were to be left in someone else’s care. Now it struck raw and she couldn’t speak beyond the lead in her chest. She nodded, not quite knowing what she was meaning. The woman was telling her how accommodating the nursery she used was, and how easily her son had settled. Carys knew she wouldn’t recall the details but bubbling within, she knew it was the next step. For her, and for Ebe.

THIRTY-FOUR

A wise welcome

As soon as she walked in, the weight in her chest dropped to her stomach and she felt sick. "Come on, Ebe," she ushered as he clung to her leg.

"Who have we got here?" An older woman seemed to be speaking to her despite the wayward gaze that looked everywhere but. Identifying which eye had the most likely trajectory, Carys smiled and announced her son's presence.

Eyebrows around the room raised as muttering behind hands muted the sound as they bent over to remove coats from their precious little angels. Carys was ready to turn and leave. Or punch each one of them and knock some manners into their thick heads.

"Ebe? That's an unusual name." the lady persisted in a dripping with honey voice

"Er, yes. It's Dutch," Carys explained. "Angela from my church said her son goes here and you are very nice and would be understanding of Ebe's... er... difficulties."

"Oh, yes, I'm sure he'll be fine. What exactly does he struggle with?"

Carys stalled. The list was endless. "Motor skills, apart from when the health visitor calls round and he builds amazing towers. Mainly speech. Everyone thinks I don't talk to him enough, but I do. All the time. Then it was suggested that he needs to socialise with other children, so my husband took him to a toddler group but it was closed, so that didn't work out. I think because he looks the way he does, people don't know what to make of him." Carys took a deep breath as the woman who greeted her turned her wondering eyes onto her son.

"Well, I think he looks very dapper."

A compliment to his tasteful attire rather than his physical appearance, Carys suspected but took it gratefully. Someone at least trying to be nice was a pleasant departure to her recent experiences. "Oh, and if ever he loses sight of me, he screams."

"That may well be a problem. We don't generally like mums to stay. We see it as an important part of a child's development."

"Can we just try to get him to socialise first? Get him used to it, and then see?"

The lady tapped a gnarled index finger against

lemon thin lips. "I suppose we could try. Wean him from you as it were. He'll be with us until he turns four, so there will be plenty of time to make adjustments. No point in traumatising him."

Carys beamed and felt like hugging the woman, but feared her frailty might mean she'd crumble in front of her. Surely, she wasn't fit enough to be caring for - she looked around the room - thirty children?

"I'm Florence," she finally introduced. "The children call me 'Aunty Flo'" She smiled a warm smile and Carys felt happy this woman was the best person to bring Ebe out of his shell. "Aunty Anne and Aunty Rene will be here in a minute, and then we'll get started."

Relieved Flo was going to have help, Carys tried to edge away from Ebe who let her move to a seat when he decided that meant she was going to stay, allowing him to begin his unusual assessment of his surroundings focussing firstly on the cable that ran around the room to half-a-dozen sockets. He then gazed with eyes of wonder at the dangling florescent tubes that made a noise that would give anyone sensitive a headache.

Catching his mum's eye, he directed her gaze upwards and stared until she acknowledged the wonder of the bright illumination. Carys expressed as much enthusiasm as she could and mused on the possibility that one day, perhaps, she might leave him here and seek more age-appropriate conversation for herself. Not likely, she thought with a shake of her head.

The other mums made loud exchanges with Aunty Flo about the progress of their cherubs and Carys suspected it was for her benefit, demonstrating the superiority of their children and, therefore, their mothering ability and their family. Carys felt it and it smarted. Mother to an oddball alien child at nineteen was not what she had planned for her life. But she hadn't really planned anything and now she wouldn't change it for the world.

The muttering grew louder as the mums passed and Carys detected 'weird-looking' and 'pathetic that he can't be left.' Digging clenched fists into her legs, Carys felt proud she didn't disgrace herself and Ebe with a regrettable outburst. This was important.

Left leg swinging over her right, it fascinated her how well Ebe took to the different surroundings. Oblivious to the other children, he listened with a disturbing intensity to everything the aunties said. As they read a story with the children sitting on the carpet, Ebe stood and with every turn of the page he jumped in the air landing on one foot when he would hop on the spot and clap, his twinkling eyes turning to Carys to share the glee. Everyone will say I should read to him more at home, a guilty gulp displaced her smile momentarily.

When it came time to leave, Ebe waved with

gusto at the aunties and even made some guttural noises. After just one morning, it was a very promising start.

THIRTY-FIVE

The hum

Carys sat, legs swinging, feeling like pulling her bottom lip over her face to escape the dull monotony of seeing the same little shits play the same stupid games for three weeks.

On a positive note, it meant she was ready, just as Angela from church had predicted, to leave Ebe behind. Ebe, however, was not ready to be left. Not ready at all…

Her instinct not to sneak off was approved of by the aunties. They agreed it could increase Ebe's anxiety as he would never trust she wouldn't be there. Instead, she had told him she had to go and would be back in five minutes. Her plan was to not even leave the building but watch him from a distance and return as soon as he showed the first sign of distress. Unfortunately, as she could have predicted, the moment of catastrophic distress occurred before she even left his sight.

Collapsing into the too small plastic chair beside him, she watched as he splashed in the water table, and built ever-more impressive Meccano and Lego. It was beginning to have an effect. The other children saw the superiority of Ebe's building skills and started looking at him like a small adult, so it seemed to Carys. No words were spoken, not by Ebe anyway, and the other children gave up trying to elicit conversation from the mute little man. But there was communication of sorts and it was a revelation; a huge step forward. Despite the difficulties, it was clear coming here had been the right thing.

The other mums had cooled their ire towards her from morbid curiosity, she suspected; wondering why the mum with the odd-looking son was allowed to stay when they had always been dissuaded. It had earned her a grudging respect. Not that she cared. She had envied their independence. Was she destined to suffocate and, evermore, have Ebe clutched to her?

There was a particular boy, Charlie, older than Ebe, who was more spellbound by Ebe than the rest. In turn, Ebe had noticed and sought him out. The opportunity seemed too good to miss when one day they played together. Well, Ebe's eyes turned the brilliant hazel glow they always did when he was excitedly following a cable or had discovered a new LED on a piece of equipment at home. And Charlie was enthusing appropriately. Most wouldn't call it laughter, but Carys could tell he was pleased.

She did what she said she wouldn't and snuck out of sight, ready to return the moment he showed concern at her absence.

Minutes piled on minutes until an hour later, she returned and told Ebe she was back. He barely looked up before returning to Charlie. Charlie was the godsend she'd prayed for. A friend. Who would have thought it?

Charlie had told his mum about Ebe. "Lights fly from his fingers, Mum! He's magic!" And he had tried to show her when she'd collected him, but she smiled and ignored him and just talked to Jared and Alys's mum. "But, Mummy! Mummy! Look what Ebe can do!"

"In a minute, sweetheart," she'd said, ruffling his hair and then Ebe had gone with his own mum and Charlie was frustrated. Tomorrow, he'd ask if Ebe could do anything else.

"I'm pleased it's going better," Marco smiled. Might he get a wife who can perform normal wifely duties like feeding her hardworking husband? Or sharing intimacy? It was early days, but he had to grasp onto any hope there was. If he could be left at nursery, might he stay in his cot? In his room? His heart fluttered. "Do you think you'll be able to leave him there the whole time soon?"

"I don't know. It seems a possibility. Thank god for Charlie."

"Yes! Encourage other friendships in case Charlie is ever ill. Or, heaven forbid, moves away or something."

Carys chuckled. "Not sure what I can do, but agreed. I'll thrust other children at him at every opportunity."

"Maybe we should have a party? A belated birthday."

Carys's lips vibrated as sceptical air blew through them. "I think that might be pushing it, but let's be optimistic." It wasn't just the unlikelihood of Ebe having enough friends to fill a party, it was the thought of those friends' mums. And controlling the little monsters. The aunties had skills she could only watch awestruck as thirty little bums sat riveted to story time or any other activity they required.

It all seemed so unlikely as the bedtime nightmare routine began and ended as it had for three years, with Ebe stuck to his mother's chest, face pressed into hers and Marco on his own on the cold, dark side of the marital bed.

Ebe didn't notice for the third day on the trot when his mother hid around the corner. Nor, when she left the building and peered in at him from the window. And he didn't notice when she disappeared and ventured fifty metres to a café across the car park in the Span Arts centre. Eyes fixed on the door, ready to abandon her latte if an aunty popped a beckoning arm from the doorway. But he didn't, and it was beginning to be strangely emotional. She couldn't complain, though. She wouldn't complain.

1997

Charlie was never far from Ebe, and despite his mummy's continued lack of interest in Ebe's odd abilities, other children had been persuaded to look when he'd said, and now they were captivated too.

Supervised free play tended to be a circuit of play themes in the room. Toys were shared, and turns on the police motorbike, and pedal car, limited to fifteen minutes or less if there was a lot of interest. And if one group of friends got the Wendy House, which they called ty bach twt (lit. small neat house), on one day, then another would get it the next. It was important to get at least half the session in the little play house or there wasn't time to act out the activities, which mainly centred on cooking and eating. Recently, three-year-olds, Adrian and Vanessa, had got 'married' and were enjoying role-play of holding hands and telling one-another they loved each other frequently. The others had embraced the roles, and instead of taking the house for themselves, would visit the new couple and drink tea from empty cups and eat the plastic peas and ham before bidding cheery farewells and allowing the next visitors inside. They were quite the socialite pair, despite their limited accommodation and same ol' menu.

Nearly all the other children visited them. But never Ebe.

On his own in the corner, he spent his time at his unofficial toy repair shop. The other kids would bring toys to him with a variety of issues from needing new batteries to parts falling off, and Ebe would source batteries from similar close by toys that weren't being used, as well as screwing, taping, or, on occasion creating replacement parts from cardboard or Lego, all the broken toys. It impressed the aunties. But they didn't know the half of it...

Not all the children visited the 'newlyweds.' Charlie and a few others kept close to Ebe in case he did one of his special things. Not that mending things wasn't cool. It's just what they had come to expect from this tiny adult. The really special things were far more extraordinary than that.

Charlie remembered the tears in his eyes when he'd cut his finger with the paper scissors. They were supposed to be safe but Charlie had tested that claim by deliberately putting the loose skin between his thumb and index finger as close to the scissor handles as possible and had succeeded in proving the manufacturers, and Aunty Flo, wrong.

It hadn't bled. It was more of a nasty red pinch, but it had hurt. When the hand holding the scissors shot into the air, the odd-looking boy had met his gaze with fiery orange eyes. It could have been the shock that stopped the pain, but by the time Ebe placed his hand over his, even the redness disappeared—like it had never happened.

The compulsive curiosity which led him to try to bust the official safety claims now compelled him to test if what he had witnessed was true. So, he did it again.

The pain was already less. Was it because he was expecting it? That he was prepared? Or was it because Ebe's burning eyes still bore into him, before he'd even moved his hand and removed all traces of injury once again?

When Ebe went away, Charlie tried one more time. He stopped when the smallest pressure shot pain through him and tears flooded his eyes.

"Careful with that, Charlie, bach!" Aunty Ann whisked the scissors from him and guided him to the water table. "Meghan, Hannah, I want Charlie to join you at the water."

Hannah frowned. "There isn't room!"

"Well, perhaps you'd like to play in the ty bach twt?" A glance across the group showed there was already a crowd in there. "Or do some sticking?"

Hannah dried her hands and skipped to the sticking table, halting abruptly as she spotted the odd boy's huge tower. "Can I do that, Aunty Ann?" she asked. She'd never seen anything quite like it. Why weren't they falling? Were they glued?

Ann did a double take and wondered the same thing. "What are you doing with those, Ebe?" she inquired with a smile. The unintelligible mutterings accompanied with the excited flashing eyes and bobbing up and down was the answer she anticipated from their newest charge, so she knew she'd have to examine the building blocks for herself. They appeared stable, but at such an improbable angle. Convinced they must be stuck together, she plucked the top brick off the pile and watched, horrified, as the entire stack collapsed to the table and onto the floor.

Quickly looking to Ebe to apologise, she could see that wasn't required as he hopped on the spot, clapping his hands in delight. "Sorry, Ebe!" she said, anyway. She sat where he had been and attempted to build the blocks up again. When they got to the expected maximum height, they wobbled and fell, much to Ebe's continued glee. "I don't know how you did that, young man, but well done!" Ann watched in wonder as Gareth, a robust but quiet boy, brought a toy over to them and even though she held out her hand, he passed it to Ebe. Ebe fiddled with it for a moment and handed it back for Gareth to run happily away with it before Ann had time to consider what was wrong with it. Shaking her head, she smiled. "Come on, Ebe, story time."

Ebe waited for all the other children to sit down, then sat on the very edge of the carpet, as far away as it was possible to get whilst still being on it. No-one spoke to him or acknowledged his presence, and he sat rapt for the story.

The damp response from some other important people thwarted the pleasure in Ebe's progress. The health visitor, initially pleased that he was at least enjoying the company of others to a certain extent, was worried he had yet to emulate their speech. She arranged appointments with paediatric doctors to look into Ebe's issues further. It was time to get the specialists involved.

Not specialists; not officially at any rate, Natalia and Dan purported their skills as parents and grandparents, along with their status as dreaded in-laws, to give their own input, as per usual.

"He's nearly four!" Natalia repeated, shaking her head over crossed arms as Carys tried to defend why he still wasn't talking, and tonight's after dinner topic of why he still didn't sleep in his own bed.

"Marco, son. And you, Dan: move Ebe's cot into the nursery. How will he ever settle in there if he's always kept with you? When you have more children, they can't all sleep in bed with you."

"More children?" Marco roared. "We'd need to have sex occasionally, or at least once, for that to happen!" his face burnt at giving away their family secret: for Carys, who was glaring at him now, and for his own manhood. He was denied the very essence of married life and not demanding the very least intimate affection from his wife made him feel pathetic. It was only his holy virtues that kept him close to sane. Grateful to leave the room, he and his dad grunted the heavy cot from beside their double bed, across the landing, and into the nursery. With a satisfied nod, they went back downstairs.

Carys wore the face of defeat and seemed to have forgiven or forgotten his discrepancy and was offering Ebe for inspection and good-night kisses, which he endured inanimately. "Remember, leave him if he cries," Natalia wagged a finger as Carys lugged him up the stairs.

Marco opened his mouth to speak, but too late, his mum had sauntered after and now stood on the landing, arms still folded, checking her advice was being adhered.

After the inevitable crying and objections, she shooed the hapless couple away. "You're probably making it worse, Carys, dear. He can sense your tension and it's upsetting him. Her mission of making Carys feel like the worst mum ever complete, she closed the front door behind them after strict instruction to go out of earshot. "Take your wife to the pub or something, Marco, she snapped. "I guarantee when you get back, Ebe will be sleeping like a lamb."

Eyebrow riding high on her forehead, arms welded together, she rejoined her husband in the lounge and closed the door on the cries from upstairs. Dan bobbed approvingly.

The television flashed its wares and a series they followed came on. On his wife's approval, Dan pointed the remote control and turned the volume up. Someone did the same to Ebe, and as the speakers and the child's lungs competed through the floorboards and the screen declared '30', their ears agreed it was uncommonly loud. Natalia smiled as though it was all going to plan.

The smile etched on her face sharpened as the plot of the television show was lost to the cacophony. How was he so loud? What would the neighbours think? They weren't her neighbours, thankfully, and she was determined he'd settle soon.

The credits rolled and none of it had made any impression on the Paulos. "How long do you think it will take for him to calm?" Dan bravely inquired.

The glare deepened as Natalia took her frustration out on what she considered a stupid question. "I don't know, do I!" she shrieked. "Perhaps if that girl had taken my advice from day one, we wouldn't be in this situation, would we? A rod for your own back–I told her, didn't I."

Dan agreed, grateful his absent daughter-in-law was getting the flack, and not him.

"Three, nearly four, is a bit late in the day to train him, but what choice do we have?"

"Do you think you should check on him?"

"Why!?" she shrieked again. "He sounds healthy. His lungs work, that's for sure. No. If he sees anyone, he's won and we'll have to start over." Calmed by her own advice, Natalia sat back in her chair and smoothed her trousers over her bulging thighs. "And I can hardly go against what I told Carys, can I. No, we'll ignore him and watch a film. Put subtitles on if necessary!"

'If?' thought Dan, scrolling through the menu. A war film with lots of shooting and less dialogue seemed a good choice, and one they'd seen before. The opening scenes were quiet and Ebe's screens drowned out any hope of hearing anything else.

"What's that?"

"What?"

"The heating or something. A dreadful humming noise. That won't be helping, will it? I bet that bothers Ebe's young ears more than mine."

"I can't hear it," Dan shrugged.

"Well, it's something. Go and check."

Before he'd found, as countless before him, that the source of the sound could not be deciphered, the front door burst open to frantic Carys who pushed past them and bounded up the stairs as Natalia called after her admitting, "He hasn't stopped!" Clenching her fist she added to Carys's back, "I'm sure he'll settle before long."

Carys didn't hear the further excuses of the strange noise, and how she really should have taken her advice much sooner, as she rushed to her son.

Separation from his mother was never something Ebe had contemplated. She had always been there. Always.

He knew her terror whenever *they* were near, and he understood. He shared it. Their coldness. Their unfeelingness. It frightened him too. And the only thing that stopped them was her.

They loomed in every shadow and reached for him in the darkness. He had to cling to his protector, or he didn't know what would happen.

They were here now. He sensed them. He could *hear* them. Why had she left him at their mercy?

Early wails were from the fear that always filled him whenever he couldn't place exactly where she was. But as the sound grew louder, he lost control. He had to get away; free from the confines of the cage she'd put him in. He knew he could, but then where would he go? Was it safer in the cage, or out of it? The turmoil of the decision ripped him apart until, with his own hands, he tried to do it himself; clawing at his face and arms, sprinting on the spot, a peculiar taste on his tongue fuelled the pain, and he swooned before gripping the bars in fresh determination.

On and on the humming intensified, him screaming over it, desperate to block it out.

Forever passed, but then relief came. She was there again, and he was in her arms. The wails had already formed within him and had to suffer their prescribed liberation, reverberating through the walls and bouncing sharply back to his ears.

The water over his face, he didn't like, but soon he was wrapped in warmth and snuggling into her. Her heart beat in his ears; ba-bum, ba-bum, ba-bum and soothed him.

Today was a special day. Was that why they had come? Perhaps, but she had protected them and now it was bright sunshine and he knew he was safe.

After slipping from her arms, a gleeful bubble in his belly, Ebe scampered down the stairs. Hopping on the spot, his eyes flashed and he knew what he wanted to do.

Yanking at yarn, he tied it around everything he saw: up high, down low. Patterns formed and when he noticed, he traced the shadows and bounced in glee as the light sources confounded and delighted him.

What would happen if he blocked brightness coming in? He could control the shadows! He'd need something big, and it would need to be high up. The chairs; yes!

With a hop to the kitchen table, he enveloped

the back of the chair in his folded arms and lifted it. It was hard, and there was one way to get it high enough to place on top of the table with this method. His bright eyes cast around the room.

Wool that he already had, bound together would be strong enough to haul from the other side. Wool tied to the far length of the long church pew bench that lined one side of the table, he tied the other end to the back of the chair. As he pushed the pew under the table, it lifted the chair with no effort.

Retying to the back of the other chair and looping it (after several frustrating attempts) over the seat of the chair he'd just craned up, he pushed the bench back, and it swung the other chair up abruptly to land on the first. It was so easy, Ebe wished he made more chairs to build a tower, but that wasn't what he was doing today and the sun was rising fast.

Tying wool in interesting patterns around the chairs, he looked to where their shadow might cast. Right on the lounge wall and reflecting from the glass of a picture he didn't like. He hopped.

The front door was at right angles to the kitchen window, so when the sun rose to meet the corner of the house, the beam of light would be split between the two. If he made a scaled down pattern high in the hallway, it would cast its shadow in the same spot as the wool from the chairs on the table in the kitchen.

The excitement warbled in his throat and he muttered incomprehensibly to himself as he pushed the bench one more time, and balancing his high dinner chair on top, was able to tie wool around the light fitting. His quick mind calculated where it would cast its shapes.

If he had to get up and open the door in the middle of the sunrise, it would spoil the surprise, so he tied sturdy thread around the handle, made sure it was unlocked, and took his place on the floor in the lounge.

With barely contained excitement, he sat and waited. Jigging as he sat, it was exactly as he wanted. He'd love to show her, but he didn't want to leave the amazing light vortex he had created.

Then she was there. Cooing at him with that lovely sound she made. With a leap, he had to hug her. His joy was hers. She had saved him from them and now he was having such fun, all thanks to her.

He could tell she shared the ecstasy as she held her sides and gripped him close. Of course, she was happy. He had made a great thing.

From the shadow cast from the window, he knew it was time. Yanking at the right strands of wool, Ebe leapt back to his spot on the lounge floor and hoped he hadn't spoilt the moment by leaving his post, but as the door swung open and the light from door and window combined, he knew he'd done it just right.

Basking in the glory of his creation, he allowed

himself a brief opening of his flashing amber eyes to glimpse his mother's reaction. Convinced she was as thrilled as he was, there was nothing more to be enjoyed from the moment. It had been perfect, as he knew it would, and now it was time for something else.

The anti-climax, or hunger, made him grumpy, and he tugged at his mother's clothes to get her attention. She read his mind at once and soon he was walking next to his wheels and heading into town. His mother muttered about where they should go, but Ebe had little care so long as it was quick.

Bumping into a shop, the smells were strong and delicious, making him even more hungry. Distressed they didn't immediately sit down to eat, Ebe hurried along clonking outside again. Where were they going?

Wherever they headed didn't look like a better place to eat than where they had come from. Why were they on grass now and heading towards more countryside? Just as he considered his tiredness, they paused and his mum sat him in the chair and strapped him in. Ebe smiled; she had read his mind.

The relief for his tired legs was spoiled by the rattling and jostling as the wheels caught in potholes and ruts in the uneven path.

Birds made noises in the tree canopy above, one of them hammering its head against the bark alarmingly, but even over all that Ebe heard it and was wondering why his mum was reacting so calmly. He was certain he wasn't mistaken. It was definitely the humming.

The trees cleared, and they were out in the open and in danger. Ebe scowled and jiggled in his seat to get her attention and make her understand. It worked. Facing the other way, they darted back under the cover of trees.

Nowhere was safe, but the more difficult they made it, the longer they put off the inevitable. Inescapable as it was, and as futile as any attempt to resist might be, the urge; the compulsion, to be away from them was overpowering.

Ebe didn't mind the bumping over holes. Anything to be free. Home, tucked up with her. That was the only safe place. To get to him, they'd have to prize him from her chest and he knew she would fight that with her last breath. They must hurry. The sound was loud and they were very close.

Screeching, he couldn't believe she had stopped. She never talked to anybody, why was she stopping now. Women sat at a table chewed on the awful fiery sticks some people love. Noxious fumes spewed from every hole in their heads and Ebe pressed himself into his seat and tugged at the straps, his distress at the noise momentarily thwarted. Then they were off again. He recognised the street. Not long and they would be in the confines of their home.

Quickly pulling in his arms so they wouldn't hit the wall, his pushchair was yanked and jerked into the hallway where Ebe was at once comforted and amused by his earlier creation. But then she pulled at it. What was wrong with her? He screeched and glared at her. She had chosen to take them out and parade them in front of them like bait on a hook, and now she was set on taking from him his only distraction. Eyes closing to a squint, he was satisfied she had read his thoughts again as she stopped. Thank you, he thought.

Plucking him from his chair, she held him close, just as he wanted, and carried him up the stairs. Instead of heading to the bedroom, she ducked into the bathroom and turned on the taps. He would bathe with her, her knew, and it would calm them down ready for whatever they were soon to endure. He smiled. She did have good ideas.

Warm and soothed from the hot bubbly water, they lay skin on skin, wrapped in fluffy towelling with the duvet pulled over them too. Slowly, Ebe felt his head relax and sleep pull him in.

"What on earth!" the loud irritation woke him at once.

His hopes for a normal life, and a normal wife, seemed as far away as ever. After last night's spectacular failure to move Ebe into his cot in his room, marital closeness looked futilely distant.

Reaching the top of the stairs, his wife and stepson were wrapped in towels on the bed and the room was humid after their bath. Nice they were having such a relaxing time rather than clearing away the mess so he could walk into his own house after a hard day at work, he thought sarcastically, as Carys moaned at him for not being utterly thrilled.

And then she brought up last night, inevitably, and it surprised Marco that, despite agreeing it hadn't gone well, he felt angry. "My mother was just trying to help. She was trying to save our marriage!" Too late, he'd said it now. Whilst the effect was predictably unpleasant and, so, regrettable, it was the truth. Marco wasn't sure how long he could go on if a flicker of hope for normality didn't spark soon.

His mind regained focus just as she was telling him to fuck off. Well, maybe he should. His lack of response seemed to help. She was excusing herself, but as she did, or perhaps more so the excuse she used riled him ready to blow. It was the humming noise again. And, now, she was suggesting the wool tied to everything might be protection from extra-terrestrials, and that Ebe had built it; lifting chairs, tying knots when he can't tie his shoes, and reaching the ceiling. The preposterousness might have calmed him by reminding him she was not mentally sound, but the rage kept burning. "Should I call the doctor? Or the police?"

"No!" Carys squealed.

"I won't bother asking what's for dinner! I can smell, or rather I can't smell; it's nothing, isn't it?" Jaw clenched, he yanked a bag from under the bed and threw some things from the drawer into it, more for show than for practicality. "I'm going to my 'terrible' mother's for some food. Don't expect me back." Tears tracking down Carys's cheek stopped him, but a glance to Ebe, his supposed stepson's glassy emotionless stare, he knew it was too late. He'd had enough.

Without another word, he stormed down the stairs, flinging his arms at the woolly obstacles in his way, throwing them to the ground, and slamming the front door behind him.

This was *his* house. He would be back, but not tonight. Tonight, he needed to be away from mentally ill wives and their ungrateful children and find some peace. Admitting defeat to his mum and dad could be unpleasant, but surely after their own shortcomings last night they would understand how difficult it was.

Regret wrenched his shoulders down as he drove in silence the short distance to his parent's. Food after a day at work would be welcome, at least.

His mother looked up, nose pointed in pensive anticipation, "Carys and Ebe not with you?" and as he shook his head, she relaxed and her nostrils crinkled softening its sharpness as she smiled. "What brings you here alone, then, son?

Natalia, and Dan gleaned no more sense of his situation, occasionally squeezing his chin in contemplation. “I thought we were done with these demons, but if she really is mentally unwell, perhaps it’s a chemical imbalance in her brain. Prayer might help, but it maybe God’s punishment for something she had done.”

“Oh, don’t be silly, Daniele,” her Italian pronunciation ridiculing him even more. “That would mean he’s punishing Marco, too. And Marco is a good boy.”

Yes, he was wasn’t he. How many men would have stuck by a wife and child who seemed to resent him. His studious following of his faith kept him going no matter what.

Sitting to enjoy linguine smothered in a tasty fishy sauce was heaven. Much better than his own attempts, particularly as he wasn’t worried he would get it thrown at him, or that his stepson would ignore him the whole time. For all the years he’d resented their expectation, and control of him. But he enjoyed the comfort of their familiarity now.

“What’s that noise?” Natalia paused from slicing tiramisu, a deep line tarnishing her severe features further. “Daniele, check where it’s coming from, would you, please? Isn’t it the same sound we heard last night and I said was Marco’s heating? Well, it must be outside, mustn’t it. Marco, what’s wrong?”

He'd heard it before she had. Head tilted, and then a quick plunge with a cupped hand to rid him of what he hoped might be a brief bout of tinnitus, earned him quizzical stares from his parents. And now his staid and sensible mother had confirmed its place in the real world and not just in his mind.

As his dad stood and cocked his head to the fridge-freezer, then walked to the front door and back with a growing scowl, when he returned to the table and dismissed it with a shrug whilst reaching for a bowl of dessert, his nonchalance was scant comfort for his son.

Carys's childhood accounts had seemed unbelievable. He'd always professed to be on her side, but he realised now, he had humoured her because he wanted her to love him. As her predilection for mental health problems reared its indubitable head, he'd found it even easier to dismiss her claims as folly. But now he heard it too, and just like his wife, he was terrified.

"Marco, whatever is the matter? Don't tell me you're giving your crazy wife's notions house room? Careful, you'll end up like her."

He hated the admonishment yet found it oddly comforting. These first three years of marriage had not been the blissful 'honeymoon period' they were expected to be. He'd watched his beautiful bride shift from the envy of the town, to the subject of behind-hand gossip.

And instead of being nurtured with fine home-cooked food, he'd grown accustomed to cooking his own and providing her meals to low levels of appreciation.

His excitement at becoming a dad; a duty at first, soon had become a burning desire, rewarded with a stepson who barely acknowledged him. And as for making the family bigger, it seemed ever-unlikely. If this was how the three-year mark looked, how did they fare for the infamous seven-year-itch?

So, with all that going on, of course he was stressed. And if he was stressed, no wonder he saw the oddities in the mirror. And why would they take the form of anything else, given his unstable wife's propensity to lap up every alien conspiracy theory going? It was normal. A perfectly rational sound that any number of harmless rationalisations could explain.

With a yawn, keen to avoid conversation that might sully his resolve, Marco excused himself. "I slept badly last night, so I think I'll go on upstairs for an early night."

"Not just staying for dinner then?"

Marco shook his head. "I just need a break. I bet after a good sleep I'll see things clearer tomorrow." A grin forced his mouth into an over-the-top- expression of carefreeness. He hoped he could convince himself.

His mother waved him through the door, excusing him from clearing away the dishes, and called out after him, "There are clean sheets on your bed."

Her keeping his bedroom as it was struck him as odd despite her occasionally referring to it as 'the guest room. "Thanks, Mum, you're the best!"

THIRTY-SIX

Unexpected meeting

He felt like he was floating. The humming noise was deafening and he didn't know where he was but it seemed to be the very heart of the noise. His eyes were closed and as he tried to unshut them and couldn't.

The floaty sensation surrounded him. He wished his eyes would open because he was sure he was flying.

"Open your eyes."

Ebe smiled. His wish had been answered and his lids released their glue grip and he saw his surroundings for the first time.

He wasn't flying, but sitting in a chair. A wonderful comfortable chair that was hard and accommodating at once. A man approached and Ebe laughed. He didn't have any clothes on. He looked odd and Ebe hid his face. No, no, no.

Ebe had met no-one without his mummy close by before. The usual wrench of desperation rattled his chest and tears stung his eyes. The man moved closer and a familiar yet peculiar smell made his nose twitch and his eyes water. Or, they might be a lady. He couldn't tell without clothes, and the head didn't have hair, so Ebe didn't know if it was meant to be short or long.

The seat held him firm as he shuffled back from the figure moving closer. A cry stuck in his throat and he frantically searched for her. How had he missed it? How had he not known who this was? The icy chill as they reached him forced a shrill squeal from his lips. Dark eyes pointed in his direction and he struggled to match their gaze. A rattling sound drew his stare down and he saw his legs trembling against the cold hard curve of the seat.

"Ebe," the person with no hair and no clothes said without moving their mouth. "There is something I want to show you; someone I'd like you to meet..."

THIRTY-SEVEN

Orders

Marco's peace was soured by the guilt. He was sure it was nothing sinister, but equally definite it was real. He'd heard it. His mum and dad, too. And he knew it would scare Carys. She didn't have his gift for rationalising everything, and of seeing God's will in all that we do. He considered going home, but if they were sleeping, he'd disturb them, and what then? Reassure it was all right? That was just as likely to upset her and make her question his loyalty.

His full belly added to his remorse. Had she eaten? Was she too angry to prepare anything? When he'd seen them, they were cosy and warm. Carys was a fully grown woman. Surely, she would feed herself and her son.

He fooled himself that sleeping, and giving himself the rest was the most sensible thing, and snorted; why shouldn't he ask for supper when he needed it? What was good for him was good for her. It was God's way.

Planned sleep was always hard to come by. At home he'd shuffle resentfully on his side of the king size bed, and heed the nudging from his wife that he was snoring because if he woke Ebe whilst he was lashed to her face, she would more likely send him to the couch than attempt to move that boy. As he grunted his contempt, he checked himself. He understood. Ebe asleep on her face was preferable to him crying. At least she could settle knowing he was safe.

What was wrong tonight? Room to roll around his big bed in his old bedroom to his satisfaction. Teeth clenched, he shook his head. Thrusting back into the pillow, he gave up lying on his back and shuffled onto his side, bringing one knee up and tucking a crooked right arm under the cold side of the pillow. The familiar scent of his mother's fabric softener soothed him and sleep wove its silken threads around his thoughts.

Sudden panic cut through and woke him. Propped up on his elbow, he scanned the room in the dark. That cursed noise was even louder. With a sigh, he folded one half of the pillow over his head, blocking both his ears.

Swapping arms and ears covered by the pillow, he kicked his legs in frustration. And just when he gave up on ever getting rest, consciousness left him like a light turning off. From nowhere,

Marco was in a deep and peculiar dream. Or so he would try to convince himself when he woke up...

The humming noise was intense; like he was part of it, and it was part of him. His eyes scrunched against a searing light all around, but a voice forced them open. He realised, rather than speech, he was hearing a multi-timbral animal squeal, while in his head he understood the words clearly:

"We do not wish to harm you, but you must do as we say." Despite use of the plural pronoun, Marco only detected one... One what? His mind baulked at the word 'person', and so his self-narrative used 'speaker' instead.

Marco widened his gaze and thrust back in his seat. It was only then he even noticed he was sitting down. But, where was he?

All he saw was stark white, illuminated by unseen lights. The creature in front of him looked exactly how Carys had described: a diminution, naked figure, with a large head and pale white flesh. He was reminded of Ebe, not because of his appearance, more from his wife's claims of his extra-terrestrial parentage. He had scoffed at that; well, anyone would, wouldn't they? Was there really a similarity between his stepson and whatever this was?

"Marco."

His own name reverberated around his head

whilst the animalistic screech filled the space in front of him, only to quickly absorb into the room beyond and become drowned out by the humming noise.

"Marco, we have an important mission for you."

From nowhere, the almond eyed creature was joined by several identical figures. Only the first one spoke to him. "Ebe is about to undertake his next stage of development. He will need your guidance."

How can I guide him? What important mission? he wanted to scream, but when he tried, his mouth clamped closed.

"Ebe will begin asking things of you. Crucial questions of monumental importance. You may believe you don't have the answers, but when the time comes you will be assisted. Come, let us show you."

Not against his will, but out of his control, Marco rose from the smooth seat and floated after the creatures a few pace-lengths behind. Doors opened, or rather, disappeared to reveal light so bright it prevented him seeing.

If not for the dread in his chest and the weird people he was following, Marco thought it looked how he had always pictured heaven. Travelling, drifting at a speed it was impossible to determine with nothing familiar to reference: no landmarks, objects, no breeze against his skin, as though they were stationary but for the odd creatures moving their arms and legs in a walking motion.

They arrived at the same spot, but when the doors vanished, the room beyond was darker and another diminutive figure sat as he himself had a minute before. A strangely familiar figure. Marco smiled. No wonder he had been thinking about him. Stepping inside, his stepson looked as surprised to see him. His mouth moved for the first time. Dreams were funny like that. "Hello, Ebe," he said. "Fancy seeing you..."

THIRTY-EIGHT

Ebe the chatterbox

Ebe laughed. When he was told he was about to meet someone, he didn't think it would just be Marco. Feeling smarter than them, if they weren't even aware that he and Marco were already well acquainted, then what had he to fear from them? And they were being nice to him. Eyes flashing the orange hazel they always did when he enthused, Ebe let his view take in more of his surroundings.

Yes, it was white. Everything. But there had to be something making the noise; something powering the doors; keeping them flying. With excitement bubbling in his belly, he ogled in every direction. It was a thrilling game of hide and seek, or 'Where's Wally'. Where were the wires? His greatest desire now was to search the room and find out everything he could. With a squeal of joy, he jumped down from his seat but stopped when an unseen force held him still. Fear flickered again, but then when he looked at the big faces they hadn't changed. They weren't angry, they were just doing something to him to stop him from moving. Adults do that sometimes. His fists clenched, and he stared more.

When Ebe laughed, a shudder rocked Marco. What was there to find funny? Marco gulped. Of course, he understood them, didn't he? "Ebe? What's happening?" What was the point in asking? He had never said a word, not even an intelligible sound.

"Marco," the creature's voice sounded in his head. "Ebe cannot yet speak. Soon he will and this is the reason we have brought you here. The direction of Ebe's studies will need guidance for him to reach his potential in a timely manner. We are on a schedule that requires his education's completion by a specific time.

"You are wondering how you may influence the child, but the answer has been presented already, and a while ago. There was another before you created for this purpose who unfortunately ended his existence before he served his purpose. We will not allow that to happen to you.

You will retain control of your daily living in much the same way. The minutiae of human existence are of no interest. But when opportunity to expand Ebe's knowledge is witnessed, another will use your bodily vessel to further the greater purpose. We will now demonstrate."

The screeching timbre echoed in the white space beyond Marco's comprehension. In front of him, a slice opened in the room and created a portal. Beyond was not another world, but something far more mundane. It was a mirror; or at least some method of offering a reflection, because Marco could see himself. It surprised him to be naked and his hands flew instinctively to cover his genitals.

He expected the change. The creature had hinted that he had been prepared, but nothing equipped him for the metamorphosis. The mirror image swelled and sprouted upwards whilst his skin rippled in scales and a lizard tongue licked the air.

It couldn't be real, it couldn't. A look at himself would show it to be an illusion. A screen overlay or something. He remembered squealing with joy on the family's trip to Orlando on the Haunted Mansion ghost train when a ghost appeared in the car with him and his dad. It had looked so tangible. This had to be something like that, didn't it?

His reflection repulsed him. Tearing his disbelieving stare away from the compelling shock, as he tried, beyond his control his head tilted, forcing his gaze. Eyes fought him to stay open and his stare was directed at his hideous reptilian flesh. "Nooo!" There was nothing he could do; no movement functioned. And then, he left his body, or rather, what used to be his body. From a distance, not above, or below, or in front or behind, but from an unperceivable sense of detachment, Marco watched as the lizard walked to Ebe and picked him up.

'Leave him alone!' he screamed in his head, but no sound came. As the monster held Ebe, who stared wide-eyed but calm. Tears prickled his face. The creature shrank effortlessly back to his usual form, then into the huge beast again, before changing one more time back into Marco, but not naked, fully clothed in his usual work clothes.

Ebe laughed and clapped his little hands.

Fifty times in a second, like a crazy Marco/lizard man strobe effect, he changed rapidly, wearing everything he remembered he owned and him watching from a distance of all around and nowhere like he was in the back of his own head and seeing things from his mind's interpretation of reality.

With a jolt, he stood, Ebe in his arms, both reflected in the mirror. The child hugged him like he never had before then wriggled free from his grasp as Marco instinctively lowered him to the floor. With a brief look back, he ran into the darker room beyond where they all remained and smoothed his hands over the walls, giggling as he ran.

A creature stood in front of him and took his hand. Together, they disappeared into a growing brightness.

"Ebe is ready to undertake his next step of integration, where conversation will become necessary. It has been avoided until his mind became less impressionable. His brain may be filled with what is important and not the frivolous folly humans learn when they are at their most impressionable. He will soon speak verbally rather than merely telepathically, and then we expect you to guide him in certain interests. In the meantime, you must return home to your wife and provide a stable environment for him to grow up. It is vital he have no worries in order to fully develop as we wish."

Tears wouldn't be stopped. The creatures didn't care or didn't notice. Still, only one of them addressed him.

"You may enjoy a normal life to a point. What that point is will depend on your level of cooperation. Do you understand?"

If he didn't obey whatever they asked of him, the lizard would take over and live his life for him. He understood. He struggled to believe it, but he understood. And as he patted his torso and legs to confirm he was still able to and that he felt like he expected, the cotton of his T-shirt and boxer shorts familiar and reassuring. As he looked up to nod his confirmation, he gasped.

The ceiling rose in the bedroom he'd spent years of his life staring at swirled in front of him in the breaking dawn.

Jumping out of bed, heart thumping, he breathed hard. "That was the weirdest dream," he said out loud to make sure he had the capability. The humming sound was gone. Night time road works or something. Noise travelled oddly in the small hours, he knew. A tentative glance in the mirror and he laughed. Completely normal. Touching his hands to his face, the giggles of relief echoed.

He looked at the bed. It was early. Much earlier than he wanted to get up, but rather than risk resuming sleep and falling back into the peculiar nightmare, he crept from the room to make tea.

THIRTY-NINE

Reunion

Hand held, the funny naked adult guided Ebe. Doors vanished in front of him and he jumped joyfully in an excited attempt to break free. He couldn't, so he returned to the slow walking pace.

In another room, a man who, to Ebe looked a lot like Marco; a taller version with light coloured hair. Around him a glow of many colours, effervesced in swirls. Ebe sprung up and landed, clapping his hands, smiling at the naked man who had brought him in, who must have let go of his hand.

"Greetings, Ebe," the new tall man said as he came in. Ebe frowned. Where was the sound coming from? This was the best place he'd ever seen. "Be still. I have something to share with you."

Ebe did as he was asked, either from desire or

compulsion. He didn't know because he made no attempt to disobey. The tall man approached him. Lowering his hand, it hovered over Ebe's throat. "Open your mouth, young man, please."

Ebe did. "Your father says it is time for you to speak. Your brothers and sisters will be learning too, but it is thought you have a skill beyond many of the others; an understanding and a fascination with matters of great importance. It is my belief you will go onto achieve greatness. For my kind, you are an asset which we must protect."

Ebe stared at the man. A shudder rippled down his spine. He understood every word, and they were kind happy words. The words were not the cause of his fear.

His eyes bulged as the tall man put his hand into his mouth and grasped hold of his tongue. The taste was vile, like the smell when he had been in the car with Marco and they had stopped for fuel.

Ebe tried to pull away but was glued to the spot. A cold, icy stare met his, and the man removed his grip. Turning to the other person with the translucent grey skin and big head, the tall man spoke in a screeching roar and the small man grasped Ebe's hand again.

A window came into view as they walked from the room to a hazy corridor. Children: some like him, and some like the tall blonde man, cupped hands around their eyes to peer out at him. Ebe waved but none of them returned the gesture. And then he was alone; floating again, the sound of sobbing encroaching on his mind. With a shake of his head, he ignored it and craned to see the other children like him, but a fuzzy feeling in his chest made him cry out past a tightening in his throat. The cry was his mother's. He moved instinctively to her and wrapped his arms around her as he felt her do the same to him. Did she know what had happened? She must have, or she wouldn't have let it. She was his protector, and he needed her. Tightening his squeeze, she whispered, "How?" he didn't answer. Instead, he fell back to sleep, peaceful and keen for what the new day would bring.

She shook him awake. His eyes burned. He had so much to tell her.

FORTY

Hunger

Marco cupped the mug of tea to his chest and stared through the kitchen window, taking occasional sips. That was too weird. Guilt for his scepticism of Carys's extra-terrestrial stories, combined with tension after their row, and being under his parents' roof; that's what must have done it.

The next sip made him wince. Ice cold. How long had he sat here? Dawn had broken over the valley. From waking far too early, he was at risk of being late. Showering took longer than the four minutes he usually allowed because his mind kept playing snippets of last night in jagged, non-ordered clips. The sight of them; of himself. "Thank goodness it was all just a dream," he stated out loud, challenging the powers that be to strike him where he stood if he were speaking untrue.

The shower didn't suddenly grow scalding hot, and he wasn't visited by an extra-terrestrial forcing him to believe the unthinkable. And whilst he shaved, his tentative looks to the mirror grew more confident, as he didn't morph into a reptilian humanoid. He let out a little laugh. "You'll be joining Carys in the nut house at this rate!"

His parking space was untaken at work, which was never guaranteed, so that was a pleasant start to his working day. When he reached the large office with its multiple desks, he was whistling a show of frivolous gaiety. So, it deflated him more than it might have when a colleague shrilled, "Marco, you look terrible... What happened to you?"

His lips moved, but he had nothing to say as his shrug elicited a knowing smile and a nose tap from his co-worker. Marco considered what his presumption meant: he'd been drunk? Lucky with the ladies, or both? He had no energy to ensure he reached different conclusions and was relieved the deliberate wink was unlikely to indicate he had any idea that he looked so terrible after a simple nightmare, so he returned the smile and tapped the side of his own nose.

By the time his phone rang after lunch and his wife probed him to come home for dinner, he'd virtually forgotten it. But what she said brought it chilling back to life...

"You won't believe what Ebe can do!" she

gushed. “He’s not stopped talking since his first words this morning. It took a while to understand him, but he’s getting clearer and clearer.” Marco heard her gulp. “And just now he said ‘Marco doesn’t like my wool formation!’ What do you think of that?”

“Wool formation?” Marco couldn’t trust it was true. Anyone would struggle to accept their mute stepson learning to talk after four years of not even a grunt. But after last night’s nightmare, this was much harder to take. “You’re reading too much into it,” he blustered. “I bet. It’s good he’s making sounds, though. Nursery is paying off.”

He put the phone down, having agreed to go home for dinner. In his head, Ebe speaking was unimaginable. The feeling of dread that he actually might witness it in a few hours sickened him. Exactly as his dream had prophesised. All the times he’d seen reptilian reflections swam around his mind; head shaking to dispel any attachment to the possibility he would have to accept it was true. Eyes down, he tapped on his keyboard and hoped a juicy case would take his attention.

The clock whizzed on like a stopwatch and the hour of reckoning came upon him in a flash. Heart thudding in his chest, he made his way slowly to his car, and prepared for a laboured drive home. He could stop and buy flowers. A nice gesture, he persuaded himself, not allowing the knowledge it was a delaying tactic to get a foothold.

Ebe felt tired, but his mummy shook him awake. Instantly filled with a desire to communicate, her words to him were overwhelming. Did he want breakfast? Which jumper did he prefer? Walk, or be pushed in his stroller? Answers formed in his head, but his unaccustomed lips couldn't form the speech, and before he tried, she asked him something else.

Finally out of the house, they seemed to be going a different way to nursery to their usual route and the change excited him. Eyes widened in flashing anticipation as they arrived at a gate, behind which a large horse meandered over to them. He knew what this animal was called, although he wasn't sure how. Still words wouldn't come and all the while she kept on at him 'Did he like the horse?' he was becoming frustrated.

They pushed on further, and she continued on at him, congratulating him on walking such a long way. He blocked her out because something else had his attention and he was determined to coax his mouth into working as he wanted it to.

They moved closer to the strange object, and Ebe's lips trembled in eagerness "Do you want your pushchair, Ebe?" He had to try now or never. "There's a feather in the river!" he cried. It didn't sound right, so he repeated the words, and then again, and again. When his mother echoed them, he knew he'd got it right.

Pleased with himself, responding to all her questions and ask some of his own. His language was basic compared to what he wanted to say, but he knew he had to learn. This was a skill he was prepared to perfect.

The smell of garlic and onions would normally spark his appetite, but with the anxiety building since Carys's phone call, it made him feel sick. Desperate to seem normal, he still said, "Something smells fantastic!" as he walked through the door. Flourishing the fresh flowers from behind his back. "I'm sorry I left you to cope on your own last night."

His gesture was not met with the gratitude he hoped as his wife bristled with rageful resentment. 'Why had he left her if he thought she was unwell?' she argued. But then she triggered his logical arguments and gave him a crutch to beat his fears with when she said, "Because you disrupted the formation, they made it into the house. They almost took Ebe!"

But as he scoffed and claimed she was crazy, her story of what happened to her in the night: the humming first; then *them* taking Ebe. It all sounded too similar to his own nightmare to be coincidence. He could hear his voice and hers, but he wasn't involved in the conversation. Nausea had too firm a grip on him now.

Through it all, his denial and logic presented the best arguments. If he shouted loud enough that it was all her mental imagination, he could will it to be untrue.

But then, cutting through his argument like a scythe, Ebe bustled into the room. "Mummaay! Mumaay? Wot iss dinner?" he asked.

Marco struggled to keep his anxiety in his mouth as he witnessed a conversation about dinner, and then without looking directly at his face, he accused him of being angry with him and not liking his 'wool formation.' Just as Carys had said. "Bloody Hell!" And it was hell. His own personal hell had manifested right in front of him, and there could be no escape. Carys laughed, and as Ebe joined her, Marco forced his own laughter too, but it caught untruthfully in his throat.

"Aw, Marco, you're all choked up. You must have been more worried than you let on about Ebe talking."

She didn't know how right she was. But not for the reasons she imagined. Aware vaguely that she had thanked him for not showing his concerns and making it worse for her, now she was peering at him, awaiting his reaction. As he choked out a response, dewy eyes and a gentle pat on his hand told him he was excused to take a moment for himself. He squeezed his eyes closed, too, and stood up, returning the affection rubbing her arm and mumbling about needing the toilet before padding from the Kitchen and up the stairs.

How could he be pleased? His nightmare was coming true. Ebe had spoken, and not just nonsense but full complicated sentences... Just as they had said.

Guilt bubbled within at his bluster that Carys had made it all up. Especially as she had taken it so well. Logic in his mind was giving up the fight. And when she said they had come last night and their wardrobe had wooshed across the room and crashed into the wall, it was too easy to dismiss it as her being crazy. Combined with his own odd night, and Ebe's conversational eloquence, it pointed to a worrying truth.

Not wanting to stop at their bedroom in his need for solitude—its location directly above where Carys and Ebe sat at the table was too exposed for the apprehension he was feeling—first, he had to peek in the bedroom and see for himself.

The scrapes on the wall were clear to see, and he gasped. Then with a sneer and a shake of his head, he decided it proved nothing, as logic once again clawed for a foothold on his sanity. If she was mentally unstable, she might have moved it herself, heavy as it was. Much more logical. That returned his nightmare to just that. But what about Ebe?

He crept along the landing to Ebe's unused

nursery. *Click*. The door closed behind him and he was alone. They wouldn't hear his cries in here. Arms shook, but then the violent vibration rippled through his chest and down his torso into his legs. His voice, a warbling cry, escaped his dry lips and echoed around the lifeless room.

Marco dropped to his knees, the trembling taking a gentle steadiness with sporadic convulsing as he hid his face in his hands.

It was too many coincidences, wasn't it? Carys's story, his dream, Ebe's sudden ability to speak? The hum had the same associations for them both, now. There had to be perfectly logical explanations for all of it, but in a fit of fear that denying them might bring forth the other thing that showed itself whenever it wanted, he couldn't allow himself to consider them. And if he feared that, then to all intents and purpose, he may as well accept it: They had been here. In his house. They had taken Ebe and made him talk. And they'd seized him and forced him to look at that... That...Thing. And threatened him. That's what it amounted to; do as we say or lose control of your life. No-one will even notice that your personality is completely different.

What would they ask of him to make such a threat necessitous?

Marco sobbed, not only for himself, but for whatever was to happen. Whatever they guided Ebe to do, they would force him to help him. The trembling stopped. Marco lowered his hands to his lap. He had no choice.

He pasted a smile on his face and showed what he hoped was appropriate enthusiasm for Ebe's latest development, and it saw them through until bed.

Oddly comforted by the normal routine of his stepson sleeping nose to nose with his wife, and himself pushed to the edge of the bed, in spite of the difficulties they'd faced. What they had yet to face could be harder than anything he foresaw.

His purpose in taking on Carys and Ebe seemed more relevant than ever. A justification for his very existence. No-one else offered what he did. And all the problems he and his parents had associated with his wife, he now knew was the truth. *They* had been the problem. But now he, Carys, and Ebe would be a team against whatever was to come. The three musketeers.

Marco woke early. Carys and Ebe seemed not to have moved all night; a skill Carys had forced upon her due to Ebe's propensity to wake and scream at the slightest disturbance. It didn't matter now it was morning, but Marco crept around the bed and tiptoed from the bedroom and closed the door and that of the bathroom to minimise the noise of showering.

When he creaked back in to get dressed, Carys's eyes were open, and she smiled at him across the room without moving. He grinned back, but emotion caught in his throat and he turned away. What was it, guilt at how he hadn't believed her? Or fear now that he did?

The thoughts lingered as he drove to work. The frost covered hillsides didn't take his attention as they usually would. His focus remained entirely within the ten-to-two portion of his steering wheel as his fingers pointed forward like daggers securing his way.

He pulled into the council offices car park without being aware of completing the journey, and he frowned and pressed his lips together, whitening a line of a smile as the gate man opened the barrier for him to enter.

Taking his usual spot, he didn't push the door open as he expected and head into work. Instead, he sat and stared at his hands, still on the wheel.

Something sharp between his teeth made him run his tongue over his lips to dislodge it, and he soon realised his hands must have left the wheel at least long enough to find their way to his mouth to chew his nails.

That was a habit he didn't want to return to, so now he was cross as well as guilty and afraid and whatever else he was feeling. Ramming the car door open, forcing it to pay the price for his temper. It had quick revenge as it swung back on its hinge to bang Marco sharply on the shin. "Fff..." he controlled himself; his ministerly demeanour not lost yet. "Golly, that was unfortunate," he forced an over-the-top grin onto his face and only let it slide for fear anyone he encountered would suspect he was insane; and he didn't have the energy, or the inclination to convince them otherwise.

Sighing repeatedly up the two flights of stairs, he flumped into his chair behind his desk with one final humph, and opened up his computer.

It was difficult to look busy when anyone who passed by might glimpse his screen. He had to have something to conceivably be studying so as not to arouse suspicion. An indecipherable spreadsheet of people waiting for housing benefit outcomes was boring enough to only attract the attention of the most resolute evaluation.

Occasionally clicking on a figure randomly and pinching his chin in mock deliberation, Marco attempted to settle his thoughts. He soon wished the database was as engrossing as his performance would lead one to believe.

He looked up at just the wrong time to catch the eye of the colleague he scared shitless in the bathroom yesterday. As his cheeks filled with bile, he fought the need to rush to the toilet again and swallowed it down. But not before imagining his colleague's terror-struck face if Marco had pushed his chair back and rushed towards him.

He laughed, spluttering and re-catching his breath, and falling into silent guffaws. Calm down, Marco, he tried to subdue the hilarity. It's not even funny. "It's not even funny," he repeated out loud, his voice hoarse now produced a silent muffled noise.

A crowd, from within and out of his own office, sidled up and asked him what was so amusing in an increasingly aggressive tone. "Sorry," Marco managed at last, pushing back his chair and dashing from the office. Down the stairs, he rushed through a back door that led to the river.

A fast-flowing weir, metres away, had Marco headed there for the privacy the penetrating white noise afforded.

Steps in the river bank, installed to calm the flow when it flooded, gave easy access to the clear curtain of water. As close as he could without slipping in, Marco screamed at the top of his lungs. He couldn't even hear himself, so he knew no-one else would know what he was saying. "What the FUCK is happening? God, I can't believe you have forsaken me this way. To go against everything I've ever believed about you to serve what? Aliens? Demons? And if I don't, I'll be lost forever."

Marco collapsed to the floor. Splashes from the weir helped disguise the streaming tears, as well as the gut-wrenching sound of his sobs.

But he was watched. Everyone in Pembrokeshire County Council offices was peering out of the closest windows to the river at a man on the edge of everything. Some with gossipy judginess, others with concern for his safety. Then, as a shoal of mackerel, they returned to their seats as the man stood and brushed himself off and looked up at the windows.

By the time he came back to his desk with one final, “Sorry,” no-one questioned him. They didn’t know if one more might send him over the edge.

A small amount of work achieved, Marco ventured to the vending machine for coffee and a snack. As he pressed the buttons to turn the carousels around, nothing took his fancy from the sugary snacks. A forlorn ham sandwich attracted his attention. It looked foul and forgotten, but he had to have it.

His money in, he watched drooling as the plastic pyramid circled to the tipping point and committed kamikaze over the edge. Door flap unlocked, his hand pushing past and he snatched the sandwich, ripped the packet, and plucked the small pink meat slice from between the bread and a soggy leaf. In one swallow, it was gone and Marco knew he needed more.

Insatiable, he bounded back down the stairs and out of the building. He didn’t even know if it was lunchtime yet, but he didn’t expect anyone to pursue him. And he didn’t care if they did.

The scent of meat from SubWay caught his nostrils first, but by the time he drew closer, other smells of bread and salad and sauces dampened his appetite. Meat. He needed meat.

Raw animal protein caught the air and Marco followed his nose, surprised when he had to walk much further than he would have expected aroma to reach, he knew sometimes the wind was funny like that.

His place in the queue was torture. Two people in front of him seemed to be there more for the social interactions than for the purchasing of meat products. Fury swelled within him. So easily he could throw them aside and get to the front, but that was ridiculous. If he was the butcher and someone did that, he would refuse to serve them. The wisdom calmed his ire, and he waited his turn.

"What can I get for you today, sir?" the butcher smiled.

But Marco hadn't spent the time deliberating his choice, which would have been a worthwhile distraction from his murderous thoughts. "Meat!" he blurted.

The butcher laughed. "Yes. You've come to the right place. What sort of meat? Pork?" he said loudly and slowly, assuming Marco to be a non-English speaking tourist, or someone with a learning difficulty. "Chicken?" he pointed to different cuts. "Beef?"

"Beef," Marco clenched his fists. "And pork. And lamb. Yeah, lots of lamb. Give me lots of beef chicken and lamb, please."

"Do you want it diced?"

Marco shrugged.

"How about half a pound, or a pound of each?"

Marco gave a thumbs up. "A pound of each." He stopped himself ordering two pounds.

The butcher seemed relieved when he announced, "That'll be twenty-three pounds, then, please," that Marco handed him money and he wasn't forced to return the meats to their display. A very odd man, he thought, as he scurried through the door with his bag of flesh.

Marco clutched it to him. What was he going to do with it? He couldn't wait until he got home, he was starving. But there was nowhere to cook the meat at work.

The craving gripped his stomach and waiting wasn't an option, he had to do something. Odd looks from passers-by sent Marco searching for privacy and ducked down by the river again, following the path under the bridge.

There was evidence of homeless living, but no-one was there at the moment. "What an idiot, Marco," he shook his head. "What are you gonna do with this lot?" he slumped down on the floor, the cold of the chilled raw meat aching in his hands. He swallowed down drool a few times, his mouth whetting at the thought of just biting into the flesh.

He could stand it no longer. Slashing open the bag, his teeth sank into the first flesh they encountered as he gulped it down, his craving growing with every bite.

One bag finished, Marco tore into the next'

"Oh my god, no!"

Marco paused in his meal. Had he missed him before? or, had he returned to his collection of street life acquisitions?

"Oh, my god," the man repeated. Marco had no words, but as he looked at the man, he saw his fingers covered in scales. Aware know of his perspective much higher, he gasped, wondering how he didn't notice before.

The man backed away, scurrying up the bank of the river. Where was he going? What if he told people about him? Marco had a new priority above devouring the packs of raw meat...

In one leap he almost reached him, the next caught him and he flung him to the ground, staring down at his scruffy clothes, coat fastened with twine, shoes with holes. What a pitiful sight.

Privacy restored; the hunger returned. Finally sated, he threw the bags to one side and lay back against the arch of the bridge, gasping in satisfaction.

His consciousness flowed back into him and he repealed the sticky bags on his lap. Raw chicken. He'd eaten it all. But raw chicken! That could kill him. He knew he should throw it up, but he couldn't bear to. All that lovely meat and its wonderful protein. It would be sacrilege to purge himself of it, and he wouldn't do it.

He felt fine; better than fine. A wash would help, but he was ready to return to work. Turning his hands over again and again, Marco was convinced he was his usual self. It was almost impossible to believe otherwise. Memories of not being himself faded like a dream. The harder he focussed his mind on remembering, the more distant his recollection became.

A bag which previously contained meat fluttered in the breeze, then stopped as it caught on a pair of worn-out boots with holes in them a few feet away. A stark memory of the homeless man flashed in his head. Where was he? And why had he left his shoes? And his coat?

Marco couldn't let himself consider what had happened. His gaze flitting around the hidden area, he was sure he was alone and no-one had seen him.

Splatters of blood on his jacket made him gasp. Then he remembered eating the meat. It wasn't blood. People often were mistaken that it was, weren't they, but he knew it was just juices from the muscle ligaments. Proteins broken down, not blood at all. He would still need to clean himself up, though.

Taking off his stained jacket, he folded it over his arm. It wasn't warm weather, but the exertion of the walk kept him comfortable. Once back at the council offices, Marco headed straight to the bathroom.

His reflection shocked him. Not reptilian, thankfully, but haggard. The meat juice had crusted around his mouth, and he was grateful not to have seen anyone.

How to concentrate on work? He had no choice. If his quota wasn't reached, awkward questions wouldn't help his situation. But not today. Today would have to pass with him staring at random pages of spreadsheets and emails and attempting to appear busy. Anyone interested enough to look would quickly tell he was winging it. But no-one did. Everyone gave him a wide berth.

A slow drive home filled him with dread. would today be the day Ebe needed to learn something of vital extra-terrestrial significance, and that... Thing... would be called upon if he were unable to provide sufficient support? Why not today? And if not, why not tomorrow; or the next day, or the day after that?

He couldn't live like that

FORTY-ONE

Ebe the genius

2019

Despite David's grumble, there was plenty of data. Ebe had known for a long time, as long as he could remember, what the plan was to be in December, 2020. Marco had shown him when he was very small.

It was very dangerous. And it wasn't just the flare of high frequency on arrival they had to be concerned about. As the current frequencies reacted, there would be a swing -back effect. Ebe liked to imagine whenever he was in the bath, that he was demonstrating the effect to a rapt audience, then he would become highly embarrassed that he would be naked on stage. Basically, as he shifted up and down the bath, the water rose one end, sloshing over the edge, but then would gush back in a sometimes more ferocious back flow to flood over his chest and onto the floor that end too.

What that meant in terms of the present situation was, apart from the immediate loss of water, there was another loss of equal measure from what was demonstrably an opposite force. If Earth's frequency soared high, then in re-stabilising, it might drop dangerously low. Anything below 5hz would turn the insides of every living thing on the planet into goo, killing them instantly. David wouldn't have considered that.

Despite the challenge, Ebe was confident there would be a way. There were methods to control and predict frequency surges that he would implement. As he'd said to his mother back in St Caradogs Hospital for the Mentally Disturbed - Marco doesn't understand it like I do. And it seemed Marco wasn't the only one.

In the room of one hundred Ebes, each prodigy was expected to work on ways to bring the supreme race to Earth safely. With one hundred minds, they projected teams of brilliance to thrash out the problem together. In reality, only a few had savant skills in the area needed. Lots came up with sci-fi solutions in line with an episode of Doctor Who. Without the good doctor to make things work, and a good scriptwriter, they were little short of ridiculous.

Ebe was thrilled that he had gravitated toward

Molly. Or she to him. And less pleased that David had seen fit to join their coupling.

Ebe had quickly learned that Molly had no knowledge that might be useful. She was ace at maths; solving equations and calculations quicker than a machine, but putting the results into practical situations appeared to cause her distress. Ebe planned to use her as a rubber duck. That is, to explain the problem to her from beginning to end in the hope the solution was already known to him and would show itself.

A rubber duck who capable of completing the calculations without him taking his mind away to use the computer was ace. She had asked some searching questions, too. But before Ebe had a chance to consider and answer, David butted in with a workable but flawed response every time. Ebe had enough.

"The problem is bringing the Aryans here will disrupt the frequencies, but we don't know what frequency they vibrate at so we will need to allow for more than is likely just in case."

"Why are they coming?"

"I don't know," Ebe began.

"It has been prophesied in almost every religion. Not usually by name, but by reputation. They have abilities to manipulate what we all see as matter because they utilise the space in-between. What seems ordinary to them will seem like miracles to us, and the humans of Earth.

"Why is it important?"

"I told you. They promised, and lots of religions have foretold it." David was flustered. His answers usually proved thorough enough. He sighed; anyone human. Of course, a fellow hybrid would want deeper answers. Only now did he realise he hadn't thought. What would happen if they didn't come?

Ebe was thinking the same. "It must be important. A lot of effort has been put into our development. The rewards are likely to be great enough to take the risks. That's promising to me. It says they think there will be a solution they just don't know what it is. They trust us to find it. Probably if we don't, they will reconsider their position. We owe it to the furthering of our shared species to seize the opportunity. I'd like to do the things I imagine they can, wouldn't you?"

Molly touched his hand and smiled. "Yes," she said. Ebe stared at her hand in wide-eyed wonder. Being touched by strangers was never something he tolerated lightly. But this felt good. In fact, it felt wonderful.

"But you made an excellent point with your question. If it's fulfilling a prophecy and to show their evolution to further ours, then perhaps one being, coming alone, may be the answer. If they need something from the planet's rich mineral deposits and that's the real reason they're coming, still sending one scout is a marvellous idea. We'll see exactly what happens, gain a datum for frequency, even if we have to assume a range of double, or treble our own, we should have much better data." Ebe's eyes flashed.

Molly gripped his hand and yipped, "Yes!"

"Yeah, I suppose," David agreed.

"I'll ask Marco." Ebe stood up and walked to the door. When the handle wouldn't work, Ebe rocked on the spot. "Oh, no! Oh, no. Oh, no..." Shaking the door, pushing, pulling as though the idea they were locked in was unthinkable.

A loud buzzing preceded the door opening and Marco stood at the door. "What is it, Ebe? Are you okay?"

"Why is the door locked? What if there was a fire? I hate being locked in."

"Stay calm. It's for your own safety; all of your safety. There are bears and other animals that might do you harm—serious harm—if any of you wandered off. You're so important, and we care about you. We just need to be sure where you are, that's all. Why were you trying to leave?"

Ebe weighed the options. It made sense, although it would have been nice to be told. Perhaps they were. He often missed things people said when he was thinking about something else. Marco would probably have said, to pass the blame to Ebe, not himself. Ebe would discount it this time. There were more important things to discuss. "I have a proposal..."

"Already! Well done," Marco clapped.

"Just the early glimmer of a plan."

"Go on..."

It took only moments for whoever was in charge to express admiration for Ebe's idea. One Aryan representative would arrive as soon as precautions had been made, then the real work would begin.

FORTY-TWO

Oumuamua

It was all happening rapidly. An Aryan ambassador was due to visit in a few days. It was deemed no special preparation was needed and that one being would be no more significant than a solar flare. Reports of aurora borealis being visible much further south than usual were predicted but not feared.

Studies could then be conducted and appropriate measures taken for their mass migration. Ebe was worried. He'd gone from concerned but confident they would find a solution, to considering the operation a little too rash. There were things to do even without sufficient data that would help with a radiation surge. Staying indoors; making sure predicted weather wouldn't send the radioactive material swirling around the globe. Hazmat suits and breathing apparatus were precautions

Ebe thought were sensible. It was a big thing to introduce to the world without the main population being made aware.

It wasn't even Ebe's field of expertise. His voice was ignored and the so-called experts' advice tolerated as gospel. He hoped they knew what they were doing.

Meanwhile, the one hundred special researchers working with Ebe were at a loss with nothing to do apart from hang around the mess hall. Not permitted to venture beyond the base unsupervised due to the threat of bears, Ebe felt hemmed in. There was consolation in the form of Molly who had scarcely left his side. David had relinquished his role as her best friend and had taken to sitting a couple of tables away and pretending he hadn't noticed them.

"What do you think about all this, Ebe?" Molly stroked his arm again, a sensation he was growing fond of.

"All what?"

"Oh, you know; us all being hybrids with particular skillset to bring the supreme race back to Earth."

Ebe shrugged. "I suppose I wasn't keen growing up. Always feeling different from everyone else. I never really got other people: what they were thinking, or why they did the things they did. I learned to decipher most of it over the years."

"You used the past tense a lot there. Do you think this is it for the human race?"

Ebe gulped. His mum in the hospital, waiting on his promise to return when it was safe. He had to believe he'd see her again. She was the only person important to him. "It will be okay, I think."

"I hope so. I'd like to hang out with you when all this is done with. Would you want that?"

Ebe's eyes flashed, a smile playing on his lips as he quickly agreed. What now? He had no clue. So, he was surprised and thrilled when Molly threw her arms around him and held him in a tight cuddle.

"What's all this, you two. No fraternising on duty." Marco stood over them with a frown. "I'm responsible for you, Ebe. If you get distracted and don't perform as well as you should, I'll be seen as culpable."

"We're just having some fun, Mr Paulo," Molly smiled at him. "While we wait for the Aryan to arrive from Oumuamua."

"What do you know of that?"

"I know it's an interstellar craft that has been in the earth's solar system since November 2017. I follow NASA findings. It's a passion of mine."

Of course, it is. Marco shook his head. "Well, make sure you don't get too distracted, either of you, okay?" Marco's smile dropped as soon as he turned away. Ebe had long accepted Marco's explanation and version of what to expect. He did his own brief research. He wouldn't buy a pair of shoes without Googling all the features and benefits of every shoe on the market. Fortunately, he was surprisingly disinterested in what was to come. 'We'll see,' had been his pat response, but what if Molly filled his head with different data? Who was she even here with? Some of the extra biological entities had not the benefit of Marco's unique perspective. Whoever ran the project must have had their reasons for developing skills differently in different ones. As far as Marco was concerned, Ebe was all that was required and all the others were failed attempts at creating him. And he'd tolerate nothing to interfere with his progress. Bide his time. Not cause undue stress when things were so delicate.

FORTY-THREE

Takeover

1997

He arrived home as he had at work: by surprise, with no recollection of the journey. Numb, he pushed open the front door.

Carys seemed pleased to see him and he was astonished dinner was underway. It was amazing what a bit of support did for someone.

"That smells nice, my love,"

"Roman Lamb. My mom used to make it."

A pleasant evening passed, but Marco couldn't focus on anything, and if quizzed he wouldn't be able to recall any conversations, or what they watched on TV.

And then he woke in bed, with a jolt.

"What's the matter?" Carys was sitting upright,

Ebe thankfully still unconscious, drool sliding from his mouth onto Carys's nightie.

With a shrug, he said, "I don't know. I had a nightmare, I think."

"You were screaming. It's a miracle Ebe slept through it."

Marco closed his eyes, but there was no way he was going to go back to sleep. With a jerk he swung his legs from the bed and let his feet hunt around for his slippers. Locating one, he knew the other couldn't be far. On his hands and knees, he soon found it shoved under the bed. Stood up at last, he asked in an exaggerated whisper. "I can't sleep, would you like a cup of tea?"

"No, thank you." Carys closed her eyes but as he reached the door she called out, "You may as well make me one. I can leave it if I fall asleep."

As the kettle bubbled, Marco's dream strayed into his thoughts demanding explanation.

He was under the bridge again. The man lay motionless beneath him as he spat venom into his face. Still and silent, it was clear slamming him into the ground had killed him.

The hunger took over then. It would satisfy my, er... my needs, and get rid of the evidence, Marco justified his horrific idea.

Razer teeth cut into the poor man's throat as sharp claws sliced and scraped the clothes first, then the skin. Frenzied, his teeth and claws ran all over his body. The memory might have been vague, or he was protecting himself from the worst of it. The next image was post-feast and there was no sign of the homeless man. Blood on his hand, he knew what he'd done.

The taste of the man's flesh, good and meaty as he liked, also had a tang that repulsed him. What had this creature put in his body?"

Waking with a start and Carys asking what was wrong didn't fade the memory. It was with a sickening surety, he knew that's what it was.

He would return to the scene of the crime and pray the homeless man was back with his belongings. Sleep was too dangerous tonight. Carefully taking Carys her tea, Marco returned downstairs where he waited wide awake until morning.

As soon as dawn broke, Marco had to see again the site of his crime. Or not crime, he prayed.

Four minutes in the shower, he was grateful they were still asleep, he plucked his clothes from the chair in the bedroom. Clutched in his damp arms, he dumped them on the landing and put them on at the top of the stairs.

With a gentle call of, "Bye," in case Carys was listening, he scurried downstairs and out to his car. Crunching into reverse, Marco didn't wait for the windows to defog and screeched from the close.

The roads were busy as always. Where was everyone going in this underpopulated corner of Britain? He wondered what their stories were. He doubted any of them would believe his own, and that was a comfort.

Parking closer than the civic centre car park, Marco scampered down the embankment and headed to the bridge. When he reached it, he laughed. It had all been a nightmare; a vision. Palm on his face, he chortled more. “Marco, you are cracking up.” Stress of work, of Ebe, of a mentally disturbed wife, lack of sleep. It took its toll. The reason for his positivity rolled over in its sleeping bag and gasped.

Marco gasped too. This was an unfamiliar face. Very different. This one belonged to a girl. “Excuse me. Is this your stuff?”

The girl sat up and glared at him. “Of course, it is. Find yer own.”

She can’t have assumed he was homeless in his smart, clean clothes. “There was a man here yesterday. I imagine it’s his gear.” Would she answer, *‘He’s dead’*?

“It’s mine. Get lost, buddy.” Marco’s stare searched under the bridge for signs of the other man. “Look, leave me alone now. Unless you’ve got some spare change for a cuppa?”

This was exactly what he spent his working day trying to alleviate. Mums with four kids by different dads were priority on the housing list. Or rather, the kids were. It wasn’t their fault their mother hadn’t worked it out just yet. People without homes were given a grant to buy a tent or a sleeping bag. It occurred to him the other man might have been trying to steal this girl's belongings rather than the other way around. He mellowed his tone as he searched his pockets. The guy who was here yesterday, I'm trying to locate him. Do you know where he went?"

The girl shrugged. "In the river for all I care."

Marco's world collapsed once again as the straw to which he'd fixed his hope blew away. Of course, it was true. He hadn't really ever doubted it.

2019

"Is he always so controlling," Molly scowled after Marco as he left the mess hall.

Ebe shrugged again. "He's been good to me. He's not my dad. My mum said my biological father was one of the others."

"A Grey?" Molly shuddered.

"Yes. Why, aren't you?"

"Apparently not, no. It's just that I'm super-interested in a bunch of stuff. They diagnosed with Asperger's Syndrome when I was eight or nine, but it's never really bothered me."

"Me too," Ebe grinned. "I assumed we all were, and for the same reasons. So, who's your dad?"

"He's called Alan. I'm not sure if he is my real father, but I've never really asked. We're nothing alike, and I have heard Mum and Dad arguing about it, but I was never that interested. He was there. He provided for me and loved me. Who cares if someone else planted their seed? Not me."

"I sometimes wish I didn't know. When I was little, I didn't believe it. My mum is a bit of a nut case. She's even in mental hospital in Wales right now."

"So, why do you believe her? I don't think you're a half a grey alien. You look lovely to me."

It was the first such compliment Ebe had ever had. He liked it; before suspicion overtook. It was like those texts promising you'd won a competition you had never entered. Ebe refused to respond to those, and he wasn't sure he shouldn't treat Molly the same way. "It bothers you then, if it's true?"

Molly laughed. "Not at all. It's really cool. Imagine if I am mixed species too. It never occurred to me, but it's amazing to wonder."

"Marco's a reptilian," Ebe blew through his teeth, keen to see her response to his startling information.

"No way? He looks normal. Human."

"He does most of the time, but sometimes when it suits him, he changes. He said that part of him exists at a different frequency and he tunes in to it whenever he wants as easily as switching a radio station. I always think of it as another window open on my laptop. Two windows can be open with vastly different tabs, and you can switch between them at once."

"I bet you were scared to get on the wrong side

of him growing up."

"At first, I was terrified, but he showed me he was in control and I was fine. He really shaped me. More than Mum. Mum was just frightened all the time, but Marco understood things. Things that gave me a path when, being so different, I had no direction. I've been preparing my whole life for this. That's how I know it will work."

"Now you realise you're not so different after all, do you feel better?" She stroked his hand, and when he sighed that he did, she squeezed her arms around him again. "I'm pleased you're here, Ebe. I really like you."

"I really like you, too."

1997

Carys was in a black mood, and Marco wasn't coping. He was pretty sure it was down to him, and to find out he was about to do something he never expected he would do: ask Ebe. "What's wrong with Mummy, Ebe? Has Daddy done anything wrong?" Ebe looked blankly at him and he revised the question with a sigh. "Has *Marco* done something wrong?"

"Mummy was upset watching her program."

Marco thought he knew the answer. "What program, Ebe?"

"Aliens and U.F.Os"

"Was there anything in particular that upset her about aliens and UFOs?

Ebe shrugged. "Are they real, Marco?"

What should he say? From a parenting perspective there was one answer, but what would *they* want him to do?

He didn't care. Despite the compelling power, he hated them. Hated them more because of the power. It was what made it all seem so hellish; the exact opposite of what he'd been brought up to understand. Maybe that was the difference. Some people confronted with the possibility of the kind of strength he wielded would be thrilled. Perhaps that was the test. He had been, too. But look where that got him. It was time to fully accept what he was: a murderer. He needed to become as far removed from whatever they had in store for him as possible. But it terrified him.

He could deny the pleasure in feeling so... so... strong. He felt sick remembering his brief glee. But the thing that took over him was undeniable, and if it decided he wasn't providing the answers they required, he might lose himself to the beast completely. Then where would Ebe, and Carys, and everyone else for that matter, be?

So, he answered thoughtfully, but truthfully. "A lot of intelligent people, including your mother, think that they are, and others are adamant that they aren't."

"What do you imagine, Marco?"

He coughed. Why was he being irritatingly persistent? "I have days when I believe, and days when I don't." "And what about today?"

For heaven's sake! "Okay, Ebe, today I'd have to say, on balance, I think I probably do believe in aliens, yes. I didn't before, but now I do."

"Because we saw them on the spaceship?"

Marco felt faint. "What do you mean?"

"We went on the spaceship. I saw you. And I met my dad, and he showed me lots of my half brothers and sisters. He said I was going to work with them one day."

That was a lot to be telling a four-year-old. "I had a dream about seeing you on an alien craft, yes. That doesn't make it real."

Ebe ignored the objection. "Do you suppose they're nice? They seem nice, but they say things that aren't good."

Marco's heart thumped and ached. "What sort of things, Ebe?" he winced in anticipation.

"That humans are silly."

"Well, that's not very friendly, is it?" Ebe shook his head. "So, I'd probably have to say they're not good."

Marco felt the change happen instantaneously. What would transpire? Would he kill and eat his own stepson?

Just like under the bridge, he was taken completely with no notion of what he was doing.

He came round however long later in bed, Carys, stroking his chest. "Thank you," she said.

"For what?" He panicked, "Where's Ebe?"

"Asleep in his cot."

"What? Are you sure nothing's happened to him?"

"He's fine, look."

Marco peeped over the covers and saw Ebe peacefully snoring. "Why did you thank me? What did I do?"

"Ebe said you reassured him about a dream he'd had about aliens, and that you'd promised to protect him. It meant a lot to him. He's been bugging me all day about who his dad is and upset me. He said you explained it all."

What had he told him? Marco didn't recall saying anything. And it was all very well him being taken over at will to teach Ebe, but Marco vehemently disagreed with those teachings. And as for the other sickening indulgence, he wasn't prepared to risk those he loved, nor anyone else. He had to rid himself of this torment for good.

After a wonderful night's sleep cuddled up to Carys, Marco still felt restless. He would until he could get rid of the reptilian takeover. Having watched his dad purge countless members of his flock of demonic presence, he accepted it was where he would start. Not the same, but the thing inside him had evil intent and Marco was sure directing the power of God Almighty toward it would make things unpleasant for it, at least. He didn't need to understand how to deal with it. God knew, and that's all that mattered.

"You're early," Dan greeted him at the front

door in his dressing gown. "Come in. I can see something is bothering you. Carys?"

Marco shook his head. "Not really. She's being great, but I've got a problem."

"What sort of problem?"

Marco's throat constricted, fear and relief fought to express and all Marco could do was press his lips together and direct a pale smile at his dad.

"Give me ten minutes to shower and dress and I'll be with you, okay?"

"Of course. Thanks." He wanted help right now, but he shouldn't be unreasonable. Ten minutes would make no difference.

He stood and filled the kettle and the coffee machine. His dad might need some stimulation to wake up. The drip, drip, drip as the dark liquid percolated alerted Marco's bladder to the nearness of a toilet. Now he had thought it, he wouldn't relax until he went. And he didn't want to interrupt his dad mid-exorcism.

The smell of Palmolive delighted his nose and put him right back in his childhood; safe, even if he wasn't free to be himself. Maybe being himself was the problem. This demon had jumped on his taut emotions because he'd moved away from his father's teachings; away from God.

As he washed his hands, he glimpsed his reflection.

It was there.

In the mirror.

"If you continue with this, I will take over your body and execute your father, and your mother, and eat them in the vilest way. I'll bite their heads off and rip them apart. Or tear them inside out whilst they're still alive as a punishment for producing such a disloyal son. You have to tell your father you don't need him to do anything and leave."

"That's just what a demon would say. You're scared."

The lizard cackled. "It would be inconvenient and detrimental to Ebe's development for your annoying parents to become involved in his upbringing. You have to step up and do the job they have intended you for, or I'll do it completely myself and I will murder your parents just to show your ghost how fucked off I am. So, no. I'm not scared. But you should be. And if you're not, you will be."

"Are you in there, Marco?" a knock on the bathroom door and his mum's voice.

"Fine, Mum."

"Who are you talking to?"

"No-one. I'll be out in a minute."

Her slippered footsteps shuffled to the kitchen and Marco heard the making of coffee and tea.

"Excellent. I get to kill her first."

"You're afraid, demon. I'll never let you win. We'll see how you do against the power of Jesus Christ!"

The lizard shook his head. "Have it your way."

The last thing Marco remembered was seeing his arms change to scales and his skull crashing into the hanging light fixture as his height soared.

And then he woke up at his desk.

FORTY-FOUR

Fighting back

Punching the contacts in his phone, his thumb bending the screen to almost breaking at his urgency. "Come on, pick up the phone."

'You have reached the Paulo residence...'

Over and over Marco dialled, a whimper, caught in his throat, escaped into the room and drew the attention of hie colleagues.

"All right, Marco?" one leaned back in his chair to ask.

"Did you see me arrive? Did I seem okay?"

"Very calm and pleased with yourself. I assumed something had put a smile on your face. I'm surprised you're not bragging. You look the complete opposite of that now, mate. What's wrong? Lost a pound and found a penny?"

Marco frowned. What was that supposed to mean? Ignoring him, he wondered hopefully if they weren't answering because something his other self had said offended them, and not because they... Not because they couldn't.

He had to find out. "Er, something's cropped up. I'm going to have to leave the office for a bit."

His colleagues looked up like they couldn't care less. A few well wishes reached his ears before the door closed.

Sat behind his steering wheel, he turned onto the dual carriageway and he checked the mirror.

"They're dead, Marco. You must know that. And if you go back now, you'll be caught at the scene of the crime. You'll go to prison. *I'll* go to prison, and then Ebe will be left without his mentor."

Through the torture of picturing his mum and dad's bloodied remains, Marco had the half-thought that being in prison would be for the best. If we're in prison, we can't hurt anyone.

"It's not merely that I'm recommending you don't go back, Marco," his lizard reflection sneered. "I won't allow it. I won't let you go there."

Heart racing, he knew it was true. Any instant now the beast might take him over and there was nothing he could do about it.

Or was there?

A split-second decision. Careful to keep his mind blank; it was time for action, not thought. His thoughts could be read, but his actions. Well, he could make them count.

Something so vital without counsel from the

Bible, or his holy father was unthinkable, but what did that matter now? If he spent time thinking of a good plan, the lizard him would know about it and stop him. He had to act fast. Keeping his mind on triviality; the clouds, the birds, the traffic, he drove slowly, exiting the roundabout towards the council offices.

At the last second, he screeched around a corner and headed for the castle. Up, up, clipping the narrow stone gateway, he locked his knee straight and accelerated.

Even if he changed now, the speed and trajectory made his plan inevitable. Thirty, forty, fifty miles an hour, the car crashed through the fence at the end of the car park and burst into the air above a steep ravine. Out twenty feet before the nose dipped, he plunged towards the ground, and in less than a second, the bonnet splintered in two as it hit a tree.

In less time than that, Marco changed. As the car shattered, the strength and quickness of the reptilian escaped and landed feet away, unhurt and quietly pleased. Turning immediately back again, Marco; new Marco, whistled and walked from the smoking car. Unseen, he witnessed people far above peering over the edge and pointing at the crash.

A snapping twig caught his attention. A lady with a small dog stared at him, lips making silent Os as she stood trembling.

"Sorry, I can't afford to have witnesses." Marco

changed and leapt on the woman, tearing at her neck.

Nips at his ankles made no impact, but irritated, so Marco flicked the dog and laughed as it landed in a bush, scurrying in the opposite direction. "You won't tell anyone, will you, scamp?"

No remains were left of the woman. Any cloth that didn't have enough flesh to make it tasty, the beast forced down for convenience before changing effortlessly into Marco and strolling back into work.

"You feeling better again, Marco? What was wrong?"

"Notification on my phone. Someone broke into my car. It's gone."

"What? Oh, no! That's terrible. You look happy now, though."

Marco grinned. "Well, I've been thinking about selling it, and I just remembered it's insured."

The colleague smiled, bobbing his head, but as he looked away, he rolled his eyes and shook his head. "Weirdo," he sighed under his breath.

Marco had swift regrets about the full takeover he'd badgered old Marco into allowing. The council work was as dull as anything he could think of.

He called the local police and reported his car stolen. When he had an incident number, the insurance would pay out and he might enjoy trying out some new cars. He thought of Carys.

That was something else he could enjoy. He phoned the doctors and made an appointment to discuss a vasectomy. They couldn't take any chances. Offspring would be most incompatible and undesirable.

Then he tried to focus his mind on the figures in front of him for homelessness in the county and possible solutions. He smiled. Well at least he'd helped get one off the housing list, he thought, and laughed again.

With a sigh, he'd had enough. Dialling from the office phone, the mobile presumably destroyed in the crash, Marco bobbed his head listening to the ring-ring.

"Hello?"

"Hi, Dad. Can I ask a favour? Would you mind picking me up from work? My car's been stolen."

"Oh, Marco, that's awful. Yes, of course." Dan gave a cough. "What happened this morning? Woke me up, and then disappeared without saying goodbye."

"Sorry. The office phoned. Some poor homeless guy needed my help urgently."

Dan's pride was almost palpable. "You're a good boy, Marco. If you still want help when I pick you up, I'm free all afternoon."

"Thanks, Dad. But I'm fine. Never better."

"Apart from your car being stolen."

"It's merely material. Insured material, at that. I'm really not bothered. I'd rather not inconvenience you, that's all."

"Not a bit of it, son," Dan oozed pride. "Glad to help."

Marco stood up. "My dad's picking me up. I need to get back home and sort out this pesky car business. What with getting married, moving house, and having a baby, I can't remember what I've done with the paperwork."

"Tell me about it!" his colleague chuckled.

Marco merely rolled his eyes and jutted his chin to get another laugh. It might be boring, but this being human was a pretty easy gig. And it was all for a good cause. Perhaps the worthiest cause of all. If there were a few casualties along the way, in the scheme of things, it didn't matter.

FORTY-FIVE

A new man

With a glint in his eye, Marco offered to take Ebe for a stroll, having witnessed Carys stressing over dinner. Her curves made his mouth moist, and he shook his head. He'd have to pay privately for the sterilisation of his human host. Resisting temptation would be too difficult to wait for the National Health Service waiting times. He could be seen within a week, and until then, he'd have to feign a headache.

"Where are we going, Marco?" Ebe asked as he was guided into the passenger seat.

"Just getting out of your mother's hair." Seeing the confusion on Ebe's face and anticipating him arguing that they'd been nowhere near her hair, he corrected his statement. "Giving her some peace to cook dinner without stress. There's something I want to show you."

As they drove, Marco set the scene. "You've expressed curiosity about the extra-terrestrials your mum watches on the telly. I may have been a bit vague before in my answers, but I want to come clean with you. They're real, and they are good. They are our friends."

Ebe stayed silent as Marco pulled through a gateway into an area of woodland on the edge of the town. "I'm taking you to meet one of them. Don't be scared."

It was difficult to tell if he was or not, but he had a future already cast and it was time his mother's negative indoctrination was shaken up. "Come on. Don't dawdle."

Further along a muddy track, into the trees they went, until the only sound was birdsong. Marco had deliberately taken a few turns so that if Ebe ran off, he wouldn't make it to the road before Marco could easily catch up with him again.

"Are you ready?"

Ebe nodded, eyes wide and unblinking.

"What do you think the alien will look like when you meet him?"

Ebe gulped and said nothing.

"Do you think he'll be naked with a big head the same as the ones you met on the spaceship?"

He nodded again.

"Well, not this one." Marco morphed into the eight-foot-high lizard, and within a second changed back to human form again, ready to reassure his protégé everything was fine. Ebe stared wordlessly, so Marco changed a second time. This time, still as his lizard self, he spoke. "I bet you didn't know I was an alien, did you?"

Ebe shook his head in jerks. "How are you doing that?"

Marco shifted again. "It's complicated, but basically, I'm two very specific beings existing at distinct frequencies. I can switch any time. The reason I've brought you out here because most people are scared when they see my other form. I knew you wouldn't be frightened, Ebe. That's why I've trusted you. But Mummy would be afraid, wouldn't she."

"She is scared of aliens."

"That's right, Ebe. So, we'll keep this our little secret, okay?" If he didn't agree by choice, Marco knew he could scare compliance into him if he needed to.

"I won't tell."

"Good boy. But now you know, there might be other secrets I have to tell you as you grow older. Don't worry. It's nothing you wouldn't like. In fact, I'm certain you'll like it very much indeed."

As Ebe grinned up at him, Marco considered how well it had gone. His stepson really was special. And now at last, thanks to him, the world could be allowed to find out just how special he was.

FORTY-SIX

Arrival

2019

Ebe was disgusted. He and his comrades were once again locked in the room, for their own safety, they were told. In case the radiation from their visitor hurt them. They were far too important to the big picture to risk.

He had tests he wanted to conduct. Being inside should protect from immediate radiation, but the vibration was another matter. What frequency would the evolved Aryan vibrate at, and could he rely on him being a typical subject? The ambassador must have been picked for a reason. Once deemed safe, Ebe was desperate to test some theories.

He knew that groups of people emit a higher frequency than individuals. From his vast understanding about light and sound waves, the intensity would be multiplied. It was the incentive for suggesting that a singular Aryan to come first. But he didn't yet know how multiple humans together would affect the Aryans. Would destructive interference cancel one another harmlessly, or would waves of energy grow so huge as to be catastrophic? Thousands of calculations confirmed by computers had predicted infinite possibilities, the vast majority of which were not good news. Not for homo-erectus anyway.

It would be a tough thing to test, of course. But measuring the frequencies separately would negate the risks and Ebe could quickly calculate infinite probabilities as to the safety, or not, of the rest of the supreme population returning.

He knew testing would be done, but would whoever conducted them in the most useful way? People often missed out the most crucial information because they didn't understand. He would have to wait and see. Perhaps there would be no need to put himself in danger.

Marco wasn't allowed in the greeting party either. But unlike Ebe, he was pleased about it. Real Marco might have been fascinated, calling her an angel, or questioning everything he had spent his life believing. But new Marco, the shapeshifting Alpha Draconis reptile couldn't care less. He hoped the tests would be done quickly to begin the age of Aquarius officially and his kind secure what they had been promised.

For now, eating and drinking the American snacks suited him well whilst he waited. His first taste of Hershey's had disappointed, but he acquired a taste for it over the week. And with a lack of available meat, filling up on sugar took his mind off his cravings.

Unwrapping his third bar of the morning, he wondered if there would be a detectable shift when he arrived. He suspected not. Not at once, anyway. But when they all came, there would be a shift in climate, and related natural disasters within weeks. What could the EBEs do about it? He understood everything broken down into maths equations, but that didn't automatically provide the wherewithal to do anything. Knowing a bullet is travelling towards you at twelve thousand feet per second doesn't make it easier to dodge.

Marco bit into the gooey chocolate and nodded to his own logic. But his brownie points for trying were assured. That was what really mattered.

He had become used to the daylight hours and was surprised they were much the same as back in Wales. He had expected days of darkness and other days of never-ending sunlight, but that didn't happen. So, when darkness enveloped the small island, Marco was once again shocked. Until he stepped outside.

Covering the sky and blocking out the sun entirely was a huge football stadium sized spaceship hewn from solid rock. He'd never understood how those things stayed in the air. Species from around the universe had explained to him how it absorbed energy from stars and transmuted it into useable power for flight. That didn't explain what he saw.

Hovering high above them, the cigar shaped rock looked like a skimmed stone, paused; a Hollywood special effect. What would the tourists think? Oh, he remembered. The island had been closed for a few days for military manoeuvres. That meant, despite its size, the Cambrian cigar wouldn't be seen by anyone they didn't want to see it. The nearest landmass being thousands of miles away meant they were effectively shielded.

No dramatic shift in energy came. Just a big rock floating in the sky.

Marco noticed the tapping on his arm. Where was he? He quickly realised he was lying on the floor outside the mess hall. He'd fainted? How embarrassing.

"You were told to stay indoors. We can't have you disobeying orders because you assume you know best."

He could mutate and rip this human to shreds in seconds. Fists clenched, he knew he had to keep in control. It wouldn't be tolerated. But he was so hungry and this arsehole was pushing it. On his knees, he wobbled, and the officer hooked an arm under his to help him up. Why was he so weak?

With a step back, the officer regarded Marco. "The guest is in the main hall over there. The Greys are with him now, but they want someone reptile next, to see how you're affected."

"Well, you can see how I'm affected. I fainted."

"Perhaps in your other form you can withstand it."

He wanted to say, 'Find someone else,' but he felt filled with sudden confidence. And how impressed would Ebe be if he met the supreme being? Enough to listen to him about staying away from the weird girl? "Okay, when?"

"Tomorrow. Let them get their baseline results, and then we'll know how you affect one another." The officer looked down at his shoes, then back up at Marco. "We will need a hybrid, too. Probably not your boy, though. He's somewhat indispensable, I understand."

That would be a tough one to sell, but Ebe had no choice. If he came up with a solution, he would be able to visit the supreme beings as much as he wanted. And if he didn't, then it would be the least of his worries. "Okay. How should I prepare?"

The officer laughed. "I don't know. What can you do? Maybe ask your boy." He held a smile for a while, then turned abruptly. "Right, I'll be getting off, and see you tomorrow after you've had something to eat."

Ebe was pleased to see him.

"So, son, I'm going to be one of the first to make contact. I fainted yesterday just from being outside."

"Yes! I knew it. Keeping inside will help when the rest of them arrive. Keep an eye on the weather, Marco. There will likely be bush fires and tornados."

"Good. It'll warm the place up."

"Not here. It depends on the wind direction. Maybe Japan, or south to Washington, or California."

Marco felt out of his depth. "Well, I'm going to see him in my other form. Like this," he indicated his body, "I'm no use. I can't even reside safely on the same island."

"Good luck."

"They want one of you, too."

Ebe's face drained of colour. Molly looked over from another table having given them privacy, itching to come and see if her new companion was okay as she locked gaze with Marco. Don't upset my friend, she implored. "I can't do it. Not without more figures. If it knocked you unconscious; and you're used to shifting frequencies; I couldn't cope."

"Don't worry, that's what I told them. I've convinced them not to take you, but they will insist on one of the others. Data is needed, or you all may be at risk."

Ebe's gaze glistened, and he gulped, grateful and guilty. Who was it that would be forced to do what he was too scared to? Her eyes burnt into him and he jerked round to meet her stare. No, not her. He glared and shook his head, but then he realised she wouldn't understand what they'd been talking about, so she'd be puzzled. Forcing a smile, seeing hers drop, he stuttered to Marco that he had to go.

"Not to see that girl."

"Why? She's confused." Shit, he wanted her out of Marco's head. Go away, Molly, go away.

"You're getting uncomfortably close to her, son. It's not healthy. You have an important job to do."

Ebe remembered a significant fact. "She'd be no good for meeting the Aryan. She said her dad is human anyway."

"Well, she's wrong."

Ebe shrank into himself, arms folding over one another in continuous motion like mating snakes, sweat beaded on his forehead and dark circles grew in his pits. Marco sighed. "Don't worry about her. Worry about me. What can I do to prepare myself?"

Subject changed, Ebe took the instruction not to fret about Molly at face value. "I don't know, Marco. I have no data for your species so can't have an opinion on whether your other self will survive. Against radiation, I expect, but not against a drastic and abnormal change in your vibration. But I don't know what vibration is normal for you. Humans are around three to seventeen hertz. Quite a variation. You've always said your other self exists at a different frequency. Do you know what that is? Is it higher or lower?"

Marco shook his head. "You know I have no clue."

"Well, I think you should refuse. You might not survive."

"This seems ridiculous. I've lived twenty years in an alien body, spent time with species from other times and dimensions. What's so special about the bloody Aryans?"

Ebe shrugged. "I'm not religious. But I can tell you that your own rate rising or falling rapidly is likely to induce an expected physical response. You must have heard how whale song knocks divers unconscious? And in World War II, the French and Germans both experimented with frequency disturbances. Attempts to knock planes out of the sky with sound were unsuccessful, but imagine!" Ebe danced on the spot. "In France, they developed a lower than three hertz sound that melted the internal organs of participants, so they gave it up as a bad job."

"So, you're saying that could happen to me?"

Unnaturally bright, Ebe grinned. "It might. You may well faint, and then afterwards drop into a pile of goo." He laughed, then halted. "But seriously, you could."

"What are the chances I'll be unscathed?"

Ebe tilted his head from side to side, "Well, as a shapeshifting being yourself, you are used to living at different frequencies. You're like a bull shark."

Marco pulled his head away. "How am I like a fish?"

"They live in the sea, which is salty. But they mate in rivers. It's a whole different process for breathing. Some animals even thrive purely on sulphur in the centre of the planet. Who knows what you're capable of?"

Fear blew through Marco's lips. What choice did he have? Recalling times when Ebe had made simple things sound the most complicated decision in the world, he had to put his faith in those willing to risk it. The all-wise Aryans would know, wouldn't they? No, Ebe understood. The supreme beings were a misnomer. Enlightened in otherworldliness, useless in practical terms. Like an absent-minded professor, ace at his specialist field, can't make a cup of tea. He would have to excuse himself and remind them how important his continued existence was to the mission overall. "Thanks, Ebe. Don't worry. You have persuaded me it's a bad idea."

Ebe grinned. "I'm glad you asked me."

There was no obvious chain of command. They'd been shown around the base briefly. Just where they were expected to go; the EBE room, the mess hall and the bunk house. Everywhere else looked the same but had purposes unknown to him. He wouldn't simply await his fate to be collected by someone in a uniform he didn't recognise, to take him to what was unlikely to be good for him.

Wandering around, going from door to door, none of them opened to him but he suspected his disoriented wanderings would attract attention and he was right.

"What are you doing out of confines?" a question from behind, he turned to a heavily armed scowl. The gun muzzle jerked to direct him back to the familiar sites.

"I'm due to meet our guest tomorrow but I have some misgivings."

"Misgivings?" The soldier snorted. "I bet you do. Why are you out here?"

"I need to speak to someone. I'm going to make other arrangements."

"Get your ass to quarters, and I won't have to shoot you."

"If you shoot me, I won't be able to meet our guest."

"You won't be able to meet anyone..."

He barely got the word out when Marco flipped to his full form, swiped and knocked the soldier to the floor. Gun yanked from his neck, Marco threw it out of reach. "Oh, dear. You can't shoot me now."

A net shot over Marco and men holding it scooped him into a ball dropping him to the floor. "Easy, there, you lizard freak."

The first soldier, brushing himself off, stepped over him. "I could shoot you now, you stupid fuck." He spat on him. "Take him away. I'll tell Colonel Alan we've got a cowardly lizard on our hands." Bending down to Marco on the floor, he sneered, "You won't get out of it that easily. And this display of disloyalty has made you all the more disposable."

The rough ground hurt as his eight-foot bulk was dragged away. He knew he'd be punished, but if he convinced them of his significance, at least he might stay alive.

He returned to his human form to calm his captors. At a table, sitting on a chair, free to move if he wanted, he waited for the colonel to come and tell him what a naughty boy he was and what a disappointment. He didn't care. So long as he wouldn't have to confront the being that might turn his insides into goo just by looking at him, a bollocking was nothing. He was pleased not to be tied to the chair, but he knew the machine-gun toting guards would quickly immobilise him again if he became violent.

The door swung open and a bustling officer stormed into the room. As he pulled out the chair opposite him, it scraped the floor with a sharp screech. "Now, what's all this, Marco Paulo, eh?"

"All what, sir," Marco added grudgingly.

"They tell me you're not keen on meeting our supreme guest tomorrow. Is that right?"

Marco shook his head. "My genius stepson has convinced me I may not come out of an encounter alive."

"Nonsense. Of course, you will. It's a great honour to be asked."

"I'm sure it's less of a privilege than you and your cronies deciding I'm the most expendable reptilian here."

"You're the only reptilian here."

"Now I know you're a liar. There was another introduced to us on the first day we came."

"True, but he has been called on another mission."

"What's more important than what we're doing here?"

"Nothing. I didn't say it was of greater importance. Like I say; chosen to represent your species meeting the first arrival of the Aryans is an honour, and you will do it."

"Why is it so important? Why do you care if my species are wiped out when they arrive?"

"Frankly, Marco, it would suit me if you were. But mine is not to reason why. Mine, like yours, is to do as I'm fucking told. Now you will meet our Aryan arrival tomorrow as planned. Understood?"

"What if I refuse?"

"I see I'm going to have to restrain you. It's a shame. I'm told the added stress can have a negative effect on your vibration. We'll have to take what we can get, though."

"Don't restrain me. I'll do it."

"I'm not sure. You might be planning an escape. You wouldn't get very far, but it would be an awful inconvenience to come and find you. And what if you got eaten by a bear or something before you escaped to safety? Or, what if someone gave the order to shoot to kill the traitor? It might be better to make sure you don't try. You only have yourself to blame."

"Please, no. I won't be any trouble."

"It wouldn't be difficult to explain how you turned violent and we had to shoot you. Remember, I don't give a shit about you. Don't make killing you the easiest way to stop the pain in my ass."

Marco sighed. "Fine. I hope you know what you're doing and I survive unscathed."

"I never said I knew what I was doing," the colonel chuckled, "But I hope you make it out alive too, for what it's worth."

One day, I'll get you alone and rip your snivelling head off your shoulders, Marco thought as the door closed and locked behind him. Even though his freedom had been an illusion his whole life, being physically detained stuck in him; a festering splinter ready to burst.

FORTY-SEVEN

An unwanted honour

Marco hadn't slept. If these were his last moments on Earth, he didn't want to spend them unconscious. He didn't believe they were, but somewhere inside he must have feared it. Reassurances were scant, that was for sure. Unrestrained for the entire night, he had been brought his chosen selection from the mess hall breakfast menu which he devoured as heartily as ever he had. It surprised him he had an appetite. But then, death row inmates were always famously enthusiastic about their last meal, weren't they? If he believed this was his, he'd have preferred the colonel's head instead.

The door locks clinked open and two armed guards appeared. A third man whisked his tray away, and the colonel entered behind him. "Time to do your duty… I mean, time to receive the greatest honour your species has ever known. On your feet, son."

Was he determined Marco should kill him? Marco smiled and stood. "I can't wait."

Flanked by the two armed men, as they approached a building away from the main site, Marco's knees buckled. The men with him had turned a nasty shade of ill, and had slowed their pace. "You can't seriously expect me to go in there?" Marco shook his head.

"Change now. You'll be fine. Then follow your nose."

"What? You aren't coming with me?"

"Love to, son. But we're not up to it. These guys will escort you."

Radiation-suited men appeared from a doorway. "Your vibrations will be monitored and if they get dangerously high, or low, we'll alert you, don't worry."

"Too late. I'm worried."

"The radiation is raised, but tolerable for a brief visit. Particularly in your other guise."

"Don't I get one of these radiation suit thingies?"

"You won't need it. There are other things we need to measure where that would be a hindrance. It's important to the supreme beings that you are not harmed, so just trust. That's my advice."

"Thank you," Marco said, morphing into his other self.

"Good luck," the colonel said, as Marco walked

through the door. He didn't thank him.

The corridor was lined with unfamiliar material. From the barrack quality shacks dating from the sixties, this seemed incongruously futuristic. "How far is it?"

"A way. We're not sure what a safe distance is. The room is vacuum sealed and coated with four feet of concrete. But people on the base are still suffering the effects. You'll be okay for a while and we can see what it does to your vibrations. The door is at the end of the corridor. We won't follow you, for your safety as much as our own."

"So kind of you," Marco sneered.

"Larger groups emit more, or sometimes less vibrational energy because of wave enhancement or destructive interference. It's just physics."

"But I'm sure you'd love to join me otherwise, wouldn't you?"

Ignoring the jibes, the instructions continued. "As I mentioned, it's a vacuum. That means going through an airlock to access the room. Open the first door; it isn't locked. MAKE SURE to fully close it before opening the second door or it could slam back and slice you in half."

"Your limbs grow back anyway, don't they?" A previously silent guide piped up.

Marco glared and added him to his kill list. "Okay. Let's get this over with," he said, glad to leave the humans behind. If it was safer for reptilians to meet the Aryans, maybe their arrival would be more fortuitous than he had given thought to. There was reason to be excited for it to happen that Marco wasn't in on. Perhaps the eradication of the Aryan pet species was worth it.

Unsure if it was his vibrations altering, but a throbbing, pulsating humming noise made him giddy. *OwooOwwoOwwoo* pulsated all around him and when he reached the doors, he could barely stretch his scaly fingers out for the handle. Should he really be going in? His mind screamed no, but he felt oddly compelled. Not because he cared about disappointing his human colleagues, but something far greater. His leathery scaled hand touched the metal, and he jolted from the shock. Still in his grasp, he turned it and the door opened. He remembered the instructions to close it fully, but they seemed unnecessary as it slammed into place. He checked the seals anyway. There was no way it would shut firmer.

The second door felt impossible to open, but when he prized it a crack, it flew back on its hinges and smacked the wall behind. Inside, the *whobwhobwhob* of the humming was painfully intense. Against his better judgement, he pushed the door closed again. He was now in the vacuum with a power he had never imagined. A nuclear core brightness of every colour on the spectrum burnt his lidless eyes, blinding him.

From the brilliance, a voice came, feminine in quality, but oddly male in another sense.

Androgynous, Marco decided. "Greetings, dear one," the voice echoed through the room. "We thank you for your bravery in sitting here with me today. I shall try not to keep you for too long, as your wellbeing is of utmost importance."

In his mind he said, thank you, but he had no words. Filled with a sensation of surrealism, he wanted desperately to see who was talking to him. As though reading his thoughts, the being of light honed into view, blocking just enough of the brightness to be visible in the shadow.

Marco was less sure of the gender of the being when he saw it. It was the most beautiful living thing he had ever seen. His mind baulked at the attraction of another species, but, of course, his kind's interaction with humans had been in place for centuries. And human was what this looked like.

Shoulder length platinum hair, bright blue eyes and flawless complexion. Looking slightly down on him, the being was tall. "I sense your vibration soaring, dear one. It is time for you to leave soon. Do you have anything you wish to ask?"

Marco's mouth wouldn't work, but the being of light responded to his thoughts.

"You are aware, are you not, of the real reason for the hybrid children?"

'Yes', Marco thought, his head bowing slowly.

"The simple solution to a simple problem has caused them great excitement, just as was predicted. Thank you for keeping the secret."

'Well, it wouldn't do for them to know the human species isn't expected to survive.'

"We expect them to survive, dear one."

'I've seen the predictions. 51% survival of some of the species. That means a lot of them won't make it.'

"The enlightened will be fine."

'And the rest?'

"Will cease to be, as their frequency falls to dangerous vibrations. That's if they don't murder one-another first."

The being looked to Marco as though he/she was smiling, but it didn't seem much to smile about. Anger at the injustice grew in his chest.

"Let your negative emotion go, dearest one. It will be instantly transmuted to light. Your reptilian body is robust, but your animalistic rage could be your downfall. Guard against your anger, dear one. Your vibrational frequency has already risen higher than you have ever experienced. In stabilising, you may find yourself prone to unusual bouts of anger.

"Go for a walk. Let it pass and you will be fine. Not everyone will. Only light can exist in our presence, but in eradicating the darkness, there will be casualties of those unaware of shadows they harbour. Disease, war, pestilence, famine will all visit upon our human creation and what will be left will be worthy of survival."

'They see you as gods. They are so eager for

your arrival, but I see you as evil.'

"Everything we do, we do from love." Marco snorted, and the Aryan smiled. "People ask 'If God exists, why do bad things happen?' We greet this question with love and wry amusement. We have provided free will, and they have used it to destroy their beautiful home. When frequencies shift and many of their number return to God, they call it a disaster. But a disaster for whom?

"They accept death as part of life, and therefore as part of God's creation, yet when it happens, they cry that God cannot be real. All those for whom the higher vibration is too much; whose bodies do not cope will be returned to their creator as the light they have always been. As, indeed, you and, ourselves have always been. It is not sad. It is not a disaster. It is not evil. Quite the opposite. It is a reset for the planet; for our experiment. It has been fascinating, and now it's time for the new age."

"What if I tell the humans the truth?" Marco found his voice at last.

"It is of no consequence now. Those who are here for you to tell must surely already be aware. The hybrid children would be alarmed. Their preoccupation with their simple task was a genius idea, but as I know you are aware, they are here as our safeguard. If all of humanity is destroyed, our creation will live on at least partly."

"So you want them to procreate. I assumed

offspring would be an abomination."

The being beamed. Her appearance changed to a dark-skinned masculine figure. Equally beautiful and equally perfect. "It would be a fascinating experiment. But as I stated, we are expecting a survival rate for humans that will repopulate the planet with a newly enlightened generation. Heaven on Earth. Utopia. Call it what you will. We are very proud of our creation.

"Bringing the hybrid children here to safety is our insurance for this unpredictable planet. A contingency plan. A breeding ground for a new species if it should prove necessary. That isn't to say we are not interested in continuing the experiment, whatever happens.

"I hope our hybrid friends have the data they need to smooth our safe amalgamation into the ecosystem. Their program of research isn't entirely without merit. We have many new things to share and will be delighted if we discover more enlightenment than is predicted, whilst happily resolved to the alternative plans if enlightenment has failed. It is the right time.

"Our presence has been sensed and predicted for millennia. I see the blurring of sexuality and genders has already happened, and a growing population favours the planet's ecology over established governments. It is definitely time for our new age of divine rule. It is the age of Aquarius."

His handsome face creased with concern. I

detect it is becoming overwhelming for you, Marco. So with gratitude for all you have done to safeguard our arrival; and in keeping our secrets, I thank you, and bid you farewell for now."

Marco couldn't speak. His throat constricted, and he edged to the door. The male/female being waved, and before it slammed shut, he heard them say, "Much love to you, dearest one."

FORTY-EIGHT

Transparency

"Are you okay?"

The voice came from nearby and he didn't recognise it. Was it the Aryan again? A touch of his arm and he knew it couldn't be. Eyelids still in defence mode from the searing spectrum of light took time to adjust to the lack of threat and allow themselves to be opened. It was a hospital type room. Not like Withybush, more like MASH. A nurse wearing green coveralls peered at him from beside the bed.

"You've been out for quite a while."

It was a croak, but Marco found his voice. "How long is quite a while?"

The nurse checked her watch clipped upside down to her pocket. With a squint and side mouth she answered, "Twenty-nine hours."

Marco blew through his lips. When had he returned to his human form? He smiled. "That's a good sleep. Er, how am I doing apart from that?"

"Medically sound. Normal observations. Definitely different to when they found you." The nurse fondled the hem of the bedsheet and looked away.

"Come on, you can't leave me hanging. What changed?"

"Obviously you were unconscious. It was still apparent when you came in. I know because I was working this time yesterday as well."

"What? What was obvious?"

"You were glowing. No, it was more than that; like you weren't really there. See-through almost. You look perfectly normal now."

Marco didn't want to assume the nurse knew his dual identity but had to ask. "I looked human though, did I?"

"Human? Yes. A see-through glowing human. Vibrating at a whole new frequency I was told, but I don't know about that. It must have dropped to normal now."

"Or your frequency has risen to join mine," Marco replied.

Her face swelled, eyes bulging, "Is that a thing?"

Marco shrugged. "Maybe it's something I've heard. But it makes sense, doesn't it? If you think about radio stations. If you hear a fuzzy noise, it gets clearer when you tune into it. Perhaps you've tuned into me."

A uniformed guard entered the room. "You're

looking better." He turned to the nurse. "When is he safe to come out and re-join the base?"

"A couple of days, I don't know. We don't really understand what we're looking for."

"No, I suppose not. There are some tests we want to conduct that would be safer in the lab, that's all. Time is of the essence."

"Okay, well, like I say, we don't understand the risks, so it's a bit hard to tell. Ask Doctor Roberts."

"Captain Roberts?"

"Correct. Now, Marco, is there anything you fancy to eat?"

"Meat. Lots of meat."

The uniform shook his head. The patient was back to normal, it seemed.

FORTY-NINE

Ebe the healer

"Are you worried about him?" Molly held Ebe in an embrace, his head flopped on her chest. He probably wasn't, but he'd say he definitely was if it meant she would keep cuddling him. "I'm sure he's fine."

"I'm more bothered about why he hasn't come. Marco can look after himself." The reptile rage Ebe had witnessed enough to fear filled his thoughts. If Marco hadn't survived an encounter with the Aryan visitor, what hope did the population have? "Especially as I warned him not to do it. He said he understood and would refuse to participate."

"They probably didn't give him a choice. I mean, is this really where you want to be? Stuck in here with all of us?"

Ebe couldn't imagine anything more wonderful. Molly made him forget. A change of priorities swirled in his mind. The successful implementation granting the Aryans access to Earth dropped to a woeful second place after keeping Molly safe. Perhaps finding a solution wasn't the best thing he could do with his time after all. Maybe, proving it would be a catastrophe would. But he wouldn't lie. It wasn't in him. The facts were the facts, the truth was the truth.

"Oh, here he is," Molly tried to inject glee into her tone, but something about Marco bothered her. "I'll leave you to it. I know you'll want to catch up.

Marco pulled out a chair next to Ebe and put his hand on his knee. Molly smiled a micro-smile and wandered away. "Well, you weren't wrong, Ebe. I was nearly a gonna by all accounts."

Ebe spun in his chair to face his step-monster-dad. "As, you know..."

"Yeah, of course. They could have sent any human in. I'm the only saurian here. The other one conveniently fucked off at the right time, didn't he. But after shining like a glow stick for a day, here I am unharmed."

"Glowing? Were you transparent?"

"Apparently, yeah. Why?"

"Do you know what your vibrational frequency rose to? That's really dangerous. It's what I feared. Are you radioactive?"

"Whoa, I don't have all the answers. Apparently, I make a Geiger counter click a bit, but in a range they have assured me is normal. Vibration, I don't have a clue. It went off the scale of the accelerometer thing they had, but it's back to healthy now."

"Around eight hertz?"

"Lower than that. About one or two. So, I'm well recovered."

Ebe frowned. "That's lower than normal human range. Lower than the fatal French experiments?"

"I'm not a normal human, am I."

"How do you feel?"

"Great. Better than great. More alive than ever."

"I suppose that's good then. I'd be concerned the extra-low frequency is due to swingback. You know, an over-reaction while your body stabilises. Like a swing. It doesn't just swing up and then stop at the bottom of its arc, it swings back almost as far."

"It's been three days. You said I'd turn to mush." Marco made a show of pummelling his stomach. "Hard as rock. I think I'm fine. Sorry if I worried you," he said hopefully. He suspected Ebe wouldn't even notice if he hadn't come back.

"Molly was more worried."

"Why did she care?"

"She cares about me." Ebe blushed. "I think I love her."

"Fuck's sake, Ebe. It's less than a week. It's what's known in the dating game as a holiday romance. They never last."

"We're not on holiday. She hugs me and cares about me. It got me thinking; if one Aryan coming here is so intolerable for even you, is bringing the rest here even sensible after all. What if I'd rather settle down with Molly and start a family?"

"Ebe, you know you can't do that, yeah?" Why was he lying? The Aryan had seemed keen on pursuing inter-hybrid procreation as a logical next evolutionary step. But for reasons he didn't appreciate, he knew he didn't want that. Not with Ebe and Molly, definitely. "Don't let anyone hear you saying your priorities have changed, either. Not everyone here is our friend. But anyway, I mean, biologically procreation would be most unsound. Your paternal genes are too similar. Any offspring would be an abomination."

"Like me?"

"No. You're not. You are special. Carefully selective breeding to bring about the best in species is what you are. The thing is, the best Greys in species may well be the same individual, I don't know. They'd have no reason to mix it up. Your proliferation isn't on their agenda. She's probably your sister, for Christ's sake." Ebe scowled at the floor. "Sorry, mate. I had to tell you. Take the hugs, but don't get other ideas, yeah?"

"She said her dad's human."

"I told you, Ebe, he bloody isn't. Molly wouldn't

be here in this room with you if she wasn't *like* you. Do you understand?" Ebe remained motionless. "Do you?" With no response, Marco gave up and pushed his chair back in. "Think about it, Ebe. Do as you're told. It's the only way to get out of here."

Maybe he didn't want to get out of here. Maybe he wanted to stay here with Molly forever.

"You're upset. What did he say to you?"

Ebe had no words. How could he tell her Marco was against them having a family, and that he had to agree it would be a disaster, when it was all he wanted in the world? How could he say that, when he realised Marco was right. Love? He didn't know the meaning of the word.

"He doesn't want us to be together, does he?"

Ebe gasped. Were they 'together?' His heart beat as unfamiliar chemicals flooded his neural systems. He shook his head.

"I'm going to talk to him."

"Don't!" Shocked, Ebe's his hands shot to Molly's shoulders. "He's dangerous."

"We're surrounded my armed military who have our safety as their main protocol. I want to *talk* to him. Not pitch my skills in an interspecies MMA battle."

"There's no need. We can..." Ebe paused. *'Be together'*? Is that what he wanted to say? If so, wouldn't it be polite to ask Molly first?

Molly scowled. With a swift turn of her head,

she flounced away. Ebe stared at his hands. That wasn't what he wanted. *'There's no need...'* the words echoed around his head. "There's no need to talk to Marco because we can do whatever we like without his permission. That's what I meant! Molly!" But it was too late. Her mousy pony-tail swished just as the door slammed behind her.

Should he rush after her? When his mum was upset, he would advise leaving her to calm down. Whenever Marco insisted on pre-empting her, it rarely ended well. Sitting on his hands, Ebe screwed his eyes shut and pressed his lips hard together. I must resist. Leave her to cool off. I must, I must. I'll explain later and we'll laugh about it.

2000

Relief enveloped Ebe as he listened to the radio on the first day of the year. Worry had turned to panic. Leaflets from the government had plopped onto their door mat and he had read them avidly.

His mum and Marco had been less concerned, but he thought that was because they didn't understand. Odd, because Marco seemed to understand a great deal. Or, maybe that was why he appeared nonplussed. Because the Millennium Bug had turned out to be nothing. Not nothing. That would suggest it had been a fuss for no reason. But thanks to tireless work from software engineers around the world, it had transitioned smoothly after all.

When plonked on Santa's knee at the shopping centre and asked what he wanted for Christmas he replied, 'A solution to the Millennium Bug' and everyone had laughed and said he must be the only five-year-old in the world to ask for such a thing. He wasn't stupid enough to think his wish to Father Christmas had influenced the matter. Or to believe the man upon whose knee he'd perched was the real monk of legend. But his wishes being answered from any source, be it Divine, fate, magic, or merely coincidence, he was grateful today.

Festivities over, he was keen to get back to school to use the computers. An interdimensional portal he was designing was stored on one of them, and he was anxious to proceed with it, now all the fuss was over.

He generally enjoyed school. Teachers all approved of him, due to his cleverness. And he still revelled in stories. And the bountiful cafeteria.

Unlike the rest of the children, playtime was his least favourite time and he always longed for it to be over. Some boys were unpleasant to him, and some girls too. Others appeared nice but Ebe wasn't sure if they meant it, or if they sought approval for being kind to the strange boy. He couldn't help it. The way they saw things was not the way he did. Pretending seemed futile;

pointless, and it didn't even work. Nobody was fooled.

In pre-school it had been the same until everyone realised how skilled he was fixing things. The problem of big school was the lack of toys. They had some, but they all seemed in good working order. The opportunity to demonstrate his ingenuity in repairing them didn't exist in the same way.

Sometimes, permitted to stay inside, he'd finish off on the computer, other occasions he was encouraged to 'get some fresh air.' Friendless, he spent those break times walking the perimeter of the playground until it was time to go inside again.

Years passed and whilst his thoughts developed, the routine, and the route, remained the same. Killing time until he could go back inside.

The opportunity did come one day, a few years later. Not to make friends, but to gain a following more befitting his status as saviour of the world...

2005

With dismay, Ebe resolved himself to not being able to wait until he got home to use the toilet. Fortunately, he'd coped until break time. Putting his hand up and asking in class would be excruciatingly awful.

And he'd succeeded in being the first one in so he could select the least disgusting cubicle. Dry seat; a lock that slid as it was supposed to, and hardly any toilet pap*ier-mache* stalactites dangling above his head.

Fresh paper rolled from the dispenser to line the seat, and with enough in reserve for when he needed it, Ebe was almost ready to unbuckle his trousers. Nervously he watched himself so he would remember the fastening procedure in reverse.

Just in time. Wiped and in the process of re-buckling his belt, Ebe stopped mid-loop as the toilet door flew open.

He recognised the voices and he didn't like them. Unsure of their names, he'd struggle to pick their faces from a photograph. But they were familiar, and if they saw him alone and unsupervised in the bathroom, they wouldn't be nice to him. Marco would scare them, but Ebe just wanted to keep out of their way.

Breath held, he would wait for them to leave, or at least lock themselves in their own cubicles so he could exit unseen.

"What's the matter? You too chicken?"

"No, it's not that. But, well, it is pretty dangerous, isn't it?"

Two or more boys laughed. "Only if you don't know what you're doing. Jason's done it loads..."

"It is well lush, boys, I'm telling you. Better than wanking."

"Then, you can wank *and* do it, and that's even better!"

"But I'm not a wanker."

"Yeah, whatever!"

Laughter again.

"Here, use this."

Ebe didn't have any idea what was going on but felt certain he wanted no part of it. So, he held his breath even tighter before realising his error when oxygen starved air threatened to explode from his lips. Opening them as little as he could he let the air out. It worked, coming out almost silently.

Until the last moment.

When it whistled.

Head trembling as he awaited the cries of 'Who's there?' but they didn't come. Too enthralled with whatever they were doing to notice him. Still nervous, he drew inhalation slowly, and controlled the in and out so he wouldn't risk noise again.

Sounds he couldn't recognise. The laughing stopped. One of them was being sick, it sounded like. And then someone said, 'Shit!' and another said a name and repeated it. Then they left. Footsteps scurrying through the door, and it slamming behind them.

Alone again, Ebe slid back the bolt and pulled open the cubicle door.

That's when he saw him.

The chord from someone's hoodie was round

his neck and he lay completely still. Ebe closed his eyes and shook his head. Knee crooked, he bent beside the boy, loosened the string and listened for breath. None came, and his chest wasn't moving. He was turning blue.

Ebe held his hands over him. Heat burned his fingers as he moved them around to find the right spot. The room glowed gold, then red and blue. When the spectrum filled to bright white, the boy gasped for breath. His eyes pinged open and he stared right into Ebe's face.

Feet sliding, he rammed against the wall and pulled himself to standing, not taking his eyes from Ebe.

Later, as Ebe continued his usual perimeter perambulate, as he had for over five years at the school, a larger boy stopped him abruptly. "What did you do, Ebe? I thought… We thought… How did you bring Kieron back to life?"

Ebe shrugged, and the bigger boy raised his eyebrows. "You won't be telling anyone what we were doing, will you?"

Ebe shook his head.

"Say it. Say you won't tell anyone what we were doing."

"I don't know what you were doing."

"That's the spirit. Good boy."

And from that day, sure everyone knew his power, he still had no friends. But that was from his choice. Everyone tried to converse with him, he just didn't want to. "Who was that?" his mum would ask when they needed to go to the shop after school and other children would say hello.

But Ebe had no idea, and despite his supernatural fame, still felt unsure if they were being genuine. "Dunno," he answered.

If Carys had been so-inclined, she could have asked them; spoken to their mums and arranged them to come over. Perhaps involved them in treats to local theme parks, or even beach barbecues. But she was as awkward around people as him and seemed almost pleased he hadn't recognised them and she was off the parental hook.

And so it transpired on his first day at Oxford University, they left him standing in a hall full of newcomers as socially inept as ever. He didn't care. Unlike many of them, from what he'd overheard, he wasn't there to party. Mathematics and its application to life on Earth was all he cared about. Marco had told him of big plans set out for him. A guaranteed job in Alaska on what he called the most crucial mission of our time.

"I don't want to leave him." Carys, had hugged her son a fifth time and Marco guided her away.

"You have to, Carys. This is good for him. This is where he needs to be. And it was. If anyone knew what was meant for Ebe, Marco did. And developing without his suffocating mother he believed necessary, too. "Come on, Carys. You can't Molly-coddle him forever."

Would he ever learn? Sometimes, morphing and teaching her a lesson she would never forget was very tempting. But he considered keeping her in the dark crucial. If anyone could steer Ebe away from his destiny, it was this woman.

It would have helped if they were leaving him amongst a gaggle of new friends, but that had never been likely. Did he have to look so lost?

From a distance, they observed as he sat alone, other students milling past. "Should I at least introduce him to someone?"

"To whom? You don't know anyone. He'll be forever remembered as the kid whose mum tried to arrange a play date."

"I don't want to arrange anything. I want to help. He's never going to communicate with anyone without help, is he?"

"And he never will if you insist on doing everything for him."

"But... I just"

He'd got her, because, however hidden his agenda, he was right.

2017

Professor McKinley was worried. Ebe had been very keen to attend lectures when the term began. Now, he hardly saw him. Upon asking the other students, none of them said he was out partying, which meant he was the other type: - the overwhelmed type. The type who is terribly homesick and who falls into acute depression. He'd have to act soon, because the university losing such a brilliant mind was unthinkable.

Dormitory number procured from the front desk, the professor made his way to the boy's accommodation block and quickly found the room. *Knock-knock*. Cans rattling and paper bags sorting underfoot, he waited patiently for an answer.

"Hold on. Just coming."

The tone sounded bright. But often, those suffering the most with depression seemed the happiest. The door opened and Ebe framed from the chink of light beyond. "Oh, I thought you were my mum."

"Sorry to disappoint. I'm worried about you. I haven't seen you in lectures for quite a while. You don't want to waste your opportunity." (And we don't want to miss the prospect of having you here, he thought.) "Is anything the matter?"

"No, not at all," Ebe said, pulling the door open further, then pausing abruptly. "Er... Excuse the mess." His gaze shot to the floor and dozens of soft-drink cans.

It was in disarray The professor's original fear returned. It appeared a lot like depression. But not Ebe's face. His hazel eyes flashed with excitement. "I'm pleased you're here. Look!" He ploughed his way through flooring debris to his computer monitors. Aiming the cursor with the mouse, he opened spreadsheets he'd been working on. The professor gasped. The more he saw, the more amazed he became. Everything he'd taught in his lectures, and a lot more advanced mathematics than that, were displayed on the screen. At random, he indicated one equation and asked, "Can you explain this to me?"

Ebe's eyes flashed. As he re-wrote the numbers, his astonishing aptitude was undeniable. The professor chose another and another until it was apparent Ebe's non- attendance had nought to do with a lack of interest. There was nothing he could teach him. His grasp of the subject already outstretched his own.

FIFTY

Life and death

2020

"You're alive."

Marco turned and locked eyes with the colonel and pointedly refused to respond. His neck prickled and he didn't trust himself not to react in the worst possible way. Go for a walk, the Aryan had suggested. You'll be fine, he/she had said.

"I say, hey, son. Good to see you alive…" Ignored again, the colonel shouted, "Where ya going, son?" Marco continued on in silence. "There're certain areas prohibited on this island. Make sure you stay in the barracks."

Marco turned and spat ferociously, "I'll go wherever the fuck I want." In a split second, he morphed into the eight-foot lizard, then back to his human form.

"Okay, son. Don't come runnin' to me if a bear bites both your legs off." Marco was twenty yards away when the colonel called out again. "Say, where do yer clothes go when you morph into that thing? Why don't they rip like the goddam hulk?"

Marco ignored him. Why did nobody get it? It was on an entirely different frequency, as easy to recall as switching tabs on your phone. And when you did that, you didn't expect the people in the tab you left open to wind up with no clothes just because you Googled a photo of a whale. "Just keep going," he ordered himself. "Carry on, and maybe you'll find some peace."

He wasn't sure how long he'd walked, and reaching the shoreline didn't mean much. The open ocean still felt claustrophobic with huge mountains looming across the crescent of the bay. "Shhhiiit!" he screamed at the snow topped hills. "Shit shit shit!" he yelled again, not even knowing why. The elation he'd experienced in the presence of that being had left him deeply unsatisfied with his normal levels of happiness - if that was an emotion he recognised. It boiled down to: did he have a problem, or not. And now, he thought he had a problem.

He'd sacrificed a lot for that boy, and for what? A contingency plan for if the humans were wiped out? A pet project of a supposedly enlightened species who had forced him to give up any other existence in favour of baby-sitting a hybrid child?

And what thanks did he get? The love of a good woman? No. Of their child? Again, no. Ebe had never called him 'Dad'; had never said he loved him. But now in the space of a few weeks he was inseparable from Molly. 'I love her,' he'd said. What a fucking joke. What a fucking insult. Why had it taken him until now to realise? He screamed again at the sky.

They were coming if Ebe and his cronies uncovered a safe passage or not, that was obvious. Why go through all the pretence that they care? All those not 'enlightened' would fulfil God's great plan and die, and be grateful or be damned! Fists balling, fingernails cutting into his palms, he was so angry. They were all going to die, and no-one cared. He should never have become embroiled in this god-forsaken planet.

Humans wouldn't be the first advanced species to become extinct. They were outgrowing their planet and the spiritual enlightenment the Aryan's offered was their last salvation.

They talked of God. Of a higher being who created them. The Greys talked of a universal divinity. But they all admired the ridiculous humans who had to be genetically modified to even exist. Was their fondness for them a bias towards their own creation; made in their image? To the humans, they were gods themselves.

There was always a bigger god, so it seemed

to Marco. He didn't care for all that. Ironic, inhabiting the doner body of a preacher's son.

And now, having done his part. Having sacrificed his very existence to bring Ebe into being; to guide him to what needed to be learned; to fetch him here to this hierarchy of extra-terrestrial weirdness. After all that, he was cast aside for a creepy-looking girl he barely knew.

And then she was there. The figure of all his angst; his rage; his fear.

"You made Ebe cry. I thought you were supposed to care for him."

He didn't answer the allegation. Morphing, the shock registered on Molly's face just before he drove his razor talons at her neck.

Ducking away, she was too late. It had all happened too quickly. Hands thrust to her throat, blood seeped through her fingers and she fell, gurgling, to her knees.

"Marco! Stop!" Gun shots rang out. The colonel aimed high above his head.

Marco remembered his promise to himself. In a leap that bridged the gap between them, he roared as the colonel brought the gun down and let out a shot that ripped into Marco's shoulder. Piercing the armour-plated scales, he squealed, fuelling his fury as his claws tore into the colonel's chest.

A dozen more gunshots echoed round the bay, and eight of them hit their large but motile target. Marco morphed rapidly back and forth either in a desperate attempt to escape the fatal blasts, or in a seizure of death throws. At last, he collapsed on the ground in a pool of his own sticky plasma in front of the colonel who clutched at blood oozing from gashes on his torso.

"Are you okay, sir? What happened?"

"I think we just witnessed the backlash the lab guys keep on about. If the Aryans come, everyone could turn out like this."

"Turn into lizard people?"

"No! become unaccustomedly, savagely, murderously enraged. It won't be pretty. Not pretty at all."

It was hard to take the threat seriously. And they had all those hybrid boffins on the case. It would all be fine, of course it would. The millennium bug, other conspiracies, they all worked out. You didn't spend this long working on a problem to have it go wrong. It was very un-American.

Holding one another up, they collapsed further at the sight in front of them.

On his knees, the big-headed boy Marco had brought with him, hovered his hands over the girl's neck. Golden glowing light changed to blue, red, and green and the boy stared on intensely.

With hurried steps they moved to watch the miracle as the gaping wound on her throat healed in time-lapse rapidity. Her eyes opened suddenly and she gasped. With a hand to her back, the boy helped her sit forward. From dead, to gasping her first breath, she stood. Shaky for a moment, she took a step, then another. “Ebe, you saved me. Thank you!”

Tears in his eyes, it was a feeling he'd never experienced in his life. And then his neutrality was challenged again as he looked at the wheezing corpse of his step-dad. But it wasn't him, was it. He'd shown himself to be a malevolent monster. As he lay in his grotesque reptilian guise, Ebe still wondered if he should heal him. The light of divinity, whilst harnessable by any wretched soul, could only ever perform good. If he tried to heal the monster and it worked, it was Divine Will.

He hesitated still. If he hadn't disobeyed his own advice and scurried simpingly after Molly, it would have been too late to save her. If he brought this creature back to health, who was to say he wouldn't hurt her again? He would make things difficult for them at the very least. There was no need for him to intercede fate, was there. What was done was done.

He had these thoughts whilst edging closer to Marco. Tentative, slow, shuffling steps to appease his moral compass more than to hurry his help along, moved him to the shoulder of the beast. Once more, Ebe knelt. Hands outstretched, the golden glow lit and extinguished at once. Either he was too late, or healing Marco was not the will of the Universe. Whatever the reason the outcome was the same. Marco was dead.

Marco was dead and Ebe had seen it happen. He had never taken bad news as people might expect, only ever using his mother's reaction as a gauge. If she was upset, he was upset. But she wasn't here. Would she care that Marco had been killed?

From what she'd said, she was terrified of him, only realising his true nature months ago. She would more likely care about Molly because she cared about Ebe. Which must mean he cared about Molly. Which was probably why he felt as bad as he did. He could have saved Marco if he'd been quicker. But he prioritised a girl he knew little about over someone, who in one guise or another, had been in his life since he came screaming silently into the world.

But he was a menace. A monster. Perhaps the enlightenment from the Aryan arrival would have lifted him above that side of him. But did he deserve it? Ebe had to believe that he didn't. That if he had, the healing would have been a compulsion with no choice but to obey. The power of the Universe hadn't wanted to save him, and that was that. Ebe dusted his hands as he'd seen in old black and white movies. It was to show whoever was watching he was done with thinking about it. There were more urgent matters to attend. And with Molly at his side, there was nothing he couldn't achieve.

The colonel suspected he understood the true reason for the hybrids being brought to the island, although nothing had been confirmed. Seeing fellow humans become so ill; and then Marco's uncontrollable rage. He feared their arrival more than ever. If it wasn't too late, maybe the hybrid boffins would think of something he didn't understand and bring them in safely.

Fortunately, losing his stepfather didn't demoralise him as the colonel feared. Without any facility to process grief, and with guilt at choosing Molly over Marco swiftly dealt with, Ebe threw himself into the problem undistracted. He had vague justifying thoughts that Marco would want him to finish what he started, and Molly did too, for that matter. And the promise he'd made to his mum to get her when this was over. If anything, he was spurred on

FIFTY-ONE

Ebe gets to work

"So, the problems are firstly radiation, akin to a solar flare."

"If they come in winter, people will be indoors more," David suggested.

"Good idea, except it's not winter everywhere at once. We need to tell people to stay indoors."

"Because of radiation?"

"Well, yes. I expect everyone is aware of the risks and will want to stay indoors. That's not the biggest hazard though, as you know."

"So, how do we tackle the vibrational changes?"

"Use what we came up with previously."

"Keeping people in small groups because crowds vibrate more intensely."

"That's exactly right, yes." Ebe and David had a truce as David assumed he was mourning his dad, and he was being sensitive; just as he'd learned. He vowed to help him cope by staying with him whilst working around the clock for a solution. "The planet has already shifted. It's a shame we don't get news broadcasts, but the personnel have confirmed unusual weather patterns like bush fires and tornadoes much earlier and more ferocious than usual. I think we're seeing the shift due to the arrival of our Aryan scout."

"But if humans in crowds are more susceptible, won't a crowd of Aryans cause a much more dangerous surge and backlash?"

"Well, yes, but what I'm saying is it's started. The Earth is becoming accustomed to the new frequencies. The next wave might not be as bad. And don't forget, no humans are going to be expected to have direct contact with the Aryans like they have here; merely exist on the same planet with them."

"How long will it take to get them here if they stagger it?"

"Depends how many there are, doesn't it? But if they bring a few, see how it goes, bring a few more, we'll get more and more data and be able to make more and more accurate predictions."

"Seems pretty simple. Why didn't someone else think of this already?"

"A lot of things seem simple to me that no-one else thinks of. Marco told me they'd used computers and all the models pointed to disasters of varying magnitudes. But they all assumed they would arrive or not arrive. The idea of staggering the arrival seems not to have occurred to them."

"Weird," said David.

"Weird," agreed Ebe.

Big buildings give off vibration, so keeping away from those would be a good idea."

"Tell people to work from home."

"Yes," said Ebe, "But some people's homes are bigger than where they work. Imagine a big apartment block."

"I'd say less people live in blocks than don't and working in their houses would be safer. But perhaps communities in large complexes could move out to friends in the country like evacuees in the war?"

"Yeah, that could work. But there might be people travelling all over the place to enable that. I think individual governments will have to carry out their own plan, depending on the prevalent industries, etcetera."

"Do you think all countries will tell people why?"

"I don't suppose any of them will. They'll blame a solar flare or something, but then astronomers may wade in with arguments that it's false and people might not believe it, so won't stay in."

"I bet they would if they knew the actual truth."

Ebe laughed. "But they'd never leave their houses again!"

"Well, what will they tell them?"

"That's not for us to worry about. Say some

sort of virus; bird flu or Ebola or something like that, I expect. Some countries could just declare martial law. Not everywhere enjoys the freedom to question the government that we do here and back in the UK."

"It might be over in a couple of months."

"Yeah, maybe. We'll know more when more arrive," Ebe agreed. "Not everyone will make it, you know. A lot of people won't survive the increase and will just die. It could be a real lot. I still think the benefits will be worth it. Aryan enlightenment is what everybody spends their time praying for, in one way or another."

"It doesn't matter its appeal. We don't have a choice."

"That's exactly right," Ebe repeated his new favourite key phrase. Everything was either wrong or exactly right; from theories of how to bring extra-terrestrial supreme beings to Earth from another dimension, to the toppings on a pizza. But in this instance, it seemed appropriate. They had no choice at all. "And then there's the backlash. Millions of people reacting adversely to the opposite to elation."

David snorted. "Even more reason to keep them apart then, I suppose."

It wasn't perfect, but in the face of the inevitable, they had concocted a solution that would save lives. Not all of them, but a lot of them. How many would be a worrying wait and see game, the repercussions of which may last for months or even years.

FIFTY-TWO

Aftermath

September 2022

Most of the others left weeks ago, but they'd kept Ebe. And Molly. The mission was over as far as they were concerned. Quarantined on incommunicado island, they'd learned what they'd been told and nothing more. After all their hard work in isolation, they had expected a fanfare for the big arrival. Instead it happened in sporadic spurts around the globe, and the locations an international secret. They already knew so much it seemed pointless.

Gratified his gradual technique had been used, unfortunately, it soon became clear months had been a very optimistic prediction. With the first wave, the planet's weather went mad. The hottest, the wettest, the coldest, the driest, the windiest, stormiest, most unpredictable meteorological conditions since records began. Climate change theorists were having a field day, and, it seemed, wildly supported here on the base.

Closer to them, dangerously close, was something else the Aryan had predicted: War. And on 24th February, 2022, Russian forces invaded Ukraine again. Suddenly, Alaska didn't seem so safe. Or perhaps it was the safest place in the world. Too near to Russia for nuclear attack. Not that there was anything here now for them to be concerned with. Everything secret had already happened. It would play its course. The vile act presumably part of the backlash, or swing back of the higher frequencies, along with the retaliation of the western countries.

Ebe and Molly longed for the days it stabilised and the promised land delivered what it pledged. Until then, they were disinclined to mention their roles to anyone. It wasn't as though they'd had a choice. And they hoped, dire as the world situation was, they had helped prevent it from being graver.

It was all part of the larger plan. Whilst not everything going wrong was being attributed to the correct cause, and some were laughably inaccurate to those who knew, the changes they rang were what was needed: what the Aryans wanted.

They called it 'A New World Order'; a time predicted in almost all holy texts. A government of governments chosen by the people to truly better the planet.

Ebe lapped it up. Having been instrumental in its passing, he had little choice. To believe it was all for nothing was unthinkable.

"You're leaving us soon," a kindly man in casual uniform pulled out the chair next to Ebe and Molly at the table.

"Only to fetch his mum," Molly spoke up. Her own family had yet to be in touch. Covid; the war; abandonment? No-one was sure, or no-one was saying, but for now, Molly was without a family home to return to. With a disinterest akin to Ebe's, she'd vowed to stay here in Alaska with him instead.

But he knew exactly where his mother was, and a promise he'd made to her seemed more important to him than anything. Molly had been angry, but Ebe remained adamant. "I said I'd fetch her when all this was over. It's time now. Don't worry, Molly. She's going to love you." He'd convinced himself it was true but had no idea how she would react. She didn't do well with strangers.

"And then what? When you've fetched your mamma here?" the officer asked.

Ebe shrugged. Start a family, he wanted to say, but that wasn't allowed. "Keep her safe," he said finally.

"Good idea. You're gonna find it's a little... different out there, son."

"Oh, no, Ebe. Don't go. Stay here," Molly clutched at his sleeve, but Ebe didn't flinch. "I have to go, Molly. I promised."

The officer chuckled. "I'll tell purchasing to order in less food." Ebe shot a sharp look his way, and the man raised his hands in surrender. "Joking, joking. Sorry. I'd eat a lot, too, if I'd lost my dad."

"He wasn't my dad."

The man shrugged. "I got into a lot of trouble for that. We're not meant to kill the lizards. They're protected under a treaty, but I reckon he'd have killed us all, given the chance. The hate in those lid-less eyes frightened the shit out of me.

"When I filed my report, they told me they were supposed to test him. Him going crazy was a predicted side- effect of the higher vibration; that he'd dropped back to a much lower vibration, or a less evolved, primal state. They needed the data and they couldn't get it with him dead. I said they should tell us more what the fuck is going on if they want us to know these things. They said..."

Ebe had stopped listening. they were right. The statistics had been vital. He gulped. He'd made very particular calculations based on very specific reports. The planet, the ecology of countless species, was a finely tuned work that, if out by anything, could have devastating consequences. A surge of guilt at saving Molly over Marco gripped his chest. Choosing sentiment over a monstrous step-dad was one thing; but choosing it over their mission was not something he felt proud of.

Somebody needed to tell him exactly what was happening in the world. With another gulp, he began breathing faster, catching his breath becoming harder and harder. There was nothing he could do. It was too late.

They cohabited here. The planet shifted and whatever devastation that had happened, Ebe reminded himself. He had taken everything he knew about into account, including the potential swing back of Earth's vibrational frequencies as the planet steadied in its orbit. The effects on humans successfully predicted and guarded against as far as it could have; keeping in small numbers, indoors was the safest scenario. So, it didn't make a lot of difference that Marco had swung back so hard he almost killed Molly. And once he was dead, the data was lost. Could he have made his point clearer? Made sure Marco refused to go? Throat gripped with emotion he didn't recognise. He knew he could have done more. He could have saved them both.

For the first time in his life, he had the human ambitions to start a family. It was a concept he never previously considered. In moments he hated Marco; the old Marco. Weak and incapable, forcing the other Marco to walk in and take him over. And he became the monster who terrified him. At other moments, he detested himself for not persuading Marco firmer, or for becoming attached to Molly. If he hadn't, she wouldn't have risked her life tackling Marco, and he wouldn't have reacted. He knew it was because Marco had made him sad.

With all this hatred inside him, there existed only one person he wanted. And today, his long journey back to her would begin.

Nerves at how she would be; and of how he'd manage the travel arrangements, had reduced his fingernails to raw skin, and then, perversely, he missed Marco. At least with him around, he felt safe. Provided with plenty of money which had been part of the arrangement for taking him out of society, Ebe was ready.

"Ebe, before you leave us, there are some things I need to tell you about what to expect."

Ebe's heart dropped and swirled all the Molly and Marco guilty feelings around until he fought to keep them in. What was he about to be told? Tabletop gripped in reddening fingertips, he braced himself for the worst. His mother was dead? The world had collapsed in balls of fiery tornadoes?

"We kept people inside and in small groups, as you know. It was considered the best way to achieve that was with a virus."

"You told people the illness they felt as a result

of the radiation and vibrational anomalies was caused by a virus? Did they believe it?"

"Well, yes. Because it was true."

Ebe squinted. If Marco had been there, he'd have wondered if he was being deliberately thick, as he sometimes seemed to do. Ebe wanted the truth quickly, so filled in the gaps. "You made an actual virus? Couldn't that have weakened people so they would cope poorly with everything else?"

"A consideration, yes. But there would have been too many questions we couldn't answer if they'd skirted the truth. So, they made a new truth and quickly cobbled a new strain of a largely familiar virus with the aim of it being severe enough to frighten people into taking the precautions you outlined, but which would mutate into a form akin to the common cold to which it's closely related.

"Given how long it took to bring the supreme species here, things were made rather more of than we intended. Casualties occurred besides the unavoidable deaths. Businesses which relied upon people going out went out of business. But what else could we have done? Sometimes, Ebe, I wonder if telling the truth might be better. But it's a cat that once out of the bag can never be wrestled back in. And the consensus that mass panic would ensue is one I agree with on the whole, but still, it's been a tough few years and we're lucky we were here living life the same as ever."

Ebe was quiet. "Was… Was my mother one of the casualties?"

The officer shook his head. "No, no, Ebe, she's fighting fit and thrilled about you coming home. She hasn't been told about your stepfather. We thought it best that came from you."

Ebe blew through his lips. That was a big ask. "So, I can go?"

"Yes. Just one or two more things related to this pesky virus thing, I'm afraid. You may need to wear face coverings and keep to what they're calling social distancing. It's different in various states and countries. In England and Wales, they abandoned restrictions as soon as World War Three loomed. It's not much of a humanity you're going back to, Ebe, I'm afraid. But I reckon you expected as much, huh? As soon as you get access to the internet again, you'll see it all. I didn't want you being overwhelmed."

Ebe raised an eyebrow. "I don't know if anyone told you, but I'm considered to be pretty smart."

The man smiled at Ebe, the smartest dumbass he'd ever met.

"I thought it would be Utopia: heaven on Earth," he said, eyes moistening as he immediately ran the probability that all the sacrifice had been in vain. "I'm still confident it will be. It's just gonna take some time, that's all. The Age of Aquarius is upon us. That's the main thing."

"Well, I hope you're right, son. Now you get off to your mama and have a great time. And Ebe?"

"Yes?"

"Thanks. Oh, and Ebe...?"

"What?"

"Sorry."

What passed as a teary farewell to the girl he called his girlfriend, took place with a kiss on each cheek and an awkward hug. Eyes failing to meet, they whispered goodbye and good luck before Ebe turned and left. He would miss Molly, but there remained another woman he stayed excited to see. And she'd waited on his promise to return for far too long.

FIFTY-THREE

The journey home

The sight of masks and barriers and one-way systems and arrows and lines on the floor was like he had walked into a dystopian future. It suited him well enough: keeping crowds at bay and avoiding people were things he yearned for in everyday life. The masks too gave a sense of privacy, having his face mainly hidden meant less judgement of his appearance.

It felt safer, seeing people regularly rubbing sanitiser on their hands. Maybe it wasn't a dystopia and was the beginning of the Utopia he'd promised his mum.

His phone, now charged, had pinged into life but had required updates that so far hadn't achieved sufficient 4G or WiFi signal to implement. In the hotel now, he browsed the internet for the first time in over two years and got up to speed on what the world had been told of the situation.

Not that he hadn't considered it, but his lack of understanding of others' motivations, rather than lack of empathy, meant he wasn't ready at all for the crisis the world appeared to be in. "It will be okay. *They* are here now and they will take care of everything, you'll see," he said to the empty room.

There were good news stories. The air and the sea were already cleaner. People were using the momentum to influence climate change at a rate that should have been done ages ago, in Ebe's opinion. Hopefully it wouldn't be too little too late.

Mushrooms that ate plastic.

Fossil fuel cars being illegal to manufacture within eight years.

Eighty percent of energy coming from wind turbines and nuclear power.

There were a lot of changes already on the horizon, and Ebe wondered how directly the Aryans had played a part. Were they sitting on the council advising, or was it simply the evolved frequency people were now living in, unbeknownst, that was affecting the change?

Governments had become less and less trusted, so if the Aryans offered a solution, they might well grasp it with thankful hands. History showed these things could be terribly slow, or very rapid. On their last occupation thousands of years ago they were revered as gods. Monuments, such as the pyramids made in their honour, pointing their origins out for all to see. That was a baby step to what they had planned now. Heaven on Earth was the reality they longed to achieve. To be successful creators themselves, putting them closer in their spiritual evolution to their own almighty god.

Brief forays to the planet a couple of thousand years ago had seen them depicted as angels, foretelling many godly good deeds. And now they were here to fulfil their own prophesies; their own promises.

Yes, Ebe decided. Reading through all the media fluff, there were already a lot of signs things were going to plan. The grin on his face grew so wide it threatened to cramp.

His mind at rest, the thing he'd missed more than the internet called to him. Walking down to reception, he asked for a taxi. Despite the short distance, he had spent so long in a room with no exercise and unlimited mess provisions, he had lost a bit of mobility. And the idea of scouring his memory to find his beloved cuisine was bringing him out in a cold sweat. A taxi door to door would solve the issue. And he was the instigator of all the good that was happening in the world right now. Without his genius, everyone may have disappeared or dissolved in a low frequency glob. His eyes flashed with excitement. He deserved a treat.

One double Big Mac didn't quite hit the spot. He still craved the taste after the third, but fitting in another would be regrettable. And he really shouldn't have had the large banana milkshake. He pitied the aeroplane toilet tomorrow. If it evacuated over the sea, he might be responsible for a tsunami. He laughed to himself and choked on the last mouthful.

"Are you okay there, buddy?"

Ebe regained his breath. "Fine, thank you." Hailing another cab, it took him the short distance back to his hotel. Tomorrow, Seattle, London Heathrow the day after. Then he'd travel straight to Wales and get a hug, or a cwtch as she always called it, from his mother. She'd be so pleased with him, wouldn't she? Ebe struggled to sleep through the emotion and excitement.

Eventually, he dropped off an hour before his alarm call. As he staggered into the elevator and caught his reflection, he looked away. Hopefully, sleep on the flights will make me look a lot better, he thought as the doors swished open.

Touchdown at London Heathrow after an eventless stopover in Seattle where the temptation of the golden arches didn't sway him from sleep. He had awoken feeling proud. If he were to lose weight, resisting McDonalds, and plenty of rest would help a lot. Now back on UK soil, he was confronted with his favourite food before he even left the airport. He indulged, but only what he considered a normal meal.

Still hungry afterwards, he shook his head wondering how the measly portions had ever become popular. What did Americans think of the poor reproduction of the famous chain found here? It was probably enough to cure him of his cravings.

He had impressed himself with his ability to navigate the continents the way he had. Without help from Marco, he'd done perfectly well on his own. He just had to catch a train now and by dinner time he would be with his mum.

FIFTY-FOUR

The faces

Ebe jumped into a taxi which was waiting outside the train station in Haverfordwest, South West Wales. He was shattered, but there was no way he was going to sleep until he'd seen her. "St Caradog's, Withybush General Hospital, please." The cabbie gave a knowing smile.

The screams and horrific out-of-tune guitar accompanied screeching were loud from the car park. Ebe winced, feeling for his poor mother. A person appeared at the glass door dressed in everyday clothes, identified as a Psychiatric Nurse by a lanyard around her neck, which struck Ebe as a dangerous apparatus to be wearing around the murderously unwell. "I'm visiting Carys Ellis; my mother."

"Ah, yes, Ebe. I remember you. I'm so pleased you're here. She has been very excited." Ebe grinned. "I'm pleased to see your mask. Don't be alarmed by patients who haven't got one on. They are exempt for a number of reasons but they've all been tested and they're all clear. Would you mind using the hand sanitiser? That'd be grand?" she said, smiling again.

"Follow me. I'll find you a nice private room, then fetch your mum, okay?"

The window reflected him as darkness squeezed over the land. Why was he so nervous? It was only his mum. But he had a lot to tell her. Was she well enough to hear it?

Noises outside caught his ear. "Fuck off, Richard. I swear I'll drop you if you come near me. And, Mark, if you play that guitar one more time, I'll wrap it round your fucking head!" more noise ensued and his first glimpse of his wonderful mum in over two years was her fending off a guitar as it splintered on the wall in front of her. The nurse shouted at them all to calm down, "You'll lose your privileges. Back to your rooms. Now!"

The door banged open and his mum and the nurse balled in. "That was silly, Carys. You're meant to be going home. How are you going to convince the doctors you're better if you behave like that, eh?"

"Only the insane would put up with it," Carys sneered.

"I put up with it."

"Well, more fool you. No, sorry, Andrea. You're one of the good guys. I just can't stand it anymore."

She turned as though she hadn't realised why she'd been brought to the room, and her face burst with tears as she ran over to her son and threw her arms around him. "Oh, my god, Ebe. You're here!" She held him for ages before pulling back, frowning, and pummelling her fists on his broad chest. "Took your fucking time, son, didn't you?"

"I'm so sorry, Mum. I've been locked away on an Alaskan island since I last saw you. No McDonalds or anything!"

"Well, you look like you've been eating fine. What was it, seal blubber?"

Ebe's bottom lip quivered. She'd never been mean to him before.

"Sorry, son. It's been hell in here. I was told I was well enough to leave about eighteen months ago. All I needed was a family member to vouch for me. They couldn't get hold of you or Marco, my dad seems to have fallen for the allure of a Thai Bride and is living on the beach in a bar he's bought in Thailand. Never even came to see me!" Her face hardened. "I don't know if he cares if I'm alive or dead. I only heard about his Thailand exploits when I called Dan and Natalia. They couldn't possibly have taken me in. Loads of excuses, all bollocks. So, I've been stuck in here waiting for you. You could have phoned, or something."

"We weren't able to. I've been a virtual prisoner myself."

"You're here now. So, we can go home." Noticing him going silent, she tapped his arm. "Ebe?"

"Marco has the house rented out."

"Well, tell him to kick them out! It's my home, too, and I need to get out of this place. I swear to you, son, it's driving me insane. If I don't leave here now, I may end up staying for the rest of my life."

"Marco's dead," Ebe blurted. He waited for her reaction. Would she be sad? She had been terrified of him last time he'd mentioned his name. She shunned his touch as he reached to hold her when she surprised him by breaking into sobs. "What? How?"

"It's a long story, I'll tell you later."

"Do you not have anywhere to go, Carys?" the nurse asked from the corner of the room where she did a poor impression of someone not listening.

Carys glared at Ebe. Not one for picking up even the least subtle of hints, Carys answered. "Ebe will be with me, and we'll go to a hotel until we sort something more permanent."

The nurses face screwed up in lines all pointing to Carys not leaving.

"Please, I have to get out. I've wait two long years. I haven't done anything wrong. You can't want to keep me here."

"I don't, Carys. But we have a duty of care. It's just, we could be sued if we let a vulnerable patient out into the community to be homeless."

"There's plenty of money for us," Ebe assured. "And the house will be yours after probate is completed. We'll just stay in a nice hotel until we can find somewhere permanent. It'll be fine." He didn't want to upset her telling her about Molly and Alaska just yet. Maybe Molly could come to Wales anyway.

"Hmm," the nurse drummed her fingers on the table. "I'll need to ask the doctor."

She returned five minutes later. "He says if you can find accommodation for at least a week, he'll sign the release forms. Check in here again after that to make sure you're settling in okay. The world is a very different place to when you were out last, Carys."

She left them alone to their arrangements. Ebe hated using the phone, so Carys took it and searched for likely candidates. "How about here? It looks lovely and has rooms available for a few weeks."

"Ebe looked at an Edwardian mansion that boasted sea views and peace and quiet in a small village on a peninsular. "Looks perfect. Book it and I'll pay."

Carys beamed. "And then you can tell me what on Earth has been going on, young man." She took his hand and they left the room.

Papers quickly signed, it seemed almost as if the staff were as keen for her to leave as she was to go. She didn't care. Breathing outside air for the first time, she felt like falling to her knees and kissing the ground. She didn't. There would be plenty of opportunity for that when they got to their hotel.

In the darkness it was difficult to appreciate the scenery, although the city skyline of lights from the refinery had its own beauty, to Carys, everything was amazing. A trip to a rubbish dump would have been the most exciting thing she'd seen for years.

The night didn't spoil the sight of the hotel as it loomed into view across the field. Crenellated walls and a turreted tower made it look like a castle. Ebe didn't notice the tears on his mother's face as the taxi swerved around every bend. She squeezed his hand extra-tight and as they pulled up on the gravel drive, she wiped her eyes with her sleeve readying herself to meet people from the outside world.

"Oh, you don't have to wear masks here. Hospitality is exempt," a young pretty girl greeted at the door as they plonked their bags at their feet. Ebe kept his on, eyeballs darting fervently. He'd never heard anything so ridiculous. And as he'd been insulated from all UK bugs for years, he didn't want to have a catchup now.

"You should leave yours on, too, Mum."

"Oh, it's fine to keep them," the girl blushed. "Whatever makes you feel comfortable. Be aware other guests and staff won't be wearing them, as per Welsh Assembly Government recommendations, so you may wish to avoid communal areas." That sounded like Carys and Ebe's perfect time.

The room was wonderful. Large and atmospheric. It would be the first time Carys had slept with no nurses checking her every fifteen minutes. And without waking to Mark murdering songs on his guitar. It was the perfect opportunity to sleep, but it was also the ideal chance to watch television without some arsehole changing the program, or interrupting by throwing the TV out of the window, or something equally irritating. She could sleep all week if she wanted, so she indulged her desire for mindless viewing.

Ebe lay next to her on the bed scouring his phone. "Do you care what I put on?"

"No. I don't watch much telly, mum. Unless it's Rick and Morty, and you're not keen on that."

"I don't mind. I'd rather watch it with you."

By episode two, the screen flickered without them, the warnings that the TV would switch off displayed unheeded.

Ebe woke at dawn. Carys lay snoring peacefully,

and he tried not to wake her as he pulled back the covers and did a wee that sounded like an elephant having a shower. It was a beautiful day, and he was loath to waste it, but he couldn't bring himself to when she needed sleep so badly. A hasty note left on the bedside table, Ebe closed the door quietly behind him and ventured down the stairs.

Breakfast was being started by early morning staff. "We're not serving until seven, sir, sorry."

"That's okay. I'm just going outside," Ebe smiled back. The sea air as he stepped out onto the palm-tree lined garden hit him with powerful ozone notes and he breathed it in deeply. Sea gulls catching the current guided his eyes to the ocean, and he began his stroll. It was the furthest he would have walked in ages, but he was determined to make the half-a-mile stroll.

As a ship passed on the horizon and the Atlantic glistened in the morning sunlight, he wondered how it differed from his unwelcoming home for the past two and a half years. The distant mountains of the Preseli Hills were much smaller for a start, but there was more to it than that. A calm poured over him. Was it because it was all over now? Just a wait for things to get better and better?

It was an optimism he would hold for the briefest time.

The Globe Hotel was in chaos when he

returned. From upstairs, screams pierced the ears of everyone listening. Staff had abandoned their posts serving breakfast and were knocking on the door and calling, "Whatever is the matter, Mrs Ellis?"

Ebe pinched the bridge of his nose. He hadn't expected his first day with his mother would need him excusing her mental behaviour. She'd been in their care for ages and declared well for the past two years. How could she not be ready to come out?

Carys had leant a sleepy arm across the bed to stroke her son and comment on the beautiful morning. Not feeling him there, she had forced her eyes open, eyelids knotting to confound her.

At first, she was sure she was imagining it. It was even quite amusing to watch the pictures swirl around her mind from the wallpaper. It was the only pattern, other than stripes, she had laid her eyes on since her admittance to the mental ward.

Everyday objects; a car, a little wheelbarrow, she saw initially. Then faces. Two in particular. She shuddered at their grotesqueness, relieved they were confined to her imagination and the wallpaper. But as the faces grew more and more detailed, she sat up straight in the bed and pushed herself away from the apparition as it left the wall and became real.

She did not expect to yearn for the safety of

the ward, but she'd been taken in after seeing her husband morph into a reptile in front of her, and now her first time out and the walls were coming to life.

Innocuous to begin with, the images grew more and more realistic and it was impossible to see only the pattern. Even the car and wheelbarrow escaped detection.

Then it looked at her.

Knowing that she saw it too, the creature climbed out of the wall, long spindly arms reaching for her as it moaned a grotesque hellish growl.

Heart cramped, recalling herself as a six-year-old desperate to wake her sleeping parents, Carys screamed for help. The monster jumped angrily from the wall and loomed over her. The dark shadowy figure's gaping mouth looked ready to swallow her.

This time, she wasn't alone. The door banged and the cries of, 'Is everything okay?' turned more and more alarmed and she heard the police being mentioned and felt grateful. They'd been good to her over the years. She didn't know what they could do to help her, but she hoped they'd come soon.

Sergeant Rex Austin took the call. "This sounds like your cup of tea, sarge."

"What is it?"

"A long-term resident of St Caradogs is on

respite at The Globe Hotel, Angle Peninsular. She says the walls came alive and attacked her."

Rex rolled his eyes. It hadn't been long ago he'd become the scape goat after becoming involved in some dubious beast-in-the-woods reports. He was retiring soon, and it couldn't come early enough. So, he figured he may as well be the one to investigate this nonsense. "It sounds like a job for mental health services."

"I agree, but the hotel staff are adamant there was someone, or something in the room with her. Two voices, although they described it more as an animal. They all seem pretty shaken up, and I said somebody would attend, so..."

"Okay. A pleasant drive to Angle will get me out of the office."

"That's the spirit, sir."

FIFTY-FIVE

A new fear

He didn't need to ask who was expecting him. A lady rocking on the sofa by a fireplace, chewing at her fingernails was clearly troubled. "Mrs Carys Ellis?" he enquired. She stopped gnawing just enough to look at him and nod. "I hope you don't mind. One of the staff called me to say she heard noises like an intruder in your room, and screaming. That was you, I presume?"

"The intruder, or the screaming?"

Rex stammered on his words. She was joking, presumably, but her sour face suggested otherwise. "Why were you screaming?"

Carys sighed. "I'll tell you, but I don't expect you to believe me."

"It's best if you tell me the truth as you understand it. Then I can have a look around the room."

"And decide I'm a complete nutter..."

"Not at all. If you are suffering some psychosis, that's nothing to be ashamed of, and if there's truth in what you tell me, I'll do my best to get to the bottom of it."

"Psychosis? The staff have told you then."

Rex flushed red. "I didn't know it was confidential. Sorry."

Carys waved a dismissive hand. "The walls came alive and attacked me. There. Do you want to go and look at the nothing that's left behind? I saw faces in the wallpaper pattern. It happens all the time. I'm always seeing faces in things: the fronts of cars, clouds, smudges on walls.

"At first, I was impressed with my ability to construct something so real with my imagination. But it *saw* me. It seemed to really piss it off and it loomed over me on the bed and I really believed it was going to eat me." She broke into maniacal laughter. "It was going to bloody eat me, I swear." Back and fore, she rocked, laughing little titters and mumbling, "It was going to eat me..." over and over.

"Er, I'll have a look, shall I?"

"Room eight," a staff member offered a weak smile.

"Thank you. Can you show me, please?" her reluctance was evident, and Rex noticed her twisting a ring on her finger as she said, 'Certainly,' with a grimace.

Something happened here, Rex sensed. Not

what Carys Ellis said, obviously, but something that spooked the staff. Then he considered having a guest suffer a mental breakdown would spook anyone.

An examination of the room with the staff member waiting outside showed nothing out of the ordinary. The wall was intact, for sure. He turned to leave and gasped. A large man with an even larger head blocked the doorway. He mumbled under his breath and grabbed a bag.

"Sorry, I'll be out of your way in a minute. I'm just checking the room after a complaint of an intruder. Were you in the room too, Mr..."

"Call me Ebe."

"Did you see anything out of the ordinary, Ebe?"

"No. My mother is mentally unwell, sir. Last night was her first away from a secure mental health unit. It must have been a shock being out in the real world. Have you heard of borderline disorder?"

"Kind of," Rex didn't want to admit his shortcomings. He winced at the word mother. Carys Ellis must have nearly died pushing this monster out.

"The sufferer has a lower stress threshold than some, and when it's reached, they hallucinate. It was obviously stressful being away from the institution and doctors, that's all."

"The staff seem pretty spooked."

Ebe's eyes flashed. "She can be scary when she's having an episode."

Rex relaxed. "I see. Well, that makes a lot more sense than an intruder coming out of the walls and disappearing into thin air."

Ebe smiled. "I need to pack a bag."

"Is she not happy staying here again? That's a shame, it's lovely."

Ebe mumbled something about going back to Alaska Rex didn't quite catch, and it was unlikely to be important. Case closed. One for mental health to take on. His reputation wasn't about to fall further foul of his colleagues.

"Rex Austin, you old bastard!"

Rex stopped dead. Turning round, he was even less pleased to see the big Texan than he imagined he would. If the gruff FBI agent was around, something was definitely up. "Nathan. Are you here about what happened last night?"

Nathan Dale, the FBI paranormal agent Rex had been embroiled with in the recent 'beast-in-the-woods' case, shrugged. "I don't know a thing about it. Just here to collect young Ebe. He's half E.T, you know," Nathan whispered with a grin, rolling his eyes.

Rex nodded, dropping down a step and then another like an insulant child called to explain a bad school report. He reached the bottom, his head raised slowly, and he saw Carys Ellis rocking where he'd left her.

He walked over and sat next to her on the sofa. She stopped rocking. Rex could feel her trembling like a Chihuahua puppy. He placed his big hand on her leg and she paused, looked at him, and gulped. With her full attention, he leaned close and spoke clearly. “I believe you.”

End Of Part Two

AFTERWORD

Thank you for reading my story. I hope you have enjoyed it.
The HUM was inspired by many true events, whilst this follow up is more from my imagination. Although I have tied fiction in with real life occurrences. The Sea Empress oil spill was a terrible time for our beautiful coast. Mother nature has done its thing and reclaimed the beaches and the ocean, and most of the species that were affected are doing better than before the spill. Nature is wonderful.

The final chapter has set the seen for what is to come. The changes in vibrations seem to have brought new creatures into our awareness. Carys has seen them, but she won't be the only one. Not for long.
Follow me on my Amazon page for updates, and you won't miss the next installments in this, or any other, of my series.

Thank you, once more, for your attention.
Very best wishes,

Michael

ABOUT THE AUTHOR

Michael Christopher Carter

The beautiful Pembrokeshire Coast National Park provides the inspiration for Michael's novels, giving a real sense of life in South Wales.

A love of writing formed at a young age, and a love of books even younger. At school it was well-known that Michael would have to be a writer one day. It took forty years for him to fulfil that dream.

A former top performing direct sales consultant from the leafy suburbs of England, Michael was brought up a Catholic with a burgeoning interest in alternative, New Age spirituality leading him to attain Reiki Master status in 1999 before becoming a full time carer for a family member.

It's from this unique perspective that he finds time for his one true passion of writing; producing paranormal and supernatural

thrillers set in beautiful Wales.
Michael writes overlooking distant mountains, the ocean, and one of the most impressive mediaeval castles in the world, and always endeavours to inject some of this wonder into his novels.

PRAISE FOR AUTHOR

"I can't wait to read more by this talented author"

"Another great read from Michael Christopher Carter."

"Another great read. Fast becoming my favourite writer..."

"...an incredible story, full of reality, crossed paths and if only's"

"...draws you in and does not let you go until the last page"

"Cancel everything in order to read this book as you will not want to put it down."

"Previously I had only read a fab short story by this author, but wow can he write a brilliant full length

thriller!"

"I think I have just found my new favourite author, this book is excellent, thought provoking twists and turns on every page ,I have already purchased another book!"

- AMAZON REVIEWS

THE HUM

The HUM is a series of thought-provoking first contact books that will have you questioning what is real, both out in the cosmos, and within our own minds...

The Hum

Just because you're paranoid, doesn't mean they're not coming to get you...

Carys is pregnant

But she's never had a boyfriend

Or a one-night-stand

She's never had contact with anyone to explain her condition

Not anyone human anyway

Her wild claims are dismissed as a symptom of her paranoid psychosis, but Carys knows she's not crazy to be afraid whenever the dreadful humming noise fills the air; coming from everywhere and nowhere. She knows what it signifies: that her and her baby are in terrible danger...

E.b.e. Extra Biological Entity

On Earth, a baby is born every minute.

But not like Ebe.

Not like Ebe at all...

Ebe has a face only a mother could love.
But for stepdad, Marco, he has no choice.
Tormented with disturbing visions of a face not his own, and nightmares of threatening extra-terrestrials, he fears he must accept his role caring for and guiding his peculiar protege toward a very particular purpose.
For reasons he does not yet understand, Ebe is special. Only he has the capacity to conclude a millenium-long alien agenda.
But is it a plan to save, or annihilate humanity?
And is there anything he can do to stop him?

BOOKS BY THIS AUTHOR

Paranormal Tales From Wales

A collection of standalone thriller novels, novellas, and series with paranormal and supernatural themes, set in beautiful Wales.

Printed in Great Britain
by Amazon